STAR-SEER

APRIL MARCOM

 5 PRINCE PUBLISHING
5PrinceBooks.com

STAR-SEER

April Marcom

5 PRINCE PUBLISHING & BOOKS, LLC

PO Box 971

Golden, CO 80402-0971

www.5PrinceBooks.com

Digital ISBN-13: 978-1-63112-217-0

Print ISBN: 978-1-63112-218-7

STAR-SEER. April Marcom

Copyright April Marcom 2018

Published by 5 Prince Publishing

Cover Credit: Custom cover by Marianne Nowicki at www.PremadeEbookCoverShop.com

First Edition 2018

For my own baby sister Melody, for whom, like Sleigh and little Blush, there isn't anything I wouldn't do.

OTHER TITLES BY

APRIL MARCOM

The Three Stones of Bethany

STAR-SEER

April Marcom

1

I t was on the night of my youngest sister's birth that my dangerous obsession was also born.

The wind blew softly through the warm air, ruffling the hem of my dress. The stars shone like flecks of gold against the velvet black sky, a bright silver moon keeping watch over them all.

It was the perfect night for those gifted with star-seership. I was just returning home from a long night at school for the youngest star-readers of my people. We had to attend classes late at night, since it was the only time the stars were available for this specialized form of studying.

The moment my circular house came into view, I knew something was wrong. Men in dark cloaks were just entering the dwelling. Their hoods waved carelessly behind them, ready to shroud the natural light cast by their pale skin and pure white hair when they reached the Surface.

Light cast by my own body must have shone brighter at the realization of what was happening: my mother had just given birth to a defect.

My feet raced over the bridge connecting the tops of two

valor trees. Our entire city was set at the highest boughs of these giants, older and stronger than anything else of our world, simply to keep us guarded from the savage defects living on the ground below.

"Sleigh, wait!" Auree, my elder sister, called after me when I followed the last man into our house. I noticed her sitting against the outside of our house with my little sister before I disappeared inside.

It was the sound of my mother's voice coming from her bedroom that stopped me dead in my tracks. It broke and came out in painful shards. "Don't let them take her, Devin. She's our daughter."

"I know..." my father's voice came just as strangely, laced with sadness, something he had never displayed before. "Auree was right to send for them, though. Think of the danger we would be putting our daughters in if we kept her."

"She *is* our daughter."

"I'm sorry, Bloom." The last transporter disappeared into my parents' room. "Every defect poses a great threat to us all. That's the entire reason the Avarice had this city built in the sky, to keep them away from us."

I wanted to follow the transporters into the room. I had never seen a defect before.

"But she's only a baby," my mother pled.

A new cry rang out. Our house began to quake. My arms swung around wildly as I fought to catch myself, falling back against the curved hallway wall. A crack split through the wall right behind me. I scooted across the floor to the opposite side of the hall. The baby's cries grew louder, a burst of fiery light erupting from my parents' doorway.

"Give this to her," one of the transporters said, raising his voice.

A moment later the baby became silent. The trembling became still and the light went out.

"You see, Bloom? To keep her here could destroy everything we've worked so hard to build. She must be delivered to the Surface. The other defects will know how to care for her."

"She's *my* child," my mother said.

"You know the Avarice would never allow it."

"There's not anything I wouldn't do to change this." My Father's voice was so gentle; I scarcely recognized it. "But we can't put our girls at risk by upsetting the Avarice."

I wondered what he meant. The Avarice was a group of six men who lived in a tree-castle at the heart of our city, surrounded by guards. They were in charge of keeping peace and order. They made certain everyone had a house and all the things they needed. They wouldn't harm anyone.

"Can't I just finish giving her this bottle?" my mother sobbed. "It's the only chance I'll ever have to feed her."

"There's a powerful sleep aid in what she's drinking that will keep her from waking until she's reached the Surface," a transporter said. "She won't be aware enough to keep drinking it for much longer."

No one spoke after that. My mother kept crying. I could scarcely make out her muttering to my baby sister about how much she loved her.

I stayed where I was in the hallway, still wanting to see my defect sister but too afraid to move.

The terrible images I'd conjured since childhood of what a defect might look like danced through my mind as I waited. A tiny body with four long arms. A giant forehead and crooked fangs. Eyes red as blood that filled your soul with evil and ice. I'd never managed to discover anything about them, because it was a forbidden subject to discuss.

I stood when I heard footsteps crossing my parents' room. The transporters were coming. The defect would be with them.

"I don't want them to take her," my mother cried desperately. There was suddenly a lot of scuffling.

"Call for the guards," a transporter shouted.

"NO!" my father shouted back. "I'll take care of her. Just leave us be."

"It isn't fair," my mother moaned.

My father shushed her soothingly and began whispering so I couldn't understand anything he was saying.

Our translucent roof let in the first feeble traces of morning's light. It was enough to reveal the transporters filing out of the room in a straight line, like ghoulish apparitions come to harvest my sister's spirit. The first three only held a bag at their side. The fourth held a bundle of blankets to his chest, concealing my sister from me.

I wanted so badly to ask them if I could see her. But the men transporting her were so grave and so haunting. Their faces were solemn and filled with shadows cast by the hoods now hiding them. Even their skins' natural light did nothing to detract from this disturbing effect.

Three more men walked past me after the carrier of the baby. None of them acknowledged me in any way. The first exited our house, then the second and so on.

My mind was racing, though my body had suddenly become immobile.

I had to see my sister. Nothing could make me want to face the transporters, though. They were, perhaps, my greatest fear.

Secretly, I had always wanted to visit the Surface, if only to see what the world below was like. At fourteen years old, I was young but not afraid. There had simply never been a reason good enough to risk trying to sneak down the only passageway connecting the two worlds.

Until now.

HENNA'S GRANDFATHER WAS A TRANSPORTER. As her best friend I was her keeper of secrets. Therefore I knew she had one of her grandfather's old cloaks hidden beneath her bed due to her own curiosity about the Surface. It was one of the reasons we've always gotten along so well, the forbidden wish we shared.

She kept the cloak in case she should ever find the courage to sneak down through the passageway. It was only a dream, though. I knew she would never do it.

But I would.

My non-defective sisters were crying where I'd left them when I walked outside our house. No doubt the loss of Blush had hit them hard. That would have been the baby's name.

"D-did you see her?" Eve, the youngest of the three of us, asked.

I shook my head, then walked quickly toward the short bridge connecting our house to a neighbor's. Every house and building was constructed alongside a valor tree, with a decent-sized landing running all the way around the structure.

"You just got home. Where are you going?" Auree called to me.

"For a walk," I called back before quickening my pace to a jog, then to a run.

The night still offered enough cover that I felt well-hidden racing around houses, over bridges, and under irrigation pipes.

We lived in the section of our city most heavily populated by star-seers, those who can see forthcoming events by reading the stars. Since we're most active at night, this was the most challenging area. The other four talents would still be resting, or just barely waking up, not likely thinking of coming outside just yet.

Builder housing lay just past our area, where those primarily responsible for constructing, repairing, and adding on to our city resided. It was the only part of my city separating me from the weavers, who provided us with fabric and clothing. This was where I would find Henna. Although she was also a seer, both her parents were brilliant weavers.

There were also irrigators to supply our people with fresh water and healers to care for our ill and prepare medicines. I was grateful there was no need to tear through their housing, too.

I was especially careful to avoid the Avarice castle, since the most watchful eyes surrounded it both day and night.

I couldn't stop thinking of Blush as I ran. My other two sisters looked so much alike. Blush was supposed to be *my* little replica. That would never happen now.

The branches became thicker. A pink and blue sunrise began to peek over them. I knew I was close.

Then, there it was, branches hanging all around it. The overgrowth near Henna's house was always a mess. Her parents preferred it that way.

Henna's window was staring right at me when I reached the open walkway around her home. I found myself out of breath as I pushed the heavy cloth covering aside and climbed into her room. She was already in bed fast asleep, her skin's light dimmed slightly by slumber. She was a star-reader, as well, so she'd been at school all night. Star-readers generally slept through the early hours of the day.

There was no reason to disturb her. She wouldn't notice if the cloak disappeared for a day or two. And I knew she wouldn't be angry when I told her what I'd done.

I crossed the open space slowly, careful not to make a sound. There was only a short bench on the side of her room opposite her bed. Quite a few simple dresses had been laid over it. The scrolls she'd taken notes on at school rested upon them. Two pairs of soft slippers were placed neatly underneath the bench. Henna managed to keep her room tidy by hiding nearly everything she owned under her bed.

The room was all hers. She was an only child—sort of. Her parents had given birth to a son when she was two. He was a defect, which was part of the reason she wanted to visit the Surface so badly. Her parents were heartbroken enough they'd made certain not to have any more children.

Lying on the floor, I pushed dusty papers, fabrics, and hair adornments aside so I could get to the box behind it all. I gasped and bit my lip when a needle stabbed my hand through a little sack of what must have been her sewing things. I rubbed my hands together before going back to pushing things around a bit more carefully.

Finally I saw the old wooden box. I slid it across the floor as quickly as I could manage while still keeping silent. It was short, but plenty wide enough to hold everything I would need.

Inside it I found the thick, padded undershirt that would give me more of a manly look. Then I took out the boots Henna had modified to make her appear taller. It was a struggle getting them on since her feet were a good bit smaller than mine. My toes were curled under and my feet pinched tight, but I managed it. Lastly, I removed the most important piece, the transporter's cloak. I slid the box back under Henna's bed and pushed her things in front of it again. Then I put the cloak on as I went back to climb out her window.

The early morning sun shone brightly now.

The sound of water spraying outside startled me. Jordan was standing just outside his house. He was Henna's neighbor and a classmate of ours. He was tall and handsome, a serious crush of mine for as long as I could remember. Water poured from the pipe beside him into the cup he was holding.

It was a good thing my identity was already hidden within the cloak. But had he seen me exit Henna's window?

I didn't have time to worry about it. I set my pace at a fast walk to avoid looking suspicious and hurried on my way.

Watching him made me thirsty. My people relied heavily on always having water nearby, since our bodies used it along with sunlight to keep us alive, much the way plants do.

Jordan shivered at the grim sight of my attire before I looked away, walking as quickly as I could. It was important that I reached the passageway before the other transporters did or the men who stood guard there would have no reason to let me go down.

The boots were hurting my feet. It felt like I might fall at any moment. Still, I ran when I was certain Jordan couldn't see me anymore.

It would have been peculiar had he seen a transporter dashing all over the place.

My ankles were throbbing and my chest was on fire by the time I reached the bridge leading to the passageway. It was the longest one ever built and led straight to the peak of a mountain. Stairs had been cut into the mountain's side. They worked their way back and forth all the way to the ground. At least twenty men stood at the enormous ledge where the bridge met the mountain, spears in hand.

There was no sign of the transporters. Either I had missed them or they hadn't arrived yet. The latter seemed more likely, considering how much closer Henna's house was to the passageway than mine and how fast I'd gone.

I turned around so I could work my way through bridges and around trees back into the city, hoping I could come up behind the transporters and join their line. There were little more than bridges and small landings so close to the passageway. No one wanted to be near it.

My heart pounded, nearly audibly. I was as frightened as I was determined. Of being caught. Of facing an adult defect. Of what might happen to me on the Surface.

What hope I had of ever seeing my sister began to die when the first houses came into view. And then a man in brown appeared from the back side of one, followed closely by another. I felt a rush of joy at seeing the tiny bundle of blankets carried by the fourth.

My muscles seized for a moment. Everything suddenly became very real.

Ten men in cloaks had rounded the house by the time the last one emerged. Number eight's hood turned to face me. He lifted an arm to motion for me to join them. It seemed a natural thing for transporters to fall into line as they moved through the city, making what I did next much easier.

Swallowing all my fear with the help of every Surface daydream I'd ever had, I pulled my hood lower over my face and made my way to become number eleven in their line. I made certain to keep the enormous sleeves hanging down over my hands. They would have been a dead giveaway to my deception.

I turned right onto the bridge that would take me to the transporters. Number three was just passing by at the very end. My head hung lower until I could only see my feet.

The breeze blew toward them, pressing gently against my back.

It's not too late. You can still turn back, fear seemed to call from where I'd buried it deep down.

I ignored it. No matter what happened, I was doing this.

2

I glanced up when I took my first step onto our final bridge. Number ten was only a few paces ahead of me. I hurried to catch up, wishing the world was still shrouded with night.

Watching my feet and the fat, overgrown branches below, it was easy to let excitement win out. Valor trees were so enormous and full of foliage, it was impossible to catch even a glimpse of the Surface. I'd explored every part of our city available to me more than once, trying to sight any indication of the Surface, and failed at every attempt.

The stony gray mountain with bits of blue and black crystal embedded within broke through the branches below. I'd never gotten close enough to make out the stairs. Now I could see them snaking back and forth toward the mountain's peak.

A minute later, I was stepping onto the ledge, hoping with all my heart that no one would realize I didn't belong.

"Another defect?" a gruff voice asked.

I didn't bother to lift my head.

"Yes. A little girl, born to Devin and Bloom." I recognized the voice of the transporter from my parents' bedroom.

"We'll put that in the records. Go on and follow the guards. I'll make sure every transporter has a gathering bag. It's been forty-eight days since the last defect was born. We'll be needing every useful thing you can find down there."

The heavy footsteps of the muscular guards moving toward the dark tunnel in the mountain were jarring. My anxiety over being so near to the transporters was doubled at the guards' presence.

A moment later a bag appeared beside me. A meaty arm led away from the handle. Being careful not to reveal any of my hand, I took hold of it. The guard's arm drew away. I relaxed a bit.

This was happening. I was pulling it off.

The transporters began moving toward the tunnel. Soon I was walking into the shadowy cavity at the inside of the ledge. A steep stairway went downward and wrapped around to the outside once more. Then we were descending, winding around the mountain's exterior, turning left and then right. The path could hardly be called straight or consistent.

It wasn't the descent that made my knees feel shaky, though. It was the long line of men that could have looked back at any moment, right into my hood. That's all it would have taken and everything would've been over.

The bits of blue stone glittered in the sunlight at my aching feet, like stars of sapphire in a stormy sky.

Such direct sunlight would have usually made my skin beam brightly. Our cloaks prevented that.

For a split second at a sharp turn in the stairs, I caught sight of a tuft of dark hair poking out of Blush's blankets. I'd never seen hair that wasn't white before.

Everything seemed to darken as we sunk lower and lower into a world completely shaded by valor trees. Their branches began thinning out. Weepy trees and dots of color growing along their trunks came into view. A long walk later and I caught sight of the ground. The dots of color became berries.

Then I could see so far I wanted to reach out my arms and twirl around. The Surface seemed to go on forever. It was an amazing sight, worth every risk I'd taken to get there.

A tiny whimper drew my attention back to Blush. Her head bobbed up and down against the shoulder of the transporter holding her, causing the blanket to fall off her head. A pair of little balled-up fists wriggled free of the blanket as well.

"Halt," her transporter called. Everyone stopped so he could feed her the rest of her bottle.

Her eyes opened for only a moment, revealing giant black irises in contrast to the icy blue color of my people's eyes. Her skin was a beautiful light bronze color instead of pale. It lacked any light at all. But aside from that, Blush didn't look so different. She was quite lovely, actually. My love for her went so deep already, it wouldn't have mattered what she looked like.

It wasn't long before she'd drifted off to sleep and we were moving once more.

Halfway around the mountain our feet finally hit the ground. I paused for a moment, fascinated by the way the top layer moved about when I rubbed my boots against it.

I followed the transporters through the woods away from our city. It was disappointing to find very little growth aside from the trees. We passed by a patch of moss or tree shoots now and then, but nothing more.

"Guard." A transporter broke away from the line, followed by one of the guards. They both went to rip vines from around the base of a valor tree and put them into the transporter's bag.

Fifteen steps later another did the same. Then another.

I realized they may be expecting me to return with a bag full of something useful.

Luckily, Auree was a healer so I'd learned enough from her

to recognize what plants I should gather. She was the only one of my family without the ability to read the stars. The gift of healer came so naturally to her, though, there was no question as to whether or not she'd been born with her own special talent.

We began walking alongside a thin stream. The water gurgled and splashed against pebbles and roots. It reminded me that I was painfully thirsty, but I continued to follow.

Fragments of sunlight broke through as the valor trees became farther apart.

A transporter broke away to harvest some shrubbery I knew fought infections of the skin.

My eyes widened when I saw a rare graceling flower growing behind one of the giant trees. A film coursed through its stem that could pull venom right out of your body. Only the transporters ever needed it.

I hoped another transporter would see the vital plant. There was no way I was breaking away with no cover to hide me and prevent a guard from tagging along. But no one noticed. So it was left behind.

"Almost there," a guard called back.

The ground began sloping downward up ahead, the stream breaking away to the right. A valley lay before us. Right in the center, a house built of thin branches that had been woven together stood alone. Even the roof was created after this exquisite patterning.

Tears clouded my vision. This was certainly where my sister was destined. I didn't want to be there anymore.

The pain was too much. I stopped when the transporters began their descent. I'd loved that baby for so long. And now she was being handed over to a complete stranger. I felt protective of her, but helpless to do anything.

So I followed the stream away from the others, where I could get a drink and cry until they returned. The water washed through a thick growth of bushes and pint-sized trees to an opening of sunlight and serenity. The tip tops of wild vegetation grew in uneven rows all around. The water pooled into a small pond where I knelt and cupped my hands together to get a drink. My eyes closed as I swallowed the refreshingly chilled liquid.

My sister is a defect, I thought to myself. *I'm never going to see her again...* I couldn't help but cry noisily. It hardly mattered if anyone heard. What punishment could I possibly receive for coming to the Surface that hurt more than this?

The defects would get to watch Blush grow up, while our family was left with a gaping hole where she belonged. Or what if they abused or starved her? We would never know anything of her life.

I flinched and stood up when I heard leaves rustling nearby. My moment of careless defiance had passed. I realized very quickly how much I truly cared if my sin was discovered.

The sound of footsteps drew nearer, but not from the direction of the transporters.

My heart pounded at what might be approaching, as I wiped both eyes on my sleeve. While I was somewhat familiar with healing plants, I had only my imagination to tell of what dangerous beasts might dwell down here.

I thought for a moment of running away screaming for the guards, but a hand appeared pushing the brush aside so someone could get through it. Then a young man of great stature stepped through the overgrowth. He couldn't have been more than a few years older than me. His eyes were dark, his lashes thick and long like dozens of delicate butterfly antennae. He had the same dull skin as Blush.

He approached the other side of the pond and stared at me sympathetically. "I heard you crying," he said in a powerful, harsh voice. "Are you lost?" It seemed he was trying to sound kind, though his voice wouldn't allow it.

I swallowed hard. Here before me stood a defect. He was no monster. On the contrary, I found him enchantingly attractive. I was afraid to speak for fear of him discovering what I was.

"Are you injured?" he asked, crossing the pond. The smell of burning wood danced through my nostrils as he drew closer.

Without warning, he reached out and pulled my hood off. I sucked in a deep breath and stared at him, petrified. No doubt my skin was shining as it never had before.

He didn't look surprised at this, though. Instead, he turned my head gently from side to side. "You seem to be alright," he rumbled, "but you of all people shouldn't be this close to the accursed luminaries of the sky. If you were discovered, they would probably take you to their city and you would never see your family again."

What could he mean? I wondered, but grief got the better of me. I bit my lip as tears began streaming over my cheeks.

"Oh, come here." The man put his arms around me.

I was too sad to be surprised. Instead I leaned against his chest and let out a long whimper.

"Whatever it is, time will heal it."

I loved his voice. As scary as it sounded, it was also very comforting. Knowing that this powerful being was on my side made me feel safe.

Without warning, something red leapt out of the water toward me.

"Look out!" the man cried, grabbing me with both hands and throwing me behind him. I fell hard to the ground.

The man landed on his stomach beside me, howling in pain. The earth shook violently. He rolled over as I saw something long and red slither back into the water.

Pond water sloshed around ferociously and splashed onto

the surrounding dirt and grass at the earthquake. I screamed and fell over on top of the defect. I'd never known the world could shudder so horribly. A crack opened in the ground on the other side of the pond before everything became still. Water spilled into the fracture.

"Get back," the man said through heavy breaths, struggling to sit up and scoot away from the water. He was holding one arm between his elbow and shoulder in clear agony.

"Are you alright?" I asked, scooting back with him.

"*Of course not*. That was a red devil serpent. I'll be dead by nightfall."

"It bit you?"

He answered with a look of intense hatred.

He turned his head to vomit all over the ground. Fire poured from his lips with it, spreading away from us.

I leapt to my feet at the thought of the graceling flower. "I can save you. A defect body can't be too different from ours."

"Defect?" The ground began to tremble again. "You're from the city in the trees. You'd love to see me die." He leaned over to cough up more vomit and fire.

"I would not."

"You stay away from me," he choked out as he struggled to crawl away over the fire. It was fascinating to see that the flames did him no harm.

I had to focus on his wound. "Just stay here. I'll be right back."

The man collapsed in the fire.

Tearing the boots off and tossing them to the ground, I ran along the stream as fast as I could. No sign of any transporters or guards. I wondered if the earthquakes had sent them fleeing home and I had been abandoned.

It was far more important to worry about saving the man's life who had offered his for mine.

When I was close to the flower, I saw my original companions hurrying toward the passageway in the distance. It would have been so much easier to follow them. The threat of angry defects appeared to be reason enough to have left my bag behind. Two transporters were empty handed.

But it was my fault the defect was dying back there. And I was no coward.

I ran around behind the valor where I'd sighted the graceling flower and was happy to discover dozens of them filling a spacious inward groove of the tree. After grabbing two handfuls, I took off in the direction from whence I'd come.

3

T he bright rays of sunshine felt good against my skin
when I broke through the clearing.

The defect was lying unconscious in exactly the same spot where I'd left him. There was little more than ash of the grass surrounding him. The final breaths of his fire crept up over a small tree nearby. His clothes were a bit charred, but still intact.

Dropping the flowers in a pile, I sat down and began trying to pull his arm out from under him. It took a lot of yanking and budging but it finally came free.

His arm was already red and swollen to nearly twice the size it should have been. Two holes where he'd been bitten oozed a thick green pus. I squeezed as much of it out as I could so whatever it was the flowers offered could go directly into his body. The holes went deeper than I'd expected. I wiped the pus coating my fingers onto his pants before picking up a flower.

While I recognized the striking purple plant, I had no idea how best to extract the anti-venom. I pressed my thumb and finger together around the top of the stem and squeezed as I went down. It was a good thing I was holding it over the wound.

Halfway to the bottom, a dark slime began seeping out into one of the holes in the man's arm. I got out every bit I could before reaching for another. One glimpse told me I'd grabbed six gracelings with one hand and five with the other.

I cast the first graceling aside and did the same thing with a second one, alternating between dripping the slime into each hole.

At number six, the skin around the wound looked dry and papery. Blood began oozing with pus from the wound. He groaned unconsciously when I squeezed and cleared as much out of his arm as I could. My hands became caked in the disgusting secretions just as before. Again, I wiped them off on the side of the man's pants and got back to work.

Secretions from the eleventh flower had hardly sunk into his arm when he began trembling all over. He rolled onto his side and cringed forward, crying out in pain. "*OOOOHHAA!*" The fingers on his hand curled inward unnaturally.

One leg jerked forward and kicked me accidentally. His skin was freezing. Removing my cloak, I laid it over him, careful to leave his injured arm free. One way or another I needed that cloak to get home. I preferred not to wear his still-flowing seepage.

His teeth were bared in silent pain when I stood to gather dry brush to set a fire beside him. The tree had gone out, but a few tall, spindly shoots were still ablaze where the thicker growth began.

Fire has always been forbidden in my city, since it's said to be capable of burning it to the ground. Every sort of luminary, as this man called us, was taught at a young age which elements were most flammable and how best to extinguish a fire. So I knew enough to get it burning big and warm.

The man's eyes fluttered open when I sat beside him and put a hand on his cheek, then they closed just as swiftly. He had finally become motionless. His skin was still freezing, though he was clearly not dead. Already, the swelling in his arm had gone down somewhat.

I decided to gather enough wood to keep the fire fed for a while and piled it all up beside him.

Then I took my heavy shirt off and laid it over his torso before sitting against his back, where I pulled him carefully toward me. The man was quite large and heavy as stone, made up mostly of muscles. But I did eventually roll his back onto my legs, his head resting against my side. For a long time I rubbed my hands over his arms, hoping my body heat would help to warm him. Occasionally, I added more wood to the fire.

Aside from that, there was nothing to do but mull over the consequences of my actions. Like what my parents would say about me disappearing for so long. Or what the Avarice would do if I was discovered. It was nearly enough to have me quaking as the man had been.

I didn't want to think on it anymore. Instead, I put an arm under the man and leaned over to hug him against me, rubbing my whole other arm back and forth over his far side.

I wished I'd never come to the Surface. The man in my arms could very well die because of me.

At that thought, he rolled over to face me, pressing his injured arm into the ground between my crossed legs and draping the other around me simply because it had nowhere else to go. I had to maneuver the cloak to cover him properly. My legs were beginning to tingle with the weight of his body cutting off sufficient blood flow.

I stretched them out straight and continued running an arm over his back.

Hours must have passed by. The firewood I'd gathered eventually ran out. The man's body had warmed enough that I stayed right where I was.

Morning was becoming afternoon when he groaned and pressed one hand against the ground to sit up with. I leaned back and scooted my legs out from under him.

"How are you feeling?" I asked timidly.

"Awful," he mumbled, reaching for the wound. It was still pretty red and papery, but considerably less enlarged. The oozing had also stopped. He scooted on his knees toward the running stream to lay down, cast his face into the water, and drink great mouthfuls of it.

"You probably shouldn't do that," I said as I stood to fetch the cloak that had fallen from his shoulders. "Remember there's a red devil thing in there."

He ignored me and continued drinking.

I waited behind him, wondering if I should try prying him from the water. I decided he would have probably rather been bitten again than to have me touch him. Clearly, he detested me for what I was.

He swayed and nearly fell over when he finally stood. He stumbled back away from the water before he turned to face me, looking unhappy. I wasn't sure if it was all the pain he was in or if he was just dwelling on how much he hated me for the city from which I'd come.

"You must be a healer," he said in a raspy voice.

"My sister is a healer."

"Then I am grateful for your sister, but I'm forever in *your* debt. I'm Gabriel."

"You saved my life first, Gabriel. And my name is Sleigh."

"You could have left me for dead, though. So you've earned my eternal trust. I can help you get back into your city. You're not a transporter, so you obviously weren't meant to come down here."

I wondered how he knew so much. "There's only one way to get back in, but I doubt you'll be able to help me with that."

Gabriel shook his head, wincing as he twisted his arm inward to look at the wound. "Your people underestimate us. They think of us as nothing more than ignorant barbarians, don't they?"

I stared at my feet, unwilling to answer.

"They're the ignorant ones. There isn't a tree we can't climb right into your city. We know all about your kind... What is it that drove you to come down here, anyway?"

"My sister was taken this morning for being born a defect. I only wanted to see her."

His eyebrows dipped down momentarily. "You're wrong to call us defects."

"I'm sorry. If I had known anything about your people, I would have never grown up calling them that."

"It's alright," Gabriel rumbled, sounding more like himself and still looking severe. "The Avarice control you with ignorance. They don't want you thinking for yourself."

"No, they don't. It would be anarchy without them."

"Come on. You need to get home before anyone notices you're gone."

Gabriel went around the fracture in the ground to the tall grass he'd initially emerged from, leaving me to gather my things and follow him feeling puzzled. It seemed like he should make me nervous, the brutish voice and overpowering physique. I found it impossible, however, not to feel a certain unexplainable bond to a man who had taken a fatal blow for me and offered a lifetime promise of trust.

"If you knew I was dressed like a transporter, how did you not know I was from the city?" I asked him.

The brush thinned out the farther along we went.

"We find things that have fallen or been thrown away by sky luminaries all the time. It wouldn't be unusual for someone to wear a transporter's cloak."

Gabriel stopped to untie something fastened to the trunk of a tree that hardly stood above his head. It was brown and blended perfectly with the tree's bark. He began unrolling a thick piece of cloth with dark sludge smeared all over its insides. I could barely make out two more of these rolls tied to other trees.

"What's that for?" I asked.

"You can never tell your people about this," he replied. "Not your closest friends. Not even your family."

"I won't."

"Which direction is your house from the mountain passage?"

"East, about halfway through the city."

"I'll get you as close as I can." He began walking through the open trees.

I fell in step beside him, still feeling the painful loss of Blush.

"Will your people take good care of my sister?" I asked.

"I'll see to that myself. Does she have a name?"

I smiled fondly at him, feeling better at the thought of him looking after her. "We were going to call her Blush."

He nodded. We walked in silence for a minute or two.

There were so many useful things we walked past, but I didn't want to put Auree at risk by having her smuggle it to the healers.

"You should probably leave all that behind." Gabriel gestured to the boots and clothes on my arm.

"But I took them from my best friend. I've got to give them back to her."

"I didn't think there were any female transporters."

"There aren't. The cloak was her grandfather's."

"Then you'd be doing her a favor. Once in a while a luminary sneaks down here when a baby is taken from them or someone they love falls ill and your city is lacking the resources to heal them. If they risk going back to your city and the Avarice find out, the luminary is brought back down during the night and put to death."

I stopped walking to stare at him in horror.

"If you or your friend were ever found with that cloak, you'd probably be killed."

"They kill people? Are you sure?" It was true that someone went missing now and then. Their disappearances were always attributed to a fatal fall, though.

"Yes. My people have seen it happen. We're always watching, remember?"

"Have *you* seen it, though?"

"Only once. My fath—an Avarice read him his charges before he had him killed."

"Your father's an Avarice?"

His face became acidic. "Spencer is my father."

"Hm." I could see a slight resemblance in the shape of their face and mouth. Spencer's hair and skin were so much lighter, though, the similarities ended there. And he always looked so exhausted, certainly the grumpiest-seeming of all the Avarice. It wasn't hard to imagine him rejecting his own son. "I wonder if their guards know they've been killing people," was all I could think to say.

Gabriel lifted an eyebrow. "They're the ones who handle the killing part. Now come on. You need to get back to your city before anyone notices you're gone."

My pace quickened beside him. "But—what if I ever want to return to the Surface?" The image in my mind of the Avarice was quickly becoming distorted and chilling.

"What? To live with a bunch of defects?" He offered a playful smile.

"I guess they wouldn't have a luminary, but you've made the

Avarice sound so wicked." My desire to get home undetected was steadily growing.

"Only the luminaries from your city, Sleigh. They are born to our people as often as we are."

"Really?" I'd never thought of that.

"Really. And none of them are ever rejected."

His words gouged at my heart, drawing a painful sigh. "I didn't reject Blush, you know, and neither did my parents. My mother begged to keep her. I think my father might have even had to restrain her from fighting against the transporters."

"Yeah?"

I nodded sadly.

"Well, I guess it doesn't matter." He stopped beside a valor tree and unrolled the cloth completely. It was a great deal longer than his arm span. He stretched his injured arm back and forth gingerly. "As long as your people bow down in fear to the Avarice, they'll keep stealing your children and we'll keep fighting to protect a people who have rejected us. Now get on my back and don't let go."

"Okay." Throwing my arms over his shoulders, I jumped and crossed my legs around him from behind.

Gabriel flung the cloth upward and blew fire against the inside of it. The black gunk began to crackle and spark. All of a sudden, it blew violent gusts of wind against us as we shot upward. He flinched at the weight pulling on his arm.

"What is that stuff?"

He ignored me and continued breathing out fire.

When I looked down and saw how high up we were, I hugged tighter to him. Heights had never scared me until I was dangling from this man.

I nearly screamed when he jerked one arm forward to avoid hitting a fat branch. The higher we went, the more maneuvering was required. He seemed an expert in avoiding obstacles from above, in spite of the vision block. It amazed me even more that no holes ever burned through the cloth.

It was impossible not to enjoy myself in spite of my fear. Gabriel was truly a good-looking man. It felt good to lay my head against his shoulder.

The ground began to disappear beneath the valor branches. I was certain I would see my city at any moment.

And then the fire stopped. The sparks went out. We floated gently to a nearby limb. "Titanasaur feces give off an enormous airstream when ignited," Gabriel whispered.

I wrinkled my nose, though there was no scent in the air.

"Follow this branch to the edge and it should take you to one of your bridges."

"Wait." I had so many questions left to ask. "What did you mean when you said your people fight to protect mine?"

"Sleigh, there isn't time."

"Please don't make me wonder forever."

He let out a sigh as he glanced through the thick foliage behind me. "There are hordes of ferocious centaurs who collect your kind for servants. They take one of us now and then, but it's the luminaries they really want. They don't know about your city because we never let them near it."

This left me even more confused. "Why would you do that for a people you believe hates you so much?"

"Because it's the right thing to do. Even if they hate us, they're still parents to many of my kind."

I smiled in admiration. This man alone had rearranged all my points of view. "I hope I do see you again someday."

"Yeah?"

I nodded.

"Maybe I'll come back up here and leave one of these gliders behind for you, just in case."

"Okay." I smiled and put a hand on his forearm, part of me

wishing he could come with me. "Thank you again for saving my life."

He lifted his other arm and laid his hand over mine, returning the smile. "The same to you." We stood frozen in time for only a moment. I wished we weren't from two different worlds.

Then I turned away to leave. The branch was plenty wide enough to make me feel safe. When I reached the smaller branches, covered with shoots of leaves that twisted through one another, I paused for one last look at the man I would never consider a defect of any sort.

But he was gone.

On the other side of the cluster of smaller branches I saw a bridge not far off. There wasn't a soul in sight. So I ran over the largest, central branch and lowered myself carefully down until I was only three feet or so above the bridge.

Wait. What's a centaur? I wondered, dangling from the tree. I shook it off because there was nothing I could do about it now.

Then I jumped and ran to Henna's house as fast as I could.

4

"Henna, get up." I shook her elbow after sneaking back into her room.

She lifted her head and turned away from the wall to look at me. Her long bangs she usually swept to one side dangled over her eyes. "Huh?"

"I went to the Surface." My voice came out a mere whisper.

She plunged her head into her pillow. "I'm dreaming."

"No." I sat on her bed against her side. "My mother gave birth to a defect. I took your grandfather's cloak and went with the transporters."

Henna finally sat up, shoving her bangs to the side and looking somewhat alert. "Are you serious, Sleigh?"

"I met a defect down there. He said the Avarice would have had you killed if they found you with that cloak or if they found out I went to the Surface."

She jerked her head back and opened her eyes wider. "The Avarice? How does he even know about them?"

"They're not what we've always been told, Henna, the Avarice and the defects—"

A thunderous detonation brought us both to our feet. We

raced to the window and watched a second explosion burst in the sky. A third skyrocket would mean that everyone was to meet outside the castle immediately. This was only used in absolute emergencies.

I watched a stream of sparks sail through the sky. The third explosion boomed through the air. My heart hammered. My life was in jeopardy.

"Henna," her mother called. "Henna, wake up. We've got to go." She opened the bedroom door and stuck her head inside. Henna's mother was a quirky woman who always had a dreamy sort of look on her face. She didn't seem at all surprised to find us together. We'd been visiting each other through our windows for years. "Sleigh, how nice to see you. We had better hurry and go see what's wrong. Quickly now." She waved an arm toward the hall.

Henna grabbed a hairbrush from under her bed before we followed her mother through their wide living area toward the front door. She was able to get her straight hair brushed and as beautiful as ever by the time we were walking outside.

Henna's father stood on their porch waiting, fiddling with the seam of his silk shirt at one cuff. "The threading's coming loose, dear. How did I not notice it before?" Both of Henna's parents were weavers and overly concerned with these sorts of things.

"Let me see what I've got here." Henna's mother reached into a pocket on her dress as we all began our journey to the center of our city. She pulled out a threaded needle and took to sewing as we walked.

Henna and I kept several paces behind. "Did anyone see you?" she asked me.

"I don't think so."

"You've got to pull the stitches tighter if it's going to blend with the natural threading," Henna's father protested.

"Oh hush now," her mother responded. "I made this shirt for you. I know what I'm doing."

A flock of yellow birds flew from one branch to another. It was such a beautiful, sunny day, the sort I would have usually spent outside to enjoy.

Jordan ran ahead of his parents and brothers when we walked past the bridge leading away from his house. A new round of adrenaline coursed through me. Even in the face of imminent danger, I couldn't ignore the butterflies dancing in my stomach at his approach. It was so rare that he paid me or any other girl attention.

The intense look in his big blue eyes made him look more grown up than usual.

"Hey, Jordan," Henna greeted him.

He ignored her, walking close enough beside me to whisper. "I know that was you this morning."

My face hid the panic building up inside me remarkably. "This morning? As in when we left classes?"

"As in you leaving Henna's as a transporter. You can trust me, Sleigh. What were you doing in that cloak?"

I took a deep breath and stared down through the paper-thin spaces between the boards of the bridge we were crossing. I didn't know him nearly well enough to trust him. Regardless, he knew my secret. "My mother gave birth to a defect."

"So you actually made it to the Surface? Did you see a defect?"

"Yes."

"Are the skyrockets because of you?"

I shrugged.

"Man, that was fearless. Maybe I could walk you to school tonight so you can tell me what it was like, you know, if you're not in too much trouble."

I nodded, feeling sick in both a good and a bad way.

"You're going too fast." Jordan's little brother came running at him from behind, cutting our conversation short.

Jordan nearly put his lips against my ear, causing me to shiver. "If you need an alibi, just let me know."

Then he turned around and stopped to talk to his brother. "You don't have to keep up with me, Lane. Go walk with Shade or Jax."

"But I don't want tooooooo."

"Mom, do something." He was sounding less grown up already. I smirked inwardly at the thought.

Henna slid her arm through mine and smiled, the silver rings on her thumbs reflecting the sun brightly. It was easy to put fear aside if only for a little while to giggle with her at what had just happened. We'd spent plenty of late nights whispering together about him or some other boy at school.

The walk was quiet after that, except for Henna's parents going on about the best fastenings for what the builders of our people wore.

Gabriel filled my mind. His short-furred pants, like the skin of some wild animal. His golden, rustic skin. The midnight-black dreads of his twisted hair. Those magnificent obsidian eyes.

Though I was no artist, I could have filled books with all the drawings of what I'd seen that day. If I did make it home alive, there would be plenty to put in my journal.

The closer we got to the castle, the more people appeared, moving over the bridges. They wrapped around trees, filling the landings, pressing against the safety rails. There was no way I could find my family in the sea of faces.

The castle was just ahead now. Five stories of meeting rooms, sleeping chambers, and who knows what else glistened in the sun. The Avarice had silver paint covering the wooden exterior reapplied once a year, so it never seemed to age. The outside walls were all perfectly straight, from the bottom floor to the roof. The corners were sharp and even. It was flawless, not a scratch or a chip taken out of anything.

The wide balcony on the second floor hosted Draver, Arachne, and Spencer waiting for everyone to gather. All three wearing their finest black suits with gold trim. Half the Avarice weren't even there. And the guards didn't seem to be searching through the crowd for anyone in particular. Both were good signs.

Henna's parents led us through a side bridge to a landing with just enough space left for the four of us.

I noticed Jordan watching me as his family went in the opposite direction. He waved, making my stomach flutter. The day was shaping into something wonderful for me.

Of course the Avarice could turn all that around. My attention was drawn back to the three. They were no longer my great protectors. I would never again see them as peaceful heroes. They were murderers in my eyes now.

Spencer seemed the greatest traitor, though. Anyone with as much power as he had who would cast out a man like Gabriel was truly a defect at heart.

"There's your family, Sleigh." Henna's mother pointed to a bridge packed full of people. My sisters were waving frantically in my direction.

My father stood behind them, not paying us any attention.

"But where's your mother?"

"She had her baby this morning," Henna answered for me.

"Oh, how lovely. Was it another girl?"

Henna pulled on her mother's shoulder to whisper something in her ear. I turned to stare at the people pressed together beside us, trying to ignore the quiet conversation taking place behind me.

Her mother's arm went around me. I didn't have the heart to shrug her away.

"Good afternoon, citizens," Draven began, speaking into a funnel-shaped voice magnifier. The fine jewels sparkling all over his neck and fingers sprinkled the audience with glints of sunlight. "We have called you all here because of a breach in our security. One among you has thought to threaten us all by their actions. A defect was born and taken to the Surface this morning. A transporter who accompanied it cannot be accounted for. This tells us that one who went below was in truth no transporter."

My muscles tightened. My jaw clenched. I fought back terror.

"The guards tell us the imposter has yet to return. If the offender attempts this, the guards will take them. When you all leave, however, we require that you return to your homes. Guards will be visiting each of you soon to see what citizen is missing from our city. Rest assured, we will find the guilty person and deal with them accordingly.

"If you know anything about this, find a guard immediately. Withholding such vital information will put you just as much at fault as the one who has threatened us all by risking a disturbance to the defects. *You* will be punished exactly as they are. Now, return with your families to your homes as quickly as possible. Be careful. Look after one another. Be safe."

Hollow words. The Avarice didn't care. They wanted me dead.

"See you at school." Henna gave me a reassuring look.

If only I could take back what I'd shared with her. She could be in danger now, too.

It was a lot scarier to think of the other person who knew my secret, though. Jordan was someone I hardly knew. From this day on he held my life in his hands.

Henna and her parents began moving with part of the crowd toward their home.

I searched the faces until I found Jordan's. He winked, assuring me that he meant no betrayal. It was better that he didn't understand the true consequences of what I'd done if it was ever discovered, better that he never found out.

It was too late for Henna. There was no holding back with her, except of course for what I'd sworn to Gabriel never to tell anyone.

As I moved slowly over a bridge where I would merge with my family at the end, my thoughts returned to Gabriel. He saved my life by getting me back into the city before the Avarice called this meeting. He saved my life by getting me into the city a different way than I'd left it. He promised to watch over Blush himself.

Whatever gratitude was owed, whatever good I felt, was all due to him.

5

Over the years, following that day, my secret founded a friendship between Jordan, Henna, and I that kept us extremely close, Jordan and me in particular. Neither one really knew the depth of how the events following Blush's removal had affected me, though. A day didn't go by that wasn't filled with daydreams of defects, especially Gabriel. My life seemed hollow somehow, like it was missing what should be right at its core. Only my fear of never being able to return home prevented me from revisiting the Surface world.

But I did walk with Auree to healer's school some mornings to smuggle books away from their library one at a time, returning each one before taking the next. I took notes and learned everything I could of the Surface. Of course there was nothing of centaurs or defects in any of these texts.

Years passed without incident. My misdeed was never discovered. And then my eighteenth birthday came.

At midnight on every star-reader's eighteenth birthday, the Avarice pays a special visit to our school. The star-reader's family also joins them, as well as any others they've invited.

When midnight comes, their mind is suddenly opened to more revelation than it ever will be again, a momentary glimpse directly into the future. The stars literally take flight to their eyes alone, forming all sorts of things to come.

When Jordan turned eighteen several months ago, he saw the death of Arachne approaching and the Avarice's son Hecate taking his place of supremacy. He saw one of the city's older bridges weakening and falling unexpectedly, making it preventable. There were lots of smaller things, as well.

Usually, I was responsible for walking Eve to night classes. She was also a star-reader and had come of age at twelve two years ago. But with my family coming to observe tonight, I was free to sleep at Henna's and spend the rest of the day with her and Jordan before class.

At about sunset, we were sitting on the landing outside Jordan's house, playing a strategy card game most popular among the builders, which Jordan's father and two of his brothers happened to be. I had a scroll laying across my lap, studying it feverishly as I tried to play along.

STARS MOVING EASTWARD-SIGNALS TROUBLE, *Stars moving westward-signals joy*
   Clusters of 3:
   Blue to my eyes, illness
   Red, love approaching
   Green, love dying
   Purple—

"SLEIGH! IT'S YOUR TURN." Jordan put a hand on the center of my back and began kneading my tense muscles.

"Why are you ever worried about your notes?" Henna asked. "You won't need them tonight."

"I know. I'm just really nervous and this is the only thing taking my mind off of it. The Avarice are coming just to see me." They both knew the Avarice frightened me terribly, though Jordan still only knew half of it.

"You're as good a star-reader as I am. You have nothing to worry about," Jordan said.

His arrogance was always his greatest flaw in my opinion.

I stared over the landing's edge at the thick fog swirling around and swallowing everything below us, not wanting to think of this night. It felt so much better to let my mind wander to what Gabriel and my sister might be doing right now. I couldn't help but grin.

"Look, the first star's out," Henna said, taking our cards and shuffling them with hers.

"Of course..." I let out a nervous sigh. "Even with all the fog, the sky's still perfectly clear."

Usually star-readers were ecstatic on the night of their eighteenth birthday. But I would have given anything to skip it altogether. I didn't want to stand out to the Avarice in any way, even if it was only for this one evening.

"You want to give these back to your father?" Henna handed the cards to Jordan. He disappeared inside his house.

"I've had this feeling all day that something terrible is going to happen tonight," I whispered to Henna.

"Aw, you're just nervous. Don't let it get to you, Sleigh."

"That's not it. The feeling's stronger than any I've ever had before. I *know* something bad is going to happen."

Lines of concern crisscrossed over her forehead. She'd long since grown out of the bangs that once hid them so well. "You can't miss school tonight. It's more important even than your twelve year choosing, when you find out exactly where you belong in this city."

"I know. I just can't stop worrying."

"Hello, girls." Jordan's mother stepped outside, smoothing down her short hair. A whistling wind blew through the tree branches behind her, giving the illusion of giant arms waving this way and that.

"Hello, Sage," Henna and I answered together.

"You must be so excited about tonight, Sleigh." She took in a deep breath and exhaled slowly. "I remember my eighteenth birthday. It was the night I knew I was meant to marry Jordan's father. Until I saw it in the stars, I wasn't sure. Builders can be very difficult, you know, but he's just been wonderful."

"How sweet," Henna answered. "I can't wait to turn eighteen. Only seven weeks left."

"Yes, that's about the time Lane turns twelve. I do hope you'll both come to his choosing. We're so looking forward to finding out if he'll be a builder or a star-reader."

"*Nooooo*," someone howled from inside Jordan's house, followed by a series of mini-crashes. "Moooom! Shade destroyed my model home. I've gotta turn it in the day after tomorrow and now it's wrecked."

"It's okaaay," Shade called out. "He wasn't even doing it right anywaaay."

Sage rolled her eyes. "Let's hope for a star-reader, huh?" she whispered before disappearing inside.

I wondered if perhaps she was hinting at wanting an invitation to my star-reading tonight. Jordan and I were something of a pair. Regardless, there was no way I was inviting anyone else to attend whatever horrible thing was happening tonight.

"Bye, mother," Jordan called behind him on his way out the door.

I gathered my scrolls and we set out for school.

We crossed a bridge without speaking a word, then another. Halfway over the third bridge, we passed a bundle of leaves hanging like a handful of flowers being delivered to us. I grabbed a couple and turned around so I could walk backwards, watching them twirl round and round one another when I let them go. One by one, the fog and darkness claimed them.

The thought of where they would eventually land was nearly enough to press my eighteenth birthday out of mind. There was nothing I dreamed about more than returning to the Surface, except perhaps for the defects themselves. It was an addictive obsession I doubted would ever release me.

The bridge came to an end, tearing me from my brief reverie. I turned around to face forward and saw a few men standing on the landing we'd just reached, speaking quietly to one another about the stars. They seemed to be in a bit of a disagreement over a small cluster in the night sky:

"They're signaling a great storm, of course," one said. "We'll need to let everyone know to be prepared."

"No, it's only a bout of cold weather. That's nothing to worry about..."

They didn't even notice us pass by.

"I had this made for your big night," Jordan said when we'd nearly reached where our classes were held. He put one arm around me and reached in his pocket to remove a length of twine with an oval of hardened amber hanging from it. A tiny safftara flower had been set in the center. The blue flower with layers of yellow-tipped petals was boiled and given as a drink to those who had bad hearts. It had a healing effect that reversed years of aging and damage to this integral organ.

"It's beautiful," I said. "But how on earth did you get a safftara put in here?" They were nearly as hard to come by as gracelings.

"That I have promised never to tell." He winked mysteriously.

Auree, I thought. There wasn't anyone else with access to something so precious that would have done such a risky thing for me.

I stopped and wedged the scrolls between my knees so I could hold my hair up against my head. There was a lot of it to hold out of the way. I'd grown it out long and taken to tying it in tight braids while I slept so it was full of waves when I let it down every afternoon. It wasn't often I exposed my hair underneath since I began dying a few dark streaks into it to remind me of Blush. It was dark enough outside now to hide it.

Nobody else that I knew of had ever done it. I doubted much that anyone would understand. My family got it, though, and Jordan loved it.

He tied the necklace around my neck.

"We're almost there," Henna said, smiling knowingly. "I'll go on ahead and give you two a minute."

Jordan put his hands over mine to withdraw them from my head. His white locks of hair had a silvery-blue look about them with the moon's light glowing right behind him in the sky. "This is a big night," he said, pulling me closer. "You're coming of age and we'll both finish school soon. It seems like the right time to say I love you."

My fingers tightened around his thumbs.

"You've been on my mind since the morning I saw you after your defect sister was born. Auree's getting married in a few weeks. We could get married on the same day, make it twice as special for your family."

No.

I took in a deep breath when I realized I wasn't breathing. Jordan had never really made it from the crush in my head to the love of my life. He was gorgeous. He was popular in every crowd. There was undoubtedly any number of young women who would have traded places with me in a heartbeat. And I certainly didn't want to lose him.

But he wasn't the right man for me, not for marriage.

"It's okay," Jordan said with a confident grin. "I know what your answer is. Your family will all be at school tonight, so we can tell them then."

"I need time to think about it," I cut in. Time to think of a way around it.

"No, you don't." He laughed.

"Jordan, please. This is a big decision. Just give me some time."

"Oh, alright." He rolled his eyes and winked at me teasingly, like my need for more time was a joke.

My jaw clenched shut.

As irritating as his ego was, it was difficult not to think of what a good husband he would make as he took my hand and we resumed walking toward school. It just didn't feel right.

A warm sensation filled me inside when I thought of the awful feeling I'd been having. A slight smile crept over my lips. Jordan's proposal had to be the bad thing that was going to happen. It left me feeling awful. At least it had nothing to do with the Avarice, though. I could finally put it aside, and try to be excited about midnight.

As the night wore on, however, the feeling refused to go away.

Darkness brought a chill to the air. I was grateful that my parents thought to bring me an orange shawl when they showed up with Eve.

Star-readers attended school on a wide landing that had three rows of five benches each, along with a comfy stool up front for the teacher, Clovis. He kept a dark, wooden box beside his stool, which was full of supplies. One bench could easily seat four people. There was plenty of room for my family to join us, with only thirty-three students ranging from age twelve to eighteen. Star-readers were always the fewest in number among our people.

Six rather extravagant chairs with padded, velvet armrests had been placed to the left of the teacher's stool on this night. Ornamented with diamonds and shiny baubles, their backs were unnecessarily tall. Even before the Avarice arrived, it felt like they were making a show of their superiority and power.

Clovis had us split into groups of two as soon as everyone had arrived, an older student with each of the younger ones. Eve and I always paired together for these sorts of lessons. Then we all studied the stars, the elder students explaining to the younger students how to interpret their observations.

Jordan sat beside us with his young partner.

Eve and I always had fun together. We usually got off topic making jokes about Auree's boyfriend, Pat. He was so soft-spoken and clumsy. He was too adorable a man not to get a good laugh at. It was the only time we could get away with it, since no one else in our family was there.

Not on this night, though. Auree and Pat sat in the back center row beside my parents, waiting patiently for midnight to come.

The Avarice arrived well before the destined hour. Everyone stood to bow to them. Spencer and Arthur took the first two throne-like seats, looking grumpy and severe. Draven, Hecate, Felix, and Karan looked friendlier. Their presence was still just as unnerving as that of the first two.

Jordan and I returned to our seat, back to back as before. I felt him move away to brush my hair to one side and kiss my cheek. "It'll be alright," he whispered.

Time seemed to slow down. I couldn't concentrate with the Avarice watching us, and I couldn't wait to escape them.

The unpleasant sense of something terrible approaching became stronger. I tried telling myself it had already happened, that there was nothing left to fear, but the dark feelings absolutely would not subside. Whatever my misfortunate would be on this night, it certainly still laid in waiting.

6

E

ve and I studied quite seriously under the scrutiny of the Avarice for an hour or so more. Then finally, Clovis went to stand in front of his stool, a bit of his wispy hair swirling on the breeze like a miniature tornado. "The moon is nearly at the hour of midnight. Sleigh—"

I flinched.

"—how will you choose to observe the stars?"

"Um... could I do it from the top of that tree?" I pointed to the valor tree behind my teacher, holding up part of the platform. There was a top branch just right for laying back on, where nothing would obstruct my view. "I could see all the stars from there."

His eyebrows sank. "What an odd request." He turned to the Avarice.

Five of them looked at Spencer, like vultures to their master. "Take someone with you to record everything you see," he said to me.

It was the first time an Avarice had ever spoken directly to me. I blinked a few times, feeling like I might faint. At least I wouldn't have to worry about them while I observed the stars.

Making the decision of who to take with me, Henna or Jordan, provided a slight distraction. I didn't want to hurt the feelings of either one. Eve was the perfect alternative.

I barely got my mouth open to ask her if she'd come with me when Jordan stood. "I'll get a scroll and something to write with." He went to lift the rickety lid on the supply chest, leaving me to stare at him in surprise.

Hopefully Henna would forgive me.

Jordan removed several sheets of parchment and a stick of fine charcoal. Then he looked up at me and nodded toward the tree.

I handed my scrolls to Eve.

Then I walked past him and grabbed hold of the branch behind Clovis' stool a bit begrudgingly. My legs swung up so I could pull myself into the tree. I didn't mind Jordan going with me, only that he'd taken the choice away.

Pushing sticks and foliage aside, I snaked my way upward through the branches, higher and higher. Twice, my sleeve snapped a twig in half when it got caught on it, and I sustained a good scratch on one elbow. The branches thinned out a great deal before I reached the final hearty bough, where both Jordan and I had plenty of room to sit.

He rested his back against the last stretch of trunk. I laid down just as planned, watching the stars and waiting. My body relaxed at the sway of my hair and skirt left to hang over the edge. All my cares seemed to melt away from up there.

"How close do you think midnight is?" I asked Jordan. Telling time by moonlight is something I've always struggled with.

"It looks like midnight to me," Jordan answered. "It can't be long now. I'm glad you decided to come up here where I'm the only one by your side for one of the biggest moments of your life... like we're already married."

I returned his smile. It was a nice thought. Maybe the stars would help me to answer his question, the way they had for his mother.

"Has a student ever taken to the trees before?" a man's voice came faintly from below. It sounded like Hecate.

"Not to my knowledge," Clovis answered.

"What do you think they'll see?" I heard Eve asking.

Henna answered, but enough voices picked up that I couldn't understand her. I hoped they hadn't heard Jordan's remark.

The night was perfectly clear. Watching the stars has always had a way of putting my mind at ease.

Two heartbeats later, the stars began to bleed. Silver trickled away from them over the sky. My eyebrows drew closer together as I surveyed the heavens above. This wasn't how any star-reader had ever described the revelations of their eighteenth birthday. The stars began moving, zipping around so quickly they left traces of light behind them. Some moved closer together. Some farther apart.

I took in an excited breath. "It's happening!"

An unfinished building took form. A flock of twinkling birds attempted to fly through a window and knocked an entire wall down. "Birds are going to damage that new house the builders are working on... The builders will start construction on loads of new houses to the north, past irrigator housing. It looks like the perfect place to build onto the city... I see Eve. She must be at least my age." I gasped when I saw her standing before an Avarice, getting married. "She's going to marry your brother."

"Which one?" Jordan asked.

"Lane. He'll be a star-reader."

The stars drew different women walking around each other. The shapes came and went so quickly, I couldn't recognize who they were. But each one was pregnant. It seemed a strange thing for the stars to reveal, until they all appeared to have finally decided on one woman—Henna's mother. But she wasn't pregnant. Instead, her face was in anguish as she held a baby in her arms. Stars swished and sparkled together beside her, forming transporters as they came to take the baby away.

"Henna's mother is going to give birth to a defect," I told Jordan quietly, not wanting everyone to hear. I sat up suddenly, speaking even more quietly. "Don't write that down. The Avarice don't need to know."

Jordan stared at me, looking startled.

I gazed up at the sky again. I saw things like our head builder passing away and Auree living in a house full of little children that must have been hers. Jordan got it all down on paper.

Then the stars began to darken. For a moment I thought it must be over. But the tiny lights danced around one another before laying out curved lines. A man took to strolling across the sky, a man with twisted dreads of dark glowing hair who took my breath away. More stars came to join him, producing a little girl who strongly resembled my mother and me. My vision blurred with tears at the sight of Gabriel holding the hand of my tiniest sister. I wiped at them vigorously to clear my sight, keeping it all to myself.

"What is it, Sleigh?" Jordan asked.

"Blush," I whispered. "She's so pretty."

The look on Gabriel's face suddenly became strange. He picked up Blush and looked around, like he was searching the emptiness for something. Then strangeness became fear. He turned and ran away as an enormous figure came out of the distance chasing after him. This new figure was something of a half-man, half-beast, with four muscular legs attached to an animal-like body that grew from his waist down. More of these creatures gave chase from behind the first. It was so intense, I could actually hear their feet beating against the ground.

Gabriel set Blush down, turning to face the creatures and drawing a sword to buy her time as she kept running behind him. Tears fell from her eyes like sparkling rain from the sky. He cut deep into two of the beasts before one kicked him hard enough in the head to knock him out. The man-beasts ran on to capture Blush, trampling Gabriel to death as they ran over him.

"What do you see?" Jordan asked.

I realized I was shaking. I ignored his question.

The thunder echoed through my ears as the stars broke apart, twirling violently in funnels across the sky, leaving little circles and squares behind, all at the tops of valor trees. Our city unfolded, and then six sinister looking men appeared at the edges, the Avarice of course. They began wrapping thick bands around the outside of our city, their bodies growing larger and more powerful as they went. This continued until the men were so much bigger than the buildings, I couldn't tell if the city was shrinking or the Avarice were growing.

It was so unsettling, I almost didn't notice the figure walking toward a part of the restraints that was unattended. A young woman, me, approached. I was larger than the buildings but not nearly as great as the men in size. My face was obviously afraid, but also portrayed a firm determination. I took a few deep breaths before reaching back, balling my hand into a fist, and swinging a blow at the cords so hard, my arm began to blur.

Before my skin could even make contact, a cloud of stars blew toward the city from behind me. It broke my body apart, carrying it over the city and splitting the buildings into pieces as well. The Avarice seemed to howl as they broke apart.

And then stars were floating daintily back to their places, drifting across the darkness in every direction as if they hadn't just revealed something that would alter my life completely.

Thunder and horror still pounded through my mind as I sat up straight. The final vision of the night had left me confused.

but I was solely concerned with what I'd seen of my sister and Gabriel. I had to get to the Surface immediately to try and prevent the awful attack!

"What happened?" Jordan asked again.

"Make something up or just leave it all out," I said, reaching for a lower branch and swinging myself downward.

"Sleigh!"

I continued my descent. Clovis would let me go once I'd assured him Jordan wrote everything down. He always let students go early on their eighteenth birthday, just as soon as a record was made of whatever they saw. Most star-readers were exhausted after it happened. I was no exception.

Sleep hardly mattered at the moment, though. I had to get to the Surface.

My knees bent at the shock of jumping from a higher branch than was necessary. This was what the terrible feelings I'd been having all day led up to. I stood up straight, right behind my instructor. Everyone got quiet.

"Jordan wrote everything down. Can I go home with my family now?" I asked Clovis, putting on a very real yawn.

"Yes, of course, as long as he's made a record of everything."

"Thank you." I turned to bow to the Avarice, seething inside but not brave enough to leave their presence without doing so.

My family stood to join me. Pat had to wake Auree, who'd fallen asleep with her head in his lap.

Eve raced toward me from the bench she shared with Henna. "Do you mind if I stay?" she asked me. School was always her favorite place to be.

"Course not." I gave her a big hug. The pain of knowing I might never see her again stabbed at my heart.

Tears threatened to escape when my mother put her arm around me while we walked toward one of the two bridges attached to the landing. Jordan was still in the tree, probably trying to think of something safe to write down. I would make it up to him eventually, if I ever did return.

"Wait!" I turned back to my teacher. "I need to talk to Henna for a second."

He nodded, so Henna stood from her bench and started walking my way.

"You guys can go ahead," I told my family. "Auree and Pat must be exhausted and I'll only be a couple of minutes."

"Thanks, Sleigh." Auree gave me a sleepy hug. "Congratulations."

"Are you sure?" my mother asked. "We don't mind waiting."

"I'm sure."

My parents gave me hugs and told me how proud they were before they set out. Not crying was becoming nearly impossible.

Henna seemed so carefree as she approached, swinging her arms back and forth casually. I envied her that.

"What do you need?" she asked in an undertone.

I gave her a hug so I could whisper to her unnoticed, hoping it wouldn't look suspicious since I'd just hugged every member of my family. The wind blew her hair in front of my mouth conveniently as I held her close. "Blush is going to be taken captive and Gabriel will be killed. I've got to go to the Surface."

Henna gasped and tried to back away.

I pulled her closer. "If I'm not back by tomorrow night, tell my family everything."

"No. You can't go."

"Don't ever trust the Avarice. And tell Jordan I'm sorry I took off. Tell him I love him but I just wasn't meant to be his wife."

"His wife?" I let her pull away to stare at me.

"And you will always be my best friend, Henna."

She shook her head and cocked it to one side, offering a look that told me she understood. "You'll always be mine, too."

Jordan caught my eye as he climbed down behind the Avarice. He really was handsome, tall and perfect-looking.

"I've got to go," I told Henna before turning to take the bridge farther away from her. Saying bye to Henna was already painful enough. I didn't want to have to go through it with Jordan, too. He would have certainly put up a lot more of a fight, one I might not have been able to win.

All that was left to do now was make sure Auree was asleep and climb underneath my bed. I'd hidden a shoulder bag inside my mattress and sewn it closed, in case I ever needed to return to the Surface. Henna's parents were more than happy to teach me how to sew and to provide a few needles and thread. The shoulder bag was filled with a saw made into a knife-sword hybrid, a vial of graceling salve, ten feet of rope, and journals packed with drawings of Blush and the Surface, but mostly Gabriel. All I had to do was throw in a few jars of water when I got home and I would be set.

I just had to hope Gabriel was true to his word and had left me a way to return to the Surface.

7

A uree had just laid down when I got home. She didn't seem to notice when I entered our room. I sat on my bed fighting sleep until her breathing became slow and steady, which didn't take very long. She rarely stayed up this late.

A breeze fluttered through the window covering above my bed, sending tremors of dim light through the room. The weather had been so pleasant, we hadn't bothered to tie it closed in a few days.

I took the fabric cutters from the bench at the edge of my bed and scooted underneath my mattress. Without caution, I sliced through the thick material to the right of where my bag was concealed. The strap had a nick in from the cutters when I pulled it out. "Oh, well," I muttered to myself as I yanked the black bag free of its confines. I shoved the cutters and two jars of water at my bedside into the bag before climbing back onto my bed.

Pressing the window covering to the side ever so slightly, I peeked outside. No sign of anyone.

I glanced back at my beloved sister before I climbed outside. *I love you*, I whispered to her.

As I walked around the side of my house, I heard my parents' voices out front. That meant I had to go out of my way to avoid them.

I took a side bridge, rounded two houses, and then took off running. The only other person I saw was merely a shadow on a porch when I was about halfway there. The long bridge at the east edge of the city was desolate, as usual.

The branch I'd fantasized about transporting me back to the Surface had grown larger and closer to the bridge. I'd also grown a bit taller. It wasn't difficult to jump and wrap my hands securely around it. Then I swung my legs upward and heaved myself onto the limb.

My skin shone much too brightly at the sudden surge of adrenaline. I could hardly believe this was happening. As desperately as I'd always wanted to return to the Surface, it was still terrifying. There was little chance of me ever returning to this city, or to my family.

My feet raced over the branch. I loved my youngest sister as much as Auree and Eve. That love was more powerful than any amount of fear. I even began to feel some excitement for seeing her again as I knelt close to the valor's trunk and began running my fingers all over it.

The more I felt around, the more afraid I became. I had no alternative plan. There was no other way down. But I certainly couldn't go home and do nothing.

I was practically clawing my way over the branch when I felt a rope. It was too dark to make out much of it, but I could feel it wrapping around the massive heart of the branch. Pressing my body flat against the tree, I reached all the way underneath and felt something with my left hand. I grabbed it and slid it out, withdrawing a dark, rolled up cloth.

Another shot of adrenaline coursed through me.

Running my fingers over it, I decided it couldn't be very old. Gabriel must have been here recently. The thought made me smile, putting a new excitement for reaching the Surface into me.

As I began unrolling it, I wondered how I would navigate my way down. There wasn't time to dwell on it, though. I took a deep breath, threw the cloth upward holding tight with both hands, and jumped into the darkness. My skin shone bright enough at such fear that I could see branches coming as I floated gently toward the ground. Each time I saw one approaching, I kicked against it, away from the branch and farther from the tree's center. It wasn't so frightening once I got used to it, although my arms began to throb. I wasn't used to bearing my own weight for more than a few seconds.

I had nearly knocked myself away from the tree completely by the time I could see the ground. Once I landed, I ran to the tree's trunk and drug my knife through it, forming an X. That way I could find it easier when I came back, if I came back. Either way, I'd marked it *my* tree forever.

The darkness of night and the moonlight shrouded by trees was frustrating once I reached the Surface. It slowed me down considerably to have to be so careful with where I was stepping.

I could only hope I was going in the right direction to find the house where Blush had been taken.

Memories of three and a half years ago raced through my mind as I dashed over earth. This wasn't half as frightening as that experience had been. I knew enough now not to feel like I wasn't in danger, for the time being, at least.

The thing that weighed heaviest on my heart as I jogged along, of course, was my fear of never being able to return home. If I was gone for too long, it would become impossible to go back.

It felt wonderful to be surrounded by land that went on forever, though. There was something liberating about it that I only felt while on the Surface.

The mixture of fear and untamed freedom was disconcerting.

The trees opened up and moonlight revealed more of my surroundings. The ground dropped down up ahead. I ran to meet it, only to find an empty valley at my feet.

A light was flickering in the distance to my right. It seemed I'd gotten somewhat off course.

I ran along the top edge of the slope, loving the feel of earth beneath my feet. The light wind caused me to shiver.

A small house took shape. I could see a fire burning through one of the windows. I slid one hand into my bag and wrapped my fingers around the handle of my long, serrated knife as I approached the dwelling.

Anxiety over coming face to face with a new defect washed over me. I was acting as I went, having no plan as to how I would save Blush or what consequence my actions would bring. It was the only way I would get through it. Thinking it all out might have been enough to make me change my mind.

Hoping the knife wouldn't be necessary, I knocked on the door with my free hand.

I was surprised when an old woman nearly half my size opened the door. Her hair was gray and wiry, but her dark eyes reflected the light I radiated like black buttons made of glass.

"I knew you'd be coming." Her voice was not nearly as deep as Gabriel's, but the power it radiated was just as present.

She smiled and held out a hand, welcoming me into her home. It was certainly inviting, with three pink chairs set before the fire, bigger and softer-looking than any in my city. A fraying blanket had been folded and draped over the top of each one. Shelves of books and boxes lined the side walls. A steaming teapot had been set with two porcelain teacups upon the little table between the chairs, suggesting that she truly had been expecting someone.

"You don't even know who I am." I stayed where I was, suspecting a trick of some sort.

"I saw it in the stars, young darling."

"You're a star-reader?" Just when I thought defects couldn't become any more fascinating...

"That I am. Now won't you come in and have a word with old Livia?"

I couldn't bring myself to trust a defect I'd only just met. Aside from all that, I didn't have time to sit around and chat. There was no way to know just when Blush and Gabriel would be ambushed. "Thank you, Livia, but I'm in a hurry. I was hoping you could tell me where to find a man named Gabriel."

"Gabriel? He lives in the village north of those mountains. It'll take you all night to get there. Why not have a rest here first?"

"I truly wish I could," I said, stifling a yawn, "but my sister's in danger. I've got to get to her as soon as possible."

"I understand. There was more in the stars I saw for you, though. At least hear me out before you go."

"For me?" My heart stopped worrying for Blush just long enough to be concerned with myself.

"Yes. I saw that you will bring peace to the land. No more fighting. No more of our children taken. It will require much sacrifice, but through an unexpected and true friend, you will accomplish what no other has managed to do."

"Me?" I began shaking my head, taking her for a lunatic. "How do you know it wasn't someone else you saw in the stars?"

"You flew down from the trees, didn't you? You're from the luminary city in the sky. That's where you've come to visit me from, have you not?"

My breath came out short. I swallowed hard. Perhaps there was some truth to her words. "What else did you see in the stars?"

"Nothing more, darling. Only that a centaur will become your greatest friend and truest ally. They will be the key to everything I've promised."

It sounded like I wouldn't be returning home any time soon. That was the only place I wanted to be at that moment. I didn't want any centaur friends. I didn't want to end so much fighting. It was all too overwhelming.

Livia reached for my free hand to hold in both of hers. My other hand still held tightly to the knife within my bag. Her skin was so warm, it seemed to take the chill right out of the air. "Don't worry, darling. The stars are in your favor."

I didn't know what that meant, but I finally let go of my weapon to lay my hand over hers. "Thank you for your help, and for taking in the children the Avarice have taken from my people."

Livia smiled and gave my hand a good squeeze. "Good luck, darling."

As I left this kindly old lady behind, I couldn't help but wonder how much more trouble I was about to get into than I'd bargained for.

I RAN as much as I could. My star-reading had taken so much out of me, though, and skirting two giant mountains was no small task. I was forced to walk for a great deal of my journey.

The sun was threatening to rise by the time I saw houses. They were all similar to Livia's, woven beautifully of limbs. Their greatest difference was their size. They were so much larger than hers had been. A few of them had some ornamentation to set them apart. One had life-sized carvings of bears in the yard. Another had yellow flowers painted all around it at the bottom.

Everyone still seemed to be asleep. With no time to wait for the town to awaken, I took up running again, heading for the nearest house. It was the smallest one, without even a window on the sides that I could see.

A man appeared coming over a hill to my right, pulling a wagon full of dead animals I couldn't identify behind him. My course veered toward him.

It struck me just as it had with Gabriel how much more attractive I found defect men. They looked so much healthier and mightier than luminaries. Of course this one lacked the appeal Gabriel possessed, since he could have practically been my father by age.

He stopped when he saw me running toward him, scratching his chest as he waited.

"I'm—I'm looking for Gabriel," I said, completely out of breath, the moment I thought he could hear me. "He's in danger."

He leaned against a cart handle without taking his eyes off me. "I've never seen you before. Not from around here, are you?"

"Please, it—it was written in the stars. You must help me find him."

Clearly he was unsure of what to make of me, but he nodded northward toward some thick forestry. "He lives in the woods there. Got a pond and swings hung all over the place for that little girl."

"Thank you." I took off for the forest, catching sight of a girl with pitch-black hair staring at me through a window. She smiled and waved. I couldn't help but feel a rush of joy as I returned a little wave to the pretty child. Everything about the defects was so captivating.

Branches whacked into my shoulders and swept over my back when I entered the trees. They weren't nearly as tall as valors, but stood like giants nonetheless. I began following a path, weaving more safely through the trees.

A house built unevenly on a small hillside had strings of shiny red beads hanging from the roof all the way around. They hummed a simple tune as the wind played them like a harp. It was obviously not the right one.

I ran deeper into the forest, keeping to high ground. Another house came and went. The broken remains of a vacant, decaying house went as well.

Then I saw a newer-looking house not far ahead. It was more or less a pentagon in shape, with a few younger trees in the yard. They were perfect for holding the swings that had been hung all around. The little pond on its back side remained hidden until I was nearly there.

Knowing I could be so near to coming face to face with Gabriel once more brought on something nearly as powerful as the fear I'd been coping with all night. It was a fluttery feeling deep inside, one that brightened everything around me. I wondered for the first time if Gabriel might not still be single, and suddenly felt a stinging in my chest.

A laundry line had been drawn between two trees where men's clothing sewn from animal hides hung to dry. A few chairs sat at one end.

Racing around everything, I rapped three times against the door. No answer. I knocked harder, panicking inside. Still no answer.

Feeling dazed with exhaustion, I ran around the house and nearly slammed into an older woman when I rounded the corner.

"My goodness!" She threw a hand over her heart, then fought to catch the basket of colorful, little dresses she'd been carrying. She missed catching the handle she'd let go of. I flung a hand over the clothes to stop them from spilling out everywhere. "Thank you, miss. You startled me there." She straightened her bonnet and dusted off her apron.

She was about my height. Her form and demeanor were not unlike the women I was accustomed to. It seemed only defect men were given to such a fierce physique. She also had the look of someone who was completely overwhelmed. If I hadn't been in such a hurry, I would have offered some help.

"Sorry about that. I'm looking for Gabriel. Does he live here?"

"Oh, how lovely to have such a pretty young lady calling on my son. I'm afraid he's not here at the moment, though. He's taken his little sister out camping. We've had to keep her cooped up inside for so long with illness. He thought it would be good for her to get out since she's been feeling better."

Camping? I wasn't entirely sure what that meant. "Do you know where I can find them? It's really important."

She adjusted the basket so it rested higher against her waist. "It's possible they're in the treehouse he built in the old oaks on the other side of a field south of here. It's just that way." She pointed behind me, nearly dropping her laundry again.

"What was your name, miss?" she asked. "If you don't find him, I'll let him know you stopped by."

A bit of ice pumped through my blood at her words. If I didn't find him, she would never get to deliver that message.

"It's Sleigh."

"It's lovely to meet you, Sleigh. I'm Gabriel's mother, Felicity. I do hope I'll be seeing you again."

"Thank you. I hope so, too."

I turned and sprinted a couple of steps before I stopped. The woman smiled when I looked back at her. Like everything I'd done that night, I was filled with trepidation at what I was about to do. My heart's desire left no question in my mind of whether or not it had to be done, however.

"Are there other young ladies calling on him?" I asked.

The woman's face shone with a mother's pride. "Not one, miss. He's a fine man, but a bit of a loner at heart. Blush has filled it so well, I doubt it's bothered him much."

I nodded before turning back to run without stopping. I would do whatever it took to save this woman's adopted son.

It gave me absolute satisfaction to know he had given the past few years of his life to my sister. It was almost like he'd given them to me, knowing what she meant to my heart. A part of me hidden so deeply inside that I hadn't known it was there until that moment, even wanted to save him for myself.

8

I could just make out a treehouse up ahead when I finally stopped jogging to take a drink of water. It seemed small and close to the ground compared to what I was used to.

My hands were becoming shaky. It wasn't helping that the sky was so cloudy. Sunlight would have done me almost as much good as sleep at that moment.

Mist began falling as I tucked my half-empty jar back into my bag. It reminded me of the rainy days when my sisters and I climbed into our mother's bed and listened to her stories.

Never again... A lump formed in my throat at that thought.

I finished crossing the field and ran around a few oaks to the one holding up a little house.

"Gabriel!" I shouted, a fit of nervousness swelling inside me. "Are you up there?"

No response.

Shaking my damp hair behind my shoulders, I climbed the ladder to a small terrace and peered through a window. There was nothing inside but a few rolled up blankets. They looked *so* inviting.

I went down the ladder and studied the ground below. Dirt

was quickly becoming mud, but I saw a partial footprint behind the tree. There were three more a little ways off. I followed their course, finding another print every now and then.

The trees opened into a small gorge. The grass was considerably thicker here. All footprints disappeared. I followed the direction I'd been going to the tallest tree on the other side of the ravine. Then I began climbing rather slowly. Fatigue had all but won out.

Cold water dripped more heavily against my skin. It felt good.

At the top of the tree, I could see forest all around me, with little breaks here and there. I felt at home up here. The leaves at the end of the branch I stood on shook as I leaned one hand against the thinning trunk and turned slowly around.

Movement caught my eye at the base of a mountain to the east. Two distant figures were sitting in the grass with a pile of something between them. They scooped the last of it into a deep basket before they stood and started walking in my direction. They were so far away, it was impossible to recognize them, but it was certainly a defect man and little girl. It had to be Gabriel and Blush.

Relief fell over me with the fast-falling rain. I wasn't too late.

The sensation hardly settled in before a greater movement caught my eye farther south. A large group of something very animal-like with the upper body of a man growing at their fronts was tromping slowly toward me, the beasts from my vision. Sooner or later, their paths would cross with the two coming from the east.

I lowered myself from branch to branch with a new burst of energy. There was only one way of saving my sister, by offering myself in her place and hoping she would escape unnoticed.

STICKS CRUNCHED beneath my feet as I tore over the forest floor. My skin lit brighter with near-crippling anxiety. Every part of my body ached far greater, though, with the fear of not making it to the beasts before they found Gabriel and Blush.

Uproarious laughter came from ahead. The beasts' voices were not unlike ours. Clearly, they could hold on a conversation as well as any man.

My course veered to the right. Hopefully I would run past the brutes on their side, drawing them further away from my sister. The distance between us was closing. Something dark moved through the trees just ahead.

"There's a someone coming," one said.

"A someone who?"

"There. Luminary! Run her down!"

My course turned all the way to my right. A shriek escaped my throat when I heard them chasing after me.

Just let Blush be free, I said to myself. All that mattered was my sister's safety.

The predators were so close now, I could see them coming around me out of the corners of my eyes. My head was pounding. I kept thinking this would have been the perfect time for my body to finally give out. Sleeping through whatever they were about to do would have been so much easier.

My light burned brighter still, pulsating rapidly to the racing of my heart.

"Star-seer," someone shouted maniacally.

They cheered as a hand reached out and pushed me hard enough from behind to bury my face in the mud. I coughed and spat the sludge out, pressing my body away from the ground.

Larger bodies quickly surrounded me. I shivered at the sight of their flattened faces and the long, dark hair that grew from their heads and over the back of their necks. While their human half wasn't much bigger than a man's, their back half atop four meaty legs and long, dark tails seemed giant from where I lay. There was nothing friendly about them.

"I'll do whatever you want," I said, rising to my knees and leaving my bag in the mud. "Just don't hurt me."

Their cruel laughter beat against me without care.

"We, we don't hurt them luminaries," one said through his amusement.

I screamed when someone grabbed me under my arms, pinching into my skin, and lifted me from the ground. My arms instinctively shielded my face a moment before I was laid on one of the creature's backs. Two more began wrapping a thick rope around my middle again and again.

"What are you doing?" I yelped, fighting to sit up.

"You do what centaurs say and no hurting will have to be done," the centaur holding me down said. I shivered when our eyes met.

Their eyes were only purple orbs with a speck of black in the middle. It was more the size of their eyes that was so distressing, though, like two mouths hanging wide open and screaming.

The centaur restraining me looked up as several knots were tied against my waist. "Tipios, get the someone's sack. We take the star-seers straight to Elyxeos' colony. The someone will buy us feeding like we've never had before."

Their voices remained excited as we began our journey through the forest. It sounded like star-seers might be the most valuable of any catch. I was too frightened even to wonder how they knew that's what I was.

By the time they were finished tying the rope around me and had taken off in the direction from which they'd come, the only things I could move were my legs and my neck. Kicking and fighting them would have been pointless.

I would never see my family again. I would never be near my best friend. I would never get to tell Jordan I wouldn't be marrying him. It was probably already too dangerous for me to return home.

I could only hope these fiends were not the monsters the Avarice were. At least they were honest about their intentions.

My eyes roamed over our surroundings. I doubted I would be able to remember our path exactly, should I manage to escape this fate, but I was determined to try.

Just inside the overhanging branches of a fig tree, I caught sight of half a man's face. The rest of him remained well hidden inside the branches. I could only assume it was Gabriel.

My head rested against the centaur's back. If I watched him for too long it might draw attention. And it was better he didn't recognize me if it truly was Gabriel. The only thing that could have made things worse was some haphazard, suicidal attempt at a rescue.

Everything about the situation was hopeless.

Still, I felt oddly satisfied. I did exactly what I set out to do. Blush was free and Gabriel was safe. I knew when I left that I would probably never return home, but I had at least hoped for a happy ending living in the world of defects rather than being taken captive in my little sister's place.

My eyes were soon heavy. I'd never been so tired in all my life. The centaur's back was so wide and his fur so soft and warm. Before long, my mind was drifting to a cradle that rocked me back and forth, a safe place where no harm could ever find its way...

MY EYES FLUTTERED a bit when I heard men bellowing to one another. One of my arms was numb, except for the heavy thing I felt dangling from it. I only blinked twice before my head jerked up, a cry breaking free of my throat when the memory of centaurs returned.

The ropes still held me right where I was. My bag's strap had been wrapped around my deadened arm three times and then shoved under the ropes where it wouldn't fall off.

"Hush your mouth, you someone," the centaur carrying me twisted around to hiss.

"You heard my words right," another centaur was nearly shouting to be heard over everyone else. "We fetched us a star-seer. What's you offering, Amphion?"

I turned my neck as much as I could to see a different breed of centaurs, twice as big as the ones escorting me. They had short blueish-gray hair all over them, growing thickest at every joint. The silver hair on their heads was longest of all. Their eyes looked more normal, with dark rings against the whites, a speck of gold in the center. They were so tall and burly beside my captors, it was difficult not to wonder if the abductors were only children. An entire herd of these giants stood inside a wide opening between a ten-foot tall fence, formed of thick branches crisscrossing over each other with deathly sharp tips on top. Each one stood with axes in hand and bows thrown over their backs.

A good distance inside the gates behind them stood an army of centaur warriors. They were the most frightening beasts I'd seen so far, wearing brass plates studded with a row of sharp-looking spikes around their wrists. The mass of warriors were calling back commands to their mentor as they carried out each order, swinging axes, throwing elbows forward, lunging back. It was this great racket that made conversation so difficult.

In spite of it all, I couldn't help but think of how the windy ride had dried my clothing completely. The rain had stopped and the sky was nearly clear.

"Twenty baskets of feed for a star-seer," the gatekeeper answered loudly.

"*What*?!" The smaller centaurs all began complaining.

"The Bellios colony pays us fifteen baskets for a regular luminary someone. They'd pay more than twenty for a seer."

The gatekeeper let out a roar so terrifying; my captors all began to cower. The more dominant men pulled their bows off and pointed arrows at the lesser ones. "Elyxeos centaurs are the only ones with the right to own star-seers. Take her anywhere else and we will have war. You vermin scavengers are lucky we offer you anything at all." Amphion turned and put a hand to his mouth before shouting to the top of a nearby tree. "Fifteen baskets of feed!"

A centaur emerged from the limbs, running down a wide ramp that went from the tree to the ground.

"Fifteen?" the centaur carrying me cried. "You want us to just let the someone free? Twenty-five baskets."

Furious lines formed across Amphion's face, a sneer full of crowded teeth on his lips, as he ran at me. Instinctively, my body curled inward, or tried to at least. I screamed when the ropes around me snapped and then I was being lifted by the monstrous centaur, who seemed even bigger up close. He threw me over his shoulder, nearly costing me my bag. I grunted as I tipped over to grab it with my good arm and noticed that the necklace Jordan gave me had disappeared.

"How soon you do forget, if you argue a deal with the Elyxeos, you get nothing."

With that, I was being carried through the gateway and into a city of the most frightening creatures I could have imagined, hoping that my life was as valuable to them as it was to the scavengers.

9

I watched everything pass us by from behind the great centaur. A single row of trees grew near to each other in a straight line just inside the fence surrounding their city. Stands had been built high up in the branches of every third tree. Elyxeos centaurs stood guard atop each one, with shields and either a spear or bow and arrows in hand. Each one wore an ivory horn around their neck and a two-edged axe strapped across their backs.

Tall houses were scattered about, each with a large opening instead of a door that stretched from the roof to the ground. The centaur carrying me turned and ran deeper into the heart of the city.

Covered platforms stood in wide open spaces with powerful-looking centaurs crowded together underneath. One group of men looked to be in a particularly heated conversation. The darkest Elyxeos shook his head back as his shoulders seemed to bulge forward, his fists tightening at his sides.

A tall structure with muddy-looking sides was bursting with the sounds of construction, hammering and sawing to no end. A smaller building smelled heavily of rose and lavender. The one just past it was nearly surrounded in a cloud due to some Elyxeos with longer hair and softer frames waving extremely dusty rugs and fabrics out of the countless arched windows.

Then houses and buildings opened up into fields of grain. Luminaries in long, perfectly white gowns with white bags tied at their waists moved slowly through the crops. My eyes squinted at the blindingly bright light they emanated. It was so intense that their features were a bit hazy. I'd never seen anything like it. And I certainly hoped the centaurs wouldn't expect such a thing of me.

As my eyes began to adjust, I noticed that there were defects kneeling over the ground, weeding or harvesting the crops. Others were carrying buckets of water from little ponds to sprinkle over the plants. They all wore clothes made from the same animal skins Gabriel had worn.

Why don't they try to get away? I wondered, thinking of their incredible abilities.

A few centaurs stood watch over them from platforms built into smaller trees nearby. One was a bit slimmer and more feminine than the rest. She wore a beaded blue cloth tied around her torso and was every bit as menacing as the Elyxeos men. I still couldn't understand how they were any match for defect men and women who could breathe fire and cause earthquakes of great magnitude.

I twisted my neck in order to see around Amphion's shoulder. More fields lay over their land. Far away, closer to the centaur houses, several younger Elyxeos were playing a game of some sort, trying to get a ball to either end of a piece of land that had been sectioned off by burnt lines in the grass. They were no smaller than the scavengers who had brought me there, but possessed a large stature that made them so much more impressive.

The thought of how their entire race now owned me made me sick to my stomach.

I turned my gaze back to the luminaries. It was comforting to see them being so friendly with one another. They even seemed happy.

Still, I felt myself trembling, though I did not regret what I'd done.

A gap began to open between the fields. Amphion slowed to a trot.

We passed an adorable little house with a circular straw roof with planked sides peeking out underneath. I watched another just like it appear behind Amphion, followed by an entire community of these small dwellings. They all had proper doors that were closed at the moment.

Finally, Amphion pulled me over his shoulder as he slowed to a stop. He set me down carefully in front of a long, sturdy-looking house. It was rectangular and must have been two stories tall with a great many windows. Smoke poured from the four chimneys at the right side of the house. Boxes filled with herbs growing from them had been placed in neat rows out front.

Amphion kept a hand on my elbow as he led me up a ramp that led to the house. I had to hold my arm up since my head only came to his waist. We walked through the wide opening where there should have been a door, and entered a small room with an enormously tall ceiling. I guessed all the Elyxeos' houses had to be so lofty. Buckets of grain lined the far wall. A table surrounded by stools was in the center of the room. Empty bowls with smooth rocks beside them had been placed on the tabletop.

The entire place smelled wonderful. My mouth began to water, something that was new to me.

"Davion," Amphion yelled into an opening to another room at our right. "We've got a new star-seer here."

A female centaur with a long, horsey-ish neck and a hardened look on her face appeared in the open doorway. The long hair growing from her head had more of a purplish tint than the others I'd seen. Her black shirt was lined with silver beads and had clear, gooey splatters all over the front. She was holding a bowl and using a long, wooden spoon to stir whatever was inside it. The wondrous odor wafted in more heavily as she entered the room.

"Marina," Amphion said. "Is Davion here? We have a new star-seer."

Marina's flattened nostrils flared as she exhaled, offering me a look of scorn. "I don't know why you even bother asking. He's out in the fields with his precious slaves, of course."

It was difficult to decide which her voice displayed more hatred for—Davion or the slaves.

"I'll leave her in your charge then. Get her fed and housed. I do not believe she will cause you any trouble. She doesn't seem nearly as afraid as most of them do."

My eyes surrendered to surprise as I stared at him. I was terrified. My heart was broken. How was it possible he hadn't noticed either one?

Marina snorted. Her cold eyes bore into me. "Take a seat, luminary."

With no other option, I seated myself at the table, tucking my bag beneath the stool.

The two centaurs turned to exit through different openings. Amphion paused in the front doorway, turning his neck to speak down to me over his shoulder. "The guards will be watching you most closely. Do *not* leave this house without being told to."

This put the first thoughts of escape into my mind. Blush and Gabriel were safe now. No one knew I was associated with them in any way. There was no reason to stay put for very long, except of course that this was the only place I might have a home anymore.

Marina returned to the room carrying a tall glass of water and a platter covered with steaming chunks of something brown, soaked in a thin golden liquid. My lips felt like they were swelling when she set it on the table in front of me. My mouth watered even more.

"What is it?" I asked.

She stabbed a gray piece of metal with two pointed tips into a larger chunk. "Meat. You're going to eat it all, then you'll help me carry more out to the other luminaries."

"Eat it?"

"Yes, eat it!"

"I don't understand."

Her nostrils flared again, more angrily this time. "Are you mocking me?"

I shook my head. "Honestly. I was raised cut off from most of this world." Hopefully, I wasn't saying too much. It was extremely important that I didn't offend someone who held any part of my life in their hands, though.

She frowned as she turned her head to stare at the plate thoughtfully. "A language barrier perhaps." She licked her lips before she glanced at the doorway. Her long ears poking out from under her hair twitched back and forth a few times before she took the fork, stabbed it through four chunks of meat, and stuck them in her mouth. She glared at me as she chewed it up quickly. Then she took a drink of my water and opened her mouth to show that it was empty. "Now hurry up and eat the rest. I'm nearly ready to leave."

She began to turn away, but stopped when I asked, "Why do you want me to eat this?"

Her arms stiffened as she turned back to me. "Titanasaur

meat makes star-seers strong enough to shine like the sun upon our fields. Our crops grow ten times faster than any other colonies'."

I stared at the plate. My body wanted that meat. I could feel it. But I hardly trusted anything given to me by a centaur. "What if I don't eat it?" I said slowly.

Halfway to what must have been her kitchen, she stopped and stamped her foot angrily. "You spoiled little luminary!" She turned a fierce look on me. "You were the one stupid enough to go wandering around by yourself. It's your own fault you were captured."

"Don't you realize how lucky you are to be here? Every other centaur colony puts their slaves under worn tarps to sleep at night and only feeds them when they feel like it. They're beaten when they don't work hard enough and killed for any attempt at escape. Families are torn apart and traded for gain. You're all treated like royalty here and you aren't even grateful enough to accept a warm meal. You're going to eat that and there will be no more questions." With that she stomped out of the room.

I turned my attention back to the wonderful-smelling meat. Marina hadn't answered my question, but her heated speech actually left me feeling the slightest bit better. Being treated like royalty was hardly what I'd envisioned of life as a slave.

I took the fork and ate the smallest piece of meat I could find. The moment it touched my tongue, my mind was transported to a blissful place. My eyes closed. It felt wonderful to eat. The food slid comfortably down my throat when I swallowed, filling me with satisfaction. Eager to continue the feeling, I took another bite. With every piece I ate, I felt more alive. I felt stronger, more invigorated. Slowly, my middle developed a comfortable pressure.

My eyes opened when my fork could find no other morsel to claim.

10

"Are you finished?" Marina asked with a sneer, standing in the entrance with three cauldrons full of titanasaur meat beside her.

I wanted more meat too badly to be embarrassed. "I love titanasaur meat. Can I have some more, Marina?"

Her nose wrinkled in snarly revulsion. "Not one of your kind has ever called me by name. *Don't* do it again. And come carry one of these."

My heart fell as I stood. Even with the sudden burst of ongoing energy I felt all happiness bleeding away.

It wasn't until I grabbed the handle of a cauldron that I realized the light emitted by my skin was pulsating. I dropped the handle and stared at my hands.

Marina picked up the other two and began down the ramp outside. Her hooves tapped noisily against the wooden slats. "Come along, luminary."

I stared at her for a moment, wanting to ask what was happening to me. But she'd been livid when she said no more questions. I was forced to assume the unexpected flickering of my light was brought on by eating the titanasaur and follow behind with the last cauldron of meat.

The boiler was so heavy, my fingers began aching fairly quickly. Marina got farther and farther ahead.

"I didn't just go wandering around on my own, you know," I called after her. "I will admit it was my fault I was captured, but not because of stupidity."

Marina laughed nastily as she turned and waited for me to catch up. Her head leaned forward when her long neck twisted around. "Your words have only proven you a liar. Getting yourself caught and sold into slavery on purpose is stupid. You're stupid just for saying that."

I sat my cauldron down beside her. "I can read the stars, remember? I put myself where I knew I would be captured because it was the only way to save someone I love."

"A man?" she snorted, beginning to walk.

"My sister."

She stopped to stare at me strangely as I picked up my heavy load, the thick skin above one of her black eyes wrinkling as she arched it up higher. I went on ahead of her.

Together we walked through the houses quietly. Marina didn't speak after that, though she did slow her pace so I could keep up.

I jumped and nearly dropped my cauldron when a loud snort came from an open window. It was followed by a great deal of snoring. The next house we passed was much more calming. The gentle voice of a mother singing a lullaby to her baby drifted from the nearby window.

Then we left the company of the little houses and began toward the fields. There only one centaur among the people, a male sitting only a few feet from one field's end, surrounded by luminary and defect children. He held up his hands and said something with a horrible look on his face. The little ones all began laughing.

"Is that Davion?" I asked.

Marina's lips tightened as she nodded.

A little luminary boy jumped up and wrapped his arms around Davion's neck. Davion laughed and hugged him back. He looked like he was really nice. I couldn't imagine why Marina hated him so much.

He noticed us approaching just then and pointed us out to the children. The little luminaries all looked really excited as they ran away to tell the blinding lights moving around the nearby fields. The young defects left to lend a hand to the older ones, looking let down.

"Do the, um—the ones who aren't luminaries not get any?"

"Of course not. Titanasaur is much too valuable to waste on them. We feed the fiery ones from our crops. The seers provide us with enough, they're allowed to take whatever they want."

Obviously, the defects weren't treated quite as well as the luminaries here.

Davion stood, offering me a smile. He looked every bit the brute of the other Elyxeos, but his softer demeanor made him less frightening. "I see we have a new luminary." He beamed at me. "What do they call you, young lady?"

"S—Sleigh." My eyes became watery. I wasn't afraid any longer, giving everything that had happened that day a chance to settle in. I *really* wanted to be with my family.

"She has already eaten," Marina said. "You should put her straight to work."

Davion snorted, his lip curling at one side. "Honestly, Marina, how can you be so heartless?"

"*She* is a slave."

Luminaries began lining up before us, taking bowls from their satchels.

It reminded me that I'd left my bag in Marina's house! She would probably throw it in one of the fireplaces when she found it. I doubted asking if I could go get it would do any good. My hand balled up softly as I put it under my nose, a whimper forcing its way out of my throat.

"Don't worry about her." Davion leaned over to put a hand behind my back and began leading me away. "She's just mad that she has to spend all day cooking titanasaur for luminaries and she's absolutely forbidden to eat it."

I glanced back at Marina. She managed to offer a look of distress and glare at me furiously at the same time. I turned back to stare at the field we were approaching. Getting her in trouble would do me no good.

I tried telling myself there was a bright side to all this. From now on I would be surrounded by defects, or the fiery ones, or whatever they were formally called. Every question I'd ever had about them would finally be answered. Every wish I'd ever made to spend a day with them would be granted. My obsession over them would at last be satisfied. It didn't help in the least.

"Am I stuck here forever?" I asked quietly through a fit of sniffles.

Davion walked me to the edge of the second field from the little houses before he answered.

Most of the defects were watching me. I noticed a woman with particularly pretty skin and dreads of dark hair growing nearly to her knees offering me a sympathetic look.

"I am Davion. My job is to know the luminaries and to make sure they have everything they need. I fight for whatever will make your lives happiest. Honestly, I've never been in favor of making you slaves, but that's the way it is. All I can do is be on your side, and be a friend. The Elyxeos have never set a slave free, but they will always put the luminaries' safety before their own. You are very lucky to be a seer, and to serve here rather than with a different colony."

I nodded, still just as miserable.

"Do you have any other questions?"

My fingers spread as I held my arm out in front of me. My natural glow was still pulsating. "Did—" *sniff, sniff,* "—did eating do this to me?"

"Eating?" Davion chuckled. "Yes, I guess you could say that. Titanasaur meat gives your body enormous amounts of energy. Only seers are capable of truly harnessing that energy and transferring it in a sense to the plants they shine their light over. Why not give it a try?"

"But... I don't know how."

All of a sudden, unnaturally warm fingers dug into my sides. A great boom of thunder exploded behind me, making the earth tremble beneath my feet. I screamed and ran forward into Davion, a throbbing sound that beat rapidly through my ears rushing over my body.

"*AYE, NONE OF THAT NOW!*" a voice shouted from a nearby tree. "I'LL HAVE YOUR HIDE IF YOU DO IT AGAIN."

Extraordinary light shone from every inch of my skin. My body shook terribly.

"It's alright, Sleigh," Davion murmured, hugging me to his front with one arm.

Keeping my side against Davion for protection, I turned back to see the source of such noise. A defect stood behind me, a teenager who could have been my age, with his coarse-looking hair pulled back into a ponytail. "Sorry." He grinned as if trying not to laugh, though his formidable defect voice, very nearly to the age and development of a man's, took away from that effect. "Giving a luminary a good start always gets their light going for the first time. It's the fastest way to learn how."

"That's right." Davion withdrew his arm and rested a hand

on the back of my head. "The way your muscles all worked together and your mind forgot everything but survival is how to harness that energy into such light. You don't have to be afraid, or course. You only have to focus all your energy as you just did."

Allowing myself to leave the safety of standing so near to Davion, I stared at my hands as I concentrated on using every muscle in my body to produce light. The throbbing in my ears picked up. My skin flashed brighter a few times. Then it really shone. I stepped onto the field and watched a few tiny leaves shoot out of a red berry plant at my feet.

"You're a natural." The boy smiled at me, squinting as he watched me.

The world looked different from behind all the dazzling light. The concentration it took to keep it going and the great force I felt coursing through my body offered a reprieve from my depressing thoughts.

Fear was the only thing truly capable of taking my mind off the pain of giving up everything, though, even if it was equally as horrible.

"The day is almost finished." Davion's voice sounded hazy with the hammering in my ears. "Why not take her to get settled into a house, Bones?"

My light began burning out when I turned to face them, thinking more of what they were saying than what I was doing.

"Bones?" I asked.

"Yeah." The boy ran his hands over his head, pulling the loose hair in the back apart with both hands to make his ponytail tighter. "I was *really* thin when I was a child. The name kind of stuck."

"Any chance your family will come looking for you, Sleigh?" Davion asked.

I shook my head, biting my lip and fighting not to cry.

Davion turned his gaze on Bones. "She will only be needing

one bed, then. And perhaps you could get her a few gowns from Marina."

"Sure." Bones turned to the defect woman I'd noticed before and pointed to me as he nodded in the direction of the houses.

The woman offered a brief bow of the head. "Take good care of her, son," she called out.

He turned back to me. "Alright. Let's go. Sleigh, was it?"

"Yes." I sniffled.

"Good luck, Sleigh," Davion called after us. "I'll see you in the morning."

"I know you're not happy to be here, but I bet you'll end up liking it eventually," Bones said. "The daytime luminaries get to do anything they want after sunset, as long as they don't wander past the fields."

"Daytime luminary?"

"Yeah. Those are the ones out working right now. Some of the luminaries sleep during the day and spend their nights with the watch guards on the towers. They light up everything so no enemy can sneak up on us undetected. Those are the nighttime luminaries."

I nearly asked how I could become a 'nighttime luminary', since it was the sort of schedule I was used to. But I didn't really want to be with a guard every night. And arranging things to remain as they'd always been for me would probably only make me more homesick.

So I let Bones do all the talking. I needed to know about life here far more than he needed to know anything about me, anyway.

11

The sun was beginning to set when Bones finally stopped in front of one of the houses on the far side of the luminary village. Vines had been tied from two windows on either side of the front door so that there were three reaching across it.

"These mean the house is empty," Bones said, ripping the vines away and pushing the door open slightly. He bent over and reached behind it to push a fat rock out of the way across the floor, making the door easier to open. "The rock's there so you can keep your door shut."

"So I could live here?" I asked.

"Exactly. The Elyxeos like to make sure the luminaries are comfortable and well-rested so their lights will shine as bright as they possibly can."

I stepped inside to find a bed all made up with a quilt and fluffy pillows in the shadows at the back of the room. Several hooks were hung on the wall at the right side of the bed. A stack of four long shelves had been built nearer to the ground below them. On the other side of the bed, there was a shining dark wood bench placed against the wall. A low-sitting table with five corners and six stools around it sat right in the center of the room. It did seem like a nice place to live, except for how lonely I would be there.

My attention was diverted to the laughter I heard outside. Three luminary women walked past the house. One began singing and the other two joined in.

Then I heard knocking coming from the direction they'd disappeared. "The sun is setting. Time to wake up," a man yelled.

"Sorry," Bones said, going to the window. "It does get noisy here right about this time every evening. You're sort of in the middle of most of the nighttime luminaries. We could look for a different house if you like."

"This is fine."

He nodded and picked up a little bronze saucer from the window ledge. It had a tall piece of white wax with a string sticking out at the top perched at its center. There was one on each ledge, I realized, the two beside the door and two more across from each other on the sides of the curvy house. A stream of fire blew from Bones' mouth to the string when he puckered his lips, leaving a little flame to burn atop the wax. He set it back down on the ledge. "The candle will keep you from being in darkness as long as it's burning. Of course, luminaries don't usually have that problem."

"I've been meaning to ask, Marina calls you and your mother's kind 'the fiery ones'. Is that how you refer to each other, as well?"

"We're nocturnes. What did the people in your village call us?"

"I'd rather not say," I answered, staring up at the tall ceiling. It reminded me of a pointed mushroom cap, with the addition of a few sturdy works of timber running across the center for support.

"You must be tired after all you've been through. Why don't you get some rest and I'll go see if Marina has a few dresses for you?"

"She'd probably rather lose a leg than give me anything." I stared glumly out the window, watching four luminary men leave the house across from mine. They all looked so similar, they must have been brothers.

"She hates everyone, Sleigh, even her own kind. It's her job to supply us with clothing and food, though. She doesn't have a choice."

"How sad." I held up a hand mindlessly when one of the men saw me and waved. "It sounds like she's as miserable as I am right now."

"Probably. That's why you shouldn't take anything she says personally..."

I shivered when I felt his body heat move away from me toward the door. "Wait—" I reached and caught him by the wrist. "Have you been here all your life?"

"No, only since I was seven. Scavenger centaurs took my sisters while they were out in the yard, then broke into our house and took us all when they realized they were seers. Usually scavengers aren't so bold, but they were starving. We were just far enough away from any other house to make it safe for them, I think. It was so long ago; my memory might not be exactly right. My parents don't talk about it."

My voice became a whisper as I let go of his arm and moved closer to him. "Has your family never tried to escape?"

Bones gave me an *I-can't-believe-you* sort of look and took to biting his nails.

We just watched each other for a moment. He leaned his head out the door to spit a piece of his nail outside before he closed it. He picked up the rock and set it against the door. Then he went to pull panes of glass down from right above each window, sealing our voices inside.

I shivered at the level of secrecy he demanded. Perhaps I'd crossed a line.

He came to pick up the candle burning beside me and take my hand to pull me away from the door. He let go when we were right beside the table, his voice becoming more of a husky growl when he whispered.

"No one has ever escaped. Luminaries who have tried are locked in a little room inside the chief Elyxeos' house for weeks. Nocturnes are beaten half to death. My family was extremely lucky to have been kept together and given such a good life as slaves. It would be ungrateful to try and escape. My mother and I would be tortured."

Ungrateful? For being held here against your will? It would have been a rude question to ask, though, since he seemed to feel so lucky. I chose to go in a different direction. "But you can breathe fire and break the earth into pieces. All the nocturnes can. Why not use that to get away?"

He turned his head somewhat and gave me a peculiar look. "Centaurs have something in their skin that makes them as fire resistant as nocturnes." He held both his arms out and blew fire all over them until flames were dancing all along the top of each one. "And centaurs are nearly indestructible, especially the Elyxeos. No amount of upheaval in the earth would stop them." His eyes bore into mine as he used his hands to run over each arm, putting the fires out. "Did you honestly not know that?"

I shook my head.

The way his eyes squinted and watched me with such scrutiny made me shiver. "How strange...Where exactly are you from?"

"It doesn't matter now; I'm stuck here. Maybe I *should* get some rest," I said, suddenly wanting to end the conversation.

Even these slave defect-nocturnes probably hated sky luminaries. He was obviously becoming suspicious.

A knock came at the door, causing us both to jump away from one another. I left Bones to answer it.

A luminary woman and Bones' mother smiled brightly on the other side, both holding two white gowns on hangers. "Hello, Sleigh," his mother said. "I'm Daphnis and this is my daughter Parthenia. Davian gave us your name and Marina sent these for you. May we come in?"

I stepped aside in response, not feeling very friendly. They handed me the gowns as Daphnis walked toward Bones.

"My bag!" I gasped, seizing it when I saw that Parthenia was holding it behind the gowns she was carrying.

She stopped beside me. "Marina said it was yours. I didn't look through it, but I did put a bowl and fork in there for you. I would have added a jar as well, but I noticed you already had a couple.

"Thank you so much." I hugged it against me, feeling the knife poke my arm through the fabric. It amazed me no centaur had bothered to look through it, or if they had, that they'd left a weapon inside.

"I figured Bones would put you in this house," Daphnis said. "It's the closest empty one to us. It's so dark in here, though. Give us some light, would you, Parthenia? I'll get all the candles lit. It's Sleigh's first night here. She shouldn't be in the dark."

Parthenia's skin blazed white light.

"I would have also brought my other daughter, but she's home with a new baby. We won't be seeing much of her for a while, I expect."

"I was only a few years younger than you when I was brought here," Parthenia said to me reverently. "It felt like my whole life was over. Everything just seemed pointless for a long, long time."

I pressed my fingers to my mouth. I began to cry as I nodded.

Daphnis paused before lighting the fourth candle to stare at me when she heard me sniffling. "Oh, Parthenia, look what you've done."

Parthenia put an arm around me. "Don't you think it's better for her to know that everyone feels that way when they're captured?"

I leaned against her shoulder, letting out a sob.

"She needs a distraction." Daphnis put a hand under my chin, lifting my head. "Would you like for me to stay the night? I could talk long enough to keep your mind busy until you fall asleep."

"That's the truth," Bones muttered, drawing daggers from his mother's dark eyes.

I truly didn't want to be alone, but the way Bones' mother seemed to want to baby me wasn't helping at all. "Could—" *sniff, sniff,* "could Parthenia stay with me instead?"

Daphnis' eyebrows drew closer. "Well, of course she can. Why not have a few of these before hitting the hay, eh?" She reached in a pocket of her dress and pulled out a few of the red berries she'd been tending to earlier. "Strawberries are Bonesey's favorite."

"Mother! Why do you have to call me that right now?" Bones complained as I took the berries, eager to eat again. "That's such a stupid, sissy name."

"Sleigh doesn't care what your name is."

"That's *not* my name."

Daphnis rolled her eyes and turned her attention back to me. "There are barrels full of fresh water north of our houses. You're welcome to it day or night."

"Thank you."

"You're welcome, Sleigh. I'll leave you to Parthenia now. If you need anything, she'll be happy to show you where we live."

"Good night," Bores said, offering me a final curious look before he and his mother left.

"Would you like to lie down, or we could sit at your table and talk?" Parthenia said. Her high cheek bones were truly prominent when she smiled.

"I don't want to be awake anymore." I dropped the berries on the table.

She put an arm around my shoulders and walked me to my bed. Once I'd laid down, she pulled the blanket out from under me so she could cover me up. "Would you like to talk about it?"

"No. Just... just don't leave." I was quickly slipping into a state of shock, afraid of being alone.

"I won't lie to you and say things will be better tomorrow, but at least it can't be worse than today."

That sort of comment was exactly why I wanted her with me for the night. I absolutely preferred her harsh honesty to false promises.

Part of me still held desperately to the possibility of escape. It was the only part still keeping me together.

After all, I had done things I thought impossible before: slipping to the Surface as a false transporter, returning to our city undetected, going back to the Surface and saving Gabriel and Blush from a terrible fate.

If there was anything I'd learned from these most surreptitious parts of my life, it was that the impossible only existed among those who believed in it.

12

A knock at the door roused me from a dreamless sleep. I felt well rested and content. The room was warm, but not stuffy, perfect for a good night's sleep. It startled me into sitting up when someone groaned beside me.

My surroundings brought everything of the day before back to the Surface. Parthenia had fallen asleep at the other side of the bed. My stomach sank to the floor.

Thump, thump, thump. The knocking came louder this time.

"It's morning, Sleigh," Daphnis called out. "We come bearing gifts."

"We?"

"It's a tradition here," Parthenia said sleepily. She sat up and stretched her arms up high, exhaling loudly as she let them fall. "The women all get together to greet new captors. They bring something they've collected since they arrived or one of the gifts they were given that they no longer need. It's supposed to make you feel more at home. I should have warned you."

"I'd be lying if I said I don't love gifts." I grinned half-heartedly at her. We mostly only had what we absolutely needed in my city. Gifts were rarely given.

Thump, thump, thump. "I'm coming in. Don't be alarmed." The rock scooted across the floor as the door opened.

"What's the point of that stupid rock, anyway?" I asked.

"Mostly to keep your door from flying open when there's a lot of wind. It's horrible at keeping people out." We laughed as a steady stream of girls and women, luminary and nocturne, began flowing into my house.

I was surprised to feel a little thrill at the idea of this being *my* own home.

Daphnis led the march, of course. "Well, isn't it nice to see you in brighter spirits this morning. Did you sleep well?"

"Yes."

"I brought a comb for your hair." She laid a long yellow dress across my lap. Then she climbed onto my bed and sat behind me so she could brush my hair with the rib cage of a small animal. "The dress is a gift on behalf of Parthenia. She hasn't worn it in a long time, so I hope she doesn't mind."

Parthenia held it up in front of us. "Course not. But there's a little tear in the back. I'll sew it up and bring it back to you, okay, Sleigh?"

"Sure."

"I'm Alessandra." A tall luminary sat beside me, handing me a pink, circular box with a matching lid covering the top. "Daphnis said you had a book of papers in your bag. In case you're an artist, I thought these might come in handy."

I slid the lid off and found little vials of paint containing: blue, green, red, and yellow. Paint was difficult to come by where I was from. There was also a little paintbrush with a handle carved from wood and hair for the brush. I didn't recognize the fifth vial filled with a thick, clear substance. "Thank you, Alessandra," I said, offering her a look of sincere appreciation. "I've never had paint before. But what's in this one?" I held up the fifth vial.

"It's glue, of course." Her smile shone even brighter than her skin.

"Glue?"

"Have you never had glue either?" She offered the same peculiar look Bones had given me the night before.

I shook my head, wanting to take it back but more curious of what it was.

"W—um, it's a sticky liquid you use for bonding things together. You can hang papers along the wall with it. Leave it in the air long enough and it hardens."

"How wonderful." I held it up to stare at the distorted colors shining through it.

"Here's one of my dolls." A nocturne adolescent set a grinning little ragdoll with pink cheeks and blue eyes in the box. "I know you're probably a little old for her, but at least she can keep you company."

"Thank you." I gave her a smile, though I'd hated dolls since my mother's breakdown after Blush was taken. She'd seized every doll in the house and thrown them over a bridge to the Surface. It took her months to come back from losing my sister. This was something I would *have* to regift the first chance I got.

"Here's my gift," a luminary about Parthenia's age said, laying a necklace of pastel-colored seashells around the box. "I'm Sirene. I live in a house near Parthenia's."

The luminary woman beside her handed me a matching bracelet. "I'm her mother. She just got married, so we're still adjusting."

"I can't believe you're all slaves and you have these wonderful things," I said. "And the Elyxeos let you get married and have your own families... I wasn't expecting any of this."

"We *are* very fortunate."

Daphnis leaned around me to set the comb in my lap. "Once a week we have a resting day where no one works. We get to go to the river for bathing, females early in the afternoon, and males early evening before the sun sets. The Elyxeos let you keep whatever you find."

"They let you leave?" What were they all even doing here?

"Not the way you're thinking," Sirene answered. "We are very heavily guarded the entire time."

"Oh?" Sadness bled into the cracks splitting into such a hopeful thought.

"Here's my gift." A nocturne woman handed me a chunk of wood that had been expertly carved to look like an owl. "My husband made it."

"The Elyxeos *allow* you to have knives?"

"Yes, of course. There's all sorts of things we wouldn't be able to do without them."

I stared at the ladies all around me. None of them seemed to think much about my question. "Aren't they afraid of an uprising or something?"

The room filled with girlish laughter. "You really don't know much about centaurs, do you?" Alessandra asked.

I shook my head.

"You must have come from somewhere far, far away to be so ignorant about them. I hope you don't take offense. I've just never met anyone privileged enough not to have to know about centaurs."

"Besides the fact that they outnumber us ten to one," Sirene's mother began, "one Elyxeos is more powerful than ten nocturne men. That puts us a hundred to one in their favor. They're about as afraid of knives as we are of sewing needles."

That was impressive. Maybe I should keep my questions to myself. They only seemed to expose how foreign I was to their Surface world.

"They are kind enough to give us their old fabrics and things," a luminary with a high-pitched voice said. She put a fuzzy white towel beside my pillows. "You'll be grateful for that when you're done bathing."

"Thanks—"

"Good morning," a man called from the door. "Sorry, didn't know you were having a welcoming party."

I stretched my neck and women moved out of the way so I could see the man who'd waved to me the night before leaning in through the doorway. The ends of his partially wavy hair drifted away from his face.

"Just wanted to introduce myself. I'm Crew. My brothers and I live just over there. If you ever need anything, come on over and wake one of us up."

"Alright. My name's Sleigh."

"Sleigh. Hmm, pretty... I'll leave you to it then." He gave a quick wave before he disappeared.

The gifts continued pretty steadily after that. I kept my questions to myself, hoping I could figure it all out on my own. I was given a few more pretty dresses, a giant rug made from the skin of a buffalo, a slender bottle of lavender-scented perfume, and a great many other useful and non-useful but fun to own things.

I found myself really enjoying being surrounded by everyone. It was difficult not to focus all my attention on the nocturnes. I found them absolutely fascinating. Their eyes were mesmerizing. Their voices were so exotic. But they behaved as any luminary.

My life was still ruined, but at least the day was off to a pleasant start... until I stepped outside and discovered that my least favorite centaur was searching for me...

13

My eyes locked with Marina's when she saw me exit through my doorway. "*You.* New slave—you will come with me today."

My breath caught in my throat.

"We'll see you in the fields, Sleigh," Daphnis said. "Just find us when you're done." The fact that she was so unconcerned put me even more on edge.

I drifted away from the group after Marina without looking back. This couldn't be good.

Marina marched proudly through the streets. Her head never turned to one side or the other. Her step never faltered.

"Hey, Sleigh," Bones called, running at me between houses. He stopped when he saw Marina and left me to follow her alone.

The morning was windy, carrying a little swirl of dust against my skin.

It didn't take long to figure out we were headed for her home. My muscles were extremely tense by the time we walked through her front door. She continued into the kitchen. I stopped halfway across the room, unsure of whether or not to follow.

It was impossible to decide whether it was riskier to allow myself to be utterly alone with a centaur or to refuse that order.

The *tap, tap, tap* of her hooves stopped. Then it began moving back toward me. "Well, come on," she said, leaning her neck forward to stare at me through the doorway.

I sucked in a deep breath before I entered her kitchen. Four gaping fireplaces were halfway full of ash at the right side of the room. Piles of wood had been stacked at one corner. A table as tall as me was at the wall opposite the fireplaces, with all sorts of cooking things underneath. Marina was headed for the opening in the back of the room, where a ramp going upward went off to the left.

"Am I in trouble for something?" I asked as I turned to follow her up the ramp through a lengthy hallway. It ran the entire span of the house, leading to a second floor. The hall was draped mostly in shadows, with only one square window in the center.

"No. You are not in any trouble."

At the top, we turned left into a large room with a giant, round bed laid flat against the floor. It was wrapped perfectly in rich, purple sheets like a gift of slumber. Two wide crates were on either side of the bed, a collection of interesting looking things piled on top of them.

I went to one of the four massive windows, twice the size of the door to my house, in the wall opposite the ramp. The window's ledge was only an arm's length off the floor, so I stepped onto it to look out over the fields and the smaller houses nearby.

Naturally, my eyes began searching for familiar faces. I found Bones and his family in the same field they'd been in before. They were just arriving, Daphnis on the arm of a luminary man who was slightly shorter than Bones.

"Tell me if you see anyone coming," Marina said from right behind me. I turned around to watch her sit on the floor next to the window, folding her legs at her side.

"Okay." I sat on the window ledge, where I could watch the outside world and her at the same time. "Why did you want me to come here?"

She frowned as she studied me momentarily. Her face seemed to lack the deep-seated hatred it had previously harbored for me. "Yesterday I ate titanasaur in a moment of weakness. I saw an opportunity to reason that you didn't understand. If I was only showing you what it meant to eat, it would be acceptable. I knew the moment I stepped back into the kitchen that I was wrong. There is no exception to be made for an Elyxeos to eat luminary food. When Davion told you I was forbidden to eat titanasaur, you could have easily had me made an outcast. Why didn't you say anything?"

"Why would I have told him something I knew would get you in trouble?"

She shook her head, looking upset. "Because I was so cruel to you."

"Still wouldn't have done me any good."

"You'll keep my secret, then?"

I nodded uncomfortably, returning my gaze to the outside world. Marina was still my least favorite centaur.

"Thank you."

The sound of her standing and moving across the room was obvious, though I continued watching the nocturnes outside. Their work seemed so much harder than the luminaries, carrying heavy buckets of water and tending to the plants. The bright lights only had to circulate over the fields. Some of them walked in pairs, talking happily as they went. I even saw a couple holding hands as they moved about.

"You are the first slave I've known of to trade their freedom for their sister's. I know exactly what it is to sacrifice everything to save your sister."

This drew my attention back to her. She was sitting as before, with two little centaur dolls in her hands. One was purple and one was blue. Both had silver shirts on their torsos with frills around the stomach.

Marina smiled sadly at the toys. "Can I trust you, Sleigh?"

She called me by my name! I was taken aback, but careful to hide it. "Yes."

"My mother deceived my father with a Bellios centaur for a time. He only discovered it when she gave birth to twins. I was one. Nephele was the other."

She held the purple doll out to me. I took it and smoothed down the shirt, staring at the miniature smile on its pretty face.

"My coloration is not perfect, but I was born with enough of the Elyxeos characteristics not to raise concern. Nephele, on the other hand, appears purely as a Bellios. It was humiliating for my father, but my parents worked it out. Our colony accepted my sister, or at least tolerated her for many years.

"Then a great faction broke free of the Bellios, creating the Deliverance. Even though centaurs of every colony aside from the Elyxeos have joined it, the Bellios make up their greatest numbers. Suddenly everyone hated her. My father was going to make her an exile. I agreed to do the job no other Elyxeos female would do if he would let her stay. No one knows it, but she remains part of our colony. She simply isn't allowed to leave home."

"How has no one noticed?"

"Our father is the chief Elyxeos. The house where I grew up is plenty big enough, I'm sure it's easy for Nephele to go unnoticed."

"Wow. So you're the daughter of a chief. It seems like he could do whatever he wants. Why keep her a secret?"

"There's so much hatred between our colonies. He probably would have been overthrown and our entire family cast out had he not done anything."

I could only nod in response. Without knowing what the Deliverance was, it was difficult for me to understand just why there was so much hatred. My own ignorance and the danger of asking too many questions was becoming something of a disability in my understanding of this world.

If only there was someone who knew my secret as well... Marina *had* just shared a secret with me that was every bit as dangerous as mine. Still, I couldn't bring myself to trust her enough to share such a thing.

"Does Davion not even know?" I asked.

"He came as part of the job I took. There has never been anything between us. I would never trust him with such a thing."

But she trusted me, and we'd only just met. I could see how putting ourselves through so much for a sister created a bond between us. She'd been suffering for much longer than I had, though. She was obviously more desperate for a confidant than me.

"Is that why you hate your job so much? Because you're married to someone you don't love?"

Her nostrils flared as a sneer came to her lips. "I hate it because I spend all day cooking the sweetest, most tempting meat known to centaurs and I can't eat any of it. I hate that my life is nothing more than serving your people. I hate your kind because my life is being wasted on them..." She stared down at the blue doll. "But I can't hate someone who's exactly like me. We love our sisters more than ourselves. That makes you special."

I leaned over to hold the other doll out to her. "You too."

She offered me a meaningful smile as she took it.

When I sat back I saw something coming our way out of the corner of my eye. I turned to see Davion running toward the house so quickly, he left a dust trail behind. "Davion's coming. He's running really fast."

"Go to the kitchen. You must be helping me when he arrives."

Sensing the urgency in her voice, I raced across the room. She returned the dolls to the top of a crate and ran in front of me down the ramp. At the bottom, I found myself standing clueless in her oversized Elyxeos kitchen.

Marina went to the table and withdrew a cutting board with long knives all over it. "Come on. You can chop the rosemary." She grabbed another cutting board and began moving things around on the table. I could only see the giant piece of meat she set on one of the cutting boards, though.

"I can't reach that high," I said, going to join her.

She let out a huffy noise and reached down to pick me up. I gasped as I sliced through the air and was set on my bottom on the table.

Marina pushed all the knives, save one, off the other board and put it next to me. Then she took a handful of greens and put it on the board.

I stared at her for a moment, not knowing exactly what to do.

"What are you waiting for? Start chopping."

I picked up the knife and started cutting the rosemary into the smallest pieces I could. "Why is this all such a big deal?" I whispered.

"Later," she whispered back.

Only moments passed before Davion came tromping into the kitchen, looking infuriated. "Why did you take Sleigh?" he asked, advancing on Marina.

"So she could help me in the kitchen," she spat back. "The

hunters and carpenters have nocturnes helping them. Why shouldn't I have help in the kitchen?"

Davion went around her to me. "She is not a nocturne. And I'm not stupid enough to believe you'd prefer to have any of her kind working with you."

I dropped the knife when he lifted me from the table and put me on the floor.

"Are you alright?" he asked me.

"I'm fine. And I don't mind helping Marina."

"Did she threaten you into saying that?"

"No." I fought back a laugh, which was a good thing, because his words were enough on their own to send Marina over the edge.

"You stupid, pompous man. I hate you! GET OUT! *GET OUT OF HERE!*" She began pushing him out of the kitchen.

He pushed her back, hard enough that she fell over. I had to run out of the way so I wouldn't get crushed.

"I'll leave on my own. I'm not leaving a luminary here for you to torture and drive around your kitchen." Davion grabbed my hand and led me toward the door.

"I can help Marina. She hasn't been mean to me," I protested, feeling awful for her. I made sure not to look back, thinking it would only embarrass her.

"Mean or not, you just got here. You should be with your own kind at least until you've adjusted."

As we walked down the ramp away from his house, I could've sworn I heard a sob coming from the kitchen. For that moment in time, I felt more like one of the monsters I'd recently encountered when I thought of how I'd hated her so much until now.

14

Davion led me to a freshly planted field where the newest captors were sent to work. There were far less hands tending to it than were in most of the other fields.

Parthenia joined me early on. Focusing on shedding light all over what she called carrots and tomatoes, and talking with her, offered a distraction from my troubled mind, though it didn't deaden the pain. Nothing could make me forget how terrible I felt.

Midday, Marina came bearing her enormous pots filled with titanasaur meat. She kept her head down as she served it, paying no attention to whose bowl she was filling.

Time seemed to go faster when I was pouring so much energy out into the fields. The day went by quickly. Part of me regretted it, since it meant returning home, where there was little to do but think depressing thoughts.

Parthenia's light softened when Davion blew a shrill whistle to signal that our work was done for the day.

"Let's go to my house and get dressed up. After night meal, we can walk around outside and I'll show you what there is to see." She grabbed my hand without waiting for a response and began running past the edge of the fields toward the slaves' houses. It was a relief to have something more to look forward to than isolation.

Davion waved when he saw us.

"Where are you going?" Bones called out as we raced past him.

"To get glitzy," Parthenia shouted back to him.

"Glitzy?" I had to ask her.

"You know—to really make ourselves beautiful. It's just what you need."

It sounded like she planned to go overboard with getting dressed up. A little thrill shot through me at the idea of making ourselves gorgeous and seeing the miniature village with Parthenia. Our resources were so limited at the top of the valor trees; it wasn't something I'd done before.

She led me to a house central to the village. It wasn't very far from mine. The door she pushed open had the names of their family carved into it in a vertical row.

"Is Axe your father's name?" I asked, referring to the name at the top of the list.

"Yeah. He's a star-seer like my sister and me."

Parthenia shone light all over the house when we walked inside. It seemed a lot smaller than mine with three beds at opposite curves of the room and things scattered all over the shelves beside them.

"The area over there's mine." She pointed straight across the room to a bed where a section of the wall had been painted blue behind it. Rays of light cut through from the top. Little fish swam around inside the blue with bubbles painted carefully above them. She even had shreds of green fabric stuck to the wall at the bottom, like underwater plants.

"That's beautiful," I said, following her across the room.

"Thanks. My sister Milly painted it." Parthenia began taking dresses from hooks so she could lie them over her bed. "It's a good thing we're about the same size. The dress my mother gave you still has a tear, so you'll have to borrow a different one. Go ahead and pick one out while I give us some privacy."

She went to a wide panel beside her shelves that stood at least a head taller than her. She began pulling it away from a whole string of zig-zagging panels. I stared at her as they continued opening, wrapping around the outside of Parthenia's bed, until the first panel was touching the wall on the other side and we were standing in a tiny makeshift room.

"That's amazing," I stammered.

"Yeah. Families always get them when there's a son and daughter living in the same house. Now hurry and pick out a dress. I want to be finished before we eat so we can leave right after."

We spent several minutes holding up dresses in front of each other and trying to decide which looked best. In the end I chose a long dress, made with a silky pale green fabric. Parthenia wore a pink dress that began almost white at the shoulders and darkened nearly to red at the tip of her knee-length skirt.

The front door opened as we pulled them on. 'Parthenia, are you in there?" Daphnis called.

"I'm in here with Sleigh. We'll be out in a couple of minutes."

"Alright. Your father and I will start setting the table for our night meal, so you'd better hurry."

Parthenia took a long, rectangular box from her bedside. It was filled with a collection of butterfly wings. Using a dab of glue she attached a pair of green wings to the outer corner of my eyes and a pair of purple ones to hers.

We could hear the shuffling of her parents moving across the room, and the sound of things being set on the table.

Parthenia tied several thin strands of metallic ribbons into our hair—blue into mine and purple into hers. Then she painted black liner over the corner of our eyes, leading away from the wings. Finally, she brushed a deep red liquid over our lips.

"Your lips will be dyed red all night," Parthenia said. "Even eating won't wipe it away."

"You're dyeing your lips?" Bones complained. "Come on, Parthenia. I'm hungry."

"We're almost done," she snapped. "Sleigh will have a lot more fun going out tonight if she's glitzy."

"Where were you planning on taking her?" Daphnis asked.

"I don't have a set plan. I just want to show her the sights, let her know this place isn't so bad. And besides, Bones—" She went to pull the panels back around her bed. "—we're finished."

Bones and his parents were sitting around the table with plates and jars of water in front of them. Two more places had been set before the empty chairs on Bones' left. Bowls half-filled with different things they'd taken from the crops had been placed at the center of the table. Everyone stared at us as we approached.

"You both look beautiful," Daphnis gushed.

"Are you sure it's okay for me to stay and eat with your family?" I asked Parthenia.

"Course it is."

A knock came at the door just then. "Wonder who that could be," Daphnis said, going to answer it.

Bones pulled out the chair next to him when I was near, so I sat in it.

"You must be Sleigh," the man sitting across from me said, offering something of a smile. He looked *far* too serious to produce a true smile.

I nodded.

"My name's Axe. I'm Parthenia's father."

"Milly!" Daphnis cried. "What a wonderful surprise. Is the baby alright, dear?"

"Yes, he's fine. Matt's taking care of him. I really just needed to get out for a while. A new baby can be overwhelming."

"Every new mother goes through that. Come in now for a night meal with us. You can meet Sleigh. She only got here yesterday."

"Hello, Sleigh." Milly took a seat by her father, as Daphnis fetched her a plate and a jar of water. "You and my sister look so glitzy. You must have something fun planned, Parthenia."

"We're just going to explore. Maybe introduce Sleigh to a few people."

As soon as Daphnis returned to her seat, everyone began piling things onto their plates. Bones shoved three strawberries into his mouth before he loaded his plate with more.

"What would you like, Sleigh?" Daphnis asked me.

"I'm not exactly sure." The berries she'd shared with me the night before were still on my table at home.

"Ha' you never 'ad any of them before?" Bones asked, the berries muffling his voice.

"Bones," Daphnis chided. "What a ridiculous question. Don't be rude."

He took a drink of water to wash the berries down. "It's a valid question."

"No, it's not."

The light on my skin burned a bit brighter. I tried to relax when Parthenia took one look at my arm and raised an eyebrow.

"Why not try some corn?" Bones held a bowl of yellow stalks out to me, his face skeptical.

I took one and he picked up another bowl, announcing each food to me as it was offered. In the end I had a carrot, radish, apple, ear of corn, and all sorts of berries on my plate. The way

Bones kept watching me, I knew he was holding some sort of internal deliberation within himself.

The new tastes kept my mind relatively busy. Everything was delicious, except for the corn and radish. I found them to be grainy and dry.

"I bet you'll have so much fun tonight," Milly eventually said through a great yawn. "Enjoy your freedom while you've got it, Parthenia. All I think about these days is how tired I am."

"You could take a nap in my bed," Parthenia said.

"Yeah—you look like a used-up rag, Milly," Bones added.

"Bones!" their mother fussed.

"Thanks a lot," Milly said, succumbing to another even longer yawn. "I might just take you up on the offer, though, Parthenia." Milly put an elbow on the table so she could rest her chin against her hand, eating through half-closed eyes.

"Is it alright if Sleigh and I go?" asked Parthenia. Both our plates were empty.

"Yes, of course, dear," Daphnis answered.

"Can I come too?" Bones asked.

Parthenia gave me a questioning look.

"I don't mind," I said.

Parthenia let out a huffy breath. "Alright, Bones."

He ran around us to open the door. A baby's cries filled the house, along with a slight tremor.

Milly perked up, staring outside. Her eyes were wide and ghastly. "That sounds like Bender."

Parthenia stopped in the doorway. "Looks like Matt's bringing him this way."

Milly threw her head back, looking frustrated. "So much for a nap." She stood and followed us outside. A luminary man was walking toward us carrying a baby out in front of him so the flames it was crying wouldn't burn him.

"I'm never having a baby," Parthenia muttered as Milly ran toward the man.

"Let's take Sleigh to see Icy," Bones said.

Parthenia nodded. "Good idea." We turned to go in the opposite direction of their elder sister.

"Is Icy one of your friends?" I asked as we walked.

"She's a friend to everyone, really," Parthenia said. "But it's a good idea because she's an incredible artist. Her walls are nearly covered with all sorts of paintings. She keeps her doors open most evenings so people can come and go as they please. It's like an art gallery inside her home."

With no clouds in the sky and the sun gone for the evening, the night was crystal clear. A yawn escaped me. My legs were tired from having to stand all day and my body had hardly adjusted to the new sleep schedule.

I screamed and lurched back when three nocturne boys about Bones' age ran down over a nearby roof and did a somersault off the edge, which wasn't very high up at all. Bones did a terrible job of hiding his laughter at my reaction. I was more concerned with how difficult it was not to stare at the alluring young men.

"Hey, Bones," one said, wiping the sweat from his forehead on his shirt. He was the first nocturne I'd seen with hair so short, it was almost nonexistent. "We were just about to come looking for you for a game of four corner escape."

"Are you the new girl?" the boy in the middle, and certainly the most handsome, asked me. His spellbinding voice sent a shiver through my spine, reminding me of the earth's occasional response to their command.

"Yes."

"You're really cute. You should play four corners with us. You can be on my team." He nodded and winked at me.

"Go on, Crawler," Parthenia cut in. "Sleigh doesn't want to play your stupid game."

"What are the rules?" I asked, wanting very much to stay close to these young nocturne men. Parthenia came before some guy, of course, but maybe it was a fun game she'd end up enjoying.

The tallest boy held up a wad of dark cloth. He was much too thin for a nocturne, the way I pictured Bones as a child. "Whoever escapes with this flag to their designated corner of the village first wins."

"What Minz is leaving out is how much trouble they always get into, knocking people over, running through the streets, breaking things, racing over rooftops. Half the time you guys end up getting into a fight and your flag's torn to pieces, anyway."

"Maybe another time," I answered, not wanting any part of that trouble. I noticed the house they'd come off of was marked as uninhabited.

"Come on, Bones." The boy with a shortage of hair did an impressive somersault back onto the roof. He certainly had the softest voice of the three.

"I was going to help show Sleigh around."

"Afraid you'll lose?" the boy on the roof said.

"Minz and I almost always win, Pre." Bones nodded to the lankiest one, who I assumed was the other dominant winner.

"It's alright," Crawler shrugged. "He just doesn't want to get shown up in front of Sleigh."

"What?!" Bones fumed, a sneer upon his lips. The other nocturnes laughed, making him even angrier. His fingers began to steam.

"Knock it off," Parthenia said. "You know my brother's not scared."

Crawler took a step closer to Bones, putting him closer to

me, as well. I sucked in a deep breath at the magnetic sheen of his darker-than-night eyes. A shiver passed through me with the reverberation of his voice when he challenged my companion. "Prove it."

Tiny flames danced around Bones' fingernails. In a flash, he ripped the cloth from Minz's hand and raced around the houses behind us. Minz shot after him.

"Yes," Pre said as he leapt off the roof and onto another one.

Crawler hesitated, focusing momentarily on me. "I win, you hang out with me tomorrow night. Deal?"

For a moment, I was speechless, even though I was screaming *YES* inside. The more time I spent with nocturnes, the more obsessed with them I felt. And keeping myself busy was the only thing keeping me together. I glanced at Parthenia, who shook her head. "Maybe," I answered.

He winked at me again and took off after the others.

15

"At least you didn't say yes," Parthenia said, leading our course as before.

"Why?"

"He's always infatuated with new luminary girls. It only takes a few days for him to get bored and move on. It's little more than a cruel game, if you ask me."

"Has no one ever turned him down?"

"I'm not really sure. They always come so upset, like easy prey. And he is rather good-looking. It only makes everything worse when he lets them down, of course."

I shook my head, despising the young man I was so attracted to. Relationships are something I take very seriously. "I'll be the first to do it, then."

"You mean reject him?"

"Absolutely."

"Good. Don't say anything, but I get the feeling Bones really likes you. That's probably why Crawler got to him so bad back there."

We stopped outside a house to let a few luminary adolescents go inside before us. I wasn't sure how I felt about this state-ment. "But—isn't he younger than we are?"

"Yeah, by about a year." Parthenia walked inside. I followed her into a house where the walls were filled with paintings.

"This is unbelievable," I said in awe, staring at all the beau-tiful pictures. Luminaries and nocturnes of varying ages were moving around, marveling and discussing them. A luminary woman sat at a table in the middle of everything, painting a fresh picture of which we could only see the back. People were gathered around, watching her, a few of the nearest nocturnes pointing to the picture and nodding.

I went to a large painting of an all-white, man-beast with two antlers growing like ivory veins from its head. "Is that a centaur?" I asked.

"Have you never heard of the Trios?" she asked me.

I shook my head.

"That's a Trios centaur. They were at war with the Elyxeos at least a hundred years ago. When they were beaten they fled to a far country. It's said they hold a colony now where they've enslaved countless nocturnes and use them as guard dogs for their city. We can only hope they never return."

There were three more pictures of the Trios nearby. One had ten nocturne men carrying a platform with a particularly nasty-looking Trios sitting on top of it, another showed seven of the milky centaurs emerging from a cave, and a third painting captured them at battle with the Elyxeos.

"They're all so lifelike. Why don't you want them to return, though?"

"Trios are quick as lightning and just as deadly. They slaugh-tered luminaries and took all the nocturnes, torturing the ones that didn't cooperate. I can't imagine how the Elyxeos managed to beat them."

The paintings hanging above them were of purple centaurs

moving around a village. Their buildings were long with flat rooftops and were considerably shorter than were the Elyxeos'. I assumed the centaurs in the pictures were Bellios. They fit the description of what I'd heard, and I preferred not to ask more questions than was necessary.

I was clueless about the next round of paintings, though. Tall, slender centaurs with sleek black coats of fur stood atop hills and hunted small animals in valleys. "What about those?" I asked, moving closer.

"The Dashings. They can see in the dark and blend in with it perfectly. They're all nomads. I've even heard they travel and hunt with nocturnes, like wandering families. They're peaceful and neutral to everyone else's conflicts. I've always wished to see one. They hide to sleep during the day, though, and it's nearly impossible to sight one at night."

"Those are definitely my favorite centaurs so far."

"Mine too. Icy used to have paintings of the Deliverance hanging up. An Elyxeos saw them through her window and seized them to be destroyed. I think he was afraid it would inspire us to rise up and fight for our freedom."

So the Deliverance had something to do with our freedom. Perhaps they were my favorite centaurs instead.

"The red centaurs with black stripes are Striplings and the brown ones with horns are Elabans, just in case you didn't know that. They're pretty similar to Bellios. They all run their own colonies the same way.

"There's more to see than just centaurs here, though. The luminary in that painting over there is the one that first befriended Amphion. He helped pave the way for many of the luxuries we have now, and his wife was the first nocturne allowed to live here. He only died a few years ago. And those three nocturne women were the first to work with Elyxeos women in developing some of the fashions they wear today..."

Parthenia went on telling me about each painting, offering a history lesson as much as a showing of Icy's work.

Halfway through the room, I caught sight of the black painting Icy was working on. There were too many people surrounding her for me to make out more than a night sky.

"That's a painting of the river running through the village we used to live near," Parthenia was saying. "Icy lived right beside the water—"

So great was my growing curiosity of the painting being created, I hardly heard her. Stars twinkled against the edges of the black rectangle, creating a vision of some sort that drew me closer. A man moved to the side, broadening my view. It felt like a sledgehammer had been taken to my chest. I moved closer to the small crowd.

"—I even remember seeing her when I was a child. Always an artist—"

A luminary was floating down from the sky exactly as I had arrived on the Surface recently. Masses of centaurs, luminaries, and nocturnes were bowing to her on the ground.

"—Sleigh, where'd you go? Sleigh? Oh..."

I could see Parthenia join me from the farthest corner of one eye.

"So she's finally painting it," Parthenia said. "The woman in the picture sort of looks like you, doesn't it, Sleigh?"

I knew she was studying me. I could feel her bombarding me with the same suspicions Bones had of my origins. I had to get away. So I shrugged and began working my way toward the door. "What else is there to see?"

"But you haven't even gotten to meet Icy, and we're not finished yet."

I stepped out into the night. "Couldn't Icy get into trouble for painting that?"

"She'll probably keep it hidden once she's finished, unless

someone requests to see it." Parthenia stepped in front of me, her wary demeanor causing me to shiver. "Is there something in that painting that disturbs you?"

My skin shone a bit brighter as I thought of what ill feelings the Surface dwellers might have for my kind from above. "Of course not. I'm just getting tired of looking at pictures."

The door in the house across from Icy's opened. "Hey, Parthenia." A young luminary woman walked outside toward us. "Wow, you two look amazing. I was just talking to Justus about coming to see if you and Sleigh wanted to go to a watch post when I saw you through my window."

"That's a great idea, Sirene," Parthenia answered. "We haven't done that in years."

"Sirene?" I asked. "I didn't even recognize you."

She patted the hair she'd chopped off from waist length to barely reaching her shoulders. "I hope it looks alright. Just seemed like time for a change."

I might have offered a remark if I had something nice to say about it.

A luminary man who stooped forward a bit came out of the house next. "You certainly found them fast. Is this Sleigh, then?" he asked.

We all moved closer to their house when an old couple came to enter Icy's.

"Yep," Sirene answered. "Sleigh, this is my husband, Justus I thought he could tag along."

"Glad to meet y—" Justus began. He screamed like a girl and jerked back, pushing Sirene into me, when a dark figure ran over his roof and landed right behind him.

"Sorry," Bones said with an unapologetic grin.

"You alright, love?" Sirene asked, putting an arm around Justus.

Parthenia sniggered, making it twice as hard not to laugh at Justus' squeal.

"I really wish you wouldn't do that," Justus huffed at Bones. "You boys could at least stay off *our* roof."

"I would if they didn't all look exactly the same," Bones said.

"Who won?" I asked.

"Me, of course." Bones held up the winning cloth, only a moment before the other three began to emerge, Crawler from the same roof as Bones, Pre from the one to its left, and Minz on the ground.

"I want a rematch," Pre barked, a slight vibration spreading beneath our feet. "You only won because Crawler dropped it and you beat me to it."

Bones' eyes glinted atop his smug smile. "Winning is still winning," he rumbled.

"I didn't drop it," Crawler protested. "It got caught on one of those stupid bats hanging outside Vin's house."

"Excuse me," a luminary man who was approaching behind Crawler said so furiously, he nearly sounded like a nocturne. "I carved those bats, and you four mischief-makers are certainly more of a nuisance than any carving I've ever created." With that, he turned to enter Icy's home behind a few luminary girls. I recognized the nocturne woman on his arm, the one who'd given me an owl carving only that morning. She offered me a little wave over one shoulder before she disappeared.

"You all have a rematch if you want," Parthenia said irritably. "We're going to one of the watch posts."

"That might be more fun than another game of four corner escape," Crawler said, offering me a subtle grin. "It sounds like the perfect place for two people to get close under the stars."

"Give me a break," Pre said, while Minz gagged.

"You should know," Parthenia said vehemently, blazing with

angry light. "You get cozy with every girl the scavengers bring here."

"Don't be jealous," Crawler said, to which Parthenia responded with her own fake gagging.

I didn't want to flat out tell Crawler to back off, so I took another route, hoping it wouldn't end up causing more trouble than the first. "Will you come?" I put a hand on Bones' arm, feeling awkward and uncomfortable. Flirting wasn't really in my nature.

His eyebrows lifted and his lips parted like he was moving in slow motion. Then his general ease returned as he put an arm around my neck, the warmth of his skin putting heat into my face. "Yeah." He tossed the winning cloth to Crawler. "I'll play some other time."

Parthenia fell in step beside me when Bones began leading me through houses. Crawler's little gang walked behind us.

"I'm not going if *they're* coming," Justus said, hanging back when we rounded his house.

"Come on," Sirene answered. "They're harmless."

"They're idiots."

"I heard that." Crawler called back as we left them behind.

"He's right, you know," Parthenia walked backwards to say, sparking an argument between them.

I took the opportunity to put a hand on Bones' warm back and tilt my head upward so I could whisper in his ear. "I hope you don't mind. I was just trying to get Crawler to leave me alone."

He chuckled quietly, pulling me closer. "I don't mind playing along."

"Why does your sister hate Crawler so much?" I asked Bones when I noticed the uncharacteristic look of abhorrence on Parthenia's face.

"Oh, they've gotten together and broken up so many times I

lost count. He's really, *really* good at getting what he wants. You surprised me tonight."

"Parthenia gave me a warning."

"Slow down; I'm coming," someone called after us. I looked back over mine and Bones' shoulders to see Sirene chasing after us, husbandless. She laughed as she ran into Parthenia and hugged her. "Honestly, men can be so ridiculous—no offense, guys."

"It might have helped if she'd married a *real* man," Bones whispered into my ear.

I shook my head and laughed.

"Man, we haven't been to a watch post since before you even got here, Minz," Pre said. We left the housing area and entered the open space alongside the crops. "We used to race to it every night and whoever won got first pick at where to sit."

"You thinking what I'm thinking?" Bones asked him. His muscled tightened against me. Then, without a word, all four boys were off in a race to one of the long ramps leading up to an empty platform.

"Always a competition with those guys," Sirene said.

"Why didn't you tell me you liked my brother?" Parthenia asked me.

"I don't. I mean, not like that. I was just trying to get Crawler to back off. Bones said he's okay with it." The only thing about him that truly attracted me was that he was a nocturne. He was cute, but felt more like a friend.

"It sounds risky to me."

"I say take all the risks you can while you're still single, Sleigh," Sirene said. "Married life can get pretty boring."

"A week ago you were on top of the world," Parthenia said.

"I still am. Justus gets a little dull after a while is all."

"WHOA!" Bones cheered when he reached the bottom of the platform's ramp first.

"Are we allowed to go up there?" I asked.

"Just the ones inside the city, and only after dark when they're empty," Sirene answered. "We don't ever go to the ones closest to the centaur houses."

The four boys waited for us to cross the open space. When we reached it, Bones held out an arm for me to go first. "Wherever you want to sit, Sleigh."

"Awww," Sirene cooed.

"Thanks." I walked past him up the ramp, turned at the bends, and sat in the middle on the edge farthest from the tree, thinking it would offer the best view.

16

B ones sat next to me and let his legs hang over the edge beside mine.

I smiled at him, thinking of how he had beaten his alleged friends twice that night and still lacked the overly confident manner Jordan always had. The smile quickly receded. The thought of my boyfriend, if you could even call him that now, was a sad one. Our relationship would have had to end eventually, at least the romantic part of it, since I simply didn't love him the way he loved me. But he was such a good boyfriend. I missed him.

With the chill in the air, it felt good to lean against Bones' exceptionally warm side and feel his arm wrap around me.

Parthenia sat on my other side. Sirene took the place beside her, and the boys filled the edge at Bones' other side.

Crawler started talking to Bones about a girl who lived beside him, so Parthenia began talking loudly enough to Sirene that she wouldn't have to hear him.

I tried to ignore the split conversations and gaze out over the small, busy village. Children and adolescents played outside.

Adults visited with each other. There were far more luminaries to see, but the dark shadows moving about signified the nocturnes mixed in with them. One even seemed to be putting on a show for several luminaries with the flames he was producing, twirling his ignited arms and making various shapes with the tracers of light left behind.

Bright lights emanated from the watch towers surrounding the enormous centaur city. The Elyxeos housing area seemed more peaceful, with only a sparse few wandering around outside. Their windows bore no light, not even the flicker of a candle.

My attention was drawn to the forest past the crops when I heard a great deal of shouting. With all the talk of war still swimming through my mind, it was impossible not to feel a horrible sense of dread. A mass of the largest Elyxeos I'd seen so far, mixed with a good many nocturnes, entered the lights coming off the platforms. They were hauling something dead behind them. The animal's corpse was nearly as big as my house.

"What's going on over there?" I asked.

"That'll be the hunters returning," Parthenia said. "Looks like they got a full-grown male this time. That'll keep them home for a while."

"What is it?"

"Can't you tell?" Crawler said. "It's a titanasaur."

"Or have you never seen one before?" Bones asked.

"C—course I have," I lied. "But why are the nocturnes with them?"

"Those are the men crazy enough to go hunting titanasaur with the Elyxeos."

"Hey, my dad's out there," Minz said, "and he's not crazy. He'd just rather be out hunting for food than weeding all day. I'd be doing it too, if he'd let me."

"Why doesn't he let you?" I asked.

"Because of the danger involved, I guess. Dad always says it's worth the risk to be able to eat some of the titanasaur he helped kill. Hunters are the only nocturnes that ever get any."

"Titanasaur are hard to kill and extremely dangerous," Parthenia said. "It's not unusual for one of us or even an Elyxeos to die in the hunt."

"They risk their lives to feed us?" I asked.

"They risk their lives to feed themselves."

Sirene nodded. "It's all about their crops. Any one of them would gladly sacrifice themselves to ensure the survival of their colony."

"Of course we're very lucky in a sense," Parthenia said. "Even nocturnes couldn't bring down a titanasaur without the Elyxeos. The luminaries here are the only ones who will ever taste such sweet meat."

Elyxeos shouted happily from the platforms. The hunters shouted back, thunder rolling through the air with the voices of the nocturnes. "They sure are noisy," I said.

I slid Bones' arm off of me so I could lay back and look at the clear sky, wondering if I might see anything helpful. He laid back, as well, followed one by one by the others.

The rare sight of the slight movement of stars northward told me that something truly monumental was approaching. The thought of Icy's most recent creation made me shudder. Was it possible there was a star-seer here who had seen the same thing as Livia? I still didn't want anything to do with this revelation. It sounded too intense... like escaping to the Surface twice... like defying the Avarice... like getting myself captured by centaurs... I'd already been through enough. I couldn't handle anymore.

It was easier to think of the cluster of stars with a reddish tint, the ones resembling Bones' facial features. He definitely had some serious feelings for me. For whatever reason, this made me laugh.

"What do you see?" Bones asked me.

"Nothing important."

"The stars still seem to be moving northward," Parthenia said. "Are you seeing the same thing you always see, Bones?"

"Yeah, I just wish I knew for certain which colony it is."

"I wish I could read the stars like nocturnes can."

My neck turned so I could stare at Parthenia. It was killing me not to ask the question burning in my mind, what she meant by that.

"I wish whoever it is would come already," Sirene said.

"She'll be here soon," Bones said. "I know she will." His head turned to stare at me. I refused to return the attention, and hoped no one else noticed his movement.

"Really?" Sirene sat up on an elbow.

"I don't know if you should be in such a hurry," Parthenia interjected. "It sounds like things could get pretty bad before they get better."

I didn't want to listen to them talk about it anymore. And lying down was making my eyes heavy. "Do you guys mind if I head home?" I yawned as I sat up.

"Sleepy already?" Bones asked.

"Yeah, I'm still not used to all this, you know."

"Do you want me to stay with you again tonight?" Parthenia asked.

I thought about it for a moment. I really didn't want to be alone, but I would have to get over it eventually. And part of me had been preparing for it, really. Married to Jordan or not, I'd been considering moving out of my parents' home for a while. "No thanks."

Bones stood and held a hand out to me. "I'll walk you home."

"Thanks. I'm still not sure if I know my way around here well enough not to get lost amongst all the identical houses."

I looked back when Parthenia shrieked, "Get away from me, Crawler." He'd scooted closer to her and was laughing hysterically at her little episode.

"They'll be fine." Bones held onto my hand and led me down the ramp. The two continued to argue as we left them all behind.

The more alone Bones and I became, the more uncomfortable I felt. I withdrew my hand when we passed by the first house.

"How long do you want to keep this thing going?" he asked me.

"How long do you think it'll take Crawler to decide he's not interested?" I asked back.

"Hopefully forever."

The way he was watching me, I had to return his smile. "Um —thanks for everything you've done for me since I got here. I really appreciate your family."

"Sure. I'm not glad you were captured, but I am glad you're here... You can always trust me, you know... with anything."

There was more to this promise than our little arrangement regarding Crawler. I certainly needed someone I could trust with anything. It just wasn't that simple for me.

We walked quietly after that. Past sleepy houses and wide awake, lit-up houses. Past laughter and singing. For the first time, I thought of how the general air of the place lacked the tension I often felt in the valor trees. It was freeing to live without the secrecy of the Surface and the promise of a race of man so dangerous and deadly we'd cut ourselves off from them completely.

It wasn't that I loved it here or would have chosen captivity. But at least I wasn't afraid any longer. The Elyxeos would die to protect and feed us, even if it was only for their own benefit. And the Avarice couldn't hurt me here.

My mind wandered to the movement of the stars. Livia's words and Icy's painting mingled with my wonderment. Could I truly be the woman to bring peace to everyone? And what if I could free my family from the Avarice? What if they could discover the beautiful unknown world beneath their feet?

It doesn't matter, I told myself. *There's nothing special enough about me to make me the woman from the painting.* I even began to question whether or not I was the woman I'd seen in the stars, breaking the chains put around our city by the Avarice. She resembled me, but it could've been someone else. It just didn't make sense that I could do all those great things.

And I preferred it that way. I didn't want to have to figure out how to do everything required to bring down the Avarice and end slavery. I was already exhausted by all I'd done for Blush. It was someone else's turn to play the hero.

"Are you sure you're okay on your own tonight?" Bones asked, turning around a house and walking to its door. When I realized it was mine, I decided something had to be done to distinguish my door from the others.

"I've got to be," I answered, feeling like a storm had just surrounded me, drenching me in a cold, dark loneliness.

Bones opened the door for me. "Do you want me to stay with you for a little while?"

"No, I'm pretty tired." I turned inside the doorway to face him. "Thanks again for helping me with Crawler."

"I don't mind." He reached up to smooth a few loose hairs down toward his ponytail, looking shy. His mouth opened like he wanted to say something, but changed his mind. Then he tilted his head and began leaning forward. He was going to kiss me!

"I have a boyfriend," I gasped, leaning back.

"What?"

"Had a boyfriend—back home. I'm sorry, Bones. It's just too soon."

The way his eyebrows furrowed unevenly made it impossible to read his reaction. A moment of uncertainty passed by.

"I left my bag at your house," I said, cutting through the silence. "All that's in there are dishes. Maybe you could bring it with you to the fields in the morning?"

He nodded and left me alone. All alone in my very own house. I decided to leave the door open, so at least it didn't feel quite so solitary.

Figuring out what to do with all the gifts on my bed would keep me busy, I decided, at least for a little while. I got straight to work, hanging up dresses, organizing and arranging things on shelves. The last thing I did was lay the buffalo hide rug at the foot of my bed.

Then I went to sit at my table, where I'd scattered my papers. I considered drawing my family, but the thought was so painful, I had to push it aside at once. Instead, I chose to create a more up-to-date picture of Blush, based on what I'd seen of her through the stars.

As I sketched her, I ate the strawberries Daphnis had given me, absentmindedly. After sitting out for so long, they weren't half as good as the ones I'd had earlier that night.

When I was finished with the drawing, I used some glue to hang it on the wall above my bed. It would serve as a constant reminder of why I was here. That I'd done the right thing.

I considered hanging up a few of my favorite pictures of Gabriel and baby Blush, as well, but was afraid it would might raise too many questions I didn't want to answer.

The light cast by my skin all over the room dimmed when I climbed into bed.

Bones was mad at me. Marina probably thought I hated her.

It was impossible not to shed a few tears for the pain of missing my family. I'd gotten nowhere in determining what my next move should be.

But at least things were better than they had been the night before.

17

I t felt as if my head was being beaten like a drum when a knock came at my door in the morning. I rolled over and groaned into my pillow. The knocking came again. It was slightly less painful this time.

"Sleigh," Bones called from outside my door. "I brought your bag."

The soreness of my legs when I climbed out of bed, not even bothering to open my eyes, far outweighed the pain of my throbbing head. My body was far from adjusting to my new sleep schedule or to the hours of standing and walking over fields. I rubbed my eyes blearily as I stumbled toward the door.

Bones knocked again. "I'm sorry if I was rude to you last night. There's a lightning storm, so we're free for the morning. Can I come in and talk to you?"

I vaguely noticed the pattering of raindrops against the roof on my way to the door.

My eyes finally opened when I stumbled into the chair I'd left pulled out the night before. The dark eyes of a substantial nocturne man stared at me from across the table.

"AAAHHHH, *BONES!*" I screamed for help, running for the door.

The rock slid across the room when he threw it open and ran toward me, catching me in his arms. "Are you alright?" he asked, then realized there was a man now standing behind my table. "Who are you?"

"I'm her husband," a familiar, rumbling voice answered.

Keeping hold of Bones, I turned slowly around. Gabriel stared at me with a frustrated look, even larger and more powerful-looking than he had been years before.

"Husband?" I asked, breaking free of Bones. "What are you—"

"I've been searching for you since you were taken. I didn't want to wake you when I got here last night."

Something shattered behind me. I jerked sideways and only caught sight of one of Bones' feet disappearing out the door. He'd thrown my bag down where he was standing, shards of glass from one of my jars spilling out over the floor.

"Why did you tell him that?" I asked.

Gabriel ignored the question as he went to shut the door. Then he came closer to me, his expression a cross between anger and hurt. "I thought it was a safe cover. It never occurred to me you would already have a boyfriend so soon after your precious Jordan."

"Jordan?" I glanced out through the window at the pouring rain. "Bones isn't my boyfriend. What are you doing here, Gabriel?"

He let out a noisy breath as he went to the table to push a few of my drawings around. "Guess I thought you'd be happier to see me," he said, holding up a picture of himself. "You've certainly been thinking about me."

My cheeks burned. I was mortified. I hurried over to the table and began gathering up all my drawings. "I am happy to see you Gabriel. I'm just surprised—and confused. You still haven't told me why you said you're my husband?"

He held the drawing in his hand out to me. "Because it's the only way the Elyxeos will take in a nocturne." His hand rested on my shoulder. "And the only way to help you escape."

A dim ray of hope began growing inside me as I sat the stack of papers face down on the center of my table. "Is that why you're here?"

Gabriel nodded.

So he'd given himself to the centaurs only so he could rescue me. I couldn't believe this man I'd fantasized about for years was actually here, standing in my house with me—our house now. It made me a little nervous, like Jordan used to when we started seeing each other. I was more relieved, though, because I wasn't alone anymore. Finally, I had someone to help answer all my questions.

"How did you find me?" I asked. "The rain must have washed the scavenger's tracks away. And Blush isn't here, so you had to have taken the time to get her home before you went out looking for me."

Gabriel pulled out a chair and motioned for me to take a seat. "Why don't you sit down so we can talk?" I accepted the gesture, then he sat down beside me. "I've been tracking for as long as I can remember. Finding you wasn't that difficult."

"So you *were* the man watching when I was captured?"

"I would have stopped them if I didn't have Blush with me."

"You would have died."

"Perhaps... probably... There isn't anything I wouldn't do for you Sleigh, not after what you did for me, and for what you've given me in Blush."

We shared a meaningful smile for only a moment, one precious moment to soak in the fact that he was really there with me, for me. An extraordinary flash of lightning burned through the room, followed closely by an explosion of thunder.

Gabriel leaned an elbow on the table, staring at me thoughtfully. "I have to ask—what are *you* doing back on the Surface?"

"I turned eighteen two days ago. The stars showed Blush being taken, and you being killed. I came as soon as I could, but by the time I found you, the centaurs were already too close. The only way to save you was to let them capture me." My eyes began to tear up, something I was getting extremely tired of.

"Thank you for that, Sleigh." Gabriel ran his hand over my forearm gently. "I owe you everything."

A tear washed against one corner of my mouth when I grinned. I scooted my chair closer to him so I could wrap my arms around his neck. "I owe you everything, too. And you can't imagine how grateful I am that you came for me."

His sturdy arms went around my back. I sobbed into his shoulder. The immense sacrifice of giving yourself voluntarily to the centaurs was all too familiar to me. This man, who I had been taught to hate and fear all my life, had given up everything for me, and for my sister. I hugged him a little bit tighter at the thought of what a truly great man he was. I knew it before, but didn't realize just how deeply my heart yearned to be reunited with him again on so many levels, until that moment.

If we did manage to escape, I knew I had a place in this world. As a neighbor or a friend, or even the faintest possibility of something more, there was a place for me with Gabriel.

Reluctantly, I drew away, but kept close to him. "Thank you, Gabriel."

He shook his head as he wiped my tears away, removing the butterfly wings that were coming loose. "You've given up so much more than I have, Sleigh."

"Do—" *sniff, sniffle,* "Do you have a plan?"

"Not yet, but I will. Did you see anything else in the stars?"

I stared at the floor, wiping the traces of my tears away, and thinking of everything I'd witnessed. "There were a few things about our city, and a woman breaking the chains put around it by the Avarice."

"Were you the woman?"

I shrugged, not wanting to confess the possibility out loud.

"So you saw nothing of my world aside from Blush and me?"

"No."

"There have been whispers recently all over every village of the same vision given to all the nocturne star-seers. A woman will descend from your city and make everything right. It's the first time in my life people are anxious for a sky luminary to come to the Surface. I've often wondered if it might be you."

"Bones was saying something about that last night. It sounded like a savior would come blazing through, bringing peace to everyone. I've been here two days and nothing's happened. It can't be me."

"Is that how you think it'll go?" he smirked. "A woman will come blazing through, magically raining peace over everything? Something so great will take time. You should talk to your friend about what he saw. He might be able to help you know if you're the one from the vision, and what exactly will be required of you if you are, if you trust him, that is."

My thoughts raced wildly at his words.

"I know if there was any possibility I was the luminary from that vision, I would want every advantage available to me in what destiny has promised."

"But the stars' promises don't always come to pass. I watched you die, Gabriel, but here you are."

"Exactly."

"But... hmmm." He was right. In a single word, he'd provided all the finality I needed, and didn't want. I had to talk to someone who had seen a vision of what was to come. Avoiding or embracing certain parts of it might be what saved my life, or what saved me from a great deal of loss and suffering. It was just so much easier to ignore it and hope it would all go away...

"Alright, but do you mind if I ask you a few questions first?"

"Go ahead."

"Last night Bones' sister said that she wished she could read the stars like nocturnes can. What did she mean?"

His face brightened. "So, we're nocturnes now? No longer savage defects?"

I rolled my eyes, wishing he'd forgotten my former use of the word. "You never were."

"Right, well, the stars always move for nocturne seers the way they do for luminaries at midnight on your eighteenth birthday."

"Wow. I can see why Parthenia would say that, then. Are you a seer?"

"Nope. The talents I was born with are purely speed and strength. They've served me well as a hunter and craftsman, though."

"Have you heard of the Deliverance?"

"Of course. Knowing as much as you can about centaurs is vital to your safety on the Surface. The Deliverance is a mixed herd of centaurs who fight against slavery. They make attacks on colonies in an attempt to free as many as they can. There haven't been enough of them to really take over a colony yet, but they give it their best shot. They would probably be our best bet in escaping, if it wasn't so unlikely that they'd make an attack on the Elyxeos."

"I feel like I should tell you, I asked Bones if anyone had ever tried to escape the night I got here. He said no one's ever succeeded, and the luminaries who have tried were locked in a room for days. The nocturnes are beaten for it."

"I know that, Sleigh, but we can't stay here."

"I agree. I just wanted to make sure you knew... Although, it does seem strange that you would know that if no one's ever escaped."

"Don't you remember what I said the first time we met?"

"Yes." I'd only replayed it through my mind about a hundred times a day since it happened.

"Knowledge is key to our survival. There isn't a man on the Surface who hasn't taken the risk of getting too close to your city or a centaur colony in order to learn more about it."

I shifted my body to lean ever so slightly closer to him. It was surreal to be sitting there with him, just as I'd dreamt of for so long.

"There are a few nocturnes that get to go hunting titanasaur with the Elyxeos—except that Parthenia said it's extremely dangerous, so that's probably not a good idea," I said, wanting to take it back.

"It's a great idea, actually."

"I just hate for you to be in more danger than you have to be." I stared absently at my fingers as they fumbled with each other in my lap. "I've always wanted to see you again, Gabriel. If something happened to you because of me, I don't know what I'd do."

He pressed one hand over mine to still them. I lifted my chin so I could meet his eyes. "If you haven't figured it out yet, our lives have proven to depend on one another's. As long as you're on my side and I'm on yours, I think we'll be okay."

"Yeah." We shared another meaningful smile. I couldn't help but worry about him joining the hunters, but it felt good to hear those words. "You want to come with me to see Bones?"

"It'll probably go better if I'm not there. I'll clean up the glass and talk to some of the neighbors, see if I can come up with a solid plan."

"Alright. If you're hungry, nocturnes are allowed to take

whatever they want from the crops, but you probably already knew that."

"No, that one's actually new."

I put the owl and the pink box my paint had been given to me in on the windowsill to the right of the door. That way I would recognize my house when I returned to it. "I guess I'll meet you back here, then," I said as I opened the door.

The thought occurred to me when I stepped out into the refreshing rain that the charade of being husband and wife could only go so far. *What are we going to do about sleeping arrangements?* I wondered. "That's the least of my worries," I said to myself, shaking it off. *I'll figure that out later.*

18

I t took me a while to find the house for which I was
searching. I was drenched by the time I knocked on Bones'
door. The cold water felt good to my skin at first, but now I
was shivering.

"Good gracious!" Daphnis said when she opened the door.
"Get a blanket for her, Parthenia. Come on in, Sleigh. What are
you doing out in the storm?"

"I need to talk to Bones. Is he here?"

"He's right back there." Daphnis pointed to the yellow
paneling surrounding his little area. "He seemed upset when he
got home. Is something wrong?"

"He didn't say anything to you?"

"Not a word."

"Do you mind if I talk to him?"

"Go ahead. I figure you're the only one who can fix whatever
it is that's ailing him."

Parthenia threw a warm blanket around my shoulders. "You
want to play a game with us?" she asked. Her dad was sitting at
their table with a game board and loads of colorful tokens positioned before him.

"Not right now, thanks." I crossed the room and paused at the wall separating Bones and I. *Do I knock?*

"It's your turn, Mom," Parthenia said behind me.

"Can I come in, Bones?" I asked.

"Go away," he snapped.

That hurt. An inner terror that I might have lost one of my only allies in this new place began swirling around inside me.

"Bones, you had better be nice to Sleigh," Daphnis said.

My nerve faltered. I was surprised when the dormant fear I once had of defects began to awaken inside me. *Don't be stupid,* I told myself. "I really need to talk to you."

"I said go away."

"You'll cut it out if you want to eat tonight," Daphnis shouted.

"Quit being such a baby, Bones," Parthenia added.

In a moment of inner chaos and desperation, I decided to trust Bones. "It's not true, okay?"

Silence—except for the tinkling of tokens and Parthenia laughing at something her dad said.

"If you won't listen, I'm coming in." I waited a second to make sure his parents didn't object.

"Two more tokens and you win," Axe said to one of the women.

So I went to one end of the paneling and folded back a section. Bones was laying in his bed, staring at the ceiling. He rolled over so his back was to me when I entered the little space. "Come on, Bones, just listen," I said quietly. He didn't move a muscle.

This is ridiculous! I went around his bed and knelt on the floor so we were face to face. He finally met my eyes. "I'm not married, Bones," I whispered. "Gabriel and I only know each other because we have a long history of saving each other from one deadly fate or another. I'm here because I need to talk to you about what you've been seeing in the stars, though."

His eyebrows rose, then fell without care. "Why should I believe anything you say?" he whispered back. "I nearly kissed you last night and now there's a man in your house saying he's married to you."

"Can we go somewhere more private?"

"We could go to your house, if your *husband* wasn't there."

I let out an irritated sigh, fuming at his childishness. There was only one thing I could think of to say that might make him listen: "I'm a sky luminary, Bones. I came to the Surface three nights ago because I saw it in the stars that my sister would be made a slave. She was born a nocturne nearly four years ago and Gabriel's the one who's looked after her all this time. I was too late, though. I got myself captured to protect them both."

Bones sat up in bed and leaned forward so he could continue to whisper to me. "Why didn't you tell me any of this before?"

"AH HA!" Axe suddenly roared from the table, causing me to jump and bang into Bones' face.

"No way, you won?" Parthenia gasped.

"How brilliant, dear," Daphnis added. "You've been holding that card the entire time."

"Of course," Axe said.

"Sorry." I brushed my hand over Bones' forehead where I'd bumped into him.

He ignored me and stood up to take something from a shelf. With a wave of his arms, a sizable tarp popped open. Then he left the space through the opening I'd made in the paneling. "Sleigh and I are going to the watering barrels," he announced to everyone.

I followed him toward the door.

"You had better go straight there in a hurry," Daphnis said. "It's dangerous outside with all that lightning."

"Mind if I come, too?" Parthenia asked.

Bones looked at me to answer. I decided it was better she knew the truth about Gabriel and I if I was going to be sneaking around with her brother. "Sure."

"Let me just grab a tarp."

Bones spread the tarp over our heads, showing me where I should hold on to it, while Parthenia retrieved one for herself. Then we were running through the rain with Parthenia leading the way, the corners of a wet blanket in one of my hands and the tarp in my other. Cold sprinkles splashed against my legs as we went.

It wasn't long before we were breaking free of the houses and racing toward the wall-less roof covering the strong table that usually held up two barrels full of fresh drinking water. The table was empty on this morning, however. The poles holding the roof up were lined outwardly with rows and rows of open barrels, left to catch the rain.

The three of us ducked under the covering. I let go of the tarp so Bones could fold it up. "If you're not married, why did that guy say he's your husband?" he asked me, sitting on the table.

"Husband?" Parthenia's eyes widened. "What did I miss this morning?"

I went to sit on the table beside Bones, crossing my legs on the tabletop. "I'll catch you both up, but you've got to promise to keep it a secret. You said I could trust you with anything, Bones. So can I?"

He nodded.

I turned back to Parthenia. "I promise; your secret's safe with me," she said.

"And you can't hate me either."

Bones surprised me when he smiled, glancing from me to his sister. "She's a sky luminary, Parthenia."

"You were right, then," Parthenia said. "She could be the one all the nocturnes are seeing."

"I doubt that, but I do want to know more about what it is they're seeing," I answered her.

"Answer my question first," Bones said.

"My sister was born a def—I mean a nocturne a few years ago. When the Avarice's guards took her, I snuck to the Surface to catch a glimpse of her. While I was here, Gabriel and I ended up saving each other's lives. Nearly four years later, the tradition continues. I came back when I saw it in the stars that he would die and my sister would be taken by centaurs. Getting myself captured was the only way to prevent it. Gabriel saw it happen, so he told the Elyxeos he's my husband so they'd let him stay. He's only here to help me escape."

"Sleigh, no." Parthenia looked horrified. "You can't escape. No one can. And Gabriel might be beaten half to death."

"I know it's dangerous, but he's here now, and he doesn't plan on staying. I won't do it unless he finds a way that's foolproof."

Parthenia continued shaking her head.

"So Gabriel's not the boyfriend you said you had?" Bones asked.

"No. That was Jordan. He and I were growing apart, anyway, or at least I was. My relationship with Gabriel is a powerful one, but it's not romantic." Though if my heart could speak, it might have said otherwise.

Lightning lit up the area around us, followed closely by the crack of thunder.

I turned all my attention to Bones. "Will you tell me about your vision now?"

"Yeah." He cleared his throat. "It starts with a woman floating down from the trees, then moves to show her laughing with a centaur, like they're friends. Then there's a war, but it's always moving so fast and everyone's already fighting; I can never tell who's on what side or what it's about. The woman who came down from the sky rides on a centaur's back into battle, and then everything stops. Centaurs and people bow down to her—together."

Well that was it. I was more convinced than ever. "That couldn't possibly be me."

"Why not?" Parthenia asked. "You gave up your freedom for someone else's. You said it yourself, you saved that man's life more than once. I don't know anyone else who's done all those things. And the woman in Icy's painting looked like it could have been you."

"She really *does* look like you... We need to tell people that the hero from the stars is finally here," Bones said suddenly, looking as if he'd just realized something he'd been struggling with for ages.

"No!" I grabbed his arm. "You promised you wouldn't say anything."

"I won't say who it is. I'll just say she's reached the Surface. Everyone here has been looking forward to this for a long time. They're going to be really happy when they find out you're finally here."

"Don't you think they'll figure out it's her?" Parthenia cut in. "Sleigh just got here, and she's absolutely clueless. No offense, Sleigh."

"I'll just say I saw it in the stars."

"I'd be okay with that if I thought it was me," I said. "But you'd probably be getting their hopes up for nothing."

"Have you befriended any centaurs?" Parthenia asked me.

"Just Davion, I guess... No, wait..." Yesterday morning's strange exchange with Marina played through my mind. "There is one other, although I don't know if I'd call us friends."

"There isn't anything about you that's not in perfect alignment with the hero in the stars," Bones said.

"You're already a hero, for goodness sakes," Parthenia added. "Do you think maybe you know it's you deep down, and you just don't want to consider it?"

"Maybe." I stared out over the houses, reflecting on everything they'd said. It was true that Marina had the potential of becoming a very good friend of mine.

Everything pointed to me being that hero. I just really didn't want it to be.

We remained in silence as I considered all the lives I could improve and perhaps even save. The thing that really swayed me, however, was the thought of how ending slavery altogether would be the safest way to set Gabriel and myself free.

If I was the prophesied hero, and befriending a centaur was part of achieving success, then I decided I had to give it a shot.

19

Bones handed me his tarp before I set out through the rain for Marina's house. He and Parthenia raced toward their house under hers, fussing at each other for hogging all the space beneath.

I really didn't want to do this. Marina still made me extremely uncomfortable. But doing nothing except going home didn't sound better. In the end, I knew that I couldn't go about my life here without working toward some means of freedom.

Flashes of distant light and thunder rolled through the sky as I ran. It was almost a relief to enter the open centaur doorway.

"Marina, are you in here?" I called toward the kitchen.

She appeared in the doorway at the back of the room instead. Her face was blank as she approached me. "Hello, Sleigh."

"I came to see if you needed any help. No one's in the fields, so Davion shouldn't mind."

Marina nodded, looking pleased. "Davion's asleep upstairs. You can help me fold the new slaves' clothes. Seerie just brought in a bundle. She's the head Elyxeos seamstress."

I followed her into a back room with a slanted roof, which

was obviously the bottom of the walkway leading to the second floor. Shelves were built into the back of the room where the ceiling reached to just above my head. A window the same size as the ones upstairs offered a beautiful view of the forest beyond the nearby fence.

Marina went to a giant basket that was overflowing with white dresses and picked up a toddler-sized one to fold. "Just put them on the little table beside the basket once you've folded them. It'll be easier for me to sort them into the appropriate shelves."

"Okay." I picked up one that might have fit me and copied the way she was folding the smaller one.

"How did your first real day go yesterday?" Marina asked me.

I'm not sure what I expected, but her friendliness surprised me. "Better than I expected. I still miss my old home, though."

"I hear your husband joined you last night. That must have made you feel better."

"Yeah." She didn't know the half of it.

"Why didn't you tell me you were married?"

"It's still pretty new, I guess."

Marina picked up the stack of folded clothes that had formed and took them over to the shelves.

"Do you ever get out of here to have fun?" I asked curiously.

"There isn't time for that."

"Maybe if I help you fold all these, we could play a game."

She threw her hair over her shoulders as she came to join me once more. "I don't have any games here."

"So we'll make one up, like...who can fold the next ten dresses faster, GO!" I began folding madly.

Marina looked stunned for a minute. Then she started folding as quickly as she could.

We laughed when we both reached for the same dress and nearly ripped in it half.

I was just getting to dress number eight, ahead of Marina by only one, when I heard an unfamiliar sound blasting outside. Marina dropped the dress she was in the middle of folding and ran to the window. More of these blasts joined the first, a chorus of strange sound explosions. "What is that?" I asked.

"The guards are alerting everyone to danger."

I joined her at the window. A multi-colored herd of armed centaurs was running at us from the distance.

"The Deliverance is coming. We need to get you to your home."

She lifted me from the floor, holding me at her side, and ran to the front room just as Davion entered it. "What are you doing with Sleigh?" he demanded.

"Getting her to her house where she'll be safest."

"I was only helping Marina with something," I added, seeing the look of such wrath on his face. It was awkward with Marina holding me. "I chose to come."

"Keep her here," Davion said. "She could get hit with a stray arrow if you take her outside."

"But the Deliverance would never attack slave housing," Marina argued.

"I said keep her here. If anything happens to her while I'm gone, I'll have you hanged."

Marina immediately put me down.

My breath caught at his awful threat. He was definitely the problem in their marriage, I decided.

Davion disappeared outside.

Marina hung her head miserably. "I wish you didn't have to hear that. We should go into the kitchen. There are no windows in there."

"I need to make sure Gabriel's alright," I said, suddenly feeling desperate.

"Gabriel?"

"My husband." I made a dash for the door, but stopped when she caught my arm.

"You heard Davion. If I let you go out there, I could be killed."

The flames atop one of the houses caught my eye. A nocturne was standing on a roof. He was shouting something and smoking heavily with the rain fighting to douse the flames coming off the top half of his body. "That's Gabriel shouting for me. I have to go to him," I said to Marina.

"You can't go out there—Go up to my room. He should be able to see you through one of the windows. But you have to join me in the kitchen the moment he sees you."

I took off through her house without bothering to answer. There wasn't time. Gabriel was standing out in the open with centaurs preparing to forge an attack.

One glance through the tiny hallway window and I saw that the Deliverance had covered nearly half the ground between where I'd seen them before and the city's fence. Pushing myself to go even faster, I nearly slammed into the wall at the top of the long slope. Then, I tore across the room, jumped onto the ledge, and pressed my body against the glass as I waved my arms frantically at Gabriel. His back was turned to me at the moment.

The Elyxeos army I'd seen training when I first arrived was running past the fields toward the fence. They were going so fast, I thought they might break it down.

Gabriel began to turn back around, shouting and flaming wildly. My feet bounced up and down with my flailing arms in an attempt to draw attention to myself. Finally, he saw me and was off the roof, flying past houses toward me.

A flash of white caught my eye when I rushed back down the ramp. I stopped to see if it might be a luminary escaping.

Centaurs were fighting and killing one another dangerously close to Marina's house. Far away to the west, completely unnoticed by those at war, were four purely white centaurs with antlers standing on top of a hill. I recognized the lightning-fast centaurs Icy had painted so perfectly, the ones who killed luminaries and tortured nocturnes into servitude, the ones Parthenia couldn't even imagine the Elyxeos overcoming. They seemed to be observing and nothing more.

Something dark came at me from the nearby fighting. I moved out of the way before a rock smashed through the window.

"Sleigh, are you alright?" Marina appeared at the bottom of the ramp.

"There are Trios out there!"

She dropped the knife that was in her hand. Her face flushed violet. "You must be mistaken."

"Come look. They're on top of the hill out west."

Marina crept cautiously to the window and peeked out from one side. "I don't see any Trios."

I stood up and searched the horizon, but found it empty. "There were four of them. They must have gone, but they were there; I promise."

"Sleigh!" Gabriel shouted, stomping through the house. "Where are you?"

"I'm coming." I left Marina still peering outside and ran into Gabriel halfway between the kitchen and the entryway.

"We have to go," he said. "We'll never get another chance like this."

I pulled him back when he took my hand and tried running outside. "I can't, Gabriel. Not right now."

He stared at me like I'd just transformed into an Elyxeos right in front of him. "What are you talking about? The Deliverance are here. We can escape."

I lowered my voice and nodded toward the kitchen. "If I leave now Davion will have Marina killed."

"So? She's a centaur," he whispered.

"But she's my friend. If I am the woman in the stars, I know Marina is the centaur all the nocturne seers have seen with me."

"Sleigh, we might never get another opportunity like this one."

"I know, but—between you and me, she's sacrificed everything for her sister that I have for Blush. I can't be the one who sentences her to death... You, you go ahead. I'll find another way."

Gabriel shook his head angrily. His fists tightened.

"I'm sorry," I said softly. "I can't."

He stared at me and spoke with a voice more resounding than usual. "I won't leave without you."

I approached him warily, holding out a hand to rest on his shoulder. His skin was even warmer than usual. "Forgive me." I leaned into him, hoping for a kind response.

His body was rigid, but he put an arm around me.

"Sleigh?" Marina called.

"It's okay," I called back. "We need to go in the kitchen, Gabriel. It's the safest room in this house."

Marina stopped in the kitchen's doorway and stepped aside so we could enter, offering Gabriel nothing more than a condescending frown. "We shouldn't have to remain here for very long," she muttered. "The Deliverance don't stand a chance against us."

20

With all that had happened that morning, there was no working in the fields even after the rain let up. The nocturne men were forced to dig a mass grave for all the centaurs from the Deliverance who had died in the attack. No humans were lost. The Elyxeos lost very few, and buried their own kind.

Apparently Gabriel wasn't the only one with escape on his mind. Five nocturnes had been tormented for their own attempt, and thirteen luminaries were captured and currently suffered imprisonment. Only the couple and their young son who lived two houses down from Bones made it to freedom. The ones who were not so lucky served as an unpleasant reminder that we truly were at the Elyxeos' mercy.

Parthenia and I were sitting at the table looking at all my drawings when Gabriel finally came home that evening. The way he walked into the house, without a glance or a word, and dropped his bag loudly in one chair was a bit unnerving. He took the seat beside it and rested his head against the table.

"Uhhh, I'll just see you in the morning," Parthenia said with a grimace. "Drop by if you need anything." She gave me a significant look before leaving us alone.

Without really knowing if Gabriel was angry with me for that morning or not, I was nervous as I moved closer to him and put a hand on his back. He responded by simply sitting up to stare out a window.

"Are you hungry?" I pulled the bowl of food I'd gathered for him closer to us, lighting the house brighter with my own natural light.

He nodded and took the bundle of grapes to eat first.

"I'm sorry, Gabriel."

His eyebrow arched as he turned to face me. "What could you possibly be sorry for? You saved me from the worst beating of my life today."

"You hardly said a word this morning, and you've seemed so upset all day."

He let out a sigh, looking exhausted. "That's probably because I can't stop worrying about Blush and my mother. We've never had scavengers that close to our house."

"But you said they only wanted luminaries."

"They do. Blush is just so young. And you said they took her in your vision."

That was true. I let him eat in silence after that, because I couldn't think of the right thing to say.

"I met with the hunters today," Gabriel said before biting into an apple, then went on through a rumbly mouthful. "One died when he ran this morning. An Elyxeos hit him in the back with a knife. There's no telling if it was intentional or not. The rest are setting out in five days and I committed to joining them."

"Must you? Parthenia said it's not unusual for a nocturne to be killed."

Gabriel took a jar from his bag and drank a lot of water before he answered. "I know what I'm doing. Besides, it's the only good plan I've got... I shouldn't have been so impulsive this morning. I asked you to run away without even considering all the risks. I should apologize to you for being so reckless."

"No. There aren't many people who would have given up a chance at freedom to stay behind with me."

He took a couple of giant bites out of the apple.

"I saw four Trios today." Maybe *he* would believe me. Neither Marina nor Parthenia had such confidence in me, apparently.

"What?!" He spat pieces of apple over the table. "Are you sure?"

"Yes. I saw them watching the fighting this morning from a distance. They didn't stay very long."

"You're absolutely certain they were Trios?"

I nodded, waiting for his doubts and justifications as to why it couldn't have been them.

"Then we're all in greater danger than we've ever been in before."

"So you believe me?"

"Why wouldn't I believe you?" He went back to eating his apple, a disturbed look in his eyes.

"Parthenia said it's crazy and impossible. She said I probably got lucky and saw some Dashings caught in the sunlight to look white."

"She just doesn't want to believe you." Gabriel set the apple core next to the empty grape stems as he yawned. "I'm too tired to keep worrying about it tonight, though. I hardly slept last night."

"You didn't sleep sitting at this table, did you?"

"Well it would have seemed strange if I requested another bed."

"Oh, Gabriel, you didn't have to do that."

"Yes, I did. And what would your future husband say if he found out another man was climbing into your bed at night?"

"No, I mean we could take turns sleeping on the rug and the bed. I've got two pillows and an extra blanket."

"I would never sleep in a bed while you were left to lie on the floor. What sort of a man do you take me for?"

I couldn't help but laugh at the seriousness in his face that quickly melted into drowsiness, accompanied by another yawn. "Did you mean Jordan when you said 'my future husband'?"

"Who else?"

"Have you been spying on me?" I shivered.

"Not exactly. I check on you now and then to make sure you're okay. I haven't been to see you since I heard him talking to your sister about asking you to marry him. It seemed pointless with him around to look after you." It was difficult to tell, but Gabriel's shoulders seemed to slump forward slightly.

"Gabriel, I told Jordan no."

His sleepy eyes perked up to stare at me questioningly.

"It didn't feel right. Jordan's this guy I really liked when I was younger. That's carried me through the time we've been seeing each other, but he's not really where my heart is. I'm not sure if even that would have lasted much longer."

He nodded and grinned sleepily. "I wish I could stay awake and keep talking with you, Sleigh, but I've got to get some sleep."

"That's alright."

Gabriel stood and went to move the rug to the side of my bed below the hooks I'd left bare, only now there were two pairs of animal-skin shirts and pants hanging on them.

I handed him a pillow and the fuzzy blue blanket one of Daphnis' friends have given me.

He punched the pillow towards the middle on both sides before he laid down on it. "Thank you, Sleigh. Good night."

"Good night, Gabriel." I lay down so I would be facing away from him, because I knew if I didn't, I would be too tempted to stay awake and watch the first and most fascinating nocturne I'd ever met to get any sleep at all.

THE NEXT DAY was bathing day. Gabriel and I really enjoyed our morning together, in spite of how sobering the events of the day before had been. We painted little graceling flowers at the bottom of our door and rearranged things inside.

When bathing time came, Daphnis said we were more heavily guarded than usual, probably because they were afraid of another attack. Nearly everyone was talking about the rumors of the deliverer from the stars having finally arrived on the Surface. It was a relief to know they were clueless as to who it might be or even that there was a possibly she could be serving under the Elyxeos.

When the females returned from the river, and it was the males' turn to go, I went to help Marina with preparing titanasaur meat for the next day. Aside from the prophesy, it was vital to my emotional health that I not spend too much time alone at home. As long as I didn't stop to dwell on her frightening appearance, I actually had a lot of fun with her.

As day drew nearer to night, I left her to gather a few things for Gabriel to eat. I was less concerned about myself, since my body didn't seem to crave the food from their crops too much. The smell of titanasaur meat was the only thing I'd discovered so far that really brought on hunger.

I sat on my bed as the sun began to set and tried cross stitching little silver stars into the edge of my skirt like Henna's mother had taught me a few months before. The more I thought of her, the more I wished I'd told Henna that her mother was going to give birth to a nocturne. Thinking of everyone back home made me feel awful. I wished the men would hurry up and return so Gabriel would provide a distraction.

I didn't get more than three stars sewn on before I decided to rest my head on my pillow and think of what I might say to him when he returned.

SOMETHING BRUSHED against the inside of my hand, drawing me out of my rest. A cool breeze mingled with the peaceful tune someone was singing outside as it drifted in through the open windows all around me. I was lying on my stomach, I realized, leaving my hand to hang over the edge of my bed. Without thinking much about it, I let my mind wander back to slumber.

It was interrupted, however, when I felt the inside of someone else's hand slide against mine, a thumb stroking the back of it. This time, I sat up on my other elbow to look over the edge of my bed. Gabriel was lying on his rug, tracing my hand with his fingers.

"Sorry," he said, letting his hand fall onto his bare stomach. "I didn't mean to wake you."

A wonderful feeling crept over me. "I don't mind," I answered, holding my hand out to him so he would resume running his fingers over it.

He sat up and held my hand as he used the opposite one to rub his thumb back and forth over my knuckles. "Your skin is so soft..." His eyes met mine with an intensity that made my chest burn and my light increase. "Are you absolutely certain you won't marry Jordan?"

My lips and throat began to feel delightfully swollen the way they had at the first smell of cooked titanasaur. "I'm absolutely certain, Gabriel. He said he loved me and that he wanted to be with me always. I couldn't return either of those sentiments."

"So—" He swallowed and stared at my hand as he ran his thumb up over my wrist. "—if you ever found a way to return to your city, would you go back to him?"

This was more than a simple question. My grip on his hand tightened as I came to sit across from him on the floor. "Not if someone gave me a reason not to."

He slid one hand up over my arm and used the other to pull my hand to his lips so he could kiss it. Then he stood, pulling me with him, and came to stand behind me. His arms crossed over me, his hands sliding over my stomach as we swayed back and forth to the song floating through the air.

I pressed my hand to his cheek, closing my eyes and slipping into a state of euphoria. My breathing became deeper as I soaked up all the wonderful feelings of discovering my true place in his heart.

"All these years I came to see you because I could never stop thinking about you, Sleigh," he murmured into my ear. "You're such a beautiful woman."

I turned my head so I could look right into his eyes. "That's exactly why I've only been able to draw one man since I met you."

He grinned and brushed my hair aside, revealing the dark streaks. "You've made part of your hair as black as a nocturne's."

"To remind me every day of Blush, and of you."

His skin burned warmer, his long lashes drifting lower as his eyes became heavy. His arms tightened around me, his hands sliding over fabric. He leaned farther over my shoulder to kiss my cheek. His lips were hot and moist and inviting.

He turned me so I would face him. My hands rested on his back, as he brushed my hair away from my face and over my shoulders. I could hardly breathe. It was the most romantic moment of my life.

A shiver passed through me. No, it was going through him, a

subtle tremor of nocturne power for which my soul was starving.

Slowly, he leaned forward and kissed me. Like a drink of fresh water, the touch of his lips to mine washed down my throat and throughout my body. The heat burning from his skin only caused me to melt further into the moment. It was like magic.

Gabriel put one hand behind my head to rest it carefully against his shoulder. He let out a deep breath, the delicate quaking of his body passing once throughout the floor. "Stay with me, Sleigh. Whether we're stranded here or set free, be mine."

It took no time and no thought at all. "Alright." Whether I remained on the Surface or found a way to return to my family, deep down I knew, I always was and always would be his.

21

Gabriel woke me the next morning with a kiss just under my ear. I smiled at him as I sat up and stretched. "Good morning, Gabriel."

"You look just like your sister when you sleep," he said, smoothing down a few of my flyaway hairs.

"Aww." What a wonderful thing to say.

"I brought you something to eat for a change." He handed me a bowl of grapes and strawberries.

"Thanks."

He went to close the windows as I ate, giving me a chance to notice the assortment of vines and plants piled on the table. "What's all that?" I asked, pointing to it.

"A few useful things we might need. I gathered them on the way back from the river yesterday." He came to sit beside me on my bed, wincing as he rubbed his arm below the shoulder.

"Sore muscle?"

"No, it's the place that devil serpent bit me. It gets sore in the morning sometimes."

"The bite that was meant for me." I reached out to push his

hand aside so I could rub it for him. There were two small scars where he'd been bitten, uneven ovals protruding only slightly.

"I've been thinking on what you said about seeing the Trios. It's only a matter of time before we're all affected by them. You should take advantage of every chance you get to grow your friendship with that centaur."

"Why? What do you think is going to happen?"

"That's just it. The future is so uncertain. She's part of the vision everyone's seeing, so it seems important."

"Good point." A terrible guilt stabbed at me inside as I continued to rub his arm. I leaned forward to kiss the scars. "I can't believe you're still suffering because of me."

He slid a hand over my cheek and offered me a kiss. "I'd say it's worth it to have you." I smiled when he took my hand to kiss it and then held it against his cheek. "With the magic of last night gone, do you still mean everything you said before?"

"Gone?" That was absurd. "It wasn't the magic of the night, Gabriel; it was the magic of being with you. For years, every part of me has ached for you at only the sight of your face in my drawings. Last night you satisfied an inner struggle I've dealt with since you got here."

It wasn't like me to be so forward, but he made me feel safe. And things felt totally natural with him, the way I imagined real married life to be.

Gabriel smiled, gripping me at my back and leaning in for a kiss as unforgettable as the first had been.

I ran one hand over his scar when he leaned away, a small but very special piece of our history that would always tie us together. I kissed it once more before I got out of bed to put my bowl away. "Would you mind giving me a minute to change?" I asked, knowing I needed to leave for work soon.

"I'll go refill our water." He packed his bag with both our jars before he left.

Then I removed the dress that used to be Parthenia's and put on one of the white workers' dresses. I filled my bag with what dishes I would need and the single jar of water beside my bed.

I barely sat down, still feeling blissful from Gabriel's kiss, when a knock came at the door. Parthenia and Bones greeted me on the other side.

"Ready for work?" Parthenia asked me.

"Yeah, Gabriel just went out to get water."

"I'll lend you one of mine," Bones said, shutting the door to force me outside. "He doesn't even have to go to work with us, so it's pointless to wait on him."

"He's joined the hunters, then?" Parthenia asked, moving around my house.

I felt guilty leaving without telling Gabriel goodbye, but I didn't want to get in trouble for showing up to work late either.

"Yes, but how did you know that, Bones?" I asked him.

"I talked to him a little bit on the way to the river."

For some reason, I found this unsettling.

"There's something I haven't gotten a chance to tell you yet," Bones went on, looking really eager as he leaned closer to me so he could whisper. "I was able to tell the ones who escaped about you before they left."

"Okay."

"Don't you get it, Sleigh?"

"Get what?"

"He's excited because word of the arrival of the hero in the stars will spread through the outside villages," Parthenia said. "They'll all be celebrating by now."

"But we don't even know for certain that I'm that hero" I certainly still wasn't convinced. "It seems kind of cruel."

"I know it's you," Bones said with absolute finality.

"Hey, guys," Minz waved to us when we broke free of the

houses. He and Crawler weren't far ahead of us. They waited so we could catch up. "So you're married?" he asked me.

My cheeks burned. "Yes."

"I knew Gabriel before my family was brought here. He's a good man."

"He is." I hated the way he was watching me so fixedly.

"You know I get it that you were captured and thought you'd never see him again, but I hope you don't plan to keep messing around behind his back with Bones."

My eyes got huge as I stared at him, feeling defensive. "I don't! And I only did that so Crawler wouldn't flirt with me. It stopped the moment we were away from you guys. Sorry, Crawler. I didn't want to hurt your feelings."

Crawler put a hand over his heart and faked a pout. "That hurts, Sleigh."

"It would have made more sense to tell him you're married," Minz said.

"I know."

"In all fairness," Parthenia piped up, "that probably would have done nothing to stop his advances."

Crawler smirked as he shrugged and broke away to the field he generally worked on. Minz shook his head and followed after him.

"Does everyone think I'm some sort of adulteress?" I asked, feeling humiliated.

"Of course not." Parthenia put a hand on my back. "I told Sirene exactly what you just told Minz. She gets it. And even though Bones' friends really are idiots, they're not the sort to go around destroying someone else's reputation."

"They're not idiots," Bones said.

"What are you doing? You just missed your field."

"I thought I'd work with you two today. Sleigh's field still needs more workers."

Parthenia lifted a disapproving eyebrow, but said nothing.

We got to work as before once we'd reached our field, Parthenia and me enjoying each other's company as we shed light over the crops. Bones talked to us whenever we were close enough to hear him. I really hoped he understood that there could never be anything between us.

Partway through the morning, Parthenia smacked my arm gently and nodded to my side. I realized Gabriel was walking toward us. My first instinct was to run and wrap my arms around him, but I wasn't sure how he felt about things like that in public. So I only smiled and waved as he approached, dimming my light slightly and meeting him at the field's corner nearest to him.

"You left without even saying goodbye," he said, handing me two jars full of fresh water.

"Sorry. I didn't know how long you would be gone and I didn't want to be late."

"It's alright. But I didn't have a chance to give you this." He held up a thin white cord with two hand-painted charms in the middle, a little red and orange flame and a ball of blue and white light carved from wood.

I placed the jars in my bag and gave him my wrist so he could tie it on. "It's beautiful. Did you make it yourself?"

"Yes, last night after you fell asleep."

"Thank you, Gabriel. I love it." I reached up to hug him, relieved when he hugged me back long and hard.

I realized he had a thick, hemmed strip of black cloth tied around his arm exactly where it would cover his scar. A long silver arrow was embroidered in the center. "Did you make this too?" I asked, sliding one hand down over the arrow.

"Orius, the chief Elyxeos hunter, brought it to me. It marks me a hunter. If I don't prove myself on the first hunt, he'll take it back. I'm not worried about that, though."

"Aye! You get back to work!" a guard hollered from a nearby tree.

I jerked away from Gabriel, sure he was yelling at me. But I followed his gaze to a field farther over where a couple of luminary woman with dimmed lights nodded to him and burned them more brightly.

"Maybe I should get back to work too," I said nervously.

"Relax," Gabriel shushed me in a deep, husky voice. "Hunters get considerably more respect than the other nocturnes. One advantage is that we can come steal a portion of our wives' time whenever we want."

"Really?"

"That's what Orius said—as long as *you* don't mind?"

"No." I shook my head happily. "Steal as much of my time as you want."

He chuckled softly. "There is a project I should probably get back to. I want to get it finished before you come home tonight."

"What is it?"

"It's a surprise. But—can I kiss you before I go?"

"We're married, remember?" I gave him a wink. "You can kiss me anytime you want."

He grinned. "I mean do you mind—in front of everyone?"

"Gabriel, I will *never* turn down a kiss from you."

His smiled broadened as he laced his fingers through mine with one hand, holding it up so it was pressed between our hearts, and putting his other arm around me to pull me closer. Then he kissed me with plenty of passion and little restraint. My heart burst into flight. I had never been kissed like that before.

I gasped and let out a shaky breath when his lips released mine. My goodness, I began to think I was falling absolutely in love with this man. What else could ignite such fire within my soul?

Gabriel glanced behind me. "That should put to rest whatever Bones thinks is between you two."

"What?" My heart deflated, putting out all inner flames. "That kiss was for him?"

"No, Sleigh." His eyebrows furrowed. He gazed upon me with absolute resolution. "That was for you alone." He kissed my cheek before he turned to leave.

Bones was standing in the middle of the field when I turned around, holding an empty watering can sideways and staring at me. I felt kind of bad, not that I would have traded that kiss for anything.

Parthenia was still moving across the field. She waved me over to her.

"You told me your relationship with him wasn't romantic," Bones said crossly when I walked past him.

"It wasn't when I told you that."

He let out a huffy sound and left the field completely for his old one.

"Don't worry about him," Parthenia said. "Even if your marriage isn't real, he should have expected something like this. He'll get over it eventually."

I felt awful to see him looking so dejected and to know I was the one who had caused it. "I only hope I haven't lost a great friend in all this."

22

W hen I got home that evening, I found that Gabriel had woven the mass of vines into a spherical chair with an opening in the front. He'd hung it from the ceiling for me. Of course it was *just* big enough for the two of us if we were really close together. Sitting back against the vines, squished against Gabriel with my head on his shoulder, was the perfect place to get cozy and recount the day's events.

Having a man who could build and do just about anything left me feeling a bit spoiled. And more than that, I started to feel happiness again.

At the end of each day, I made it a point to crop by Marina's to talk for a few minutes before I went home. It began to feel like I could trust her, though I had no reason to reveal any secrets to her just yet.

The days passed by too quickly. And then the one I'd been dreading arrived, the day Gabriel set out with the hunters. We were both awoken at the break of dawn when one of the hunters came knocking on our door. We ate quickly, then Gabriel put an arm around me and guided me toward the front gates.

Hues of orange and pink dusted the still purplish-black sky

to the east. It was far too early for anyone other than guards, hunters, and hunters' wives to be awake. At least fifty enormously-built Elyxeos men had already gathered at the gates, along with twenty nocturne men. Eleven more joined them at about the same time we did.

"Morning, Orius," Gabriel said to a particularly scary-looking Elyxeos who approached us. He had a long scar across his chest and a terrible burn where no hair grew anymore along his hind side. He only grunted and nodded to Gabriel in response, handing him a sword and shield.

Gabriel waited until Orius had gotten a good distance away to say, "I would have requested a bow and arrows too, but the quiver wouldn't have worked with a shield over my back most of the time."

I didn't really care. My eyes teared up when women began saying goodbye to their husbands. "I know you've got to prove yourself today, but..." I had to take a deep breath. "Promise me you'll be careful. I can't handle any more loss."

Gabriel offered me a sympathetic look as he swathed me in his arms. I wiped a tear against his shirt. "I've been hunting all my life. I'll be fine, Sleigh. You're worrying over nothing."

"But you've never hunted titanasaur."

"Trust me, I promise you—I'll be fine." He placed one hand on the side of my face to guide my lips to his.

A flash of how my former life was so different from now played through my mind.

"Awright, everyone MOVE OUT!" Orius shouted.

Gabriel lifted his head and kissed the top of mine. I swallowed down a sob, knowing it would probably only make things worse for him.

A woman my mother's age came to put her arm around me as the men and centaurs bolted from the city. "It gets easier to say goodbye," she said. "The first time's always the hardest."

"How? When every time could be the last?"

"Like anything, you get used to it. Heading straight off to work'll take your mind right off it."

She turned our backs to the gate and led me toward the fields as the other women were already doing. No one else was crying, though every face wore a somber expression.

"You're Sleigh, aren't you?" the woman asked, letting her arm fall to her side. "You're still pretty new here."

"Yes."

"Well, I'm happy to meet you. My name's Lark. I've been here well over ten years, so you can trust me when I say it'll get easier."

I nodded, continuing in silence after that.

Parthenia kept my mind busy when she joined me in the field. Apparently, Crawler was trying to get back together with her and she had an endless list of reasons why she shouldn't. While I agreed with her on every one, it was obvious who she was *really* trying to convince; herself.

Early on, I noticed that several luminaries in the fields north of mine had stopped to stare at something. Centaurs smaller than the ones I was accustomed to were running along the outside of the fence. The guards weren't blasting any warning sounds, so it couldn't be the Deliverance.

"They have horns," I said to myself when they were close enough to identify. I only counted six centaur men. "What did you say those are called, Parthenia?" We'd both stopped to watch the approachers.

"Elabans. The yellow belts across their chests means they come in peace."

"What's going on?" a guard outside the fence shouted when they ran by.

"We need to speak with your chief. The Trios are massacring our villages."

"Trios?!" three guards cried from three different trees.

Parthenia stared at me like a frightened statue.

I watched Marina exit the slave lodging and run full-speed toward the bigger Elyxeos houses. She was headed for the gate. Davion chased after her away from one of the fields, calling back, "Stay where you are; keep working."

"YOU HEARD HIM!" one of the inside guards yelled at us.

Bodies began moving. Work resumed. We were all like hollow shells, though. Everyone kept glancing toward the gates, hoping Davion would return and tell us what was going on.

My mind worked tirelessly, wondering if the time had finally come to put all my trust in Marina. I knew I stood a better chance of hearing what was truly happening from her.

It started sprinkling, which felt nice since it was such a warm day. The sprinkling had come and gone by the time we saw Davion coming toward us. Marina walked beside him until they were about halfway to the fields. Then she broke away toward her house, avoiding the slaves and not speaking to anyone.

Just as before, more and more luminaries and nocturnes stopped to watch. Davion waved everyone over when he was close enough. The mass of slaves was far too large for everyone to hear him at once. So he shouted something to the ones nearest him, then sent them back to the fields so he could make the same announcement to a new wave of spectators. I hung to the back, not wanting to fight the crowd.

I only moved forward when he motioned for the last of us to do so. "The Elaban have been having problems with Trios attacks, that's all. You shouldn't worry, though. You're all surrounded by Elyxeos. You're literally in the safest place you could possibly be right now."

"What about the hunters?" I asked, feeling ill.

"They go in the opposite direction of the other centaur

colonies. I have no reason to believe the Trios will be anywhere near them."

"What if *we're* attacked?" a woman practically screamed.

Davion did a splendid job of putting on an assuring smile. "Then our colony will protect you. They're nowhere near us, though. Don't put yourself through the awful stress of asking 'what if'."

He was making it sound much too harmless. I didn't have to think very hard of what to do next. "Oh..." I put a hand to my forehead and tried to make myself look like I might faint.

"Are you alright, Sleigh?" Parthenia asked me.

"Yeah, but..." *Pant. Pant.* "I should probably lie down for a little while."

"Have you not been feeling well?" Davion asked me.

"I just get so..." *Pant. Pant.* "so dizzy sometimes...It's always been unpredictable."

"Go ahead and take the day to rest. Luminaries can't produce the light needed when they're sick, anyway."

"Davion, Trios are striking against centaur colonies!" the woman went on. "We'd be better off getting attacked by a wild pack of titanasaur."

"I'll check on you tonight to see how you're doing," Parthenia said when I began walking away.

I figured I might be there and I might not.

"They won't be attacking us, Myra," Davion said behind me.

I had to leave in the direction of my house, but my true destination was Marina's. *She* would give me the real story and I could decide where I stood then.

In spite of Davion's reassurance, everyone in the fields looked nervous, even children. I could only assume that whatever slaves the Elaban had in their charge must have been taken or slaughtered.

The people I'd come to love here were in danger. Blush was

in danger. This was real. There wasn't time to let fear or doubt rule me any longer.

It had become easier to consider the possibility of me being the woman in the stars since Gabriel arrived. I felt braver, because whatever I did, he was a part of it. He would stand behind me and carry a portion of the burden. Nothing was as scary when I wasn't doing it alone.

I stopped to rest a hand against the side of my house when I reached it, my nerve faltering. *What am I doing? I'm just Sleigh. I've spent all my life playing and studying and dreaming. Running off to have a forbidden talk of heroism with a centaur—this isn't me.*

But one glance through my window at the drawing of Blush hanging on my wall set me straight. This *was* me. From the night she was born, my obsession began. The reckless young woman I'd become, who does whatever it takes to get what she wants, was born on that night. From the moment I heard Blush's very first cries, I felt I had a sister who broke every mold and every rule I'd ever been taught. It was thrilling. It was wonderful.

With this renewed determination, I set off at a run for Marina's. Davion would never know as long as he didn't make a surprise visit home. If he did, I was certain Marina or I could come up with something.

I found her standing in the doorway, staring at the sky. Her face was paler than usual. She was so lost in thought, she didn't even notice me until I was walking up her ramp.

"Sleigh, what are you doing here?"

"I came to talk to you about the Trios. Davion thinks I went home to rest because I'm sick."

She gave me a scrutinizing look, but nodded and walked into the kitchen. I followed her all the way to the back near the rise leading to the second floor. Here, she sat down on the floor so she was more at my level and we could speak in secret.

"Davion told us the Elaban are having trouble with Trios attacks," I said in a hushed voice. "Is that really all there is to it?"

"No." Marina stared at the ceiling much like she had the sky. "They've only started with the Elaban. They're attacking the Striplings now, city by city, village by village. They kill everyone in their path who doesn't manage to escape, all except for the nocturnes. They're taken prisoner. Centaurs are abandoning their homes and gathering in the Bellios colony nearest our city. They're trying to get as close to us as they can without actually being here... I guess it makes them feel safer... Either way, it's only a matter of time until we're forced to get involved."

My heart thumped faster. "How did the Elyxeos beat them before?"

"I don't know." She shook her head slowly, like she was slipping into a dream. "Only the greatest leaders of our colony knows that. My father and six other men. They'll be talking about it when they're finished hearing everything the Elaban came to discuss. I did overhear them talking about a secret weapon once when I was still an adolescent, though, something called the Avarice. Nephele moves around our home in secret. I bet she would know more about it."

A whirlwind swirled uncontrollably in my head at the mention of the Avarice. I had to make a split-second decision: my past world, or my present one. Who did I save? The answer came to me at once as the image of myself breaking the chains put on my home-city by the Avarice unfolded in my mind.

I would save both.

"Can I trust you, Marina?"

She finally snapped her attention back to me. "After all the trust I've put in you, you shouldn't have to ask that question."

"What if I said I knew about the Avarice? Would you take me to Nephele so I could speak with her?"

"To my father's home? The *chief Elyxeos'* home?! We'd both be killed if anyone ever found out."

"Keep it down," I said. "We might all be killed by the Trios if we don't do something."

Her nostrils flared, the muscles in her face tightening. She stood and went into the front room. The only reassurance I had that she wasn't going to tell the world what I knew was that I knew far too much about her. Her usually loud footsteps were barely audible now. It was impossible to know exactly where they were taking her.

A minute or so passed by before she re-entered the kitchen carrying a large basket filled with colorful fabric. She sat the basket on the table, her eyes becoming distant once more. The way her hands were shaking made me wonder if the way she appeared so detached wasn't her reaction to fear.

Marina gave no warning before she came to put her trembling hands on my sides and lift me off the ground. She sat me beside the basket and leaned her abnormally long neck forward. "You're going to hide in this. I will get you to my sister. I'll come back for this basket after a while, whether you've returned to it or not. There's nothing more I can do."

"Thank you, Marina."

Her eyes remained unfriendly. I understood the terror they must be masking.

I climbed into the basket. Digging my way deeper into the silky material, I folded my legs inward and held my bag against me.

As I felt the basket being carried outside, I wondered how all this might tie in with freeing everyone from slavery. Perhaps my vision of freeing the sky luminaries simply came before freeing the ones on the Surface. Or perhaps it was all rolled into one great and terrible series of events that had been carefully planned for me by the stars.

23

The ride in Marina's basket was awful. The uneven motion made me feel sick. Every voice frightened me. I couldn't shake the dreadful fear of being discovered any second.

Marina was silent for a long time. Then it felt like we were rising.

"Aye, Marina," a burly voice said, stilling the basket. Everything became darker and I knew we were inside somewhere. "Your father's busy right now."

"I figured that. I only came to see my mother." The movement resumed and all was quiet, except for hooves tapping against stone.

A faint voice came and went when we began our ascent for a second time. Once at the top, and a long walk later, we climbed even higher within what I assumed to be the chief Elyxeos' home.

"Marina," a soft voice said happily.

"Hello, Nephele." I felt the basket being set on the ground and wondered if I should get up.

"I haven't seen you in *so long*," the other woman said.

"I've been really busy lately. Did you hear about the Trios?"

"No, I just woke up. What about them?"

"They've been attacking the weaker centaur colonies. I brought someone to talk to you about it." The fabric was pulled away from me.

Nephele gasped when I stood up and climbed out of the basket. She staggered back away from us. She was so much smaller than Marina, nearly as small as the scavengers had been, with beautiful shades of violet hair all over. "You brought a luminary to father's home? How could you do that?"

We were in a large room with wooden slats for the walls and floor. The only windows were in the ceiling.

"Sleigh said she knows about the Avarice," Marina answered. "I brought her here to talk to you about it."

"I mean what if she tells someone I'm here?"

"Don't you trust me?"

"What matters is that I don't trust her."

So far I liked Nephele about as much as I'd liked Marina the first time we met.

"Don't be so selfish, Nephele," Marina said. "This is about every centaur's safety, not just yours."

Her sister folded her arms and glowered at her.

Marina's lips curled upward. "You look ridiculous. I'm risking far more than you by bringing her here. I'll be back after I spend some time with mother. You had better take care of Sleigh." Marina headed toward the room's open entryway.

"I thought you hated luminaries," Nephele said.

Marina glanced back. "Not this one." And then she was gone.

"I only need to know about the secret weapon that could defeat the Trios," I said. "I'll never tell anyone you told me."

"Well—" She offered a familiar sneer, the same one her sister still presented to everyone but me. "There must be some reason my sister trusts you... What is it that makes you so different from the others?"

"We both gave ourselves to a life of servitude to spare our sisters."

Nephele got a sour look on her face, but nodded. "What we discuss, you can never tell another living soul. Neither you nor I am allowed to know of these things."

"I swear it."

"Years ago centaurs worked alongside your kind. When the Trios started fighting for supremacy, they even fought together against them. Of course that did nothing to defeat the Trios. They were an impossible opponent. Everyone was dying. Hopelessness became a plague. And then the stars gave us a gift—a secret weapon to win the war."

"What was it?"

"I don't know. But whatever it was, a group of luminaries took it from the Elyxeos after the war. They called themselves the Avarice. Centaurs hunted them for a long time. In the end, the only way my ancestors felt they could get revenge was to enslave your kind. It seemed only fair since no one would tell them where the Avarice was."

"Does the Avarice still have the weapon, then?"

"We can only assume they do. No one's ever found them... You know where they are, don't you, Sleigh?"

I only stared at her. It wasn't the sort of thing to share with just anyone. We were interrupted when the hasty thunder of heavy hooves sounded below us.

"The leader centaurs are right under our feet," Nephele whispered, demanding silence. She didn't move a muscle until long after their footsteps had died away.

"Come on," she said suddenly, hurrying out of the room without making a sound or giving me a chance to ask what was going on.

I left my bag on the floor behind the basket and went to peek outside of the room. The shining wooden hallway was lit by windows in the ceiling. It was empty except for Nephele. I followed her as she'd commanded.

I was terrified, and couldn't help but wonder if my life would ever return to normal. Streaks of light raced over me as I ran, like waves of hot fear.

One of Nephele's back legs nearly slipped out from under her when she stopped beside a doorless opening, causing her to throw all her hair to one side as she quietly recovered.

She crept carefully into the dark, empty room. Exactly in the center, she folded her legs under and lowered her ear close to the ground. I knelt beside her and did the same. Right away, I could hear men's voices as if I was in the room below with them.

"You're here because generations ago, your luminaries and nocturnes fought at our side," one was saying.

"Our side?" another roared. "They rode us like animals." I was fairly certain that was Amphion.

"They fought to protect each other, with an understanding of mutual respect. Davion, could such a thing ever exist now? Are the offenses we've committed against them too great to be repaired?"

"Against them?!" Amphion cut in again. "Chief, this is outrageous!"

"Calm yourself, Amphion. With the Wings of Hendraya taken by the Avarice and lost forever, the slaves may be our only hope. Davion, what say you of this? Might they stand beside us against the Trios?"

"I cannot speak for any person more than I have known here, but as for those who serve our colony—I believe they would stand beside us."

"ErrrrAHH! They will never ride on my back!" Amphion shouted.

"Shut up, Amphion!" a new voice returned the shouting. "The Trios are conquering and killing, drawing nearer to our city as we speak, and you're completely consumed with something so insignificant."

"I've always said we have no need for slavery," Davion said. "We could work with the luminaries. We provide them with titanasaur and they provide our colony as well as their own kind with more than enough food for us all."

"This isn't the time for that," Chief said. "Right now we need to focus on the imminent crisis. An army stands waiting for us to reach a decision as to where we stand."

A thread of purple hair caught on my breath as I inhaled, twirling through one of my nostrils. I was sent instantly into a convulsion of coughing when I felt it inside my throat.

Nephele stared at me, looking horrified.

"What was that?" Davion asked.

I covered my mouth and tried to stop, but my throat constricted, making me gag. When I felt the hair on the back of my tongue, I reached in my mouth and pulled it out, taking deep breaths and forcing my muscles to relax.

Nephele got up and ran from the room.

"Someone's up there," Amphion said. "GUARDS!"

I raced to the hallway, but found it empty. My first instinct was to yell for Nephele, but I'd made a promise to Marina. Nephele had to be kept secret.

Heavy footsteps were already running my way from the bottom of a ramp leading to a lower level. I ran in the opposite direction down the hall, taking a sharp left. Unfortunately, one side of this new stretch of hall had no wall, but looked down over the openings at the centers of two levels below. Only a flimsy railing was there to prevent falls.

Guards were running toward or up the ramp leading to the highest level where I stood frozen. "Luminary!" one shouted when he saw me, drawing a bow and arrow to point at my heart. "Stop right there or you're dead."

I didn't move a muscle. There was no point anyway. They'd seen my face. There was no escaping them now.

Amphion pushed his way through men until he spotted me. Centaurs were already surrounding me. His eyes became vicious when they met mine. "Throw her in confinement while we decide whether her crime befits punishment of death."

"I know about the Avarice," I cried as a hand clamped tightly around my arm and began dragging me away.

Anger became surprise. "Wait! How do you know about this?"

The centaur holding onto me ceased movement, but didn't let go. I swallowed hard, careful not to give too much away. "Because I grew up under their rule."

Amphion stared at me for a long moment. No one moved. The arrow remained pointed right at me.

"I know where they are, Amphion. We could make a deal."

"Terious, bring her to me—carefully."

The man aiming an arrow at me lowered his weapon. The one holding onto me led me through the hall, down the ramp, and right to Amphion. My heart pounded as the massive and heavily-armed centaurs stepped aside. Any one of them could have taken me and snapped me in half if they wanted to.

The biggest and scariest of them all was Amphion. His eyes were so intense. I shrieked when he grabbed me and threw me over his shoulder, trotting through the corridor into a large room where several Elyxeos men were seated on the floor around a low table.

"Return to your stations," Amphion shouted to the guards.

The sound of them scattering was stifled when he put me down a bit roughly and slammed shut the first centaur door I'd ever seen.

24

"Sleigh?" Davion asked. "What are you doing here? I thought you were sick."

"Sorry I lied to you."

"Why would you bring a luminary in here?" a man asked. He was rather flabby and wore a necklace of slender, pointed teeth that reached from his neck nearly to his waist.

"She said she knows where the Avarice is, Chief," Amphion answered.

"Impossible."

"She claims to have grown up under their rule."

The chief looked to Davion like he might have the answers. "Sleigh hasn't been here for very long," Davion said. "She certainly stands out against the other luminaries. She's even gained favor with your daughter."

"Marina?" one of the men asked.

Davion nodded, and they all turned to stare at me like some strange being unknown to their world.

"Well, where are they?" the chief asked.

"I want to help you protect all these people," I said, "but I also want to protect my family. Like everyone I grew up with, they're ignorant to what the Avarice is truly like. It's not their fault they follow their laws. I need to know you won't hurt them."

"You mean to say the Avarice rule over an entire kingdom?" someone asked.

I nodded.

"But we've *never* stopped searching for them," Amphion said.

A shiver shot through my back. I hoped no one noticed. "And slavery has to end. Davion's right; luminaries and nocturnes would tend to your crops in exchange for housing and food. You don't need to take away our freedom."

"Or maybe we should kill you if you don't tell us?"

"We're not going to kill her, Amphion," their chief said.

"I would die before I sentenced my own family to death," I said, sounding braver than I felt.

"You ask far too much of us," the chief said to me.

"Not nearly as much as I'm offering." For a moment it felt like I'd been taken over by someone else, like a different woman had just made home inside my body and spoken up against him.

"Let her die," the youngest-looking centaur said in a squeaky voice.

"We need her, Raytheon," another argued. "Our wives and children will be massacred."

"But ending slavery—"

"NEVER!" Amphion roared.

There was a lot of arguing and shouting that followed. The anger exploding inside those walls was like a miniature war I'd singlehandedly started.

"QUIET!" the chief shouted three times with no luck. Finally, he yanked Amphion's axe from the strap on his back and swung it over his head, driving it into the center of the table. Half the centaurs jerked back. Two gasped. Davion wrenched back against the wall. "We are getting nowhere!" the chief hollered.

"May I be permitted to say something?" the oldest-looking centaur asked. There were almost as many silver hairs growing from his body as there were blue. He was the only centaur who hadn't spoken up once since I joined them.

"Of course, father," the chief said, bowing his head. The other men watched him with a quiet reverence.

"Half my life the slaves were made up only of luminary seers. Care was not taken to keep families together, or to keep them happy. The other half of my life, nocturnes have served us here as well as the luminaries. Since Davion began looking after them, great care has been taken of our slaves. When this charge was declared, there were those of our kind who were nearly in a riot. But over time, they accepted this transition. Even though we shared whatever the slaves desired of our crops with them, our harvest has doubled. We've become the sole owners of the coveted seers. I've taken notice that with this very luminary, the quality of her own work has soared to new heights since her nocturne husband arrived."

The old man nodded kindly to me. I returned the gesture.

"The happiness of these bright star-seers affects our crops significantly, more than you've probably ever given thought. Imagine what they might produce if they were free, if it became their trade to work as they do now, but to be able to make that choice."

Amphion snorted angrily.

"Skelleon, your age and wisdom is second among us only to my father's; what do you think?" the chief asked the man sitting beside his father.

Aside from Skelleon's age and ugly scars, he was also adorned with muscles in his shoulders and neck that were so large they were nearly bursting from his skin. He wrapped one hand around the long clump of hair growing from the bottom of his chin. "I don't want the other colonies to be destroyed, but it seems needless for us to put our own colony's lives at risk going to battle when the Trios haven't even come near us."

"They were here the day the Deliverance came," I said.

"Liar," Amphion hissed.

"What do you mean the Trios were here?" Chief asked.

"I saw them watching the fighting from a distance," I answered. "They didn't stay for very long."

"You're certain it was Trios centaurs you saw?"

I nodded.

"Likely searching for any strengths and weaknesses they could find," Skelleon said.

"That's really Orius' area of specialty," the chief said. "Regardless, this changes everything."

"Why don't we send the luminary to wait outside so we can discuss this," his father suggested.

Amphion got up and led me to the door. "Terious," he yelled into the hallway.

The guard who'd first taken hold of me ran up the ramp from the level below.

"Watch over this slave," Amphion said when Terious was right outside the door. "She is to remain right here, unharmed."

Terious grunted and crossed his arms over his chest. I hardly stepped outside before Amphion slammed the door shut and his stifled voice picked up. The guard stared fixedly at me as arguing resumed within the room.

The men's voices grew louder and louder until they were shouting again, though I could make out little more than Amphion hollering about cutting off one of my hands if I didn't tell them what they wanted to know and Davion shouting that he'd better not harm me. A horrified, boiling hot sensation pricked all over me at the thought of what they might do to me.

However terrible Davion was to Marina, every part of me was immensely grateful he was there. I jumped when I heard a loud *CRACK* and someone howling in pain. The shouting continued.

"It sounds like they're killing each other," I said to Terious, who started laughing.

"They're always carrying on like that," he said. "No one's died yet."

We stood with a silence between us after that. Terious never stopped watching me. Every now and then someone would cry out like they'd taken a serious blow, but he never seemed concerned.

A time later, we heard a woman's voice from the ramp going upward. "What's she doing here?"

I forced myself to remain neutral when my eyes met Marina's.

"I cannot say," Terious answered.

Marina's teeth shone when her lips warped into a heated sneer. Then she tromped up the ramp. I figured she probably wanted to strangle her twin.

Several minutes later, the men's voices finally got quieter. All I could hear was Terious' heavy breathing.

Then the door opened and seven giant centaurs walked into the hall. Skelleon had blood dried over his nose. Amphion had an ugly bruise already forming on his arm. Neither seemed concerned with their injuries.

"I'll go and ready the troops," Amphion said before he ran away down a ramp.

The chief stood closest to me in front of the others, his fat belly not far away from my head. "We have decided we must at least travel to the gathering of the other colonies to learn more of what's happening," he said. "Since you've made yourself invaluable to us, you'll be coming, too."

"Me?" I asked.

"Yes. We won't be letting you out of our sight from now on. And once we've visited with the other colonies, you and I will discuss further the whereabouts of the men you spoke of before."

"But—" Panic welled up inside me. "My husband's gone with the hunters. He won't know what's happened to me."

"We will leave a message for him. Davion—" He glanced at Davion, who lifted me carefully and placed me on his back.

"Don't worry, Sleigh; you're safe," Davion turned to whisper. "Just hold on."

It was awkward to put my arms around his sides, but necessary if I didn't want to fall. My skirt ripped nearly up to my knee when I threw a leg over him.

Following at the end of their line, we descended two ramps and crossed a courtyard surrounded by tall buildings. The yard was surprisingly unkempt. Weeds tangled and choked dying flowers or each other. Lastly, the chief raced through an open breezeway that ran the full length inside a gigantic main building.

Then we were bursting into the open, where an army of Elyxeos stood in perfect rows, awaiting their orders. Amphion was at their head and the Elaban at their side. Everyone had packs filled with supplies strapped to their lower, more animal-like backs. It occurred to me that they'd probably made ready to leave, just in case, the moment the Elaban had arrived.

I rode with the head centaurs to Amphion. "The luminary will ride with you," the chief said to him.

"SHE—WILL—NOT!" Amphion roared.

"She may very well be vital to the survival of our kind and of hers. She will be safest with you."

"She would be safest with Orius."

"Orius may be the best hunter we've got, but you're the best fighter. The luminary rides with you."

"Her name is Sleigh," Davion said, bowing his head.

"Why can't I ride with you?" I leaned forward and whispered to Davion.

He offered me a reassuring smile as he turned and lifted me from his back. "I've got to stay here and look after the other luminaries. I'll explain everything to Gabriel, though."

"I said it before; they will *never* ride me." Amphion glowered at Davion.

"Very well," the chief said, glaring at Amphion, but not looking anywhere near as scary. "For putting yourself before the lives of your own colony, and refusing an order given to you by your chief, you are stripped of your duties as head warrior."

"You can't—"

"Therefore, you will no longer be one of the League of Royal Elyxeos Centaurs."

"CHIEF!"

"To protect the secrets kept for generations by this noble society, you must be put to death, immediately."

"ALRIGHT!" Amphion reared up on his hind legs. "Alright. I will carry the luminary."

"And protect her with your life?"

"Yes." Amphion gritted his teeth. "I will protect her with my life."

"I could carry her, father," someone said at Davion's other side. It was Marina, standing as tall and proud as ever. She held out my bag to me. "I found this in an upper floor."

"What are you talking about, Marina?" the chief asked. "You cannot abandon your place here."

"Davion could feed the luminaries until I return." She turned partially toward her husband, an enquiring look in her eyes.

He nodded, the callous look he always gave her softening.

"You've had me trained to defend myself very well, Father. I could carry Sleigh."

"That was years ago," the chief said. "She will still be safest with Amphion."

Her father came to lift me clumsily from the ground, cradling me as he held me out away from his body. Amphion's shoulder's bulged when his muscles tightened at the feel of my body against his. I wanted to argue that I should get to choose who carried me, but my nerve seemed to have stretched as far as it could for one day. I took hold of the straps keeping Amphion's axe against his back, not wanting to touch him.

"At least let me come with you," Marina said. "None but Davion knows how to look after one of her kind as well as I do."

Her father nodded, then took off through the gate, leading the wave of Elyxeos men northeasterly.

More soldiers surrounded the city outside the fencing, while the watchmen in the trees had been tripled by armed Elyxeos men and women.

The triumphant sound of men coming toward us from the south became even louder than hooves beating against ground. The sun had just begun setting and the hunters were emerging from a nearby forest. Their voices ceased when they saw the soldiers pouring from the city. Half of the Elyxeos hunters were dragging a mid-size titanasaur behind them. The other half ran faster toward us.

Amphion moved to the side of his army, allowing them to pass us by. He cupped his hands around his mouth. "ORIUS, MAKE HASTE!"

I was relieved to see Gabriel running behind him unharmed. I hated the look of terror on his face when he saw me.

It's okay, I mouthed out, holding up a hand.

Amphion recommenced running alongside his army when

Orius had nearly reached him. Gabriel was left behind to the centaurs' immense speed.

"Are you aware a slave is riding on your back?" Orius scoffed at Amphion.

I might have laughed if I couldn't see and feel his severe loathing at my being carried.

"It was this or death, according to Chief," Amphion answered.

My only comfort, aside from knowing Gabriel was safe, was that Marina would be with me. It was beginning to feel like the stars had given her to me, the same way they'd given the Elyxeos whatever gift had aided them in winning the war a century ago.

25

There wasn't enough time before night fell to reach the Bellios. So we stopped to sleep inside a muddy, smelly ditch Amphion said would be the safest place for us.

He had me lay to rest at the heart of his army, and right in the middle of the noblemen. I fell asleep closest to Marina, though. Her body warmth was the only thing protecting me from the chill of the air.

Hours later, I was awoken from a dream about Gabriel when someone slammed into my side and rolled down over my legs into the bit of water trickling through the lowest part of the channel. Marina sat up with a start when he kicked her on his way down.

A nocturne boy lifted himself from the disgusting sludge and stared at us. He couldn't have been more than eleven or twelve years old.

"Where did you come from?" I asked.

"Did our watchman not even see you?" Marina added, peeking over the edge of the ditch. She exhaled noisily, causing her cheeks to puff out. "He's fast asleep."

"Are you Elyxeos?" the boy asked desperately, causing a few

nearby men to stir. His young voice had only a bit of a growl and an echo to it. "The Trios are attacking my colony. They'll all be killed if you don't help us."

"Is that a nocturne claiming to be part of a colony?" Amphion rose up suddenly on all four hooves. Several more followed.

"I'm part of the Dashings. Can you please help us?"

"Where are they?" the chief asked him.

"In the ravine past that thicket."

Amphion drew his axe when something ran through the mud farther down the ditch, just beyond the reach of our army.

"Rayna, Lorena, everyone wait!" the boy called to them. A little group of nocturne children stopped midway up the other side. "There are Elyxeos here. They can help us."

It wasn't difficult to see the sparkle of tears on their faces when they ran toward us. "Can you please help us?" the tiniest girl sobbed pitifully. "They got my sister. I want my mama. *Please.*"

"How many of the Trios are there?" our chief asked the boy.

"Not that many. But they're so fast. They're killing everyone."

"If they're killing centaurs who are nearly impossible to see at night, they'll kill us too," Amphion said.

"How big is your colony?" the chief asked.

"Not half as big as your army," the little boy said.

"Your colony?" Amphion sneered. "He's not a centaur. He cannot be part of any colony."

"Yes I can! Dashings found me all alone when I was too young to remember. They loved me like I was their own son. My mother and father are both centaurs as far as I'm concerned."

"Perhaps we could form an alliance with the Dashings," the chief said.

"It's not worth dying for," Amphion said. "They're just kids. They don't know what they're talking about."

"Yes I do," the boy said stubbornly.

"I want my mama," the little girl whimpered, making a few of the others cry harder.

"We should at least go and see what's happening," Skellecn said. "There isn't time to waste arguing about it, Amphion."

"Yes, we'd have the element of surprise," the chief said. "We could remain hidden in the trees and open fire on them. Amphion, there's hardly a cave in this land that isn't full of Dashings. We need them on our side for this war. You stay here and protect Sleigh." The chief climbed out of the ditch and took to running along the edge of it from above. "WAKE UP! Up and out, come on."

Men began scrambling up the muddy slope, drawing weapons and shields.

"Stay with the luminary while my men are out fighting?" Amphion muttered as he sat down. "Ridiculous."

One of the nocturne girls ran up to me and took my hand. "Can they save our colony?" Her eyes were wide and glassy. Tear stains had left dark smears over her dirty face.

"I don't know," I said honestly.

She began petting my arm. "I never saw a nocturne like you before."

"She's not a nocturne, Lorena," the boy said. "She's a luminary. Our colony's so small; we've never had one before."

"I've been told there aren't any luminaries living with Dashings," I said.

"They're pretty rare, I've heard. You're only the second one I've ever seen."

"I thought luminaries were rejected for posing such danger to your *so-called* colonies," Amphion interjected heatedly. "How can they hunt or move about at night when a luminary's light is revealing them for all the world to see?"

"Sometimes nocturne families leave a colony for a village

when a luminary is born," the boy said, putting as much dislike into his voice for Amphion. "It's their choice, though. The Dashings would never send them away. You wouldn't understand that, though. You're a slave driver. You treat our kind like animals."

"Animals?!" Amphion's hand sank deeper into the trenchside as he went rigid. "Elyxeos have offered their lives to give our slaves the best food there is. We built them houses with our own hands."

The boy didn't look intimidated at all. "So they can feed you. You still keep them caged in with your fences and pound on the nocturnes just for wanting to leave. Like I said, animals."

"You had better watch your mouth."

"Well you had be—"

"Why don't you tell us about the Trios?" I interrupted, fearing for the boy's safety. "Is this the first you've seen of them?"

"They attacked my colony eight days ago," one of the girls said rather numbly. "There were a lot more of them than there were tonight. I was the only one who got away." She sniffled and wiped her nose, though she showed no other evidence of sadness.

"It sounds like they're attacking the Dashings one cave at a time," Amphion said. "The Trios must know they're too stupid to live in colonies large enough to protect themselves, or to join with the rest of us to fight. It even sounds like they're not bothering to send a proper army for an attack. And why should they?"

The kid's shoulders moved up higher, his lips tightening and his body giving off smoke. "No one's ever tried to attack us until now, because we're not stupid enough to make enemies, like you are."

Amphion stood up, gripping his axe in both hands as he advanced on the children. "I told you to watch your mouth."

The children all ran over to me, screaming and crying harder. They huddled around me, pressing against my sides. Only the boy stood bravely where he was.

"He's only a child, Amphion." Marina ran to his rescue. "If you harm him, everything your men are doing right now will be wasted. No Dashing would ever side with us."

The head warrior stared at her for a moment. His lips poked out when he used his tongue to wipe something off his front teeth. "That slave has poisoned you, Marina," he said before climbing upward.

"Where are you going?"

"To keep watch, and to get away from all the madness down there."

Marina went to sit across from me, avoiding the little nocturnes. She was surprised when the boy took a seat beside her.

"You're beautiful like the moon is," Lorena told me.

Another girl began petting my hand. "And you're soft like a baby is."

"Um, thank you." I said, then whispered, "What's that boy's name, anyway?"

"That's Slade."

"More children are coming," Amphion called to us.

Slade stood up and stretched tall enough to just see over the top. "Your sister Scaris is coming, Lee. Tana's carrying her."

"Really?" A boy wearing badly torn shorts perked up.

"An Elyxeos," a girl's voice said.

Slade waved his arms. "Over here, Tana."

It wasn't long before a little black centaur with two children on her back came running down, sliding on the muck and dropping the girl and boy.

"Scaris!" The one called Lee ran to help her up and hug her.

The children came to sit around me while Tana went to sit beside Marina.

"I'm so thankful to your colony for delivering us," Tana said. Her shiny, black hair reflected the moon's light like a mirror. It was gorgeous.

"They are fighting the Trios, then?" Marina asked.

"Yes. That's how we got away."

"Hey, Slade," I said, "do you think the Dashings would ever join with the other centaurs against the Trios, at least to protect themselves?"

"Not as long as they keep people for slaves."

Tana looked at him and nodded.

"Do they not realize what Trios do to nocturnes?" Marina asked.

"Keep quiet, someone's coming," Amphion said.

The fact that he didn't mention children or Dashings made me terribly curious. I inched myself away from the children and crept carefully toward the top of the wall of earth behind me.

"Sleigh, stop," Marina whispered.

But I was nearly to the edge. I dug my fingers into the mud, taking deep breaths to quiet my glow, and peered over the surface.

Amphion was so near to me, I could almost reach out and touch him. A streak of something colorless was racing toward him. Amphion had his axe ready, but the streak was moving too quickly. *It must be a Trios,* I thought, amazed at how it appeared as nothing more than a lethal blur in the night. Despite what an awful centaur Amphion was, I couldn't bring myself to sit in hiding and watch him die. Besides, he was the only *real* protection I had at that moment.

I realized for the first time how vulnerable I was, having received no defensive education. This training suddenly seemed mortally important, with a war I'd gotten myself so deeply caught up in at hand.

I hardly looked to the stars, hoping for guidance, before the Trios was nearly upon Amphion. They flickered back at me wildly. Each time they blinked back on, they shone brighter, and brighter, and brighter. I understood.

Amphion shouted and held his axe up, ready to strike. I swung my legs up over edge, burning my inner light like my life depended on it, and leapt to his side. The streak faltered. I could just make out a pair of ivory horns and a pale arm thrown up to shield its face. The other arm held a sword aimed at Amphion's chest.

The axe sliced through the air and into the Trios' neck, dispelling the rapidity of the swifter centaur.

Marina came racing to my side. "I told you to stay down there."

"A Trios was coming."

"That's exactly why you should have stayed hidden."

We heard the sound of little bodies crawling out of the ditch behind us.

Amphion made certain death was inflicted on the Trios before turning his attention to me. "Why did you do that?" he asked, looking appalled.

"Would you have rather me let you die?"

"I would have rather you stayed where you're safest. I swore to protect you, and my colony needs you alive more than it needs me."

"But I saw in the stars exactly what to do. I was shown how to keep me safest. Who do you think would have been next if that Trios had killed you?"

"You speak too boldly for a slave."

"But you've always admired that most about me, haven't

you?" Marina said. "And I think Sleigh may have just given you a great strategy for winning a war at night."

"Strategy? From a slave? That's absolutely ridiculous."

"I'd think the head warrior of the Elyxeos colony would be smart enough to take whatever lead is available to him in winning any war."

Amphion stepped closer to my centaur friend. "Are you insane, Marina?"

She stepped closer to him. "No, are you?"

Grrrrr, Amphion growled, puffing his chest out and throwing his axe around wildly. "You're right. You're both right! Happy?!"

"Being right's not important to me, Amphion," I said. "All that matters is saving everyone I care about."

Amphion replaced his axe against his back, still staring at me with nothing but absolute contempt. "I suppose you're going to claim I owe you for saving me."

"Maybe you could teach me how to fight." I'd never even held a weapon beyond the knife in my bag. "If I'm going to be the one on your back, it would probably be better for you, too."

"Let me be very clear. You will not always ride on my back. But—I will train you to fight. Then at least I will owe you nothing." He held out a hand to me. At several times the size of mine, it dwarfed my entire arm when I shook it. "I still hate having to look out for you."

"That's okay. The feeling's mutual."

He glared at me as callously as ever. The more I saw how determined he was to protect me, though, the less frightening he seemed.

"Look." Slade pointed toward the thicket. Centaurs of all sizes were racing toward us. Most of them had figures riding on their backs, including the Elyxeos soldiers.

"The madness is spreading," Amphion said in disbelief.

26

T he royal Elyxeos men had just settled into a circle away from the joyous reunion of Dashings and nocturnes with the escapee children. I was forced to sit beside Amphion since he didn't seem to think he could trust anyone else to watch over me.

The solemn look on the faces of the other six was unsettling.

"What happened, Chief?" Amphion demanded the moment the last Elyxeos had taken his seat. "Every single one of you rode in with a fully-grown nocturne on your back."

"You need to listen and consider what I'm about to say before you lose your temper," the chief said in a profound voice, his forehead creased with concern. "The carnage was already awful when we saw it through the brush. We shot arrows at the Trios from where we were hidden and killed all but two before they discovered us. Two Trios alone killed twenty-three of our men. We finally killed one, and the other ran off in your direction. It must have taken a miracle for you to kill it on your own."

A pause was provided for Amphion to explain. He let it pass without a word.

"We've discovered that the Dashings spread out over the

land may outnumber all the daytime colonies combined. That's not counting their nocturne counterparts. They would all join the war in our favor if we would only release the slaves."

Amphion began shaking his head. "Madness."

"Some of the Dashings have seen the Trios in their entirety, Amphion," Skelleon said. "Their army is innumerable."

"Say we gave in. How do you even know that the other colonies would do the same?"

"If they have seen or suffered the devastation we have witnessed on this night, they will certainly consider it," the chief said. He reminded me of Marina when he stared off into the sky, in spite of the absence of any physical resemblance.

"Orius," Amphion said, "what do you think of all this?"

Orius pressed one fist into the ground as he leaned forward. Even surrounded by such giant centaurs, he was quite impressive to look at. "It is madness, but I can see no other way. I suppose—" He heaved a burdened sigh. "I would rather lose our slaves than our colony."

Raytheon nodded beside him.

"I don't understand why we're even having this conversation. This *Sleigh* knows where the Avarice is." My name dripped from his tongue like acid.

"I know, but her demands are one and the same with the Dashings," the chief said. "Even if we retrieve the age-old Wings of Hendraya, they cannot win a war alone. We need every advantage available to us."

There was the mention of a strange pair of wings again. I wondered if they were the gift from the stars Nephele mentioned before. In spite of how badly I wanted to find out more about them, I was too afraid to ask during such a momentous meeting.

"What if we made that demand of the slaves and freemen?" Skelleon asked. "They fight by our sides—"

"You mean on our backs," Amphion mumbled.

"—and we set them free, thus giving us even more of an advantage."

"Why would you say that in front of a slave?" Orius asked.

"Amphion's the one who demanded she stay by his side."

"You forced me to swear her safety on my life!" Amphion shouted at them all.

"It doesn't matter," I said softly. "Why would I interfere in any way when my kind's freedom is at stake? Everyone will have to get involved in this war eventually, I imagine. It makes more sense to join in alliance with centaurs than to fight it on our own."

The chief cleared his throat. "We take our vote now. The Trios are attacking closer to our city than we thought. We haven't the luxury of putting it off any longer. We must decide where we stand. So—in exchange for the Dashings and their nocturne brethrens' alliance, and for finding out the location of the Avarice, do we choose to offer freedom to our slaves, with the option to stay and work for home and food within our colony?"

"I vote in favor," the chief's father said, raising his hand.

"So do I." Skelleon raised his hand, too.

The chief shook his head. "Because I can see no other way— I vote in favor as well." His hand went up slowly, followed by Raytheon's.

Excitement that I'd never known filled me like titanasaur meat.

Orius looked thoughtful with one of his filthy hands pressed against his forehead. His other arm rose partway, then went down.

"It's already four to three, Orius," the chief said. "You might as well vote whichever way you want. It won't make a difference."

"Hunting has been my whole life," he stammered. "I can't lose my nocturne men."

"How important can they really be in comparison to our hunters?" Amphion asked.

"You would be surprised."

I wondered if the nocturnes whose lives had always been hunting, as well, wouldn't stay to keep hunting with him even after gaining their freedom. But the decision had already been made, so I kept quiet.

Orius squeezed his eyes shut and turned his head away as he inched his hand above his head.

"You can't be serious?" Amphion cried. "What will your men say when they find out you were in support of this—this—*lunacy*?"

"What do you want from me?" Orius snarled back. "We always said the worst thing that could ever happen would be another war against the Trios, and now it's here. We nearly became extinct last time."

"When the hunters see that their leader helped to make this difficult decision," the chief said, "it will probably make it much easier for them to follow this new way of life."

"*AAHHH!* YOU'RE ALL WRONG, AND YOU KNOW IT!" Amphion hollered.

The laughter and indistinct voices of the remains of the Dashing colony became silent. I leaned back to look past Amphion and realized they were all watching us now.

"Would you keep your head for once?!" Skelleon shouted at Amphion. "Do you know how much less fighting and yelling there is when you can't make it to a meeting? It's always so refreshing, like a first breath of morning air."

Amphion clenched his jaws together, his face becoming taut with rage. "You got what you wanted, slave," he snarled at me in a most dangerous voice. "Now tell us where the Avarice is."

I couldn't help but shrink away. My voice came out small and fearful. "My family's safety hasn't been promised yet."

"No one gets hurt, as long as they give up the Avarice," the chief said. "You have our promise."

"Why should you make that decision on your own?" Amphion said.

The chief's eyes were fiery when they met his head warrior. "There isn't a centaur alive that wouldn't trade anything for a chance to slay those murderous thieves. Are you honestly going to argue with that?"

Amphion only glowered at him.

"Then it's settled. The Elyxeos are officially at war."

"When all this is through, will we at least still maintain the right to be the only colony to work with seers?"

"Absolutely. That is a right even war cannot take from us."

"I say we send some of our men back now to give the slaves the option of freedom in return for their allegiance in this war," Orius said. "That way they can prepare to set out with a number of our men to gather in the other luminaries and nocturnes for the same cause once you've returned."

"The free of their kind would never believe that."

"If we carried slaves with us who they've known in years past they might."

"They would believe you," I piped up.

"How do you know that?" the chief asked me.

"Star-seers have been foreseeing the possibility of peace being forged between centaurs and man for some time." It felt like I was giving the secrets of my people away, but perhaps betrayals like this were one of the reasons I was written in the stars as a deliverer. "They'll probably be prepared for it, even."

"Fascinating."

"A number of my men and I could set out with this slave as

well in pursuit of the Avarice, and to take back what is ours," Amphion said.

"Good idea," the chief said. "Best wait until we return from the Bellios, though. We'll have the freemen gather with the rising army to the north, as well as the Dashings, assuming the other colonies agree to our terms."

"If we're using the strategy of drawing in luminaries and nocturnes to fight in exchange for their freedom," Orius began, "we should make the same demands to the Dashings if they back down."

"Right, every advantage. I'll send the Dashings to gather in their kind. Amphion, Orius, Flank, you take half the men and return home. We'll lead the rest to the Bellios and return tomorrow. Have the slaves ready as planned. We can only hope the Trios won't attack before we are ready for them." The chief nodded behind me. "The first morning's light has just arrived. We set out at once."

The other six centaurs bowed to the chief, so I did the same.

"Come on, slave," Amphion said, leaning toward me. "You are still bound to me for now."

I stared at his lower back, almost afraid to climb on. If that wasn't what he was suggesting, he would probably throw me off violently. But asking if it was what he meant might have seemed like I was mocking him. Cautiously I climbed on, relieved when he stood with no protest.

With that behind me, all I could think about, aside from the unimaginable joy the slaves were about to experience, was returning to Gabriel.

27

"Can I ask you something, Amphion?" I said, leaning closer to his more human-like back.

Morning had nearly become afternoon and I was so bored by then, I finally decided to bring up the question of the Wings.

Amphion turned his head enough that I could see his lips moving with his voice. "What is it?" he asked, sounding tired.

"What are the Wings of Hendraya like?"

He was already leading the army with Orius and the balding royal Elyxeos named Flank. He veered to the right so he could run off to the side of his men before he answered my question.

"No one can remember exactly what they look like, but they're supposed to have all the light of a luminary and be able to burst into flames like a nocturne," Amphion said. "The wearer was able to fly and had the strength of a hundred Elyxeos, along with the speed of a Trios. An Elyxeos warrior named Hendraya wore them and helped to win the war in our favor generations ago. Then the Avarice murdered him and stole the wings before they disappeared."

"How'd they manage that?"

"They came pretending to marvel at him. They brought baskets filled with the finest foods. In those days your kind and mine trusted one another. Hendraya took no thought to eating what they'd given him. He didn't live to see the next day."

"They poisoned him?"

"Yes."

"That's horrible." I sat back a little. "Is that why you don't like us?"

"That's part of it."

I looked up at the clear sky, shutting my eyes as I soaked up the warm sunlight. It was truly a beautiful morning. Not a cloud in the sky.

Of course I was curious about Amphion's further reasoning for hating my kind so much, but it felt too personal to ask him for the rest. We weren't exactly friendly on any account.

But talking with him was more interesting than riding through unfamiliar lands with nothing to do but count how many steps Amphion had taken from one tree to the next.

"Once I show you where the Avarice is, do you think I'll have to go into the city with you?" I was really afraid of having to face Jordan, though I couldn't help but worry for his safety.

"If you want to get your family out first. Besides the fact that we wouldn't know who they were, they probably wouldn't trust centaurs."

"Yeah." As I nodded my head it was hard to imagine reentering my city and telling my family they would have to leave it for the Surface. Would they think I'd gone mad, or try restraining me so I couldn't leave them again? These were unsettling thoughts. Nothing was worse than leaving their safety to chance, however.

"WATER!" Flank shouted, bringing everyone to a stop. Elyxeos crisscrossed through each other to get to the edge of a little pond off to our left.

Amphion became still so I could climb down. "Why are we stopping?" he hollered to Flank. "We're nearly home."

"But we've been running for so long. Stopping for a quick drink won't hurt anything."

Amphion didn't look convinced, but walked slowly toward the water nonetheless. "Why don't you want to return to the city of your birth?" he asked me, making me feel comfortable enough to walk alongside him.

"Leaving the city is forbidden. The Avarice will have me killed if they find me there again."

"We won't let that happen."

In spite of the still-hardened look on his face, I had to smile. "There's also a man I was close to for years. I feel obligated to him. He doesn't know I've chosen Gabriel, and I don't know if I have the heart to tell him."

"Gabriel's your husband? The one who hunts with Orius?"

I nodded.

His eyes screwed up as he pulled his arms behind his head, stretching out his shoulders. "People should be with who they love, *not* with who they're obligated to."

"I agree, but it's—"

Amphion looked up at Marina walking toward us. The flicker of gentleness in his eyes when he saw her came and went so quickly, I wasn't even certain I'd seen it. But it made me wonder if there wasn't something between them.

"It's what?" He turned to stare at me impatiently.

"—it's *a lot* more complicated than love and obligation."

"Unfortunately, I understand that perfectly."

"Here, you two." Marina held out two wooden bowls filled with water.

"Thanks." I took mine and drank it all at once.

"You're such a mess, Sleigh." Marina moved behind me and

began running her fingers through my hair. "You can't show up looking like this."

Amphion just stood with his bowl in his hands, staring at us strangely. "I have to know, Marina, what is it about this slave that's put such a change in you?"

No one said anything for a moment. She continued smoothing my hair down and gently removing tangles.

"She chose to be captured so her sister would remain free," Marina's voice came quietly from behind me.

A slit opened between Amphion's lips as he stared at me.

"*DEVIL SERPENT!*" someone shouted. Centaurs reared back, knocking into each other. A path began to clear for one who was stumbling away from the water, clutching his swollen hand.

"YOU SEE?" Amphion shouted into Flank's face, running past him. "We stop without need and now I'm losing one of my best men!"

"How was I supposed to know?" Flank's words were lost to Amphion.

The latter raced to the side of the centaur who was now down, crying out in awful agony. "It's alright, Tiberion. You will die a most honorable Elyxeos."

I ran to his side, reaching in my bag for the vial of graceling salve. "I can save him," I said, kneeling beside Amphion.

"There is no cure for the venom of a devil serpent," Amphion argued.

"My people know of one. I bet it would work on a centaur, too." I popped the top off the vial and let a few drops of the slimy goo drip into each of the hole's in Tiberion's wrist. After reading Auree's books, I'd discovered that was all you really need.

I hardly got the top on the vial before Tiberion jerked his arm outward, smacking the side of my face and knocking me over.

"It burns like death!" he shouted.

The salve flew from my hand and shattered against a mossy rock. I barely registered it before I felt my body being lifted from the ground and held close to someone else's. Amphion scooted us both out of the way as Tiberion flailed his arms and legs wildly.

"JUST KILL ME AND GET IT OVER WITH!" he went on crying, rolling over on his back.

"You've only made things worse," Amphion snapped, setting me down at a safe distance from Tiberion.

"No, it's working." Even with his arm slicing through the air, I could see pus running from his hand down all over his arm.

"*KILL ME, I SAID! PLEASE, JUST KILL ME!*"

"What do we do?" one of the soldier's asked Amphion.

The head warrior met my eyes. One eyebrow rose like he was asking me how to respond, so I shook my head. "We leave him be."

The shouting halted suddenly. We looked over and saw the wounded centaur trembling and unconscious. Amphion and Orius both took to inspecting his arm.

"What's happening to him?" Orius asked.

"The medicine's removing all the venom," I answered. "It pulls a lot of fluid out of his body with it, but he'll survive."

Orius put an arm under Tiberion's belly. "Help me to carry him, Amphion. We need to get him home to his own bed."

"I've got to carry the slave," Amphion answered.

"I'll take her," Marina said.

I gave Amphion a pleading look, hoping he would give in.

He looked back and forth at us, then to Tiberion. "Just this once. But you'll have to stay right next to me, Marina."

"Alright." Marina came to pick me up and place me on her back. The tear in my skirt ripped to right above my knee.

I waited until the other two had gotten Tiberion on their

backs and we were racing homeward to lean over and hug Marina around her sides. "Thanks for coming with me."

She turned her head so she was facing away from Amphion and said, "It feels like this is my fault."

"No, I think everything turned out exactly the way it was supposed to." Though I still wished it wasn't true, that I wasn't the one destined to be responsible for so much and so many.

I reached in my bag to take the last drink of water from one of my jars, keeping an arm loosely around one of Marina's sides. It wasn't long before I recognized the shape of a few treetops.

"Watchtower, dead ahead," Amphion called behind him not long after. "Look, Orius, your men stand waiting for you outside the walls."

Orius chuckled. "The newest nocturne hunter's even waiting with them. That's your husband, isn't it?" He glanced at me.

"Yeah." It felt so good to see him, the only nocturne among them. Imagining life on the Surface before he came along, with no one to stand by my side and look out for me always, was nightmarish. It hit me like a storm just how grateful I was to have him. "Can I go to him, Marina?"

She looked to Amphion.

He shook his head, extinguishing a portion of my joy. "I'm not letting her out of my sight until we're inside the safety of our city. He can join her in there." Amphion turned to yell to his men, "Someone will have to ring the emergency gathering bell at once. I'll be ready to make the proclamation after I take Tiberion to his home."

Hunters stood up and began pointing each other's attention in our direction. We were close enough now for me to see the black strips with a glint of silver wrapped around their arms.

I smiled and waved when Gabriel saw me. My light blazed with all the happiness coursing through me at being so close to him once more.

The questions of love I'd been wrestling with lately ran through my mind again. The finality of it was what frightened me. I needed to be sure before I decided within myself that I truly did love him. Every time I saw him, though, the question burned more strongly in my chest, pressing me in one direction.

We finally reached the hunters, and then passed them by. I turned my neck to watch them joining the army at their rear. It was difficult not to laugh when one picked up Gabriel and carried him at his side, in spite of Gabriel's angry protests.

mphion and Orius broke free of our group once we were inside. Centaurs were already gathering in the open space where the army generally trained, right inside the city's entrance. The buzz of voices was nearly as loud as the hooves pounding against the ground. Marina stopped before meeting this inner mass. Flank and a handful of soldiers ran toward the giant structure their chief called home. The rest of the men surrounded us and stood waiting for Amphion and Orius to return.

Gabriel was fighting to make his way through them to me.

"I'm going to jump, Marina," I said.

"What?"

I threw one leg over her back and slid off before I ran to meet him. Soldiers moved more readily out of my way, allowing me to close the distance quickly.

"Gabriel!" I shrieked, wrapping my arms around his neck.

He clutched the fabric against my back with one hand and my hair with the other, pressing me against him. "I missed you like there would never be a tomorrow, Sleigh." He let go of my hair so I could look up at him. His lips graced my forehead with a soft kiss. "Davion wouldn't tell me why the League of Royal Elyxeos Centaurs had to take you with them to the Bellios."

"There were Trios here."

"I know, but why you?"

He leaned down when I spoke in a quiet whisper. "They know that I know where the Avarice is."

"What?!" He looked horrified.

A soldier stared at us as he tromped farther away.

Gabriel didn't even seem to notice. "How could you let that happen? Do you know how hard everyone's worked for generations to keep your city a secret?" It was obviously a struggle for him not to shout.

"I might have been killed if I hadn't given them a reason to keep me alive."

He only shook his head angrily. "What are you talking about? Who would have killed you?"

"It's a long story I'll have to tell you later. But don't you remember what I saw on my eighteenth birthday? I'm supposed to be the one to break the chains put on my city by the Avarice. The stars would have known I would come to the Surface to save you. They would have known my fault at not being raised to harbor such hatred and secrecy toward the centaurs. And the Avarice might be hiding a secret weapon that could win the war against the Trios."

The look of anger remained on his sullen face.

"I haven't even told you the best part." Certainly discovering that slavery would soon end would fix this. "In exchange for the Avarice's location, I demanded—"

A deafening sound pierced the air. My whole body bent inward as I covered my ears. It didn't seem to affect the centaurs at all. "What is that?" I yelled to Gabriel, but he had his ears covered as well. The sound just kept going, until I felt a larger pair of hands cover mine over my ears. I glanced up at Marina. Her giant hands kept the sound out much better than mine did.

Finally the awful noise ended, though my ears continued ringing. "That was the emergency bell," Marina told me. "It summons everyone to gather here outside the castle, even the slaves."

"Amphion's calling for you," a soldier said to me, pointing at the head of their army.

"Will you come with me?" I asked Gabriel faintly, afraid he might hate me now.

His eyes were still angry, but he took my hand and walked me through the Elyxeos to the two royals. Both had blood and seepage stains from Tiberion still smeared across their backs.

The crowd gathering not far off had tripled from what it was when we arrived. Slaves were gathering to their right. Davion stood in their midst, holding a young luminary girl on his hip.

"What's your hunter's name?" Amphion was asking Orius when we walked past the last soldiers.

"Gabriel. He made a fine hunter yesterday, too. He has certainly earned his place among us." He and Gabriel nodded to one another.

"Sleigh, you're to remain by my side from now on until your part of the bargain is fulfilled," Amphion said. "Gabriel, I need your voice to make our proclamation so that everyone will hear it."

"Wait," I interrupted. "Do you mean I can't even go home tonight?" Certainly he wasn't planning on spending the night at my house.

"I'll stand guard with a few of my men around your home. Come on, now. Flank's already on his way."

I tried to catch Gabriel's eye as we followed the two Elyxeos toward an exceptionally tall watchtower at the top of a leafless tree, but he refused to look my way. It was killing me not being able to talk to him. If he hadn't made the gesture of still holding onto my hand, I might have collapsed in tears right there.

By the time we joined Flank on the platform in the trees, it seemed the entire city had arrived. There were enough Elyxeos and slaves that the two groups were pressing against each other now, and wrapping around a few houses.

"You stand in the front." Amphion moved back and motioned for Gabriel to stand where everyone would see him. Then he waved his arm in a wide arc to the guards in the trees. The ones I could see put the horns hanging around their necks to their lips and blasted a rich, bellowing tone, demanding silence.

Thousands of eyes stared at us in quiet expectance, making me extremely self-conscious. Gabriel finally looked over at me when my light burned and dimmed at the quickened beat of my heart. He let go of my hand to put his arm around my waist. The look he gave me was still not one of forgiveness, but the concern I could see he had for me was comforting.

"What would you have me say?" he turned partially to face Amphion.

"Tell them—tell them... I can't do this, Flank. You voted in favor. You make the proclamation."

"Alright." Flank moved closer to Gabriel and spoke quietly as to what he should say.

Gabriel turned back to the crowd and spoke in a way I didn't even know nocturnes could. His low, rumbling voice boomed with such resonance, it must have carried easily to every ear:

On behalf of the League of Royal Elyxeos Centaurs, I share with you this message. The Elyxeos army has discovered that the Trios are attacking dangerously close to our city. Their forces are innumerable and unstoppable the way things are now. Two of their men easily destroyed twenty-three of ours. That said, we have no choice but to join this war.

A WOMAN CRIED out in the Elyxeos crowd. Another fainted.

I was entirely wrapped up in the unrestrained power of Gabriel's alluring voice. In that wondrous sound and looking upon his captivating face, things I had never known awakened inside me.

TOMORROW, the remainder of the League of Royal Elyxeos Centaurs will arrive. They're setting things in order for our army to join the armies of the other colonies right now. In our chief's great wisdom, he has managed to enlist the Dashings to fight on our side. They will double our forces.

Now, I am going to be straight-forward for your own sakes. This war is still a hopeless one. We will have to return to the ways of old that won the war the first time. We will ride into the fight with luminaries and nocturnes—

GABRIEL STOPPED and turned to Flank. "On your backs?" he said in his natural, but still very tempting, voice. "You're going to force the slaves to fight from your backs?"

Amphion groaned. "It sounds even worse to hear someone else say it."

"Go on and finish what I'm telling you," Flank said. "It'll all make sense when I'm done."

Gabriel looked unsure, but faced the crowds and continued:

WE WILL RIDE *into the fight with luminaries and nocturnes on our backs, as all centaurs will do with those slaves who are part of their colonies.*

I COULD HEAR Amphion exhaling furiously.

A whisper arose from the smaller crowd as slaves began looking like they were going to unravel mentally at any moment.

THIS WAY *we will stand a better chance of winning the war. If we do not do this, every luminary in the land will be destroyed. Every nocturne will be mutilated into something unspeakable. Every Elyxeos will be killed.*

I UNDERSTOOD why he needed to be so blunt, to prepare the Elyxeos for what would be said next. Still, I hated the way women and children were crying in fear. It was enough to distract me from my newly heightened obsession with nocturnes at the discovery of their voices' abilities, the one before me in particular.

IN EXCHANGE FOR THIS, *you will be granted your fr—*

GABRIEL'S ARM fell from my side. He stopped to stare at the Elyxeos behind him. "Freedom?"

"Yes!" Flank rolled his eyes and gave him an incredulous look. "Now will you please continue?"

YOU WILL BE GRANTED *your freedom.*

HE WAS FORCED to stop this time by all the cheering coming from one part of the audience and outraged shouting drawn from the other.

The watchmen in the trees blew their horns for quiet, but received no such thing.

"What are you waiting for, Gabriel?" Orius asked. "Use your earthquaking and call them all them to silence."

Gabriel had the shadow of a grin on his face when he turned to the spectators and drew in a deep breath until his chest had grown to nearly twice its normal size. Then he let out a vicious *ROOOAARRR* that shook the entire city and everyone in it. The Elyxeos behind us stepped as far back as they could. Fire that could have swallowed our house blew up all around him. I fell back in astonishment, nearly going over the edge of the platform. One hand went over my heart. I couldn't decide if it was beating feverishly out of fear or amazement.

It seemed the world stood frozen when Gabriel stopped. No one made a move or a sound. He saw me and knelt by my side. "Are you alright?"

"I—I—I've never wanted you so badly."

The way his eyebrows rose brought me back to reality. Perhaps I'd said too much. I hadn't really meant to say it out loud.

"Go on, save it for when you're alone, and not in front of me," Amphion said, sounding disgusted.

Gabriel laughed under his breath as he put both hands at my waist and helped me to stand.

"Never seen a nocturne who could put a titanasaur in its place like this one," Orius said to the other royals.

"What next?" Gabriel asked Flank. The centaur returned to his place behind him and Gabriel went on:

I KNOW THIS IS DIFFICULT, but we must take every precaution and advantage we can to win this war. We will offer to employ whatever luminary seers seek work as we do now, along with their families, in exchange for all the things they've been given as slaves. We will still reserve the right to be the only colony to have seers. Orius will still go out with his hunters. Seerie will still create our clothing with her seamstresses. Nothing will change, except that the slaves will have the choice whether or not to be here, where they are safest and where they are given everything they need. This invitation will be offered to the freemen, as well, but only after the luminaries and nocturnes have fought this war beside us. They have the binding word of the League of Royal Elyxeos Centaurs.

Tomorrow, the chief will return. Some of us will set out with a number of slaves to spread the word to their kind and gather forces. For today, there is no work, only training. The Trios could attack at any moment. For our own protection, we may even be instructed to move to the Bellios colony where everyone is gathering. Either way, we must prepare ourselves.

"THAT'S ALL," Flank said to Gabriel.

"I'm taking a small number of my men to train with this luminary," Amphion said, taking me and placing me on his back. My dress ripped an inch higher up the side. "The rest of my army will be training everyone else."

The muscles in Gabriel's arms flexed as his eyes hardened. "You will stay in the city with her, won't you?" he said.

"Of course, I will."

"Can't Gabriel come with us?" I asked.

"He'll be training with Orius and the other hunters. No ones used to fighting with a slave on their back, and the hunters will stay together to fight. They've got to adjust to one another."

I was only able to give Gabriel an anxious look before Amphion was racing down the ramp away from him.

29

A mphion allowed the sun to set completely before he called our training session to an end. We'd trained all day with three of his men in the unkempt courtyard inside the chief's housing. We worked on my reflexes. We practiced working together to deflect attacks. Amphion even taught me where the best places to strike a centaur were. Apparently the skin in their neck was the easiest to cut through and stabbing a centaur right where the torso met their beastly half was almost always fatal.

My arms were shaking halfway through when Marina brought me a pair of trousers for riding and a bowl of steaming titanasaur. I began feeling better the instant I swallowed that first bite. The men were also happy to receive a bag full of fresh vegetables and grain. She didn't stay for long.

When night fell, Amphion sent the other three ahead to guard my house so he could have a word with me alone. It was a bit nerve-racking to be left with him in the darkness where no one would probably hear me, or even care, if I cried out for help. The thumping of hooves died out through the breezeway. It was replaced by the sounds of crickets chirping and tall blades of grass swishing against each other in the wind.

Amphion sat in the grass once we were entirely alone. I stayed where I was, standing right in front of him.

"Chief is probably going to insist on me having someone on my back when we do go to battle, especially since I'm our greatest warrior..." He crossed his arms over his chest, forcing all his muscles to bulge out impressively. "You're a scrawny, inexperienced luminary. You'll be nearly useless in battle. But you put yourself in danger to save my life, and saved the life of Tiberion. I trust you. That's not something your greatest fighter could offer me. I know I said before that you would not always ride on my back, but maybe you would ride with me into battle?"

Wow. I was both insulted and honored. Having the choice offered to me alone was such a privilege. There probably wasn't a better place to be in the approaching war than on the back of the Elyxeos' greatest warrior. Of course that might also make me a target. "Would you always be in the front line of things?" I asked.

He nodded slowly. "I would."

"So the Trios may want you dead most of all?"

He cocked his head back, blowing out a large gust of his breath. "Probably."

My head and my heart clashed in disagreement. It seemed stupid to ride with Amphion, but I knew I'd never get another offer like this one. No matter what, if anyone stood a chance at surviving this war, it was certainly him. And he'd earned my trust just as I had his by protecting me so well to this point. "I would be honored to ride with you, Amphion."

He surprised me with a smile, a real, happy, carefree sort of smile.

It disappeared almost instantly, though, replaced by a colder more threatening stare. "If you ever tell anyone what I just said, I'll never forgive you for it."

"I promise, it's between you and me... But since we trust each other, can I ask you a question that's been bothering me?"

"Ask away."

"Being raised as I was, I don't know as much about centaurs as I should, so please forgive me for this. Do centaurs usually keep their word?"

He snorted furiously. "Of course we do. What sort of a foolish question is that?"

"I asked you to forgive me. People didn't *always* keep their word where I grew up. They tried, but sometimes things that seemed more important got in the way. I didn't even know what a centaur was until a few weeks ago, so the question of my family's safety has really been bothering me."

His eyebrows drew closer to each other. "Honestly?"

"Yes."

"Hmph... Well then, the Avarice must *really* be hidden..." He cocked his head to one side and narrowed his eyes to study me. "The Dashings are rumored to be extremely trustworthy, as are the Striplings. No respecting Elyxeos would put any trust into a Bellios, and the Elabans have always been so far away, they're strangers to us. But an Elyxeos' word is absolutely binding. A man who has proven his word isn't good is made an outcast and a scavenger, especially one of the League of Royal Elyxeos Centaurs. Chief promised that we would bring no harm to anyone as long as they don't stand in the way of our getting to the Avarice, so we won't."

That felt good to hear. Without having the chance to talk to Gabriel about it, the fear for my family's safety had stayed on my mind fairly continuously.

"You should go home and get some rest," Amphion said.

standing up. "We'll be training in the morning until Chief gets here."

~

IT WAS a dark night with all the clouds rolling in. I could just make out the dusky silhouettes of three centaurs outside my home when it came into view. One was obviously standing, but the other two seemed to be lying on the ground. A luminary walked past them and revealed that they were both fast asleep.

"I can take the first watch," Amphion said when we reached them. "You get some rest, Saydius."

The Elyxeos who was awake bowed as I went on to my door and walked inside. Gabriel was already asleep in my bed. I thought about lying on the rug, but decided we needed to talk more than I needed sleep. So I grabbed a handful of cherries from the bowl on the table and ate them as I went to sit beside him.

"Gabriel," I said softly, putting a hand on his arm. He offered no response. "Gabriel, I really want to talk to you." I spoke louder this time.

He finally rolled over and sat up slowly, rubbing his blood-shot eyes. "Oh, hey... I tried to stay awake, but I didn't get much sleep last night."

I kneaded the muscles of one arm as I glanced at all the windows to make certain they were shut and the cloth rectangles we'd hung over them for cover were let down.

"Arms sore?" He reached out to massage both my arms.

"Sort of. They're mostly numb, though."

"You'll be feeling them tomorrow. Parthenia stopped by to see you when everyone was released."

Even with the windows closed, I lowered my voice enough that no one outside would hear me. "I need to apologize to you."

His hands withdrew as he sat back and stared at me.

"I want you to know I'm really sorry for betraying everyone's secret. When the Elaban came saying the Trios were attacking, I went straight to Marina..."

I proceeded to fill him in on everything that had happened the day before, from faking sick to Amphion's speech on the binding word of an Elyxeos. Somehow it didn't feel like I was breaking the promises I'd made to keep certain things secret when I was telling them to Gabriel.

"...I know you're mad at me, but the Elyxeos promised not to hurt anyone as long as they don't stand in their way. And if they take care of the Avarice, babies won't be stripped away from their parents anymore. Innocent people won't be put to death any longer."

He'd listened intently to my long story and never reached out to touch me. It was so unlike him, it was beginning to scare me.

"Can't you forgive me? I don't want to lose you over this."

Gabriel shook his head darkly.

I bit my lip as tears came to my eyes. My light dimmed until it nearly went out.

"That's not it, Sleigh. I can see how this all plays into the nocturnes' prophecy of our people's freedom, as well as yours of the sky luminaries. I wouldn't have traded your life to keep that secret, either. But—" He looked down at the hand I had on the bed beside him, like he wanted to hold it. Then he shook his head.

So I reached out for him. "What is it, Gabriel? Tell me how to make this right with you." I couldn't help but cry a little.

He looked up again, holding onto my hand. "Are you sure part of you wasn't looking for a way to get back to your city because of Jordan?"

"Jordan?" Was he serious?

"I know what you said before, but more than enough time has passed for you to realize you made a mistake—"

"No."

"I need you to be completely honest with me about this. Women have been torn between two men before; I've seen it happen. Everything is about to change. I *need* to hear the truth now so I know where to go from here."

"Oh, Gabriel," I sobbed for the pain this must have caused him all day long, for the terror we certainly both felt for what was to come, for how exhausting it all was.

He wiped my tears away. His eyes began to look a bit glassy as well.

"I'm not torn, and this has nothing to do with Jordan. I even asked Amphion if I might stay behind when they go in my old city so I wouldn't have to face him." I sucked in an unsteady breath. "I love you, Gabriel. You're the only man I've ever said that to besides my father. You're the only man I've *ever* felt this way about. I can't believe you would doubt me enough to worry about this all day after everything we've been through."

He let in and out his own rickety breath. "I love you, too. But —the thought of you going back to your city—to him—it's worse than I ever thought it could be."

I scooted closer so I could wrap my arms around his neck. "I just want to be with you. Before and after everything changes, I just want to be with you."

His arms went around me, lifting me into his lap so he could hold me right up against him. "Me too. I won't doubt you ever again."

"Good." I lifted my head so my face was directly in front of his. "Because that man I saw you become on the platform today —" I tilted my head and exhaled, remembering the fiery desire I'd felt at his enormous explosion of power. "—I can't imagine he could ever leave his woman wanting for another man."

His chest rumbled with his low nocturne laughter. "The one you've never wanted so badly?"

I bit my lip again, grinning this time. "Yeah."

He smiled as he cradled my head in one hand and kissed me. A deep almost imperceptive sound began in his throat, like the warning growl of a wild animal. Then it spread throughout his body and into mine, a thrilling vibration that got every part of me going. His body got hotter. My lips felt like they were sweating, salivating for his, to fulfill my inner hunger. I pulled my arms off his neck so I could press them against his back. The growling became louder until the bed was trembling with us.

I gasped and arched away from his arms when one of his hands began searing into my back. My light was blazing so bright, we both had to squint our eyes.

"Sorry," he whispered, breathing heavily. He shook his hand beside us so I could see that it was bright red like hot coal, but quickly becoming dimmer. "That's always the greatest risk when a nocturne and luminary are married."

I ran one hand over his two little scars. "A small price to pay to have you."

He used the cooler hand to place behind my head so he could kiss my temple, then beside my eye, then lower and lower and lower, until our lips met.

A knock came at the door, making me jump. Gabriel started to move away, so I hugged him tighter. "Ignore it. We'll have all day to deal with the outside world tomorrow. Don't let it in tonight."

He kissed my cheek. "Elyxeos guards are out there, Sleigh. If they think for one minute you're not in here, they'll break down the door."

My lips blew outward when I let all the breath out of my lungs. "Fine." I leaned back so Gabriel could crawl out from under me. My light was still much too bright, pulsing to the quickened beat of my heart.

It was probably better that we'd been interrupted, I realized, trying to catch my breath and feeling the fog of lust clearing just enough from my mind. It might have saved us both from making the mistake of going too far too soon and always regretting it.

Gabriel opened the door just a crack. Judging by how high up he was staring, I knew he was facing an Elyxeos.

"Is Sleigh still awake?" a man asked.

"Yes." Gabriel's eyes sank lower. "You must be Tiberion."

"That's right. Could I speak with your wife for a minute? I'd like to thank her."

"As would I," a woman's voice added.

I got up and crossed the house as Gabriel answered, "Sure," and opened the door wider. I took deep breaths as I walked, trying to quiet my glow.

It was easy to see what had given Tiberion away to Gabriel when I joined him at the door. His wrist was massive with swelling, and his hand had puffed up so big he could hardly move his fingers.

"Oh!" The woman beside him bent down so she could hug me. Her bushy, silver hair was squashed against my face, forcing a musty scent into my nostrils. "Thank you so much for saving my husband's life." She let go but took both my hands in hers. "We have four young children together, and their hearts would be crushed without their father." She smiled at her husband and put a hand on his arm. "I would have been crushed without him."

"You're welcome." It was nice to receive their gratitude, but I really preferred to be left alone with Gabriel.

"Thank you for what you did for me. Amphion has given me permission to offer you this." Tiberion bowed and held out a thin strip of leather that was dyed blue. Two metallic blue beads had been strung onto it. "Perhaps you should tie it on her arm, Amphion. I don't think I can manage with only one hand."

"Thanks, Tiberion, but what is it?" I asked.

Amphion wore a furious look on his face as he took it and tied it on my arm in the same place Gabriel wore the mark of the hunter. "It's the mark of an Elyxeos warrior," he said. "It can only be earned by saving the life of another warrior. Each of the beads represents one of those lives."

"So one's for you, then?"

His eyes wouldn't meet mine. "Yes," he practically snarled. "You're the first non-Elyxeos to receive the honor of wearing it."

I wondered if he would ever get over the pressure he obviously felt to show nothing but loathing for me in front of everyone else.

"It was quite a shock to wake up and discover slavery would soon come to an end," Tiberion said. "It was easier to accept when I also discovered what a slave had done for me, and for Amphion. There isn't an Elyxeos that hasn't been talking about it at some point during the day. You've made acceptance easier for many of us, I'm sure."

"Thank you for telling me that." I held my arm up so I could stare at the fat, shiny beads. It was amazing to know I'd earned something so significant.

"Of course. I'll let you get back to your evening now."

"Alright."

Gabriel and I waved to them as they left. Then I went to sit at the table while he shut the door.

"So what did the other slaves have to say about what freedom will cost them?" I asked as he took a seat beside me.

He shrugged. "I didn't hear anything during training. They're probably too scared to talk about it when the Elyxeos can hear them, though."

"What do you think about it?"

"It seems strange that we're not even given a choice. Flank made it sound like we had one, then he told everyone to start training for battle. Besides that, I don't mind. We would have had to fight in this war eventually, anyway. We might as well get something out of it."

"Yeah." I nodded and stared at my hands resting against the table for a minute. "Gabriel... about before..."

His hand appeared in my line of vision and wrapped firmly around mine. "I'm sorry, Sleigh. I shouldn't have taken it so far. I do love you, and I would hate for you to think that's the sort of man I am."

I smiled over at him, remembering his mother's words when I'd asked if other young ladies had been calling on him: *Not one, miss.* I wondered if I should mention it to him, but decided to keep it to myself. "Of course not. You're the most wonderful man I've ever known, Gabriel."

He stood and pulled me close to him. "Someday, though." He stared at me expectantly, a question in his eyes.

My light became more vivid as I took in what I was almost certain he was asking. It was the strangest marriage proposal I'd ever heard of, one that could easily be withdrawn by claim of miscommunication if it was turned down. It was safe. "Someday." I hoped he understood.

He moved his face closer to me, coming just short of pressing his lips to mine. "Promise?"

I inhaled and closed my eyes, every doubt I had in my mind slipping away. I was hopelessly in love with this nocturne. "Promise." My hands slid through his hair. I leaned closer so our lips were touching and whispered, "I will always love you, Gabriel, only you, for as long as I shall live."

He let out a breath as hot as fire that nearly forced me away from him. "As will I, Sleigh... forever..."

30

"CHIEF'S COMING," someone outside called, waking me up.

"What time of day is it?!" Amphion yelled right beside one of my windows. "What do you think you're doing letting me sleep for so long?"

"It's not my fault. Marina said to let you rest as long as possible."

"She does not give your orders!"

"What are you doing down here?" Gabriel sat up on his elbows when he realized I was lying beside him on the rug.

I'd awoken filled with a sense of terror the night before, though the dream was lost to me now. All I could think of for comfort was to open the windows to let a soothing breeze in and to lie against Gabriel's back. "I had a nightmare. I hope you don't mind."

"You could have woken me up." He ran one hand over my arm.

Someone pounded against the door. "Come on, Sleigh. Chief's here," Amphion said loudly.

My eyes became desperate as I stared at Gabriel, wanting to

cry. The Avarice would fall on this day. I might fall on this day. Even the idea of seeing my family was not enough to console me. "I'm scared," I whispered.

Gabriel leaned forward and put his arms around me. "Orius chose me for a riding companion. I'll do whatever I can to be there with you."

I pressed my head against his neck when Amphion pounded on the door again. "Come out or I'm coming in!" he shouted.

"I'm coming." I kissed Gabriel quickly before I got up and grabbed my bag on my way to the door.

"Finally." Amphion picked me up and put me on his back when I opened the door, not even giving me the chance to shut it behind me, then took off through the houses. I was beginning to feel like his pet.

"I can't believe her—giving commands to *my* men," he fussed, going on about Marina under his breath.

I was too nervous to be any good at conversation.

The open area between houses and fields was full of men and women, and even children who were old enough to ride a young Elyxeos and hold a weapon. They were all training tirelessly to better defend themselves.

I wondered what Gabriel would do while his Elyxeos was in the meeting.

It was a cloudy day outside, the sort that left you feeling drained and gloomy. The looks on everyone's face matched the weather perfectly. Though it was selfish, I was glad that I wasn't alone in feeling so unhappy.

An old, graying guard bowed us inside when we reached the castle. We passed four more before we entered the silent meeting room.

We were the last to arrive.

"Sorry it took so long to get here, Chief," Amphion said,

taking a seat at the end of the table closest to the door. "Your daughter had my men let me sleep until you got here."

I chose to sit beside Amphion.

"She wouldn't even let me near the house to get Gabriel for training," Orius added.

The chief ignored them and stared at me. "This will be the third meeting you've been a witness to," he said. "You must understand that whatever you hear is confidential. You must never tell these things to anyone who is not a member of this league."

"The slave is wearing a warrior's band," Orius said suddenly in exasperation.

"*I* gave it to her," Amphion said, "for saving Tiberion yesterday, and for saving me from that Trios."

"She did that?" the chief asked.

Amphion stared down at the table for a moment, giving Orius the opportunity to answer for him. "Word is she saw a Trios running toward Amphion, so she jumped out of a ditch and blinded it with light so he could kill it."

The chief had hardly taken his eyes from me, but seemed to study me intently now. "I'm impressed."

"Thank you, Chief," I said, bowing forward slightly.

"What happened with the other colonies?" Amphion asked.

The chief cleared his throat. Then he turned to his men, looking more official. "The Striplings and Elabans agreed to end slavery without argument. Their numbers have already been reduced so dramatically; they were desperate enough to do anything for our aid and the aid of the Dashings. The Elaban don't have any slaves left, anyway, after all the Trios attacks they've suffered. The Bellios refused at first. They only agreed once the Striplings, Elabans, and the Dashings who had gathered, agreed to move everything to our city and leave theirs behind, refusing to allow them to join us here. I wouldn't be surprised if the Bellios go back on their word after the war and we have to enforce the new law among them. Any questions so far?"

"Were there a lot of Dashings?" Flank asked.

"Not yet, but they assured us that many more will come... Nothing else, then?... Alright. Amphion, you'll send a portion of your men with their luminary or nocturne to gather in freemen from their villages with the promise of peace in return for their joining us in battle. Sleigh, how many would you say are in the Avarice city?"

"Far more than you have here as slaves."

"Orius, your hunters will accompany the seven of us to the Avarice city. Amphion, choose your very best warriors to come, too. We'll need the strongest men in our colony with us."

Orius nodded.

"Will the nocturne hunters get to come, too?" I asked hopefully.

Orius arched one eyebrow at me. "Perhaps, if they really want to."

I felt a spark of happiness at hearing that Gabriel might get to go. "Most of the people in my city have never seen one. Everyone's so afraid of them; it would probably be a good idea to have them with you."

"Are you saying your people have never seen a nocturne?"

"There are only luminaries in my city. I doubt any of them have ever even heard of a centaur."

"What sort of a place is this to know so little of the world?" Skelleon asked.

I could only imagine Gabriel cringing at hearing me give everything away. "It's built at the top of the tallest and strongest trees in the world."

"What?" Orius slapped the table.

"How exactly do you get to a city at the top of the trees?" the chief asked, looking alarmed.

"There are stairs wrapping around a stone mountain that'll take you to it."

"Oh, *come on*," Amphion complained.

"Are you serious?" the chief asked.

"What's wrong?" I asked innocently.

"We can't climb stairs!" Amphion raised his voice. "Have you not noticed we only use ramps to get up and down?"

My chest burned, my light becoming brighter. "I hadn't really thought about it."

"This ruins everything," the chief said hotly, "the Avarice, the *Wings*, slavery!"

All I could think of were the feces-smeared cloths I'd promised Gabriel years before that I would never tell anyone about.

"What do we do now, Chief?" Orius asked.

Amphion glared at me like I'd just shattered all the confidence he had in me.

No! It wasn't everyone. Gabriel only told me to keep it secret from *my* people, the other sky luminaries. He never said anything about centaurs. "There is one other way," I said.

"Yes?" the chief asked.

"Can you hold your body weight with your arms for a long time?"

"Of course," Amphion said.

"Do I look like a weakling to you?" Orius asked.

The others all nodded, except for the chief's father. "I'm not so sure," he said modestly.

"What if you had a nocturne on your back?" I asked the others.

Orius only rolled his eyes. Flank gave me a look like I was stupid. No one bothered to answer.

"There's material with titanasaur feces hidden near the city. If fire touches it, an airstream shoots down strong enough to carry you right to the city. So if you can hold it over your head while a nocturne's on your back breathing fire against it, you should be able to get in that way."

"I've never heard of such a thing," the chief said.

"You're a luminary," Skelleon said. "How do you know it'll work?"

"I saw it happen four years ago."

"Very well," the chief said. "Let's just be grateful for this secondary option. The nocturne hunters will have to come with us, as will a number of other nocturnes if they're going to get us all up there. If there isn't anything else to discuss, I say we go to it right away," the chief said.

The other six bowed their heads in agreement, so I did the same.

31

The clouds had mostly dispersed by the time Livia's little home came into view. It was getting to be late in the afternoon, and terribly windy. I couldn't believe how much faster it was traveling by Elyxeos.

Amphion and I rode at the head of the men, with me directing which way to go. I was only able to do this because Gabriel had been allowed to ride with me, whispering which way to go in my ear. Amphion would have to have a nocturne with him to get into my city, so I was allowed to choose which one. Orius wasn't happy when I chose Gabriel, but he agreed. The other royals rode right behind us.

The cold stares the nocturnes gave Gabriel and me when they heard they would be helping their Elyxeos companions to fly up to a city in the trees to find and destroy something called the Avarice was scary. I ended up adding to the chief's announcement, informing them that it was part of what had been written in the stars. They didn't look *quite* as upset after that.

"We need to stop at Livia's," Gabriel whispered in my ear.

"Why?" I whispered back.

"She's the keeper of the flying hides. She'll have enough for everyone."

I glanced at Amphion nervously. When he asked about the material earlier in the ride, I'd told him we would find it hidden near the city. "We need to go there, Amphion," I said, pointing to the house. "An old nocturne woman lives there who might have what we need for flight."

Amphion looked back at me. "Your variance in word is terribly suspicious."

"I'm doing my best."

"You know what happens if this is all some kind of trick, don't you?" The hateful look he offered made it a threat more than a question.

"Yeah. You'll probably kill me and reinstate never-ending slavery."

He made a snarly face, but yelled back to his men: "We stop here momentarily for supplies."

Gabriel and I climbed down when he stopped right in front of her house. A serious look passed between us, the magnitude of what we were doing weighing heavily on both of us. I only hoped we would make it out alive, as well as my family.

He knocked on the door a few times, then peered through a side window. "Looks like she's asleep." It surprised me when he opened the door and invited himself in. "Livia, wake u—" We both had to put a hand over our noses. "It smells like death in here."

"*She's* not dead, is she?" I asked, horror-struck, though her appearance and the rancid odor had already answered my question. She was sitting crooked in one of her pink chairs with a wrist propped against her chest and her mouth hanging open.

"She was very old." Gabriel walked over to her and put his fingers against her neck, shaking his head instantly. "It's like her body knew the infant nocturnes wouldn't need her any longer.

With the Avarice being removed from power, she can finally be laid to rest."

"But what do we do with her body?"

"We'll have to send someone for it. There isn't time right now. Go ahead and take that basket of flying hide to the Elyxeos. I'll check in her back room for more."

I followed his gaze to the clamshell-shaped basket filled with rolled up hides. I grabbed it and ran from the house. The dead body in the chair was too eerie for me to endure being close to any longer.

"We found these," I said, handing one to each Elyxeos. "Gabriel's checking for more."

"Livia's passed on, hasn't she?" a nocturne hunter named Khan asked, sadly.

"Yeah." I handed his companion one of the hides.

His forehead creased as he hung his head. "She gave me both of my daughters."

I put a hand on his arm. "I'm sorry. I know she meant a lot to everyone on the Surface."

"She did." He nodded, then lifted his head to gaze at me, putting the pieces of where I'd come from together.

I only winked and went to the next Elyxeos.

"I found some more." Gabriel walked outside with a matching basket full of hides.

"That should be enough." I only had a few left, but several hunters were still empty-handed.

We ended up with ten extras. Gabriel shoved six into the strap running across his back to hold a quiver of arrows against him. He'd ended up trading the shield for them.

"What do you need all those for?" Orius asked him.

"To get Sleigh's family out of the city safely."

Half the royal centaurs stared at me, probably wondering just how much I'd told him.

Gabriel held the other four out to Orius to store in his extra-large bag. He was carrying rations for himself and Amphion, since Amphion had two bodies to carry.

"Let's get this over with," Gabriel said, lifting me onto Amphion's back and then taking my hand to help him climb on behind me.

"We need to go up that hill and follow the stream," I said to Amphion. The noisy clambering of hooves resumed as we set out.

A warmth spread through me when I recognized the growth surrounding the area where Gabriel and I first met. The bushes had gotten thicker and the trees taller. Fear at how close we were getting to my city followed.

Mud splattered my feet when Amphion tore through the stream before running alongside it. The closer we drew to my city, the more out of control I felt. I was terrified, exactly like when I'd set out to save Gabriel and Blush. As always, it was the love of my family that drove me forward.

I took in a deep breath and laid my hand over the one Gabriel had on my stomach, folding my fingers in between his and pressing them against the inside of his hand. I looked back into his dark eyes.

He offered me a reassuring grin. "I won't let anything happen to you, Sleigh," he murmured.

"The stream bends up ahead," Amphion said. "Do we continue to follow it?"

"No," I answered. "Stay this course until we reach a stone mountain. Guards will stand ready at the top of it, so we need to run past it a good ways before going up."

The thought of our paths crossing with the transporters' worried me. But the ride was completely uneventful except for an angry blue jay that flew into the chief's head right behind us.

The chief got a good scratch across the cheek, but was otherwise unharmed.

Hardly any time passed before we were racing past the mountain's base. My light was burning so bright by then, Elyxeos were beginning to complain. I couldn't help it, though. With titanasaur still coursing through my body, there was no way for me to hide my fear.

"There's the tree near the east bridge," Gabriel whispered, nodding to a massive trunk far off to the right.

I could just see the end points of one side of the X I'd carved into it. "Amphion, that tree over there borders a fairly secluded bridge. We could sneak in and I could get to my family from there."

The Elyxeos turned their course to follow Amphion toward the tree.

A rabbit shot out from under a bit of shrubbery and began darting frenziedly through their legs, trying to find a way to break free of them. A few men nearly fell into one another fighting to avoid it.

"This tree?" Amphion asked when we had almost reached it.

I nodded.

"Ready yourselves, men!" He began to unroll the hide he was holding.

"You need to have the darker side facing you when you hold it up," I told him.

"Like this?" He flung it over his head.

Gabriel pulled me back against his shoulder and looked straight up, breathing out a steady stream of fire.

"Whaaa—" Amphion leaned one way dangerously, squeezing the hide tighter with his right hand and flinging us to the side as we shot upward. His bottom half dropped until it was nearly vertical. I would have fallen off if Gabriel wasn't clutching the straps against Amphion's back with one hand and still holding me steady with his other arm wrapped around my middle. "I wasn't ready," Amphion complained.

"He can't answer you or we'll drift back down," I reminded him.

Amphion mumbled something irritably that I couldn't make out. Then he bent his neck forward so he could see his men below, all watching him in wonderment. "Come on!" he shouted.

One by one, Elyxeos threw hides over their heads. The nocturnes blew fire when it was exactly above them, sending them racing toward the sky. I had to look away before the last ones took flight. Being up so high on the downward slope of a centaur's back doubled my fear.

Instead, I watched the tree's trunk growing smaller and smaller. Gabriel let go of me a few times to press one of Amphion's arms one way or the other to avoid flying into branches. Amphion only protested the first time, then saw the massive branch that had narrowly missed his head.

When we were up enormously high, Gabriel blew us nearly straight forward without warning, through leaves and little sticks. I only saw the bridge a moment before he let us drift onto it.

I had officially returned to my home city, where the men in charge undoubtedly wanted me dead.

I—was—terrified—

Certain death became my only thought...

32

My breathing became the only thing I heard as I climbed off Amphion's back. My body tingled with the sudden added adrenaline pumping through it. Orius' hooves smashing onto the bridge and cracking a board brought me back just enough to realize we needed to move. "We've got to get off here," I said, moving toward the nearest landing with Gabriel. "This bridge won't hold all of you."

Amphion and Orius raced to join us. The other five royals landed hard against the bridge next, causing it to creek and moan.

"The Avarice live in a silver castle in the middle of the city that way," I told Amphion, pointing northwest. "Can I go to my family now?"

Gabriel began pulling hides from his strap and handing more than enough of them to me.

Amphion stared at me thoughtfully, like he wasn't sure what to do. I understood. As crazy as it sounds, it felt like I belonged with him, at least until the war was over.

"We keep your husband with us until we have the Avarice," Orius said.

"What?!" Gabriel thundered.

"Why?" I asked, filling with terror once more.

"That way we know you won't try to pull some hoax," Orius said. "All we've ever had is your word. How do we know we can trust you, really?"

The thumping and stomping of hooves fell continuously behind us. "Spread out the weight or the bridge will collapse," a nocturne shouted.

"Look around, Orius," Amphion said. "How can you call her a liar after seeing all of this?"

A hissing sound caused everyone to search wildly through the sky until we spotted a rocket cutting through the clear blue, leaving behind a thin trail of smoke.

"They know we're here," I said, just before the explosion sounded.

Gabriel drew a bow and arrow and pointed it where the trail of smoke began. He let it fly, sending a luminary plummeting toward the ground.

"SHIELD YOURSELVES, MEN!" Amphion hollered. Then he turned his attention to me. "Sleigh, there isn't time to argue. Go ahead and get your family to safety. Hide near the bottom of that stone mountain and I'll meet you there. And don't worry about your hunter; I'll keep him protected."

"Hold one of the hides over you and tight against your sides. Arrows won't be able to penetrate it," Gabriel said, taking one and throwing it over my head. I was too scared to care that animal poo was getting all over me. He only gave me a quick kiss on the lips. "I love you, Sleigh."

"Come on." Amphion knelt so Gabriel could climb on his back. "Stay close." He held the shield over their heads as Gabriel leaned against his back. Then they were off, thundering through my city, trespassers and huntsmen out for blood from the worst of my kind. Everyone would be as terrified as I was when they saw them.

I couldn't think of that now. I took off over another bridge. A red flag waving in the strong winds in front of one of the houses I passed by caught my eye. Around the landing and I saw another red flag in front of a more distant house.

Wonder what that means?

My house appeared up ahead. I barely caught sight of Eve running inside. The joy of seeing her was wonderful. "EVE!" I screamed as she slammed the door shut.

I dashed over the bridge that led to our landing. The door opened a crack when I was almost there.

"Sleigh?" She opened it wider and stared at me in amazement. Her chest caved and rose as she took in an enormous breath. Then she ran to give me a far too long-awaited hug "Sleigh, where'd you go? I missed you so much."

"I missed you too, but I don't have time to explain. We've got to get everyone to the Surface."

"We can't." She stared at me, still squeezing my sides. "The Avarice are killing everyone who tries to go down there. New flags go up every day."

"What are you talking about?"

"After you left, Henna said you went to the Surface to save Blush. Father tried to go after you. He told everyone about the Avarice killing people who've disappeared, the one's we always thought fell. He told everyone what Henna said, that defects aren't dangerous; the Avarice just want to control us by making us scared of them."

It sounded like Henna had done exactly as I'd asked.

"Sleigh?!" my mother gasped inside the open door.

That's when I noticed the red flag hanging outside our house. My breath became shallow. "Did, did they kill father?"

Eve's top lip crinkled, tears springing to her eyes, as she nodded.

I fell apart inside, gasping as the truth set in. "This is all my fault," I cried. "I saved Blush but I got Father killed."

"No, Dear." My mother hugged us both, crying too. "Your father always knew. He knew he would die, but he didn't want us to keep living in bondage to the false fear the Avarice puts into everyone."

It didn't make me feel better. This was still my fault.

"Did you say—" Auree and Henna ran outside and stood frozen when they saw me. Then they made a break for us, building on the mass hug.

Another rocket exploded closer to the castle.

"Someone else is here." Eve stepped back, looking worried.

"I brought an army of Elyxeos centaurs and defects to bring down the Avarice," I said.

"Really?" her eyes brightened. "How are you shining so much, Sleigh?"

"What's a centaur?" Henna asked.

"No time." I began handing out the hides. "I've got to get you to the Surface. Hold the two smaller edges and use them to float down. We'll be safe from whatever's about to happen there."

Eve looked over the edge. "I'm scared."

"You're a strong little girl, Eve. I know you can do it."

"What about Pat?" Auree asked.

"We have to go now."

"I can't leave him behind, Sleigh. Will this thing hold us both up?"

"Yes."

Auree took off through the houses. I couldn't blame her. I would've done the same thing for any of the people who stood before me.

"Don't jump where people will see you," I called after her,

swallowing down a sob. "Come on, Mother. We've got to get to the Surface."

"I'm too scared," Eve whimpered again.

I let out a sigh. Their lack of haste was becoming frustrating. "If I let you climb on my back with your eyes closed, can you hold on tight until I tell you to let go?"

"Mm-hm." She nodded enthusiastically.

"Alright. Come on."

"I can't go, Sleigh," Henna said softly. "A guard heard my parents talking about how you saw that they were going to have another defect, so the Avarice took them prisoner for keeping it from them."

"You mean your parents are in the castle?"

"Yes. I've been staying at your house since they were taken."

My mind set off reeling with how to solve that problem. Our limited options whizzed around as I tried to decide which was best. "Mother, you take Eve down on your back. I'll go with Henna to get her parents and meet you at the bottom of the passageway to the Surface."

"No, you won't," my mother said firmly. "The Avarice have instructed anyone who finds you to kill you at once. It's too dangerous."

"It can't be any more dangerous than half the things I've done since I left this city. Plus the Elyxeos are several times bigger than we are, and ten times stronger. They'll kill anyone who tries to harm me. We'll be fine."

"No!" My mother's expression became fierce. "I've lost your father and I won't lose you, too. You're coming to the Surface with me. And Henna, your mother would say exactly the same thing to you if she was here."

"I'm not going without them," I said firmly, a shiver passing through me. I'd never talked back to either of my parents before.

"Excuse me?"

"I lost Father, too, and I won't leave Henna's parents behind. I've loved them for as long as I can remember. I've gotten myself to the Surface and back into the city twice. I allowed myself to be captured and made a slave to save Blush. I've stood up to Elyxeos warriors and been honored for saving their lives. There's even a prophecy spread all throughout the land on the Surface made by the star-seer defects that I will end slavery and bring peace between man and centaurs. My own star reading on my eighteenth birthday foretold me freeing this city of the chains put on it by the Avarice. No part of either of these revelations foretells of my death. And the man I plan to marry is probably riding at the head of the attack on the castle right now. I love you, but I'm an adult now. I've proven myself capable of making my own decisions."

My mother stared at me in alarm. "Sleigh... I can't believe you..."

"I'm—sorry, Mother."

A faint smile graced one corner of her lips. "It sounds like you've grown to be everything your father or I could have ever dreamed. And just look at you." A tear fell as she let out a little laugh, then sucked in a great breath. "You're shining like some beautiful star fallen from the sky... Be careful, alright?"

"I will."

"And, Henna, have her put on the mourning clothes your mother gave me after the incident. No one'll recognize her that way."

Henna nodded.

"Come on." My mother squatted slightly so Eve could climb onto her back. Henna and I held my mother at the sides as she stepped onto the railing surrounding our landing. "Hold on tight now, Eve."

"Be sure to use the branches to kick away from the center of the tree on your way down," I said.

Then she jumped. Violent waves passed through both her and Eve's dresses. Eve screamed all the way out of sight. My mother must have been half-deaf by it, but she held firmly to the hide.

33

A rocket shot off again, then another. Three more exploded at once. There was no warning associated with so many detonations, only a promise of chaos and danger.

"My mother's always hated clothes of mourning," I said, chasing Henna into my house. "I can't, I can't believe she's been wearing them." My words broke.

"She hasn't. She just didn't want to be rude to my mother by rejecting the dress she made for her."

We ran through the hallway to my parents' room. Henna threw open their chest and pulled out the long red dress with matching gloves and scarf. I pulled it over what I had on as quickly as I could, nearly forgetting to tie on the belt that held my sword and grab the hides before we took off through the house again.

Then we were racing over a bridge away from my family's landing. "You haven't been gone nearly long enough to be in love with someone else already," Henna said.

"It's Gabriel."

"You mean the defect you met your first time down there?"

I saw people peering cautiously through their windows. A few stood outside trying to get a look at what was going on. No one was moving toward the castle, though.

"Yeah." I hopped over a pile of building blocks a child had left outside their house, squeezing my eyes shut to clear them of tears. "He's taken care of Blush all this time and he turned himself in as a slave just so he could help me get away."

"And he's here in our city?"

"Yes."

Henna glanced at me anxiously. "You better hope Jordan doesn't come across him. He hasn't smiled since you left. He's so worried; he comes to your house twice every day to make sure we still haven't seen you. If he found out you were in love with another man, it would probably break him."

I felt horrible. It was never my intention to hurt Jordan. And I doubted there was any way to make this right.

Focus, I told myself. *We need to get Henna's parents out of the city.*

I kept the scarf tied around my head pulled down as low as I could without impairing my vision. Seeing the light still dancing on Henna's back, it felt like all the light covered up was exploding out through my face.

"You should know that there's a division," Henna said when we were halfway there. "A lot of people are siding with the Avarice. They'll probably already be there."

"You can't be serious; they're murderers." I noticed dark smoke rising above treetops to the north when I looked over at her.

"I know, but some people are convinced that we're all safer up here. They're afraid of change and what's on the Surface."

What ignorance, I thought, shaking my head as I ran. It was terrible to think of all the luminaries who were trapped up here with no way of escaping, except to die.

The closer we got, the more people seemed to be running toward the castle armed with different weapons. I wanted to scream at them for defending the Avarice, for considering the lost children of our city defective and worthless.

The very top of the castle came into view through the spaces between limbs. Several valor trees had clearly caught on fire not far west of it. There was a great deal of shouting and thundering ahead. An explosion of flames lit up the afternoon. Henna and I raced around a landing and over the next bridge.

She stopped dead when she got her first sight of the Elyxecs. Skelleon was completely engulfed in the flames cast by the nocturne on his back. He swung an axe through the men who were running away with their clothes on fire. One luminary threw himself over a bridge, crying horribly for the pain of his burning body. A sleeve ripped off his shirt on a branch, spreading little flames where it had been left behind.

Seven guards were attacking an Elyxeos hunter. One of his front legs was bleeding badly. He knocked a man's swords out of the way with his shield, then dropped it. He took a luminary around the throat in each hand before he tossed them over the landing, as the nocturne on his back pierced another in the side.

I stopped behind Henna, searching our surroundings for Gabriel and a way to sneak into the castle. There couldn't have been a better time with all the distractions outside. "Any idea where your parents might be in there?" I asked her.

"Jordan's father said they're probably on the bottom floor, since that's where most of the guards are stationed. Structurally, it was built the strongest."

Of course the builders would have the best idea of where everything might be inside.

A line of five men ran around us toward the fighting. They were all builders I recognized easily, men I would never look at the same way again. I wished I could have lit them all up like a nocturne. Two stopped short when they saw what they were up against, and turned to run away.

Instinctively, I gripped Henna's arm when the Elyxeos chief backed up to avoid a spear that had been hurled at him. His hind legs slammed into the bridge's siding, tearing through it and sending him toward the Surface.

"What is it?!" Henna asked frantically.

The chief's center slammed into a thick branch below, allowing him something solid to grab on to. Bree, the nocturne on his back, slid off and caught onto the branch right under him. He took the rolled up flying hide from the strap on his back and clutched it in one hand as he climbed to the chief, just in case he fell on the way up.

I blew out a heavy breath. "He's alright. We nearly lost our chief, Henna."

"Look!" She pointed to the castle doors. "They're getting through."

Amphion, Orius, and three hunters, all with nocturnes unharmed on their backs, were entering the castle. I was happiest to see Gabriel with Amphion, of course.

Henna and I both looked up when a luminary was thrown through the air and slammed into the second story wall. He fell motionless to the ground, no light left in him. Even though the glowing men racing around fighting the Elyxeos far outnumbered them, they were losing horribly. Luminaries were steadily dying or falling to the Surface, while I didn't see a dead Elyxeos anywhere.

I grabbed Henna and pulled her down with me when a stray arrow came sailing our way. It soared over our heads and disappeared in the trees.

"What do we do?" She stared at me like *I* had all the answers.

I looked up when a head appeared in one of the highest windows. It only glanced outside before disappearing.

"What about the windows up there?" I asked Henna. "We could climb the valor tree that landing's built on to the right of the castle. There's a branch we could run across and, if we jump off the right way, we would float to one of the windows."

Henna followed my gaze to a mildly deformed tree. Most of the branches went straight up, but a few reached out more appropriately. One went right over the castle's roof, making it look fairly easy to glide into one of the top windows.

"We'd have to sneak through the entire castle to get to the bottom," Henna said. "And what if we don't land in any of the windows?"

"It's the only way I can think of to get in without having to fight for it."

Henna stood motionless as she stared at me. I'd never seen her look so frightened.

"If there's one thing I've learned from everything I've been through, it's that you can't waste too much time thinking and letting fear inside. When it's life or death, you have to act fast before fear can stop you."

I cringed when I heard the railing surrounding one of the landings shatter. A hunting pair fell over the edge. This time there was nothing to save them.

We needed to get moving. I ripped the skirt off my dress, revealing my trousers, and threw the fabric over the bridge. Then I slid the hides securely between my belt and stomach and stepped up on the railing to jump onto the valor branch right under us. Henna gasped. The branch was even wider than the bridge we stood on. It wouldn't be hard to run to the trunk, step to the branch beside it, and follow that one to a branch of the tree I needed to get to. From there, the strangely misshapen tree looked like it would be easy to climb.

My head was pounding with heightened fear. My skin couldn't possibly burn any brighter. "If we waste any more time talking about it, we'll never get your parents back," I said before racing over the branch.

"Henna!" a voice I knew well shouted, stopping me long enough to look back at Jordan. I watched him running toward her. He didn't look like himself at all. Sadness radiated from his weary face. Even looking so pitiful, a great love for him flowed through my body. If I wasn't so focused on what I was doing, I wouldn't have been able to stop myself from going to him. "What are you doing here? Did Sleigh come back?" he asked.

Henna still wore a look of pure fright, but turned to stare at me.

Jordan glanced in my direction, catching clear sight of my face. His eyes flashed something spectacular as he threw himself over the bridge to the same branch I waited on. He ran to me and flung his arms around my back. "Sleigh, I knew you'd come back. You couldn't stay away, could you? But why'd you leave like that? I would have gone with you."

I felt cruel pressing gently away from him. "I'm sorry, Jordan; there isn't time for questions. I've got to get Henna's parents out of the castle and to the Surface." I was grateful for the first time to have something so crucial I needed to achieve as I ran away from him toward the trunk of the tree.

Our reunion was just as I'd expected. I felt all the attraction for Jordan that I ever had. I wanted to be with him, but not like I wanted to be with Gabriel, and I hadn't the nerve to tell him so.

"Wait! You're not leaving without me again." I heard his feet pounding against the branch behind me.

I felt sick at his words. He was the first challenge for which I could see no solution.

I only looked back to make sure we weren't being followed when I gripped tree bark at the trunk and stepped carefully to the branch growing beside the first. Only Henna was in pursuit, with her hide jammed into the shirt of her dress.

"What happened while you were on the Surface?" Jordan asked me when it was his turn to step over to the new branch.

I ran ahead without answering. He was more of a temptation than I'd expected. I couldn't help but remember the years we'd shared, the kisses and laughter he'd so frequently offered me.

I only slowed when I reached the place where this branch crossed with one from the malformed tree. It wasn't as wide as the first, but plenty strong enough to hold us all. My fingers just barely wrapped around the one over my head. I felt Jordan's hands press firmly against my sides and lift me higher. My heart fluttered at his touch, the magic of my childhood crush pressing into my heart.

"Thank you, Jordan." I offered him a genuine smile once I'd made it up.

He gave me a gorgeous smile in return, one with a hint of admiration reserved only for me.

I held out a hand to help Henna up next. Then Jordan pulled himself onto the branch.

"How are you getting into the castle?" he asked.

"We're going to float from that branch into one of the top windows," I said, patting the hides and pointing to the branch we needed to climb up to.

"Right into the Avarice's living quarters." Jordan chuckled softly as I ran over the branch. "You know what I love most about you, Sleigh? It's like you're missing the part of the brain that makes fear."

In spite of everything, I had to laugh. "Thanks, but I've only learned how to ignore it." I stopped halfway to the trunk, thinking of all the knowledge of the castle he might have. "You don't know what's on every level, do you?"

"Almost every level. My father said the top two levels are where the Avarice and their families live. Each one's cut into three areas, so they're all separate. The first level's where the guards stay. The second one's where the Avarice have parties and meet with citizens. I don't know about the third floor. My father said when he goes inside for routine repairs, he only stops on a landing between the stairs when he reaches that level. There's a solid wall on both sides, so there's no way to access whatever's on the third floor."

I thought about what he said as I reached up and began climbing onto a higher branch. The Wings of Hendraya had to be on the third floor, the secret floor. I couldn't imagine how the Elyxeos were going to find it.

Jordan climbed up behind me and wrapped me in a hug from behind. "I missed you so much, Sleigh," he murmured.

My heart was torn. Part of me wanted him to stop, but it felt so good. My hands rested against his familiar arms. The scent of Jordan surrounded me and I couldn't help but be taken back to the wonderful evenings we'd shared.

"*AHH!*" Henna screamed, ripping me from my memories. She was reaching wildly for the arrow lodged in her forearm and beginning to lose her balance.

34

I reached out to steady Henna.

An arrow scared through the air and bounced off the limb beneath my feet. I took out the hides in my belt and gave one to Jordan. "Shield yourselves with these and hurry," I said, using it to guard the side of me facing the fighting below as I ran over the branch closer to the trunk.

An arrow stabbed at my shoulder through the hide, leaving me sore as it bounced away. Once at the heart of the tree, I jumped onto a branch to my right, and then another. A final arrow took a blow at my side, nearly causing me to lose my footing, before I made it safely to the other side of the tree.

I turned around and held out a hand to help Jordan and Henna get to safety.

"Are you alright?" I asked, looking them both over.

There was only a bloody circle where Henna must have pulled the arrow out of her arm. "I'll live," she said.

Jordan planted a hand on one knee and leaned forward, out of breath. He shook his hide out in front of him "This stuff's amazing—What's it made out of?"

"I'm not really sure, but we've got to keep moving," I said.

"Someone knows we're up here. Can you still climb, Henna?"

"Yes."

"Better let me go behind you," Jordan said, "just in case."

I tucked my hide back into my belt and sprang as high as I could to catch onto the branch above our heads. It wasn't as easy to get up on the skyward-curved branches. Once I made it, I reached diagonally for one at eye's level.

The sun was beginning to set, painting half the sky a lovely cherry blossom pink. It was a beautiful evening.

Three branches later, I glanced at the castle. We were nearly to the fourth floor.

I hopped to a skinny branch on my left so I could hoist myself up by three nubs to a higher limb. My foot barely got on it before Jordan shouted, "Guards are coming around the bridge."

Five luminary men were racing over a far bridge, searching the branches below us for our bodies. "Their aim'll be terrible from way out there with all this wind," I said. "We just have to get a little bit higher. The branch we need is right there." I hopped onto the branch directly to my right and pointed to the one above my head, the one that stretched out over the castle roof.

"Sleigh, they see us!" Henna shrieked.

I stepped up onto a branch and swung my legs over another. I looked down when Henna screamed. An arrow was lodged into the tree beside her head.

The men on the bridge suddenly began running away. Flames burst through the air behind them. A slight vibration passed through the tree we were on. A centaur appeared pursuing them with a nocturne breathing fire from on his back.

I stood up straight and stepped across two higher branches, like floating stairs, before I reached my objective. Henna and Jordan weren't far behind.

"Do exactly what I do," I told them before I took off over the branch.

A flash of the back-half of a centaur and nocturne passed through the inside of a second-story window. The Elyxeos were still slaughtering luminaries outside the castle, but the glowing bodies refused to give up.

A bridge hung in two pieces, both ends burning where it was broken. Fire had spread further through several more valor trees and their landings. Lucky for us, the gusts in the air were blowing westward, pressing the flames away from the castle.

I only slowed when I was near the grand building. The height of where I stood overlooking everything was so much greater than I'd imagined. The jump seemed so much more impossible. The nearest window was open but only stood about half as tall as me.

An arrow shot exactly where I had been standing only a moment before. Staying was more dangerous than jumping. So I flung the hide over my head, which was pounding madly with adrenaline, and jumped forward as hard as I could—perhaps a little too far...

The window was coming fast—I was going to make it—no, I'd gone too far— A breeze blew violently against me—I could reach out and touch it, but I couldn't let go of the hide. I kicked a leg toward it and hooked my foot inside the window's ledge. Momentum continued pulling my body sideways. My leg jerked it in the opposite direction toward the opening. I let go of the hide with one hand and reached for the window.

In that split second I knew that if my hand couldn't grab hold of something, I would fall to my death.

My hand slapped against the inside wall, sliding inward so half my arm was pressed against it. My torso and half my appendages were still dangling dangerously outside. I threw the hide into the room and barely grabbed onto the ledge with the other hand. My bottom and one leg still anchored me outside. Entry was not yet guaranteed.

"Sleigh!" Henna screamed. I glanced up and saw her move out of the way of an arrow.

With all the strength I had, I hauled my body into a large bedroom. Terrible stinging shot through my foot as I fell on the floor. An arrow had grazed it on the bottom.

Henna jumped from the branch when I looked outside. She hadn't thrown herself quite as far as I had, which sent her almost exactly where she needed to be. The way her chest was rising and falling so rapidly, it looked like she was hyperventilating. Blood dripped down all over her arm.

The guilt I felt was overwhelming.

She pointed her toes toward the window when she was almost there. I leaned out to grab her legs and yank her body toward me. She let go of the hide once she was inside to help catch herself when she flew across the room.

I snatched at the air through the open window and caught hold of the hide.

Henna stood up and walked unevenly toward me. She put a hand over her chest, still unable to catch her breath.

"I'm so sorry, Henna." I didn't realize I was crying until I heard my own voice. "It's my fault you got shot. It's my fault all this happened."

She sat on the bed beside the window, shaking her head. "Just give me a second."

Jordan was already floating down from the branch when I looked outside. He was headed right for me.

"Look out!" I screamed when an archer aimed for him and let an arrow fly.

Jordan swung his legs behind him, saving him from the arrow but taking him too far away to land near the window.

"Jordan," I called, reaching out as far as I could, though I knew it was in vain.

"What's wrong?" Henna ran to my side.

"Don't worry," Jordan said, floating below me. "I'll find you inside." He swung his body forward, straight toward the window below mine. I watched him climb in, an arrow narrowly missing him, before I withdrew.

I looked around the bedroom for the first time. A painting of Hecate with his wife and newborn son hung on the wall over a large bed of black sheets and pillows. A little crib pressed against the opposite wall. Silver thread hung from the ceiling in at least twenty different places with circular crystals dangling at the end, like it was raining diamonds. A gold saucer rested on an extravagant little table with jewelry and fancy hats sprinkled all over it. The finer things had been placed a good distance from the shining bowl. There was some sort of dark, burning liquid inside.

"He keeps fire in his own home?" I said faintly.

"But fire's forbidden," Henna said.

"I don't think anything's forbidden for the Avarice."

"Why is your skin lit like that?" Henna asked me as I moved toward the only door. It was nearly twice as wide as the ones on our houses, with gold buttons lining the bottom.

"It's the titanasaur meat."

"What's that?"

"I'll tell you about it later."

I pressed my hands against the door and slid it open as slowly as possible, hoping not to make a sound, even though Henna and I had already made such a clamor entering the room.

When the door was open just enough for me to fit through, I stuck my head out to look around. The decorative hanging crystals continued throughout a large sitting room. Two long sturdy benches with blue padding lining their seats seemed to be the centerpiece. A silver chest large enough to fit both Henna and me inside it sat between them, with a messy assortment of games and tools and scrolls scattered all over the top of it.

The thing that really caught my eye, though, was the luminary light coming from behind the far bench on the other side of the room. Someone was hiding. Judging by the way their light trembled, whoever it was... was afraid of *us*.

My notion was confirmed when a small, young forehead and pair of eyes slowly leaned over on one side to peek at us. The absolute terror I saw in these eyes before they disappeared behind the bench again told me I had nothing to fear.

I motioned for Henna to follow and walked soundlessly into the room. There were three more doors to our left. Aside from that, the only other door was a smaller one on the opposite wall against the corner closest to us.

We crept to this door and opened it silently. The light behind the bench never made a move.

Henna and I stepped onto a tiny platform at the top of a long stairway. We would have been in complete darkness if we weren't luminaries.

I reached into my bag and pulled out the saw-knife to give Henna. "Just in case," I whispered, seeing the look of panic on her face. Then I withdrew my sword and began down the stairs. They went on for so long, I wondered if they descended more than one floor. It made sense that the Avarice would have separate stairways from their homes to the third level.

Step by step, my mind gradually wandered to the Wings. If they were hidden on the third floor, the Elyxeos would never get to them because of the stairs. They would have to send the nocturnes, but they would never trust them with such a thing. Or would the Elyxeos have the nocturnes fly them over the stairs? I managed to keep my mind distracted with the Wings all the way down.

The platform at the bottom was considerably larger than the one at the top, with two more stairways coming from different directions ending there.

Henna's breath came out noisily, but her voice remained quiet. "I don't know if I can do this, Sleigh. It feels like I'm dying."

"We're already halfway through the castle. We've got to keep going." I pushed the third-floor door open quietly, preventing her from arguing. I knew the only way to keep her from giving way to her panic attack was to keep moving.

We walked into a long hallway with two doors spread apart on the left and two on the right. The walls were hung with a row of glass panels that had rare flowers pressed between them.

I walked through the corridor to the first door on our right.

"Sleigh, don't," Henna's voice came weakly behind me. She was still standing at the end of the hall, her eyes wide and unblinking. The desperation in her voice and insanity on her face were beginning to scare me.

I marched up to her and grabbed her arm. "Snap out of it. The Elyxeos will protect us when we get to the first floor. You saw them breaking into the castle. They can't lose this fight. We're *going* to be *fine*."

Henna finally blinked. She didn't look any better, but she managed a feeble nod.

I kept hold of her arm and led her to the first door. Cautiously, I pushed it open to reveal stacks of chests with locks put on them against the walls. A large window in the back of the room was covered. None of the chests were large enough to house a pair of wings fit for an Elyxeos centaur.

I pulled on the brass handle until the door closed. Then I led Henna to the door a little ways down the hall on our left and pushed it open. The room was about the same size as the first, but far more interesting.

35

The underside of a staircase filled the back of the room from the ceiling corner on the right to the floor corner on the left.

On one side of the room, there was a long black table with six chairs identical to the ones the Avarice had set in the night of my eighteenth birthday. Only these had different carvings of a man slaying a centaur on the backs of them.

But that wasn't the most interesting part. On the other side of the room near a corner there stood a complete centaur skeleton. Judging by its impressive size, there was no question in my mind that it was an Elyxeos. The painting hanging on the wall past its skull showed a blue centaur with sparkling silver wings.

Henna stepped into the room at that moment and let out a shrill scream. I smacked my hand over her mouth hard enough to bump the back of her head into the door. There was a low thud and then silence.

"Sorry," I whispered, "but you've got to be quiet."

She nodded, breathing faster again.

I took my hand from her mouth, but she grabbed it and squeezed. "Don't let go of me, Sleigh." She was trembling.

There was a giant iron box in the center of the wall on the right side of the room, surrounded by shelves from floor to ceiling. It was big enough it could have served as a small closet and had a heavy chain wrapped around it four times. I could feel an unexplainable energy when I went to stand right in front of it.

"The Wings of Hendraya must be in here," I said to myself.

"Wings?" Henna asked.

"That's why the Elyxeos are here, for these wings." I glanced at the strange back wall of the room. "They might not be able to get up here. Help me find the key."

I took my hand from Henna and began pushing around glass figurines of all sorts of animals on the shelves to the right of the box. Half of them I'd never even seen. I couldn't get over how much the Avarice must know of the Surface. They were such hypocrites.

Henna looked through a pile of books on the other side of the heavy box, holding them by the spine and shaking them so anything hidden in their pages would fall out. She couldn't seem to stop glancing nervously at the skeleton.

I was just picking up a hollow bust of a long-gone member of the Avarice who was a strong part of our history when a creaking sound came from the stair-wall. A slit opened along the sides as the bottom quarter of the stairs began to lift, a secret doorway to the room.

"...don't even know if it the wings will work..." Spencer was saying on the other side.

I grabbed a yellow blanket with leaves sewn along the edges from one of the shelves and pulled Henna toward the table with me. We crawled in between two chairs and under the table before curling up in little balls against each other. Then I threw the blanket over us to hide our natural light. I held the hilt of my sword in both hands, the cold metal pressed against my center. Henna's whole body was trembling.

"Do you have a better idea?" That was either Felix or Arthur. "Our men are all dying and we'll die too if we don't do something.

"Well I'm not putting on the wings. They might turn me into a centaur or some cross-breed monster."

The two men's footsteps entered the room.

"I'll do it, then." The second man was definitely Felix, I decided.

My grip tightened when I heard the tinkling of what I assumed to be keys bumping into each other.

"What are you doing? Go and shut the secret wall," Spencer commanded.

"What if Draven needs to get in?" Felix asked.

"You saw; they got him. There's no point in risking letting in centaurs."

The jingling was nearly drowned out by footsteps crossing the room. The same *creak* sounded as the stairs began to lower.

Metal scraping against metal seized my attention, followed by a loud *click*. I let go of the sword with one hand to slide my fingers under the edge of the blanket.

"Someone left the door open, Felix. You better bar it shut to be safe."

My head began pounding painfully again. We were about to be trapped in a room with two of the Avarice.

Henna pushed against me when she flinched at the sound of chains slamming into the floor.

I pressed the side of my face against the ground and lifted the blanket only enough to see Spencer open the iron box. A pair of dull, gray wings that were even taller than him rested in the back. They looked dusty and unimpressive.

"Hurry up. Let's get these on you," Spencer said, holding them up.

I had to do something or the Avarice might soon rule over

far more than our city in the trees, not to mention that Henna and I would certainly be killed. With no other plan, I threw the blanket off and jumped out from under the table.

"SLEIGH, NO!" Henna screamed, trying to grab onto my foot.

"Wha—" Spencer stared at me in astonishment. Felix stood frozen with one hand on the back of the open door.

My sword was ready in my hand, but mostly for show. Killing was a last resort. "Put the wings down!" I shouted, charging at Spencer. My right foot slipped when I was nearly there. I fell forward, smashing him into box and falling sideways to the floor.

I heard my dress ripping as something crawled all over my back. I jumped up and clawed at the skin under one shoulder, but the crawling thing was stuck to me. Brilliant silver glitter flashed at my right side. One of the wings was thrashing wildly around behind me.

A chill rushed through the soreness of my arms from Amphion's training, relieving their aching at once.

Spencer grabbed my wrist and jerked me toward him. "Give it back." I swung my sword at his arm, cutting it off unintentionally under the elbow.

I screamed at the ghastly sight of his severed hand still holding to my arm. I slung it across the room and slammed the door to the box shut with Spencer still inside. Then I tried to stand with my back against it. Something thick and strong, but not quite solid, was pressed between the door and my body.

Spencer threw himself against the door behind me. It opened slightly, then slammed shut.

"HENNA!" I screamed at the moment Spencer shouted, "FELIX!"

"I'm coming," a fifth voice said, racing into the room.

"Jordan, NO!" I screamed, letting go of the box to run toward him.

Felix drew a knife from his belt. Jordan didn't see him. I wasn't close enough. The knife disappeared into Jordan's back.

Henna burst from under the table, still holding her weapon. The room shook when something slammed into the lower wall with the stairs cut into it. She stumbled sideways, dropping the saw.

I drove my sword into Felix's neck without hesitation. He and Jordan both collapsed against the floor. The knife stuck halfway out of Jordan's back.

Something enormous pressed upward against my shoulder blade when I tried to kneel beside Jordan. That was when what had happened became clear. I must have fallen on one of the wings, and now it was attached to my body. It hardly mattered as I brushed it back so I could sit by Jordan and help to roll him over on his side.

Felix pressed both hands uselessly against his gaping neck not far away.

Spencer threw the iron door open.

The tremendous voice and quaking of a nocturne shook the room. The wall with the room's secret entry began smoking. Something slammed into it again. A giant crack split through it and spread in five different directions.

Spencer stared desperately at the damage, then the single wing in his hand. He slung it over his shoulder and pressed it to his back.

"STOP!" I shouted, trying to stand. Jordan's hand flopped onto my knee, drawing me back to him.

The something slammed into the wall again, doubling the length of the cracks.

"Sleigh," Jordan whispered feebly, his eyes nearly closed. "You would have married me, ri..."

I wanted to tell him to save the deathbed talk, that he was going to be fine. But his glow had all but gone out. His skin was already becoming cold. His life was slipping away.

His eyes fluttered open when I took his hand. "Of course I would have," I choked out, crying again. Even Gabriel wouldn't have had me deny Jordan this simple lie.

"Give it back or you can join your boyfriend in death," Spencer said, advancing on me again. He had a knife matching Felix's in one hand, blood dripping where the other should have been. The wing attached to his back sparkled like a cluster of a thousand tiny stars.

"No!" Henna was already running toward him with the saw-blade in hand.

Spencer only noticed her a moment before she pressed the point of it to the side of his neck.

"You're not killing Sleigh."

Jordan's grip became nonexistent. I wiped my eyes on the red sleeve of my half-dress and stood up. "Why did you have to make everything this way?" I asked Spencer in a broken voice.

An opening ruptured in the smoking wall suddenly, the top half of Amphion now visible. He and Orius grabbed the broken edges and began ripping pieces away.

When Henna looked over at them, Spencer made a run for me. He jumped back when I sliced my sword at him. I jumped backwards over Jordan when he took a swipe at me with his knife.

"*GET AWAY FROM HERRRR!*" Gabriel thundered, shaking the room severely enough that dust fell from parts of the ceiling. He'd climbed through the hole in the wall and drawn an arrow back in his bow. He let it go, sinking the tip into the back of Spencer's head.

His birth father fell face forward into the floor, still and silent, at the hands of the son he'd rejected. The brilliant dazzling of his silver wing began to soften.

Gabriel raced across the room and grabbed my shoulders so he could turn me this way and that. "Are you injured?" he asked, looking at me all over.

I shook my head, staring blankly at the floor. My voice seemed beyond my own control when it burst out of me hysterically. "He just showed up, Gabriel... Right when Felix was behind the door... He's dead because of me. My father's dead too! THIS IS ALL MY FAULT!"

Gabriel glanced at the dead men on the floor. Looking unsure, he slid his arms around me. I grabbed wads of his shirt over his chest and dug my face into it to cry.

"He wore one of the wings?" I heard Orius saying as his footsteps entered the room. More footsteps accompanied him.

"Sleigh, what have you done?" Amphion asked softly.

The wing fluttered against my back as the consequences of my claiming it sank in. The Elyxeos were here for the wings. The only way to get this one back would be to kill me.

36

My grief would have to be pushed aside for the moment. I wiped my eyes on the sleeve of my dress again as I stepped around Gabriel to face the four Elyxeos and three nocturnes who had entered the room. "I didn't mean to. Spencer was going to put them on Felix. When I tried to stop him, I fell on top of one."

Amphion and Orius stared darkly at one another. "Then we owe you our gratitude to some degree," Orius muttered.

Henna had moved against the shelves to the side of the iron box. She slid against them to the corner nearest the skeleton. It seemed the living centaurs frightened her far more than the dead one.

"Will you still fight against the Trios?" Amphion asked me.

"You're not seriously going to let a luminary wear the Wings, are you?" Orius asked him aghast.

"She already has one on. There's nothing else we can do."

"We could take it back."

Everyone became silent. I could scarcely breathe.

"You don't mean to kill her?" Gabriel said, taking a step in front of me.

"How else are we going to get the wing back?" Orius said.

"No."

Orius set his jaw and leaned forward like he would come at me.

Amphion darted in front of him. "We gave her our word."

"This is no time for honor, Amphion," Orius spat. "Our people will die if we don't get those wings."

"An Elyxeos is only as good as his word, living or dead. Who's to say she won't be as powerful as Hendraya once she wears them both? And if she dies in battle, we get them back."

Orius just stared at him, like he'd suddenly announced he was joining the Deliverance. "IT IS OUR RIGHT!" he roared. "No luminary will ever wear them on their back." With that, he lifted his axe and ran through Amphion toward me.

I backed toward the door in horror.

Amphion slammed into his back-half, sending him sprawling on the floor. "SLEIGH, RUN!"

"Henna!" I motioned for her to come on and then ran into the hall with her and Gabriel on my tail.

"GO AFTER HER, MEN—" Orius shouted to the two hunters who were with him.

"No!" Amphion hollered. "Don't move unless you wish to claim dishonor and disownment!"

I raced toward the two doors we hadn't entered yet, thinking of the third-story window just above the balcony on the second floor.

No one seemed to be coming after us, though I could hear Orius shouting, "*TRAITOR!*" at the top of his lungs, and axes colliding. I hated to abandon someone who had become as important to me as Amphion, but I was useless in a fight between two of the most powerful centaurs ever born.

One of the royals shouted dreadfully in pain. Metal slammed into metal, then scraped across it.

"In here." I wrenched open the door on my right, catching sight of a burst of flames spilling from the room we'd left behind before I dashed inside. I slammed the door shut behind Gabriel.

"Henna!" someone yelped, followed by the sound of some furniture being smashed to bits down the hall.

We were met inside by a room twice the size of the other two we'd seen on that level. The back was lined with little prison cells made up of valor branches thick as a man's leg, criss-crossing over each other. Henna's parents were locked inside one. Several irrigators occupied two others, staring at my sparkling wing. Her mother reached through the limbs for her.

Henna ran into the embrace, her father's arm reaching out to put around her back.

"You're wrong! You're so wrong!" I heard Orius shouting. A slight tremor passed through the floor.

The irrigators were too busy staring at my one wing to notice that a defect had also entered the room.

"What's going on out there?" Henna's father asked.

"We've got to get you out of here so you can come to the Surface with us," Henna answered.

We all jumped when a loud *CRASH* came from our previous room.

"The Avarice locked us in," her mother said. "No one can break through this valor wood."

"I got these off Karan." Gabriel held up a ring of five keys. It made sense he would know this Avarice by name, since he kept up so well with my city.

The irrigators finally stopped staring at me to watch him as he approached Henna's parents.

"Are you a defect?" one of the men asked.

Gabriel stopped mid-reach for the lock on their prison door.

"They're called nocturnes on the Surface," I answered curtly. "They're not defects."

The irrigator drew away, looking embarrassed.

A gentle click echoed through the room, then the chains keeping Henna's parents locked inside clapped against the floor. They ran to her as Gabriel went to let the irrigators out.

The hall had become quiet, I realized.

I went to the window and ripped the covering off to see if it was safe to exit that way. Fire was spreading and consuming a large portion of the city. One of the bridges leading to the castle was in flames. It was a sickening sight to see dead luminaries burning here and there, the sort of scene that haunted your nightmares.

All for a pair of wings...

If the Avarice and their guards weren't such evil men and the wings weren't meant to save so many more lives than were lost in the trees, I would have never been able to live with myself.

I noticed Flank and two warriors running toward the castle from another bridge. Both warriors had nocturnes on their backs, while the royal was alone. Several other Elyxeos were running in a different direction out of sight.

I moved away from the window. "This level's not safe," I told the others, all free now. "There's a balcony on the second floor under this window. We'll have to jump to it. Then we need to get to the Surface. Fire's spreading all over the city."

The outer quiet was interrupted by the tapping of hooves running through the hallway.

"Why isn't it safe?" Henna's mother asked.

"Go, Sleigh!" Gabriel said. "We'll meet you on the Surface."

I rushed back to the window. Flashes of living the rest of my life in hiding began racing through my mind. "Find me near the mount—"

The door opened. I threw my hide over my head and started to lean out the window. I stopped when I saw Amphion standing in the doorway.

He stared at me blankly as he staggered into the room. A fair amount of blood had been spilt over one of his shoulders and his front. The other wing was lying lifelessly over his outstretched arms.

The luminaries backed away against the prison rooms. An irrigator went inside one, closed the door, and frantically began trying to wrap the chains around the bars.

The hide above me drooped against my head. I let it fall to the floor.

Amphion crossed the room slowly, coming steadily closer to me.

I was afraid to move. Had he just killed their head hunter to save my life? Had I just cost him one of his fiercest fighters before an impossible war? Would he hate me always for my massive error that had cost him a friend I imagined was as important to him as Jordan was to me?

He stopped directly in front of me, bowing his head and holding out the wing. "*You* will have to lead us to battle."

I looked past him to Gabriel. This wasn't what I wanted. *None* of this was what I wanted.

He crossed the room and took the wing cautiously from Amphion. The centaur allowed him to take it, turning his head to look away.

Gabriel's eyes locked with mine. I didn't want to wear the wings. I didn't want to lead them to, or even be part of, any battle.

I stared at the floor when he was nearly behind me. There would be so much responsibility resting upon my shoulders and so much death at my hands. I wouldn't have wished it on anyone.

The awful crawling sensation spread all over my back. Instinctively, my shoulders bent forward. I ignored the gasping coming from the luminaries and the spectacular sparkling light shining at my sides. The feelings of boundless energy and limit-less power filling me inside hardly mattered. There was too much to take in, too much fear and hurt on my heart.

The wings fluttered at a single thought, lifting me a few feet off the ground. Amphion only lifted his gaze when I flew directly to him and threw my arms around his shoulders. He surprised me by hugging me readily. I wept uncontrollably as I laid my head on his clean shoulder. I felt vile for all I'd lost and for what I'd forced Amphion to do.

I folded the wings against my back and let him hold my weight up, leaving my concern over the burning city behind momentarily.

Vaguely, I heard centaurs entering the room. Amphion didn't seem concerned, so I wasn't either.

We only looked up when a hand was laid over Amphion's shoulder and my arm. The hunters and their nocturne cohorts stood beside us.

"We need to make camp for the night," the hunter touching us said. "Khan's saying the hides we were given might not hold our weight well enough to make it safe to float back to the ground. We'll each need our own nocturnes to slow the fall by blowing their fire when we're nearly there. We're short by a few of them now."

Amphion sat me down. "The wings Sleigh is wearing give her extraordinary strength. She can fly down the ones without nocturnes."

The hunters exchanged skeptical looks. "Are you sure about that?"

"Sure enough to destroy Orius!" Amphion turned his whole body to stare fiercely at the other centaurs, daring them to ques-tion him further. When they didn't, he walked over to the window. "We can't go back down those stairs. We'll have to exit the castle this way. Sleigh, you wait outside and catch me. I'll be the first to be flown down." Despite the bitter look on his face, I could see the trust he was putting in me behind it.

"I'll come back for you," I said to Henna and her parents before I went to join Amphion.

Even though I'd just used my wings to fly as naturally as I use my legs to walk, staring through the dark cracks between tree limbs and thinking of how high up we were was unsettling. The truth was, neither Amphion nor I truly knew how much of the promised abilities the wings would give me.

The numbness of remembering the two men I'd lost helped me to force myself to jump out the window, spreading the enormous wings and flapping them to keep me in place.

Amphion stuck his more human half outside. He wrapped his hands around the opening and pulled himself carefully through the window, barely fitting through it. "Ready?" he asked solemnly when all he had left inside were his back legs.

I nodded, fluttering to his back as if I was riding him and wrapping my arms around his front. He wriggled his legs free of the window. We both plummeted for a split second when his body jerked downward. I recovered just as quickly and flew us over the balcony away from the castle.

It was easy, like carrying a book across a room. I laughed inwardly at the excitement of flying down between valor trees, carrying a man-beast several times my size. It felt like breathing in freedom, just as the night I'd come to the Surface for the second time.

Once we'd broken free of the trees' branches, I flew down more quickly, being careful not to go so fast I couldn't stop when I saw the ground. It was too dark to make it out from up high. As I'd expected, it wasn't long before it came zooming toward us suddenly out of the darkness.

Once on the Surface, I wasn't sure what to say. "Thank you," was all I could come up with, setting foot on land and walking around to the front of him.

"You know, Sleigh, not only is an Elyxeos' word unbreakable, we're also loyal to the death." He leaned down so he could wrap his giant hand around my arm where I wore the warrior's band. "I hope now more than ever that I did not make a mistake in placing such trust in you."

I reached out for his other arm and flew up enough that I could rest my hand over his warrior's band. It displayed considerably more beads than mine. "If I haven't proven myself to you by now, I promise that I will when we meet the Trios again."

We both scrambled out of the way when we heard someone shouting as they fell down toward us. Fire burst through the darkness suddenly and a hunting pair shot up a little ways before the flames went out and they both floated harmlessly to the ground.

Sensing how Amphion must be questioning everything, I flew right in front of him and looked him square in the eyes. "Gather hides from the men as they reach the ground. I'll be right back for them." Then my wings flapped mightily, sending me upward toward the stars.

Glancing back at Amphion, I felt all the loyalty I had for Gabriel after he saved me from the serpent, loyalty to the death, as he'd said.

The Elyxeos were truly a great people, just misguided by vengeful ancestors.

Maybe Amphion's the centaur I was meant to befriend, I thought to myself as I flew sideways to get around a bushy valor branch. *Or perhaps it was an entire colony, or even an entire race.*

37

I was so very tired. The night before seemed endless. I spent nearly all of it flying back and forth between my city and the Surface, trying to make sure no one was left behind, luminary or centaur.

Once on the Surface, luminaries were shepherded together and told that men and women without small children to look after would be forced to join the war against the Trios. Everyone else would be dropped off in the first free village we passed. The luminaries' questions directed toward me were never-ending.

Still, I refused to sleep upon centaur-back as we traveled the following day. Trios might have been anywhere, and no one could spot them faster than me. Slumber would have been impossible, anyway, with the racing thoughts of my family.

Gabriel's village just happened to be the one nearest my city and the first that we passed. He'd spoken that morning with an elderly lady in his village about getting my mother and sisters to his treehouse and explaining things to his mother.

I communicated as much as I could to my own mother when I realized Gabriel was sending them to live so near to Blush. The look of happiness on her face at hearing she would finally be reunited with her youngest daughter was priceless. It was exactly what she needed in having to deal with another daughter leading a centaur army to battle. Amphion allowed Auree to stay behind with her and Eve at my request, which was a huge relief. I couldn't help but worry about how Blush and Felicity, Gabriel's mother, would react to all this, though.

I should have been more concerned with where I was going than where I'd been. On the other hand, my family's lives had just been turned upside down. Everyone's life had been turned upside down, luminaries, nocturnes, and centaurs. The world we knew was changing. I could only hope it was for the better.

The mood among the Elyxeos was dark and subdued. It was unlike the seriousness that had previously been hanging over their heads. It was for the loss of Orius.

The League of Royal Elyxeos Centaurs hadn't said a word when Amphion told them what happened. I stood beside him with my head down, not wanting to see what sort of vile looks I was receiving.

The hunters' first thought when they discovered Orius' death was: who would lead them? They weren't told how he died, only that he was gone. No answer was given. It would be decided after the war.

Early afternoon had hardly arrived when I caught my first sight of the Elyxeos colony. "We're almost there," I called down to Amphion.

"I know that," he snapped.

I should have known he would recognize the land surrounding his city. "It looks like everyone's leaving."

Amphion stopped dead, holding up the centaur line. "What do you mean? Are they being attacked?"

"No. I think they're going toward Bellios land. They're carrying big bundles with them. The fence around the city is down, too. They're leaving from the end nearest the Bellios colony."

"They probably did that as a sign of peace to all the slaves and freemen. Do you see Marina?"

"Yes. She's close to the front of them."

"Go ask her what's going on."

I flew ahead, drawing strange looks from everyone leaving the city. I was beginning to get used to that sort of thing, though I still detested it.

The extensive line was little more than an enormously long mess. No one seemed concerned with keeping the pace of anyone else, so most of the centaurs were passing each other or being passed themselves. Children who were too young to be traveling would dart out of line here and there. Their adult would have to chase after them and carry them back into the noisy crowd.

With all the new luminaries and nocturnes, every able Elyxeos had someone on their back. There were even extras taken from the free villages who traveled on foot among the centaurs, slowing it all down. I assumed these would ride with either the Elaban or another colony who had a shortage of slaves.

I knew I had to find a way for Henna to ride with an Elyxeos. She needed all the help she could get. She'd been refused the same privilege Auree was given since she wasn't part of my family.

Davion pointed me out to Marina when he saw me. She stepped out of line to wait, looking dumbfounded. She was one of the very few Elyxeos I noticed who still had no one riding with them.

"How did it go?" she asked when I landed beside her. She seemed unable to stop eyeing my wings.

"It could have gone better. Is everyone going to the Bellios colony?"

She nodded, finally tearing her eyes away from my back. "What happened to you, Sleigh?"

"I can't talk about it right now."

"Can—can I touch them?" She resumed staring at the wings.

"I don't care." Gabriel and Eve kept touching them curiously the night before. To me they felt like the fine, silken hairs on a newborn's head.

Marina reached out and began at the top of one wing, running her fingers over the side until she couldn't reach down any lower without sitting on the ground. I shivered at the strange sensation. Her hand dropped to her side.

"We had a late start," she said. "No one could agree on what to do with the children. We decided to take them with us in the end. I can't imagine what everyone's going to do with them when we get there. It was too dangerous to leave them here, though, even with a number of adults to watch over them."

She gasped when a little nocturne boy ran into her, laughing at the older child who was chasing him. He turned to face Marina, who looked like she might rip him in half. He burst into tears and disappeared into the long line of travelers.

Marina took to muttering something about him being too stupid even to say sorry.

"Did you not want a slave riding with you?" I asked her, noticing Amphion running ahead of the others toward us.

"I don't trust them. No one questions the chief's daughter when she refuses an order."

"Gabriel could ride with you. You can trust him."

"Your husband? Hasn't Orius already claimed him?"

"Orius is dead."

Marina stared at me unblinkingly. "I don't believe it. Fifty of your best men shouldn't have been able to kill him."

Amphion was drawing rapidly closer, with Gabriel still on his back.

"It wasn't one of my kind," I said.

"Why are you leaving so late in the day?" Amphion called hotly to Marina.

"We couldn't decide what to do with the children," Marina answered.

"Now everyone will have to make camp in the open when night falls."

Marina's face burned an angry shade of purple. "It's not *my* fault."

"Have you still not chosen anyone to ride into battle with you?"

"I've been busy tending to the slaves."

Amphion snorted and reared back slightly. His voice lowered when he spoke. "I know that it is a humiliating thing to accept one of their kind onto your back, but Sleigh has taught me that having the right one might serve as a great protection to you. This Gabriel has been said to be one of the greatest of our nocturne hunters. I'd feel better if he was with you."

"*You'd* feel better? What will that matter when *I'm* living in fear? I don't need the distraction—

"Marina."

"I don't need the distraction of—"

"Marina!"

She stepped closer to him, seething with rage. "—the distraction of some slave who could drive a sword—"

"*Stop it*, right now!"

"—right into my heart from behind! I could be riding into battle with—" Her voice was partially muffled when Amphion pressed his hand over her mouth. She slapped his arm loudly and jerked her head to the side. "—WITH THE ENEMY ON MY BACK!"

"Marina," I said softly, putting a hand over hers. "Gabriel would never bring harm to one of my dearest friends."

Her eyes softened only subtly.

"You're being ridiculous," Amphion said.

"*ME?*" Marina launched right back into defensive mode.

I couldn't help but remember his response the first time he was told he would be carrying me on *his* back.

"It'll be alright," I said. "I promise."

Marina glanced at Gabriel. She took in a deep breath and let it out long and loud. "I suppose I can accept Sleigh's promise." She gave Amphion one final furious look, then bowed her head.

"Gabriel." Amphion looked back at him.

Gabriel jumped down, pausing to kiss me, and then went to climb onto Marina. My lips were left in a warm, pleasant grin.

"I'll find another companion for battle," Amphion said.

Hendraya's wings drooped behind me. It felt like he'd just ripped out part of my insides. "Another companion?"

Marina turned and trotted away.

"Yes." Amphion's eyes left her, sweeping slowly over the ground closer to me. "I'll only hold you back now."

"I don't care. I'd rather ride with you than be by myself. We don't even know how much I can do with these wings."

"That's true... We'll find out tonight after we've made camp."

"Fine, but if I'm not riding with you, I'm riding with Marina."

38

Chief called it quits for the night once we reached the same long citch we'd slept in when we came across the Dashings. The mud was dry now, so at least we wouldn't be cold and damp and squishing around in it all night.

Henna, who'd stuck unusually close to me since we stopped to make camp, was practically hyperventilating when Amphion said he needed to speak with me in private. I felt terrible about leaving, but first I introduced Henna to Parthenia and left her in her hands.

Marina slipped me a small helping of titanasaur when I went to tell Gabriel what I was doing. I ate it as I flew beside Amphion through the trees. It felt good to see a family of young valors springing up by the way. They would always inspire feelings of home for me.

Amphion stopped and watched me fly past him before I turned my course back to where he stood. We were in an open area where only tall, itchy grass and very small, spindly dead tree shoots grew.

"Do you want some?" I held out the half-emptied napkin of titanasaur.

Amphion gave me a crazed look. "I could lose my life for that."

"I know, but no one else is around. I was up high enough I would have seen them if they were."

His eyes narrowed. "You take me for a man of little honor. Put that away."

"No, I don't." I folded it up and put it in my bag. "You're the most honorable centaur I've ever met. I just thought we were close enough friends that I could share it with you."

He was standing still when I looked back at him, his mouth in a surprised O shape. "Friends?"

"Yeah."

Amphion shook his head. "The head warrior of the Elyxeos can have no friends. There isn't time for it. But I suppose we have developed a relationship of mutual trust."

It seemed he lacked friendliness the way I lacked the ability to stay out of trouble. I would take it, though.

"Have you even tried to see how fast you can fly?" Amphion asked.

"No. I've just been keeping pace with you."

"Why not try flying to camp and back as fast as you can?"

"Alright." I turned to face the way from which we'd come. I held my head up and took in a deep breath, ready for the challenge. Then I jumped and flapped my wings as hard as I could.

I screamed when I shot forward, tearing through limbs, and then landing on my side. My body bounced four times, spinning madly through the air, before it stopped. "That was terrible." I brushed off my trousers as I stood and looked around me. Amphion had been left far enough behind to spare me the embarrassment of him seeing my awful crash.

The trees must have caused it, I thought, untangling the hair that had wrapped around my neck.

This time I leaned forward when I took off, sending me soaring just over the grass. I veered sideways to avoid hitting a tree and then flapped the wings again when I felt myself descending. Each time I did this, it sent me shooting forward with a fresh burst of speed.

The edge of the forest appeared at the end of one of these bursts. I could just see the top of Elyxeos heads milling around inside the ditch from the rim of the trees. I was certainly going faster than before, but not like the Trios.

I bent my body to the right so I would glide back around toward the forest I'd just exited, wondering if the wings ever got tired. There had been no sensation of soreness or fatigue so far. They'd even cured the aching muscles in my arms when only one was attached to me.

So I flapped my wings as hard and as fast as I could. The night instantly became a dark blur racing past me. It felt like someone bumping into me when one of the wings sliced seamlessly through the trunk of a tree. It kept beating as if nothing had even happened. I hardly heard the full-grown tree fall hard to the ground before Amphion's voice was shouting, "SLEI—" and was gone just as quickly.

My feet brushed against the ground when I fluttered the wings so I would stop and hang just above it. I tried running as fast as I could on foot and found that the wind whistled piercingly as I tore through it. My surroundings weren't quite the same smear of black, but I was definitely running faster than any Elyxeos ever had.

When Amphion suddenly appeared nearly in front of me, I threw myself sideways to avoid him and slid through the grass on my stomach, tearing an enormous amount of it from the earth.

Amphion hurried to my side and leaned over so he could help me up as I spat out a disgusting clump of dirt. "You've certainly inherited swifter speed than a Trios," Amphion said, dusting me off roughly. "See if you can make fire."

I'd hardly gotten my right arm out in front of me before it was all ablaze. I screamed, feeling absolutely terrified, and shook it around until it went out. Surprisingly, it didn't hurt at all. The short sleeve over my shoulder was still burning, so I patted it until it went out.

"I can't believe how easy that was," I said, holding out my other hand and igniting a smaller fire in the palm. It felt like something in between water running over my skin and a warm breeze rushing by, lighter than water but heavier than air.

The light in my skin had gone out. It was an awful sight, like my identity was stripped away. I closed my hand, smothering the flame. My glow returned at the mere thought.

"See, Sleigh?" Amphion said, putting a hand on my shoulder. "You're better off set free at war."

"I don't care. You're my greatest ally. I want you safe, and I'm terrified of fighting centaurs. I don't even know if I'll be able to kill them. I *need* you with me, Amphion."

His eyes were drawn to my shoulder, where he rubbed what was left of the singed fabric with his thumb. "We'll have to get you some nocturne clothing."

"Is theirs fireproof?"

Amphion's forehead wrinkled, his eyebrows pressing closer together. "I keep forgetting how you're so unknowing. Yes, we make it from titanasaur hide. It's entirely fireproof." His hand withdrew, accompanied by a long, weary sigh. "I suppose I could allow myself a friend. Just don't speak a word of it to anyone else, especially the Royal League. I'd seem pathetic." I got a good look at his long, Elyxeos teeth as he spoke the last sentence bitterly.

"But isn't Marina your friend?"

"What?"

"You were worried about her safety. That's why you

suggested she carry Gabriel. And she always looks a little happier when she sees you."

He stared at me strangely, almost painfully. I caught a twitch of a muscle here and there in his face. "There's so much more to it than what you imply. But that is a story for another time."

A comfortable silence settled between us. I could only guess at what had happened between them.

Amphion disappeared into the shadows, walking toward camp.

I spun around anxiously when I heard his feet tearing through fallen leaves, his shield and axe scraping brashly together as they were drawn from the straps over his back. I tore my sword from its sheath. The shadows were illuminated by my burning light, then suddenly went dark when fire burst in two straight lines running up over my sides.

"Show yourself!" Amphion demanded.

I was forced to ignore whatever was approaching to try and put out the fires burning from my ankles to my armpits. Part of my trousers was already flying open at the bottom where a slit had been scorched halfway up my leg.

"Relax, it's only me," Marina's voice came from the dark.

My clothes were ruined, but at least there was enough left of them where it really mattered. Light returned to my skin on command and I saw Gabriel jumping off Marina's back so he could run toward me.

"Are you alright?" he was asking. "How'd you catch on fire?"

I had to hold my parts up as I flew closer to him, since part of the waistline was split open. "I'm fine. Do you think one of the other nocturnes has an extra set of clothes I could wear?"

"I can find something for you to wear," Marina said, standing directly in front of Amphion.

Gabriel knelt on the ground so he could run his hands over the outside of my legs.

"How long have you been here?" Amphion asked her.

"I only just got here. Gabriel said he saw Sleigh flying out and into the trees like something was wrong, so we came to check on you."

"Was it the wings that gave you fire?" Gabriel whispered to me.

I nodded, taking his hand and walking toward the ditch. "We'll meet you back at camp," I told the centaurs when we walked past them. I figured they would appreciate time to themselves. Whatever had happened between them had obviously never been resolved.

Gabriel kept glancing back at my wings during our silent walk. They seemed to fascinate him.

I, on the other hand, wanted nothing to do with them. They'd been the cause of so much death already. To me, having this incredible power was hardly worth the lives it would cost. I was going to have to kill centaurs, and maybe nocturnes. No one knew if the Trios' nocturnes would be fighting on their side against their will or otherwise. The more I thought about it, the more lifeless my skin became.

"Sleigh?" Gabriel asked when I sniffled. "What's wrong?"

I shook my head, fighting to keep the lump in my throat from bursting out of me in tears.

We stopped under the last trees before the dusty field separating us from to the ditch. Gabriel ran his hand up and down over my arm. "Whatever it is, Sleigh, you can tell me."

"I don't want these wings." I hated to cry, but couldn't keep it in any longer.

He put a hand between my back and a wing and turned me to face him. Their dazzling sparkle reflected beautifully against his skin. "Why not?"

"I don't want to do any of this. I don't want to go live with the Bellios. Henna will be useless at war. She'll probably be killed before she even knows what happened. And Jordan's dead because I was so reckless trying to save the wings. I don't want to be with him, but I don't want him dead either. If we lose it'll be my fault. The Trios will be targeting me, so maybe I shouldn't ride with Amphion because they'll target him too. I don't want him to die, but I don't want to be alone. I don't want you or Marina or anyone to die. These wings are the worst thing that's ever happened to me!" I leaned back against the tree behind me and reached up to press my hands against my eyes, letting out a sob.

"I'm sorry you're so unhappy." His voice came out so low and so serious, creating a deep rumbling sound. "But don't let it put out your lovely light. Someday this will all be over, just a memory we share."

"The wings will still be on my back. The Avarice killed the Elyxeos who wore them a century ago. What if that happens to me?"

"I won't let that happen." Gabriel stepped closer and wrapped his arms around my waist, pressing me gently into the tree. "Remember what would have happened if you'd stayed in the valors. Blush would have been captured and sold off to one of the crueler colonies. I don't even want to think of what she would have had to endure."

My arms went around him at the memory of witnessing his death in the sky. It was a tremendous reminder of why I'd gone through so much.

"No matter what you're forced to face, I'll always be here for you. Try to find peace in that." Gabriel leaned forward to kiss me.

Hidden in true darkness for the first time, I pressed away from the tree and into his body. His kisses were so delicious and so very addictive. Heat washed over my skin. A peculiar scuttling sensation spread over my torso and legs. The wings opened wide when I sucked in a deep breath. They reached past my sides and wrapped around Gabriel's back, pressing him against me.

He let out a muffled groan. His hand went to the back of my head. A burst of flames poured from his mouth into mine. I finally realized a gift given me by the wings that I could truly appreciate. There was no risk of being burned by my nocturne any longer.

I heard a lot of strange crinkling sounds, followed by Gabriel's hands rubbing against the bare skin of my back. More crinkling came from all over my front when I shifted. Something dry and wispy landed against my foot.

My wings withdrew and I took a step back to see what it was. I gasped when I saw the little fires burning all over my body. One of my legs was nearly bare. A bit of curled-up, black cloth hung lifelessly over my hips and part of the other leg. And the charred pieces of my shirt left smoking across my front were mostly drifting away. The back was long gone. I crossed my wings over the front of my body as a shield, afraid there would be nothing else left to cover it pretty soon.

Gabriel was already pulling off his shirt. "I should have known that would happen," he said, holding it out to me. "Put this on and wait here. I'll go find something for you to wear."

"I can't pull that on over my wings." I stepped back and bumped into the tree, feeling mortified.

His arm fell against his side. He offered me an odd sort of look. "Don't be embarrassed, Sleigh. You're the most beautiful woman I've ever known."

My heart sped up a bit. Fire burned gently against my back. The wind brushing against my naked skin and staring at his glorious, masculine chest put desire into me.

He moved closer, so I scooted around the tree to get away. My voice rose over the branches sweeping against each other in the wind. "I want you now as I wanted you before, Gabriel. This is much too dangerous."

The hot steam coming off him blew toward me. "Don't you trust me?"

"Of course I do."

He tried approaching me once more. This time I stood still, trembling with trepidation and longing. He put a hand on my neck and kissed me tenderly and fleetingly. Then he rested his forehead against mine. "I love you, Sleigh. Any man would kill to have you for his wife."

I chuckled at that. It seemed ridiculous that we were still pretending to be married.

"Someday," he whispered, reminding me of our promise.

"Someday." I nodded.

He left me to hide behind the tree until he returned. I was careful to keep my light out as I waited.

Everything was too mixed up inside for me to say exactly what I was feeling.

I looked to the stars, hoping for guidance. It startled me to see them swirling into shapes. It was exactly like the night of my eighteenth birthday. I glanced at the wings, wondering if they'd given me the gift of seeing the stars as a nocturne seer. A second moon made up of stars lit the sky. Centaurs of every kind took shape below it, slaying one another. It was impossible to recognize anyone or to tell who was winning.

A single tear rolled down the side of my face as I thought of the only thing that bothered me more than killing someone else: the fear of watching those I loved being slain. Losing my father and Jordan was more than enough.

"Sleigh!" Henna's voice called me back to earth. She was riding closer on a woman Elyxeos' back, searching the gloominess for me.

"I'm over here." I stood and waved a hand at her, but kept my light out.

"Thank you," she said to the centaur when she climbed off. The Elyxeos bowed before she ran back toward the ditch, leaving Henna in my care.

"I can't see you, Sleigh."

"Follow my voice. I'm over here."

Henna came closer until she saw my arm waving. "Gabriel asked me to bring these to you," she said, holding out a pair of trousers and a shirt with very little sleeve. They were both made of titanasaur hide. "He said your clothes caught on fire but you didn't get burned." She turned her back while I changed.

I was grateful for him sending her with a change of clothes. I imagined he felt like me, wanting desperately to explore the dangerous yearnings we had for each other's body, but knowing it was wrong. He was a man of true honor, like Amphion. I was lucky to have him.

"Apparently the wings allow me to create fire like a nocturne," I told Henna, pulling the pants on.

I held the shirt up in front of me. The back had been cut open and little holes punched through along the sides where cord was tied to it. That would allow me to get it on without hindering my wings. "Can you tie this for me?" I asked Henna when I had it on.

"Sure." We both turned so my back was facing her now. "Your Surface friend seems nice. She got really upset when her boyfriend came over and started talking to me, though."

"Crawler?"

"That's right."

"I can't believe her," I said, shaking my head. "She'll never learn."

"She told me everyone thinks Gabriel's your husband before Crawler came along."

I stretched out my arms and legs as we took up walking back toward camp, trying to get a feel for this new material. It was a bit stiffer than what I was used to. "Yeah, he claimed that when I was taken so he could be with me as a slave."

"I can't believe how much has happened to you in the little time you were gone."

"Me neither." It was enough to change a person, too much for me to handle on my own. I was inexpressibly grateful to have Gabriel and Henna there to help me keep my head.

If only I wasn't so worried about her giving way to fear. I would simply have to add her with Gabriel, Marina, and Amphion to the list in my heart of those I was dead set on protecting when we went to battle.

39

I'd never before seen so many centaurs or people as I did when we approached the Bellios city. At first they were all focused on the enormous Elyxeos centaurs coming to join their army. People were running around, shouting that they'd finally arrived.

The attention slowly shifted to the luminary with wings in the sky. I hated the way they were all watching me. It would have been so much easier to blend in with the colony below me.

I could have ridden with Amphion if I really wanted to, but it seemed demeaning since it wasn't really necessary. Even when we were forced to fight, I imagined I would only hover over or beside him, so we could still fight together.

My wings flapped rhythmically up and down, keeping me in place so I could take it all in.

The city appeared as it did in Icy's painting. In size, the buildings were somewhere between slave and Elyxeos housing. They were long and boxy, but not nearly as tall as the centaur housing to which I'd become accustomed. Each one seemed to house multiple Bellios families. A small area of tents squished close together was at the heart of the fenced-in city; slave housing, I had to assume. A myriad of luminaries stood around them watching us.

An overflow of centaurs spilled out over the land south of the city. The smallest in numbers and loneliest-seeming were the Elabans.

Nearby, the Striplings had set up camp with a fair number of luminaries and nocturnes. They'd built little lean-tos against trees. They were all outside at the moment, though, training to fight with men or women on their backs. They wore silver helmets and a shimmering piece of armor made up of small articulated pieces, like the scales of a silver serpent, over the more human-like half of their bodies. They seemed remarkably friendly with their riders.

The Dashings made up more than half the centaurs outside the city. They'd set up hammocks between trees, with little coverings over each one. These covers were made of sticks woven together, like a giant upside-down bird's nest. Most of the adults were training to fight with nocturnes on their backs. It was beautiful to watch the Dashing and nocturne children playing together like they shared no significant differences. The Striplings were set up particularly close to them.

A group of the largest Bellios ran from their city to meet the Elyxeos. Each one wore a crown of small bones atop their heads, with jutted lower jaws and dark hair growing down the sides of their faces.

I started to descend toward The League of Royal Elyxeos Centaurs, but stopped when a strange movement caught my eye to the west. An ivory antler shook back and forth past a little hill in the distance. Another antler blended almost perfectly into the grass on the other side of the overgrown mound.

Trios in hiding were watching us. They couldn't be allowed to report that Elyxeos had joined the army they opposed.

I soared toward the royals, offering two words to Amphion,

"Trios spies!" as I tore past him toward the Bellios city. I reached out for one of the enormous support posts at the side of the main gate to their city and ripped it from the ground.

Two of the exiting Bellios ran out of my way. One reached out and tried to grab my leg when he saw the destruction I was causing. I flew fast enough he didn't even come close.

The post must have been ten feet tall and half as wide around as my body. It was robust and could easily be used against more than one centaur at a time.

I flew as fast as I could, racing to beat the terror inside, before it managed to overtake me. The air I was slicing through hissed angrily through my ears.

A fuzzy white body leaned away from the hill. It offered my first really good look at a Trios. He said something to the set of antlers poking out from behind the hillside grass. Two more Trios centaurs halfway appeared. Their frost-painted fur was beautiful. Their long bodies were slender and built perfectly for speed. But they had sort of a stupid expression on their faces, with dark wide set eyes, like they were looking in two different directions.

I was nearly there.

One shot away from the hill and the Bellios city, followed by four others. I was gaining on them, moving closer and closer to the ground. Two looked back, baring their teeth. Their eyes were like murky glass orbs protruding from their faces. One sucked in a huge breath and let out a horrible screeching sound.

I faltered, trying for a moment to cover my ears with the wings. I recovered quickly, reaching the fat post back over one shoulder and swinging it into their sides, full force.

The impact against their yielding bodies was revolting. Three Trios soared over the hill. Their legs curled strangely beneath them. Their weapons fell behind them when they reached madly through thin air for something to grab onto. I swung the post the other way and sent number four flying behind me.

Number five looked back. "Demon luminary," he said in a most disturbing voice. It sounded like he was drawing air instead of letting it out as he spoke, a raspy bird-like sound.

He began zipping back and forth, making it difficult to hit him. I zoomed straight at him, but he darted around a tree. Then he stopped short when I tried to swing at him, so I went too far. This was getting frustrating.

When I heard Elyxeos shouting somewhere nearby, I dropped the fence post and swooped straight down on top of him. I took hold of his antlers and flew us both up away from the ground. He tried to stab me with a dagger. I kicked it out of his hand hard enough to break his arm. Guilt burned in my stomach at his painful bellowing, little fiery bubbles dancing circles around the inside of my waist.

"Put me down, demon!" number five shouted hoarsely.

"Why are you attacking us?" I asked, fighting not to let him go when he started thrashing around.

He became still, cringing and holding his arm to his chest. The muscles surrounding his bulging eyes shifted and sunk inward where eyebrows should have been until they were pointed right at me. "How should I know?"

I couldn't help but shiver at his strange voice and the odd look he was giving me. "You don't even know why you're fighting and killing everyone?"

"The king commands it, so it is so."

The Elyxeos must have chased after me when they saw where I was going. Amphion's men had already killed the first three trios. Now they had number four trapped nearby inside the tight circle they'd made with their bodies. The Elyxeos warriors were swinging swords and axes so wildly trying to kill him, they were lucky they hadn't massacred each other. The unarmed Trios was shooting around between them, trying to find the best means of escape.

"Where's your king?" I asked the Trios beneath me.

"Will you put me down if I tell you?" His lack of specification in location only added to how brainless he seemed.

"Yes."

"At camp. He's in the big blue tent in the middle of everyone. Follow the river that runs through Elaban land north."

I looked back at the Elyxeos. They'd finished off number four and were now running toward me. I flew to meet them.

"No," number five gasped. "Don't put me down there! GET ME AWAY FROM THEM!"

"*Amphion*," I shouted, feeling cruel. I dropped the Trios so he would fall right in front of him.

The Trios twisted midair so he was falling face up, staring at me with those popping, black eyes. Amphion held his axe ready to slice through him when he was close enough.

I had to look away. Right or wrong, I felt rotten. My wings opened wide to allow me to float slowly down.

"You did well," Amphion said, nodding to me when I landed beside him.

"Can I talk to you in private?" I muttered.

He moved away from the others without answering. We walked across soft, green grass while the others took the corpses away for burial.

"Have you ever met a Trios?" I asked Amphion, watching my feet move rhythmically below me.

"Only the ones I've killed recently."

"That one I just had, he was like a hollow shell controlled by a king. He seemed more like a dumb animal than a centaur. Do you think they're all like that?"

"What exactly did he say?"

"He told me he doesn't know why they're attacking, except

that the king told them to do it. But it wasn't what he said. It was the vacant look in his eyes and his primordial voice. It was really creepy."

"I've never heard that about them. It's possible something's changed in the decades since we saw them last."

Our walk had ceased. Amphion waited patiently for whatever other questions I needed to ask.

There was only one more answer I wanted. "I would do anything to avoid this war," I said. "The only way I can think of to prevent any more fighting is to talk to the Trios king. Maybe I can find out what he wants, and how to stop all this."

"We don't even know where to find the king."

"That Trios said to follow the river north of Elaban land. If you tell me how to get there, it shouldn't be a problem."

"It's too dangerous. You can't go walking into a Trios' camp alone. Even if we all came with you, it wouldn't be enough."

"I've thought about that. Once I locate the king, I'll fly down from the sky and straight up with him. I can fly faster than they can run. It'll be fine."

Amphion shook his head. "It won't matter. If there's one thing I'm certain hasn't changed, it's the absence of their hearts. Trios have no care for others. Nothing you say to him will make any difference."

"What if I brought him here? What if he saw what he was up against, or his life was threatened if he wouldn't withdraw his purposes? It would be better than sitting here waiting to be attacked."

"It sounds important enough that we should consult the others of the league."

I loved that he included me in his suggested meeting. "That would waste precious time."

"Sleigh, if something happened to you, all would be lost."

"Nothing will happen." I knew at hearing his skepticism that

I'd already made the decision inside to go. "I can ask someone else how to get there."

Amphion's lip curled. "You are the most stubborn, willful slave I have ever known. But you're also the best at narrowly avoiding death... Nothing I say will change your mind, will it?"

I shook my head.

"Very well. Night will fall soon. Fly east past the Bellics city until you see Hendraya's stone. The Wings' form was carved into it just before his death. Nearly everyone's forgotten the meaning behind them by now. Once you reach it, follow the North Star past the Stripling colony. It'll be empty, but you'll know it by the pond they created between the slave and centaur housing. It's heart-shaped to remind everyone of the oath of peace they recently took. Apparently, they developed a correspondence with the Dashings only recently and treat their slaves more kindly. Continue north until you see the Elaban colony. It's a muddy mess with wooden paths built to get from one place to another, the ugliest city ever built I've been told. Never had a reason to go there and see it myself. There is a river that runs narrow through the city."

Bellios were crowding together outside their city now. The other colonies were staring at us intently. The rest of the Elyxeos seemed to have lost patience and were running in our general direction.

"Thank you, Amphion." I hardly turned and lifted from the ground before he grabbed my arm.

"Be quick and be careful. I cannot explain it, but my heart is protective over you." Though his face hid well anything to match what he said.

A smile didn't seem like enough to repay his kind words. My wings flapped slightly in reverse so I could give him a good hug. "So is mine." I drew away to hover in front of him momentarily. "I'll be fine."

"I know."

I thought of going back to tell Gabriel what I was doing as I flew away, recalling what my disappearance had done to Jordan. But he was nothing like Jordan. He knew my true nature better than any luminary who had known me my entire life. If anyone would understand my need to do this, it was Gabriel.

40

The Stripling city was easily recognizable. It was a grisly sight to see the heart-shaped pond halfway filled with dead centaurs and luminaries.

I didn't have to fly for very long after that before I discovered the Elaban city, spread out around the slimmest part of a river. As muddy as the land truly was, it was every bit as beautiful. The walkways leading from one house to another were lined with smooth white stones that reflected the moonlight like tiny mirrors. Crates filled with flowers and vegetables growing inside were set in rows above ground. Of course the number of corpses left behind by the Trios was even greater here. Even from the sky, the stench of death and decay was unbearable.

It wasn't difficult to turn away from this city and follow the river opposite the way it ran. I saw nothing but images of twinkling stars replicated on the surface of the water below me for a long time.

An uneasy shiver passed through me. I needed to get this over with. After making certain the light in my skin was completely out, I put on every bit of speed the wings had in them. The water became little more than a blurry, star-dotted line in the night.

Camp fires were suddenly beneath me. The white centaurs moving around them didn't notice me diving for the highest boughs of one tree. The leaves surrounding me were bristly and dry, scratching against my skin.

White and gray tents were set up all along the ground beneath the trees. The land wasn't nearly as muddy as it had been in Elaban land, but it was still fairly marshy, with bits of fog rolling over the damp earth.

It struck me again how mindless the Trios milling their way around appeared.

I seemed to be on the outskirts of their campsite, with nothing but water and empty land behind me. Slowly and carefully, I walked over a long branch through prickly foliage.

The only safe way to get closer to the center of their camp was to creep through the thickest part of the trees.

The deeper I went, the deeper the risk I was taking burned inside of me. Hendraya's Wings gave me a certain amount of protection, but I doubted they would make me immune from an attack waged by an entire Trios colony.

Bits of a glittering gold flame caught my eye up ahead, past stabbing limbs and tents quivering quietly in the wind. I worked my way closer until I could see poles as tall as the centaurs stabbed into the ground, surrounding a giant blue tent. An exquisite gold fire burned fiercely at the top of each one, like fallen stars.

Two Trios with sharp-looking black eyes stood watch out front. Their bodies lacked the lithe, agile appearance of the former Trios I'd seen. They were built more like the other breeds of centaurs, save the enormous Elyxeos. Their fur had turned silver. Their antlers burned a yellowy-orange, like fresh teardrops fallen from a volcano onto their heads.

I looked to the stars when I'd reached the tree nearest the tent. They revealed nothing.

There was a shadow of movement inside the tent. Whoever it was appeared to be alone. I decided the best way to do this would be to swoop in, grab the tent with the Trics inside it, and fly back to the Elyxeos. As long as I was fast enough, there should be no real danger involved.

I exhaled and flapped the wings more mightily than ever before, driven by absolute desperation to end the killing, sending me barreling into the bottom of the tent. The guards only had time to bump into each other trying to twist around and see what was happening. I wrapped my arms around the skirting, taking it all in my arms, and flew straight up until I was well above the trees.

"The king!" someone shouted below. "Call for the archers!" I was too terrified to think much on his very normal voice.

I turned my course to follow the river away at breakneck speed.

"What's happening?" the king's muffled voice came from inside the upside down tent. He was thrashing around so violently, the cloth kept slipping and pulling from my arms. I was forced to scoot it back up over and over.

The twinkling of stones inside the Elaban city was approaching. I immediately located the North Star and flew opposite the way I'd come.

A ripping sound came from somewhere inside the tangled tent. "I—demand—to know—what's happening—" An antler stabbed through a small tear below me. Fingers wrapped around the edges of the gap and tore it open wider, little by little.

"You'll fall to your death if you keep that up," I said, flying us even higher.

We were drawing near to the Stripling city.

The antler moved back and forth as the king fought to withdraw it. The Stripling city had come and gone before he pressed his face to the tent so he could see out of the hole. I shivered when the rip was turned so he could stare at me. The skin seemed to roll away from his black eyeballs when they opened wider.

"You're wearing the wings," he said. "We thought they'd disappeared from existence ages ago." His eyes became slits, like two little grins. "But we have our own secret weapon too, you know."

"You can tell The League of Royal Elyxeos Centaurs all about it." I hated the way he was looking at me. Something about being this close to a Trios was like having rats scurrying across my neck.

The hole became dark when he moved away from it and became still. I felt a little better, until he started laughing. It was a heartless sound, the sort you'd expect to hear when someone's laughing at another who's fallen and been badly injured. I couldn't wait to drop him off.

We passed the cracked, decrepit wings of stone shortly after. It seemed the return was going considerably faster than my departure. Of course I had a better idea of where I was going this time, and I was a lot more anxious to get to our camp than I was to the Trios'.

Luminaries and nocturnes partially on fire lit the massive camp in the far distance. From what I'd seen of the Trios camp, it looked like we had them in numbers. There was at least twice as many of us as there were of them. After seeing what so few Trios could do to Slade's colony, however, it wasn't all that reassuring.

Everything rested on my shoulders. And what if the Trios king really did have a secret weapon to match the power of the wings? I began feeling a bit queasy.

I searched the colonies once I'd reached the entryway to the

Bellios city. There was a new group alongside the Dashings, the farthest away from the Bellios. Here, Elyxeos slept peacefully out in the open on blankets they'd laid on the ground. Guards positioned to surround them kept watch nearby.

It was easy to distinguish the six sitting in a circle not far away from the rest of our colony. They were all awake, talking quite seriously about something.

Amphion was watching the sky so I let my skin shine full-blaze. He stood and pointed me out to the others.

"I need rope!" I shouted, descending slowly over them.

The Elyxeos stared at each other and shrugged.

"ROPE!"

I was surprised to see Bones running from the colony with a rope wrapped over his shoulder.

The king began laughing again. "You don't need to tie me up."

"You can't honestly expect me to trust you?" I answered.

"No, no. I suppose not."

Bones was handing the rope to the chief, watching me glide lower toward them.

"How'd you know?" I asked.

He returned my smile. "I saw it in the stars."

Amphion reared back suddenly and reached out for the king, jerking him downward. I pulled back. "Sorry," I called to him when I realized what had happened. "I'm dropping him."

I let the tent go and the royals all scuffled against one another, turning the Trios king onto his side. One end of the long stretch of rope was used to tie his four legs together, and one end was used to tie his arms behind his back.

He was an ordinary-looking Trios. His body was slender and beautiful. His eyes were smart. He wore no crown or adornment of any sort.

I wondered if the six even noticed that the king wasn't

fighting to stop them as I landed beside the nocturne. "Thanks, Bones. Are you still mad at me?"

He shifted to one side, staring at the ground guiltily. "I had no right to be mad before." He lifted his gaze to my face, offering a friendly half-grin. "Not to mention that you somehow talked these guys into freeing us. I can't believe anyone could stay mad at you after that."

"Good." I laughed. "You should get to know Henna. She's been my best friend my whole life and she's completely unattached to any man. She's scared out of her mind right now, and I know what a great guy you are. She could use you for a friend, at least."

"We've got him," Chief said, gripping his sword and standing over the Trios' head.

"What's this about what a great guy Bones is?"

I jumped when someone whispered in my ear. "Gabriel," I muttered, wrapping my arms around him.

"Good luck," Bones said, leaving us behind.

"End the attacks or die," Amphion snarled to the king.

The Trios only began laughing again.

"What's so funny?"

"He's been doing that off and on the entire way here," I said.

"You, you making a demand of me... like you have any power at all," the king said through his crazed laughter. "That's hilarious."

"Why did you come here?" I asked the Trios. "Why are you killing everyone?"

The laughter got quieter. He stared at me, looking very amused. "For them." He nodded to Gabriel. "For their beautiful, red-hot bleeding."

"He's mad," Skelleon said.

"You're the ones who are mad," the king cackled loudly.

"Don't you know what happens when you fill a centaur with nocturne blood?"

My face crumpled in disgust.

"Are you telling me you've been putting their blood into your bodies?" the chief asked, looking every bit as sickened as I was.

"Yes, yes. My subjects. Drained them all one at a time, then filled them up with nocturne blood."

The Elyxeos stared at each other and at Gabriel looking horrified.

"Our children all died, and most of the grown ones lost their minds, but some of them—some of them have become Trios demon lords. They'll kill your lady of the wings. They'll kill you all and have your fire-slaves' blood."

"Enough of this madness!" Amphion shouted, kicking the Trios in the stomach hard enough to draw an awful groan. "You will not persist in threatening Sleigh. End this war now or die at my hands."

The king laughed hysterically, but had to stop to cringe at his aching side.

"Stop that!"

"You're wasting precious time," the king chuckled. "Tonight we attack. My army should be here any time now." He cackled loudly, without any restraint this time.

"This is your last chance to end the war," Amphion persisted.

The king continued to laugh at his demand.

Amphion let out an angry shout as he swung his axe through the air and took off the trios king's head in one clean cut. The laughter finally ceased.

"We've got to alert the colonies," Amphion said to the other Elyxeos. "Gabriel, get to Marina. Come on, Sleigh." Everyone took off running in slightly different directions, all toward the mass of armies. I flew alongside Amphion, unwilling to leave his side in the face of such danger.

Everything the Trios king said made sense. The gasping voices and vacant faces of the spies had to have been a few of those who had lost their minds. The demon lords must have been standing watch outside his tent. Just because they hadn't looked that impressive didn't mean they wouldn't have devastating abilities.

"*Trios will attack on this night—*" Amphion rode through the Striplings and Dashings shouting.

Chief and his father were racing through our colony calling out to them. The others had entered the Bellios city and were alerting them to the upcoming attack. The Elaban were already drawing weapons and standing at attention.

Amphion had hardly gotten a quarter of the way through the Dashing camp when we heard a sound unlike anything we had ever heard before. Actually, it was a lot of different but similar sounds, coming and going as smoke being carried in every direction by the wind. Loud, angry animal-like shouting. Enormous, rolling voices, mixed with the sound of trees being uprooted and left to fall.

A fair number of women began ushering children into the forest.

Everyone left behind stood ready in arms. Some truly looked unafraid. Others failed to hide their fear. I imagined I must look petrified, though my sword was drawn ready at my shoulder.

41

I gasped and fell out of the air when I saw the monsters leaping high over the back walls into the Bellios city. They were something like the two guards I'd seen outside the king's tent, but even larger than an Elyxeos. Their bones bent at odd angles, but didn't inhibit their movement. The skin on their skull seemed to have been taken and twisted to the right, creating a lopsided face and sideways jutted jaws. There were only a few of them, but that was all they really needed. They were breathing fire and setting the whole city to flames, smashing buildings and centaurs with hammers taller than me.

Bellios were swinging and stabbing and fighting with all their might, but to no avail.

I didn't want to face them, and never would have been able to without the wings. There was no one else who stood a chance, though. So I shot over the Dashings, over the Elabans, and into the city. My hands were trembling so badly, I could hardly keep hold of my sword.

One of the Trios beasts saw me coming. He threw his arms back as he leaned forward and let out an awful shout with such power, I felt it against my skin. A burst of light was followed by fire erupting all around me. I pointed my sword for the back of his throat. Everything became a blur as I shot toward him even faster than the night before. And then my sword was buried in his mouth and sticking out of the back of his neck. I let go of the hilt when he fell over sideways.

My throat felt like fire. I was suddenly throwing up all over the ground beside him.

A hammer slammed into my side. I only felt a nasty sting as I was sent airborne over the city walls. I smashed into the ground, stunned. Cracks split open beneath me. Pieces of earth were torn and tossed aside.

Senseless-looking Trios began tumbling over me, slamming into other ones and causing a mass fall. An entire army of these creatures was running around me toward the outer city centaurs.

Amphion!

"Your king's dead," I shouted, flying over the Trios. "Stop! There's no one left to lead you!"

They ignored me.

I flew over their heads, veering toward the fence to grab another post. Dirt rained over my head when I tore it from the ground. I swung the post through the Trios as I shot toward the Elyxeos, sending the enemy centaurs flying toward our friendly colonies to be slaughtered. Most of them weren't expecting it and dropped their weapons as they soared through the air, making them more vulnerable.

The Trios at the front of their lines had nearly merged with the Striplings and Dashings. I barreled through those Trios, smashing them all this way and that.

Then I flew straight to the Elyxeos. Everyone I cared about was part of that colony. They were my greatest concern.

"Alright, Sleigh?" Amphion asked, when I swooped down

and stopped in front of him. He stood at the head of the Elyxeos with the five other royals.

"Physically," I answered, wondering if I would ever recover from the abuse and killing I'd just inflicted on so many Trios.

I sucked in a deep breath and zoomed into the Trios, using the fence post to send as many as I could flying helplessly into the Elyxeos army.

Men and women were screaming behind me. The sounds of fighting and dying were merciless.

I dropped the post and opened my wings so I could shoot through the Trios at knee-level, knocking them over and breaking bones. My stomach churned dangerously at every dreadful *crack*.

I sliced through them three times before I flew back to the Elyxeos. Gabriel held a shield in front of Marina when a Trios cut through an Elyxeos in front of her. She was next. Acting on pure adrenaline, I dove toward them, extending one wing so the Trios smashed a spiked club into it. The shield in front of Marina absorbed some of the impact. I flapped the wing so the Trios went flying toward the Bellios city.

One of the demon Trios was tearing through the Dashings now.

I searched the horror for Amphion and saw a flash of white race past him before he jerked out of the way. He'd been stabbed at his side!

I can't stand this! I thought to myself.

Then I put one arm under Marina's lower half and carried her to Amphion, where I did the same to him. Both were shouting and trying to figure out what had just happened as I flew them into the woods.

"What are you doing?" Amphion barked. His legs dangled and kicked like a marionette's.

"I can't handle having any of you killed," I said. "Amphion's been stabbed, Marina. You take care of him and keep him hidden in the woods."

"It's just a cut; I'll be fine. I'm not running like a coward from a war I've trained for my whole life."

We were plenty deep enough in the forest now that they should be safe. I flew down and sat them on the ground, Gabriel still on Marina's back.

"No," I said in my fiercest voice, forcing flames around my face to get the point across. "None of you are leaving this area. There are plenty of places to hide here."

"Sleigh—" Gabriel began.

I cut him off with a kiss, then flew away before anyone could protest. The wings smacked against branches until I'd ascended above them all. Then I flew back toward the fighting.

THE BELLIOS CITY was completely destroyed. The ground inside was littered with corpses. The ones still fighting didn't stand a chance.

I flew toward one of the demons, throwing a shoulder into him. Our bodies collided and were thrown in opposite directions. These beasts were so extraordinarily massive and powerful.

I located my sword still in the only dead demon Trios. My throat constricted when I flew down to grab it. The tip was dripping crimson when I pulled it out. I dry-heaved a couple of times before flying to one of the others. Their hammer smashed against my sword and shoulder, knocking me out of the city. The sword was destroyed.

There was no denying it; I needed help.

I decided to fly into the weaker Trios. Their lack of intelligence didn't seem to be hindering them in any way. They were cutting through everyone, leaving them for dead.

The night became little more than a blur. Forcing myself to act without thinking or feeling was the only way to get through it.

But failure was overtaking me. I was no warrior as Hendrava. Even if I was, I doubted there would have been any hope.

My eyes flooded as I looked to the heavens, fluttering away from the chaos. "Please," I whimpered. "I'm not enough. We're going to lose this war. Please, please help me."

The stars remained still. I shut my eyes and cried, considering taking Henna and Parthenia and their families to hide with Amphion, and trying to help them escape. It would never work, though. There were too many Trios. Everyone else was dying. I couldn't abandon this fight, but there was no point in going on.

An eerie quiet that seemed to burst inside my ears drew my eyes back to the conflict. Most of the centaurs had paused to stare at the silver sparks pouring from the sky, swirling like a tornado. Only the Elyxeos took advantage of the stillness to massacre every bewildered Trios within arms' reach.

A fresh group of centaurs were pouring out from under the trees, stopping dead to stare as well. Judging by the mixture of striped, horned, black, and purple centaurs, I decided it was The Deliverance. There were enough of them to make up a small colony on their own.

The sparkly funnel twisted at the bottom in pursuit of the new arrivals. Centaurs of The Deliverance suddenly scattered. They tried running away, but the funnel washed over them one by one, leaving each with their own pair of silver wings.

Their backs arched horribly. They reached frantically for the skin where the wings had attached themselves, then stopped when they saw what had happened.

An Elaban Deliverer stamped one foot into the ground and let out a violent howl full of flames before he charged at the Trios. The wounded on our side of the battle stepped aside to let the winged colony step in.

I folded my hands together and held them up toward the sky. "Thank you. Thank you so very much."

Then I sailed back into the city, where I was met with help from at least fifty aerial centaurs. Together we distracted, combined against, and slaughtered what demons the Trios king had created. Two more outside the city had already been taken down by others from The Deliverance.

I left them to finish off the lesser Trios in search of Henna. There was so much destruction and blood on the ground. The Elyxeos were still fighting and falling.

"HENNA!" I screamed, searching them all. "Henna, where are you?!"

Skelleon was dead. Davion was dead. One of the chief's arms hung uselessly wounded at his side, but he fought bravely with the other.

"Henna," I cried, flying down lower.

I saw her mother holding a shield up to protect her face and cringing behind it. Her centaur slashed at a white blur, but fell dead at a lightning-fast cut to her throat.

I shot toward the Trios and smacked it toward the Dashings with one of my wings. Then I flew back to check on Henna's mother. She had curled up in hiding between the fallen Elyxeos and her shield.

"Have you seen Henna?" I asked, landing beside her.

She peeked out at me, revealing a nasty bruise on her cheek. "I haven't. I haven't. I haven't. I don't, I don't, I don't—" She was hyperventilating, looking every bit as deranged by fear as Henna had in the Avarice castle. "I can't, I can't, I don't know what—what to do, Sleigh."

I reached out and caught her by the arm, flying her just inside the forest where she could hide.

The number of Trios had been noticeably reduced when I soared back over everyone. The Deliverance were distorted by their speed, zipping around and killing white centaurs faster than the eye could see.

Finally, I spotted Henna struggling to get out from under the centaur she'd been riding. She was crying and bouncing back and forth fighting to push the centaur off her leg.

"Are you alright?" I asked, flying to her side.

"My ankle's broken," she choked out. "I can't get him off of me and it hurts so bad."

I lifted the centaur effortlessly so she could scoot out from under it. She screamed in agony when I lifted her from the ground and flew us up. "I'm going to take you to your mother, then I'll come back and look for your father."

On the way over the dying fight, I saw one of the white streaks darting toward Bones and his Elyxeos. "Sorry about this, Henna," I muttered, jerking her around as I tore through the air to kick the Trios hard enough to break his back.

"Oooowwwwwww." Henna moaned.

Bones bowed to me when we flew over him toward the forest.

"AAHHH," Henna's mother let out a strangled cry of joy when she saw us coming.

My skin had finally become consistent in beaming luminary light.

The women hugged each other and cried as I left them to continue my search.

It became clear that the Trios were far more focused on killing centaurs than luminaries, and sparing *all* the nocturnes, as I drifted over everyone. Of course spilt nocturne blood would be a waste in their eyes.

People were cheering and celebrating even with the final splinters of battle still being fought. We were winning. There was no hope for the Trios now.

Half The Deliverance were setting out in every direction in search of any Trios who had escaped.

I quickly discovered that Parthenia's father and brother-in-law had been killed. Chief's father had fallen as well. I felt very fortunate to find that Auree's boyfriend, Pat, was unharmed and Henna's father unconscious from a blow to the head, but still very much alive. There was just as much grieving surrounding me as there was rejoicing in our victory.

Henna's father roused slightly when I laid him beside his family.

I caught sight of Marina and Amphion racing toward us through the woods. Gabriel jumped off Marina as she ran and made his way to me on foot.

"How dare you?!" Amphion shouted. "You dishonor me." Blood had washed over his side and down one leg.

"No, I care about you!" I shouted back.

Marina shook her head. "He couldn't be reasoned with."

Gabriel's arms went around my lower back and pulled me against him. He kissed me fiercely, then scowled. "Don't ever do that again. I don't care if you're wearing those wings or queen of the world, even. You can't dump me in the forest and go to fight a losing battle, Sleigh!"

"But we won."

"You left me behind."

Marina charged after Amphion toward our camp.

I stared at the ground, feeling guilty, but not regretting it. "It scared me when Amphion was wounded. I love you, Gabriel, and I'd rather you be mad at me forever than dead."

"Just... promise me you'll never do that again."

My eyebrow rose as I looked up at him and shook my head. It was a promise I knew I might break someday.

He let out an irritated sigh, a thread of swirling steam blowing away from his arms.

Centaur hooves pounded the ground drawing nearer from the battle site. My wings opened protectively, a shield to hide the nocturne and luminaries behind me, as I turned to face whatever approached. Henna's father let out a strangled sound and fainted.

The split second I saw the sword before I realized who carried it set my body completely on fire. My nerves were so on edge. But it was only the chief who entered the radiance of what light was cast by the flames. Amphion, Flank, and Raytheon followed behind him.

"The battle has ended, Sleigh," the chief said when he saw me. "Come on; there's something very important we need to discuss."

Gabriel held my hand and walked with us back toward the wreckage.

"Come on, dear," I could hear Henna's mother saying to her husband.

I watched the Royal Elyxeos as we walked through the trees in silence. The chief had bandages wrapped around his shoulder where he'd been wounded. Amphion's bleeding seemed to have stopped. Flank had a prominent limp. Only Raytheon was unharmed.

Shadows swept over us when my fire went out. The peace and quiet of the night was so lovely, I was unwilling to disturb it with luminary light.

Forgive me, I whispered, yawning as I stared at Gabriel.

His eyebrows dipped down. He shook his head, though he whispered, *always*, in return.

He let go and went on ahead when the centaurs stopped at

the edge of the forest. With the only other human gone, I felt like a child left alone beside these giants.

I saw that most of The Deliverance had returned and were working to dig a hole large enough to hold all the dead spread out over the land. The strength offered by the wings had already allowed them to dig deep enough that many of them had disappeared inside the earth.

The Elyxeos I was with waited for a fair amount of distance to open between us and Gabriel before they said anything.

"You had to be here for this meeting, Sleigh, because we've all agreed that you should be invited to join The League of Royal Elyxeos Centaurs," Chief said.

"You're joking," was all I could think of to say.

"No we're not," Amphion interjected. "Three of our members need to be replaced. You're our first choice."

"But—I'm not a centaur."

"That's true," Chief said. "We've never had anyone who isn't an Elyxeos enter the league. It would help with the transition of removing slavery from our colony, though, and luminary seers would be more willing to come work in our fields."

"You've proven you're loyal, a woman of true integrity and unwavering courage," Amphion added. "You wear the Wings of Hendraya. You could protect our colony better than any Elyxeos. Stay and watch over us and we will protect you always."

I glanced back at the wings, a certain degree of anxiety welling up inside me. "An Elyxeos is bound to try and kill me for them eventually. They were gifted to your kind first, not to mine."

"We're the only ones who know their true history," Chief said. "We've all sworn on our lives never to reveal it. Besides, Amphion would probably cut our throats if we so much as think about hurting you."

Raytheon and Flank laughed. Amphion stared at me and nodded seriously.

I wanted to accept. It was such an honor. And the Surface was still so new to me, the Elyxeos colony was the only place I felt I belonged. I also felt bound to Gabriel, though. Such a significant decision had to be made with him.

Flashes of incredible light suddenly cutting through camp seized everyone's attention. The conversation was immediately forgotten.

42

A cyclone of stars streaked across the sky and reached down for The Deliverance. The world became still once more as everyone stopped to watch in wonderment. The Deliverance made no move to flee from the twister this time. It washed over an Elaban with giant horns first, leaving him wingless, then went on to the next.

"No way," I muttered to myself. I left my companions behind for the sparkling storm washing quickly over each Deliverers back. This was my only chance to be rid of the wings.

The stars were moving so quickly, splashing over two centaurs at a time if they were close enough together. A slight burnt smell hit me when I was very near. There was also the ever-growing *whoooooshing* sound of entangling winds.

A Bellios who'd just had his wings removed bowed to the sky.

I flew right in front of the cyclone so it couldn't miss me. It turned and took a different course, the powerful rushing noise moving away with it.

"Wait," I murmured.

It moved carefully over the little group of Striplings who'd paused from digging at one end of earth's freshest hollow. There weren't many left to de-wing now.

"Don't forget me!" I yelped, whizzing through the air, flying into the swirl of stars. The swishing sound became more like the tinkling of shards of glass. It felt as if I was standing under a waterfall made of sand. I was absolutely blinded by the light. Then the world appeared around me as the stars moved on. The wings still flapped behind me, keeping me in place.

The last Deliverer lost his wings to the little, glittering tornado.

"No," I cried out when it withdrew toward the heavens. "Please—" I flew after the twinkling silver, right into the heart of the spiral. Even with my eyes shut tight, I could see the brilliant light through my eyelids. "Take my wings, too. Please take them back."

A voice answered in a soft, comforting whisper. "You were chosen years ago to restore peace and harmony to the Surface world. For too long the heavens have been forced to watch horror and suffering befall the living of the earth. Every foresight and every premonition revealed you to be the one who could end it. As long as you wear the wings, we can enjoy peace and harmony laid before us once more."

"The centaurs have promised peace between our kind and theirs," I answered. "The chief Elyxeos said they would enforce it among the other colonies if necessary."

"Mortals don't always do as they have promised."

"The Elyxeos do...If they're ever needed again, I *will* take the wings upon my back and do whatever is required of me. My word is good."

There was a rush of voices, whispering to each other in a language I couldn't understand. It felt good to listen to them, though, like having your mother wrap you in a warm blanket and a hug when you've just come in from the cold. They carried with them a feeling of concern for me.

"*Sleigh!*" Gabriel shouted from somewhere below. It was loud and angry, like when he'd called everyone's attention during Flank's announcement. But it sounded so far away. "Sleigh, COME BACK..."

I wondered how high the stars had carried me as the foreign murmuring continued and Gabriel's voice became more distant.

"Day approaches," one hissed. "He'll be here soon."

"Sleigh," the first whisper returned, "you have done so much good. We believe you deserve what you have requested. But you *must* keep your vow if ever we have need for you again."

"Yes, I promise."

Without another word, I felt the awful sensation of insects crawling inside my skin. It was even worse this time than before. I couldn't help but reach back to scratch the dreadful itchiness. There were lumps moving under my skin. The wings were disintegrating. A wave of exhaustion passed through my body.

A bit of darkness broke through the blinding light below. I opened my eyes just a crack to see the hole opening in the funnel underneath my feet. Gabriel had his hands cupped around his mouth, shouting vehemently. Bursts of fire emitted from his lips, though I couldn't understand him. The stars were lowering me slowly to the ground.

"Day approaches," the hissing voice said. "Hurry! He is coming!"

The rushing wind all around me blew harder. I moved faster toward the ground.

"He's nearly here!"

Gabriel dropped his hands to stare at me.

"Make haste or she'll fall."

I gasped when the wind weakened and I swayed dangerously to one side.

"He is here!" a watery scream echoed through the rotating wind. Then it all broke apart and I was the one screaming as I tore through the air toward the ground.

A large centaur was racing toward me. I couldn't think straight enough to know who. All I could think of was how I would either crush Gabriel or myself against the ground.

My body did a full turnover through the air. I screamed even more desperately, my heart hammering so wildly, I was sure it would split wide open.

The figure sprinting toward me put on a burst of speed. Gabriel reached out for me. The centaur extended his arms, and leaned forward, still running. He caught me a moment before I slammed into Gabriel, stealing me from the nocturnes' rescuing arms. Amphion grunted with the impact of my body, pressing me against him when I began to slip from his grasp.

I threw my arms around him instinctively. My nails scratched against his back. I was shaking terribly. "S—sorry, Amphion."

"What were you thinking?" he asked, setting me on the ground.

My legs shook with weakness. "I never wanted the wings... I suppose I'm not eligible for your league anymore." I stumbled sideways when Gabriel hugged me from the side.

"Quit running off like that, Sleigh," Gabriel said hotly. "It may be a thrill for you, but it's never knowing if I'll see you alive again for me."

"A thrill?" I jerked away from him and nearly fell over. "Do you really believe I did all this—*for a thrill?!*"

Marina appeared coming around Amphion. "Look around you, Sleigh."

I stared past her at the centaurs, luminaries, and nocturnes revealed by the stunning pink sunrise chasing away the night.

They had all turned to face me and knelt upon the ground. Marina went to her knees and bowed her head.

Amphion mimicked her, then looked up at me. "The invitation still stands, Sleigh. You've won the war for us and changed the lives of every living thing. You will be remembered always, a part of our colony's history. You have certainly earned your place in The League of Royal Elyxeos Centaurs."

Gabriel was obviously dumbfounded by Amphion's words, and slowly knelt before me as well.

It was just as Icy's painting portrayed: me floating, or rather falling, from the sky. Masses bowing to me on the ground.

Tears stung my eyes as I stared at them. Nothing they did could make up for what I'd suffered and committed. If anything, it made me feel worse. It was as if they worshipped me for getting so many people and centaurs I cared for killed, like they loved me for my sins. I put a hand over my mouth, gasping and lowering my head as I cried.

"I'm sorry, Sleigh," Gabriel muttered. "I know it wasn't a thrill."

I fell to my knees and threw my arms around his neck. All I really wanted now was to get away. I shut my eyes tight, blocking out everything but him. "Can we just leave, Gabriel? I want to be with my family. I want to see Blush." Seeing my littlest sister was the only thing that could make things right within myself.

"Of course." Gabriel held me close and helped me to stand. "We'll go right now."

"What about the league?" Amphion asked rudely.

"We should go with them, Amphion," Marina said. "There might still be scavengers out there for a while, until word spreads that there will be no more slaves." She reached out for his hand.

He pulled it away. "Honor before the heart."

"Davion was killed. I've paid my sister's debt and been made free. There is no dishonor to keep us apart."

Thinking of Davion's death was too painful for me to dwell on. He might have been a rotten husband, but he was a wonderful friend. There were plenty of other heartbreaking injustices on my mind to distract me from dwelling on him, of course.

"He was killed?" Amphion stood and turned his body to fully face her.

Marina nodded and stood in front of him.

Amphion didn't move for a moment, then took her in his arms to kiss her with incredible force and longing.

Taking Gabriel's hand, I left them to find Henna's family so they could come with us. I couldn't leave them to fend for themselves.

I found myself leaning heavily against Gabriel's side. The weakness I felt after all the happenings of the night left me wondering if I had it in me to travel.

The Deliverance bowed lower to the ground, revering me, when I walked past them.

"What do you think about me joining the Elyxeos league?" I asked Gabriel, wiping my eyes and my thoughts clean of battle.

"I never want to work with centaurs again, but I've learned by now there's no telling you what to do."

"What if we lived near enough to their colony that I could take part in it, but you wouldn't have to? We could have enough distance between us and them that we have our own separate life."

"So you do want to join their league?"

"I'd be the first luminary to do it. And I've grown attached to Amphion. He could continue teaching me how to defend myself. I'm lousy at it now."

"Could Blush come and live with us?"

My heart fluttered happily at the thought of having her with us. "Wouldn't we be taking her from your mother?" The thought reminded me to worry about how his mother was dealing with mine and how they would decide to share little Blush.

"It's not exactly what you think. My mother's Grandma to her. Blush doesn't call me father, but I've always acted as one to her. My mother expects me to take Blush along when I marry."

My skin brightened, feeling elation at the thought and trying to ignore how everyone was still bowing to me. It was nice to know his mother probably wasn't as threatened as I'd supposed.

My eyelashes fluttered as I went to my knees suddenly.

"Sleigh?" Gabriel was jerked downward with his arm holding firmly to me.

"I'm, I'm alright. I'm just so tired." I looked back when I heard Elyxeos hooves thundering toward us.

"What's wrong with Sleigh?" Amphion asked Gabriel as Marina took my hand to help me stand.

"She's exhausted," Gabriel said. "She needs to rest."

"No, I need to see Blush," I argued, knowing deep down that he was right.

"I'll bring her to you," Marina said softly, "if Gabriel will show me the way."

Gabriel nodded, then turned to me. "Get some rest. I'll meet you back at the Elyxeos colony with your family." He raised an eyebrow to Amphion.

"I'll look after her," Amphion promised.

I bowed my head, wanting to cry again. Without Gabriel, the horrors of the night would be too much. But there wasn't enough left inside me to argue any more. I'd already given everything I had.

My weary thoughts were interrupted when Gabriel put a hand behind my head and lifted it so he could kiss me. It was slow and deliberate, his mouth carefully caressing mine, easing every painful ache within my heart. "You're so amazing, Sleigh. I love you."

"I love you, too." I grinned sleepily.

Then Amphion was scooping me up in his arms and carrying me through the Elyxeos camp. He pressed me closer when he leaned over to grab a couple of blankets before he carried me to a quiet stretch of shade beneath a patch of evergreens.

"Thank you, Amphion," I murmured as he laid me carefully on top of a blanket and covered me with the other. My eyes were so heavy. "You know I love you too, right?"

His hand froze in the middle of pulling the blanket up over my shoulders.

"I love you like the father the Avarice took from me."

His hand relaxed and went to smooth my hair behind me. It was a kind enough response, and so entirely unlike him, that I knew he felt the same way.

43

"What do you want me to do?!" Chief asked, pounding his fist against the table in the royal meeting room.

My head jerked upward when he startled me from near slumber. I was still so drained.

Only a day back in our city and already Amphion was arguing nearly everything the chief said.

"It's too late to do anything now," Amphion barked. "We've lost half our slaves. We can hardly function. I'm only saying you should have thought about this before voting to end it."

I was more than a little insulted, but too dispirited to say anything. It had proven impossible to pull myself out of the dark gloom still looming inside me after the dreadful Trios battle.

Chief pressed his hands against the table, straightening his elbows and leaning forward. "Only you would say something *SO STUPID* after such an impossible victory. We'd all be dead if we hadn't freed the slaves!"

"Centaurs managed somehow before slavery," Flank raised his voice to be heard over their shouting.

Raeley and Meryon, the two newest royals, glanced at each other uncertainly. Neither had said much the entire meeting.

"All you've done since we got here is waste our time, Amphion!" Raytheon snapped. "We're supposed to be coming up with ways to fix our problem, not whining about it."

"*WHINING?!*" Amphion rose to his feet, looking feral and murderous.

The ferocity in his eyes was alarming. I sat up on my knees. I reached as far as I could for his curled fist, terrified of a fight breaking out among them and getting caught in the crossfire. "It'll be alright, Amphion," I said. "The stars have promised it."

"The stars?" Chief asked, staring at me curiously.

I'd discovered early that morning, before the sun had even considered rising, how the stars left me with a very special gift. I was able to view them as a nocturne seer.

"When I went outside last night I saw your fields and houses full of luminaries in the sky."

"How?" Amphion asked, cautiously taking his seat once more.

"I don't know, but it will happen. There's no point to this dispute."

Raeley stared at me suspiciously. He was an extra-hairy Elyxeos, a beastly-looking man, with a squinty left eye. He was Orius' replacement as head hunter. I got the feeling I made him uneasy.

Neither he nor Meryon had learned the league's secrets. They were on probation for now, forced to prove themselves before becoming a full-fledged royal. I was lucky enough to be allowed to skip all that.

"Is there nothing else you can tell us?" Chief asked me.

I shook my head, slipping back into gloomy silence. Without Gabriel there, I was filled with all the loneliness of my first day as a slave.

"Elyxeos children are frightened," Raytheon said, staring at me like he demanded an answer. "Men and women are saying our colony will crumble. Think! You must have noticed something that could help us. How do we make this happen?"

"What I saw was a day like any other before the Trios. Only there weren't guards set over the luminaries and nocturnes inside the city. They worked of their own free will. There were more luminaries and less nocturnes than you had before. That's all I witnessed."

Flank let out a grumpy sound. Raytheon stared at the ceiling, full of exasperation.

"The stars have favored you, Sleigh." Amphion said, resting three fingertips over the wrist I'd lain on the table. "I'm sure that if you go to them tonight with questions, you'll receive answers."

"Seriously?" Raeley asked incredulously. "You're going to trust our colony's future to a luminary?"

An unpleasant chill rushed through my chest. I wasn't completely surprised. Most of the Elyxeos had accepted me into their colony, but there were still some whose eyes portrayed distrust whenever they saw me.

"*Sleigh* is the only reason our colony *has* a future *AT ALL!*" Amphion's voice rose dangerously.

"How's that? The stars could have chosen anyone. Most of the ones who wore the wings were centaurs. I've—" Raeley took a deep breath. Chief raised a disapproving eyebrow, but waited for what would follow. "I've tried to keep my mouth shut, but I still can't understand why you put a slave woman in The League of Royal Elyxeos Centaurs. Her kind hates ours. How can you trust her so?"

The dark clouds floating through my head thundered and rained down harder. It didn't take much these days.

The four originals seemed to slip into silent conversation, exchanging *looks* with one another. I didn't say a word, hoping desperately that Amphion wouldn't explode. Flank concluded by nodding toward Amphion. Chief shrugged and sat back.

Amphion's fingers slid farther over my wrist as he spoke. "Sleigh has proven her loyalty beyond anything you'll probably ever know. I would trust her as I trust Chief, as I trust myself, even. The heart of an Elyxeos beats within her chest; I promise you that." His hand closed around my arm affectionately. It was so giant, my arm seemed a mere twig inside it. "If you can't accept that entirely, then you're not welcome here."

I was touched.

Raeley's eyebrows rose. Clearly, he couldn't believe his own kind was siding with me over him. His whole body seemed to deflate as he let out a breath, long and slow. "I'll try."

Amphion and Chief glanced at each other. "Know this," Amphion said rather gravely, "you will never be allowed to truly join this league as long as you question Sleigh as you do now."

I heard a slight tapping out in the corridor.

"Are we understood?" Chief asked Raeley.

The tapping became louder.

"Halt!" Terious shouted from the other side of the door. "YOU'RE NOT ALLOWED INSIDE THIS ROOM!"

The loud clapping of centaur hooves only drew nearer. Everyone within the royal meeting room stood and drew their weapons.

"*One step closer and I'll cut you!*"

"My father would have you killed," a familiar voice replied fearlessly.

"GET THAT NOCTURNE OUT OF THIS CASTLE AT ONCE!"

"Marina? Gabriel!" I cried, running across the center of the table toward the door. I wrapped my fingers around the heavy, brass handle and jerked it back as hard as I could. The door shifted toward me an inch or so. It must have weighed as much as any one of my companions.

"Allow me," Flank said, standing closest to the door.

I took a step back so he could open it for me. Gradually, the back half of Marina's form appeared. A large, brutish-looking nocturne stepped into view.

"Ah—" I shrieked, jumping into Gabriel's arms. I wrapped my arms around his head and kissed him like death was threatening to tear us apart. His hands squashed against my back seemed to pull me into him. The warmth and relief of all my cares at welcoming his mouth with mine was exactly what I needed.

"He's your husband?" Terious asked. "My apologies, Sleigh."

Elyxeos hooves tromped out of the royal room.

Gabriel seemed just as determined to ignore them as I was, pressing his fingers deeper and hotter into my back. My chest rose and fell several times, full of passion and tenderness at his lingering kiss.

It was happiness. It was healing. It was true and everlasting love, the obsession I'd had for this man for years.

"I have a surprise for you," Gabriel said when my head finally lifted. He sat me down and I realized the centaurs were shielding their eyes from the great light coming off my skin.

"Yeah?" I hoped with all my heart to find Blush on the other end of that surprise.

"Come on." Gabriel took my hand and ran through the corridor toward the front entryway. The blazing sunlight swept over us both as we ran through the beaten path in the courtyard. The grass swayed gently on the breeze. A shaded chill fingered its way through my hair in the breezeway, and then we were met with the last thing I would have ever expected:

Luminaries everywhere. My luminaries. Every single sky luminary who had sided against the Avarice and survived the

Trios. I hadn't seen them since before I woke up after the battle. Like most luminaries and nocturnes, they'd taken off first chance they got.

"Your mother and I managed to convince them to come here, where they'll have a safe place to live and everything they could ever need," Gabriel said.

The Elyxeos were desperate enough for the help, I knew they wouldn't mind that they weren't all seers.

The steady stomping against the ground behind us alerted me to the royals arriving behind me. Their bodies emerged to my left.

"So," Amphion put a hand on my shoulder, glancing at Raeley. "You were right after all."

I finally located my mother in the front of things, kneeling beside a small nocturne girl and pointing me out to her.

"Is that Blush?" I asked Gabriel, though I knew from the strong resemblance she held to me that it must be my sister.

"That's her." He grinned and nodded. "The prettiest little girl in the world."

"She's beautiful." I simply watched her for an instant, taking in the great magnitude of the moment.

Her eyes lit up when they saw me. She took off suddenly toward me as fast as her little legs could carry her. She was absolutely precious, racing a bit clumsily in her long, buttercup-yellow dress. My mother followed at a slower pace.

I knelt and held out my arms. Finally, I felt peace at being reunited with my sister. After years of separation and weeks of unspeakable suffering, all was right. Everything had been for her, the most precious young life in my heart. The freedom and refuge of a world at long last finding harmony washed over me as Blush bumped harmlessly into me and hugged me tight around my neck.

Mmmmm, she crooned. It was like she knew and loved me already, just as I felt for her.

Then she popped up and pressed her chubby hands against my cheeks. "Gama said you're my sissy. Your mom said you sabed me from the centers, and I can lib wis you and Gabwiew when you get mawwied." Little sparks popped around her enormous smile.

My mother sat on the ground to hug us both. "I hope you don't mind. Felicity's told me how much she means to Gabriel." She lowered her voice considerably to whisper, 'and you did say you wanted to marry him."

"Of course not. There isn't anything I wouldn't do for Blush." I ran my fingers through her silken, black hair. "But what about you? Would you mind?" She *was* her true mother after all.

"It would be cruel to take her from the man who's cared for her since the day she was born. Having you raise her with him wouldn't bother me, as long as I see her often enough to have a hand in it."

I stared into the gleeful, lustrous eyes of my nocturne sister. My heart filled with so much love at that moment, I couldn't help but well up full of joy.

I caught Amphion and my mother bowing their heads to one another out of the corner of my eye.

"Your wings are gone," Eve said disappointedly, joining us too.

Felicity followed behind Eve to our little gathering. "I wish I'd have known when I met you, Sleigh, just how much you meant to my son. He tells me you'll be renewing your vows at Auree's wedding." She smiled and gave me a wink.

It was the perfect excuse to marry Gabriel without everyone discovering our deception.

I tried to stand, but Blush latched onto me and held fast. "Pick me up; pick me up," she yelped excitedly.

I was more than happy to hold her close as I stood. It was incredible to think of how things had unfolded. Blush had just been given to me. I could love and raise her with Gabriel, the nocturne I'd fantasized and obsessed over for so very long. It was fantastically unbelievable.

Felicity hugged me from the side opposite the one I held Blush against. "Thank you for saving my son's life, and loving him as I do."

"Of course." I had to assume he had told her of my eighteenth birthday vision.

"You and Gabriel could take my house." Marina surprised me from behind. "You've become a leader to this people, and I *never* wanted to live there in the first place. I wouldn't mind still helping you distribute titanasaur and clothing to the luminaries, but I'm ready to retire from being their primary caregiver."

"Um—" I looked back for Gabriel. He replaced his mother at my side and put an arm around my shoulders. "Gabriel and I were thinking of building a house outside the city. Maybe we could stay there temporarily, though, take over looking after our people until someone else can do it. It *would* help with the transition, for the sky luminaries especially." I raised an eyebrow to Gabriel. He nodded in return.

"Go ahead and move your things into my house. I'll get the new luminaries settled in."

"Thank you, Marina." I led my family and Felicity toward my little house, thinking that my mother or Gabriel's might like to inherit it once Gabriel and I had moved out.

Blush rested her head on my shoulder and became so still during the walk, I suspected she'd fallen asleep.

Everything I'd gone through was worth it alone to have Gabriel's love forever.

But there aren't even words to describe what Blush meant to

me. I felt so much affection, so much satisfaction and joy in holding her close, completely safe and sound at last.

Perhaps it was all that I'd already sacrificed and undergone for her. Perhaps it was the years we spent apart, leaving me with nothing more to do for her than love and long to have her for my sister once more. Perhaps it was the strange obsession she'd sparked inside me for nocturnes. Whatever it was, there was nothing on earth I wouldn't have done or given up for my sister.

MEET THE AUTHOR

April Marcom is a Pre-K teacher's assistant and mother of three. Her greatest passion, second only to her family and faith, is writing romance. Like the characters in her stories, there's nothing more important to her than the people she loves. April has enjoyed writing fiction since grade school, but only began pursuing publication in recent years. She is the author of such books as Good vs. Evil High and Wisteria and the Pirate Assassin. Besides writing, she loves baking, hiking, watching old movies, and dreaming of faraway places.

We hope that you liked this release from
5 Prince Publishing, LLC.
Please enjoy the following excerpt
from April Marcom's

The Three Stones of Bethany

-1-

The horses' hooves beat against the warm ground, rending leaves and branches as three siblings and their dear friend rode toward the house of an old witch called Brigid. The moment they had received word that their two younger sisters had been captured by dredglings, they'd set out to see if the hag could tell them where to find the girls, only eight years old and probably terrified beyond description. They'd been riding for hours through the night. No one wanted to say it, but they were all beginning to wonder if they were lost.

Of the four, Kane felt the worst. Since his father died in battle three years before, he'd felt the weight of responsibility for his younger brother and sisters resting upon his shoulders. It was greater now even than when they'd been forced to flee the castle five years ago, the day the dredglings seemed to appear out of thin air, taking over the kingdom and infesting the land like some inescapable plague. Their blotchy vomit-colored skin, beady red eyes, and unnaturally long pointed noses made the dredglings look every bit as horrifying as their cruel nature actually was.

Kane was only fifteen years of age when it all began. He'd gotten his siblings settled into hiding with a kind family in Celestial nation and gone straight to join the war. Joy and Holt joined him in the fight three years later, only a year after their father's death, and Tor had become close enough to them both in the years they spent in Celestial nation that he absolutely refused to be left behind.

Kane was twenty now, his oldest sister nineteen, and his brother and Tor, eighteen years of age.

By the time the dredglings tore through the little Celestial village, pillaging and burning houses to the ground, only Charity and Hope remained of the royal family there. The young twins shouldn't have been recognizable. They looked and acted like the other villagers. They'd even dyed seven blue streaks into their hair as the Celestial people did. But the dredglings were able to sniff out their royal blood easily, something Kane hadn't anticipated.

"Oi, look there," Holt cried out, pointing to the speck of light at the top of a nearby hill.

"It has to be her," Joy said hopefully.

"We shall soon find out." Kane urged his horse to go faster. It didn't take them long at all to cross the plain separating them from the egg-shaped house made of dried mud and straw.

At the base of the short hill, Kane climbed down from his faithful steed and left it with the others to be tied to a towering tree. He hurried to the front door and raised one fist to knock, but was startled when an angry wrinkled face appeared in the little window beside it.

A white eyeball stared at him through the dusty glass. A hole and a shadow was all that remained of the other eye. He couldn't help but notice how hunched over her back was as she turned to open the door.

"What do you want?" Brigid asked him in a scratchy voice.

"We need your help," Kane said. "Our little sisters have been taken by dredglings and we need to know where they are so we can rescue them."

"Oh? And why should I waste one twig a' time on you?"

"You will be well-paid for it." Holt held out a brown sack as the others joined Kane at the door.

The witch stared at it for a moment, and then spread her pruney, crooked fingers as she took the bag. She reached in and held a gold coin up to the light cast by an oil lamp burning in the center of the room on a scarred oak wood table. She licked her lips and puckered them out as she squinted her one eye. Then she put it back in the bag, which she placed on the table, and turned to face her eager visitors.

"Come in then," she grumbled.

Kane stepped into the one and only room first, followed by the others. Aside from the table and a lopsided chair, all he saw was a bed and shelves and more shelves of magical instruments, jars of all sorts of strange things, and a bit of food.

Brigid pushed some things around on the lowest shelf against the wall and took a jar of purple powder before throwing a handful of it into her fireplace. Deep blue flames lit under a hanging cauldron, the thick black liquid inside of it beginning to bubble immediately. The witch went to put the powder away and took an armful of other things from the shelves—a vile of blue goo, another of glowing red stones, a jar of crinkled leafy-looking things, and three small jars of spices. She set them on the table's edge closest to the fire and hobbled over to Kane.

"It's no wonder that the young Celestial man got through the magical spell I cast around my home, but how'd the rest of you manage it?" She glanced in the direction of Tor, the blue steaks in his hair marking him a member of the most magical of the five nations in Bethany.

The day they were born, Kane, Joy, and Holt had enchantments cast on them to repel and protect them from any other magic, a privilege of the royal family. But it was better that Brigid didn't know who they were. A witch living all alone like this had cut herself off from the kingdom and bore no allegiance to it, so they didn't trust her with this sort of information.

"I did not come to answer your questions," Kane said. "I came so you could answer mine."

"Humph." Brigid gave him an ugly scowl as she reached up and plucked a few hairs from his head.

"What do you think you're doing?" Kane pushed her arm away.

Brigid ignored him and walked over to the cauldron to throw his hair into the dark liquid. "A few drops of mermaid's blood," she muttered as she took the vial of blue gunk and let some of it ooze into her great pot, where it joined the sandy brown hairs. Then she took one of the red stones and a few of the leafy things to toss in. "A fragment of dragon's heart...A pinch of dried bat wings..." Next came a sprinkle from each of the three smallest jars. "A bit of salt...A bit of sage...And the ashes of a dead man..." She replaced the jars on the table and pulled a long wooden spoon from inside her black hooded robe to stir the brew that had begun to burn orange. "Now show us the little sisters of the ill-mannered man."

Everyone backed away from Brigid as thick smoke began to fill the room. Bits of color swirled together. The most vivid were yellow, orange, red, green, and blue, the five colors of Bethany's fine nations and all its power. Slowly, a picture began forming in the eerie haze. Holt was terrified, backing farther and farther away until he couldn't see anyone or anything but the smoke engulfing them.

Gradually, a cage took center stage to the billows of gray. Two little girls lay close together inside, fast asleep. Bars protruding horizontally from underneath the small prison rested on broad shoulders, the bodies of which didn't quite take shape.

Brigid's voice deepened as she began.

"Ah, the sisters of your royal birth, captured by the enemies worst.

The time is short I feel I must warn, and then their lives apart are torn.

You will have seven days to roam, before the dredglings return to their home.

Your castle is where they lay their heads, and here your sisters will be made dead."

Holt began to tremble as the smoke darkened. In the three years he spent with the Celestials, he'd never gotten over his fear of magic.

"In three short days they pass Emerald nation. Save the girls here, north of medicine's creation.

For once they pass the healer's land, their lives are no more in your hands.

Your time is up; their lives are lost. You must arrive in time or suffer the cost...

But wait...there's more...

When your quest to save these children is done, a new one begins under Elderlord sun.

If you will seek audience with the Elderlord king, the secret of victory to your heart he brings.

There is something your father never told, the answer to the war your quest will hold."

The vision of the sleeping sisters was shaken when a dredgling leapt into view, banging his fists against the bars and shouting. The girls screamed and sat up. He began laughing at the terror he'd caused. Holt jumped back with the girls, slamming into the shelves behind him. The room was suddenly filled with the sounds of metal rattling and glass smashing against the floor.

"What was that?" Brigid screeched. "What have you ungrateful brats done?"

A black cloud arose behind Holt. "I'm sorry. It was an accident."

In the gray fog, no one saw the spinning blackness solidify but him. Kane's arm came out of nowhere, clasping his brother's wrist and pulling him toward the door. He felt his way along the wall to the door and pushed Holt through the entryway. He'd already managed to get Joy and Tor outside, since neither one had gone far from him.

"What are you doing?" Brigid waved her arms around wildly in the fog, trying to see what was happening.

Kane thought of going back in to search the darkening cloud for her, but froze when he heard a strange rumbling like nothing he'd ever heard before. It grew louder and louder inside her little home, until he was sure the entire thing was about to burst.

Other Titles from 5 Prince Publishing
www.5princebooks.com